Y0-BRC-829

PRAISE FOR
Christina Ashcroft and *Archangel of Mercy*

"I was completely drawn into Christina Ashcroft's novel and couldn't put it down. With its sizzlingly hot archangels, richly imagined world and truly despicable villains, *Archangel of Mercy* will appeal to readers who enjoy Nalini Singh and J. R. Ward. Dark, gritty and erotic. I loved it!"

—Laurie London, author of the Sweetblood series

"In *Archangel of Mercy*, Ashcroft's unique world-building blends several familiar mythologies and draws the reader in with a creative and intriguing plot involving archangels, demons, gods, demi-gods and other extraordinary races. Her characters are fascinating, the story line compelling, the romance scorching—don't be surprised if you find yourself reading this book late into the night! Paranormal romance fans could very well discover a new angel addiction in Ashcroft's series!"

—Kylie Griffin, national bestselling author of the Light Blade series

WITHDRAWN

WITHDRAWN

ARCHANGEL OF MERCY

Christina Ashcroft

HEAT | NEW YORK

THE BERKLEY PUBLISHING GROUP
Published by the Penguin Group
Penguin Group (USA) Inc.
375 Hudson Street, New York, New York 10014, USA
Penguin Group (Canada), 90 Eglinton Avenue East, Suite 700, Toronto, Ontario M4P 2Y3, Canada
(a division of Pearson Penguin Canada Inc.) • Penguin Books Ltd., 80 Strand, London WC2R 0RL,
England • Penguin Group Ireland, 25 St. Stephen's Green, Dublin 2, Ireland (a division of Penguin
Books Ltd.) • Penguin Group (Australia), 250 Camberwell Road, Camberwell, Victoria 3124, Australia
(a division of Pearson Australia Group Pty. Ltd.) • Penguin Books India Pvt. Ltd., 11 Community
Centre, Panchsheel Park, New Delhi—110 017, India • Penguin Group (NZ), 67 Apollo Drive,
Rosedale, Auckland 0632, New Zealand (a division of Pearson New Zealand Ltd.) • Penguin Books
(South Africa) (Pty.) Ltd., 24 Sturdee Avenue, Rosebank, Johannesburg 2196, South Africa

Penguin Books Ltd., Registered Offices: 80 Strand, London WC2R 0RL, England

This book is an original publication of The Berkley Publishing Group.

This is a work of fiction. Names, characters, places, and incidents either are the product of the author's
imagination or are used fictitiously, and any resemblance to actual persons, living or dead, business
establishments, events, or locales is entirely coincidental. The publisher does not have any control over
and does not assume any responsibility for author or third-party websites or their content.

Copyright © 2012 by Christina Phillips.
Cover art by Cliff Nielsen.
Cover design by George Long.
Text design by Kristin del Rosario.

All rights reserved.
No part of this book may be reproduced, scanned, or distributed in any printed or
electronic form without permission. Please do not participate in or encourage piracy of
copyrighted materials in violation of the author's rights. Purchase only authorized editions.
HEAT and the HEAT design are trademarks of Penguin Group (USA) Inc.

PUBLISHING HISTORY
Heat trade paperback edition / December 2012

Library of Congress Cataloging-in-Publication Data

Ashcroft, Christina.
Archangel of mercy / Christina Ashcroft. — Berkley trade paperback ed.
p.   cm.
ISBN 978-0-425-25349-6 (pbk.)
1. Angels—Fiction.   I. Title.
PR9619.4.A846A89   2012   2012007750
823'.92—dc23

PRINTED IN THE UNITED STATES OF AMERICA

10 9 8 7 6 5 4 3 2 1

ALWAYS LEARNING   PEARSON

For Iris and Derek, with love

Acknowledgments

First of all I'd like to thank my fabulous CPs, Amanda Ashby and Sara Hantz—you both earned gold stars with this one! Also to my awesome agent, Emmanuelle Morgen, who is always a voice of reason in my world of chaos.

I would also like to give a big thank-you to my fabulous editor, Kate Seaver. Thanks also to Katherine Pelz and the wonderful team at Berkley. In particular I want to say a huge thank-you to George Long and Cliff Nielsen for creating such a breathtaking and perfect cover. I love it.

Big thanks to Fiona Lowe for your medical expertise—any mistakes are entirely my own! I also want to give a huge thanks to my good friend Eleni Konstantine—you know why, and I hope you enjoy!

Finally, thank you to my husband Mark and our children—I love you guys.

Archangel of Mercy

Chapter One

IRELAND

AURORA Robinson counted seventeen steps east of the ancient oak, three steps north, and then narrowed her eyes at the woodland that bordered her family's property ten feet in front of her.

This was the right place.

She sank to the ground and placed the silver-framed picture on the grass in front of her. The delicate, ethereal flower that had been lovingly pressed and preserved so many years ago never failed to send trickles of awe along her spine.

Her mother had worn this exotic bloom in her hair the night she and her father had finally met for real, instead of in their shared dreams.

Aurora traced her finger over the glass. This flower was the only link her mum had to her homeland in a parallel dimension. A homeland she had never been able to return to, since that night she'd stepped from her dimension into Aurora's dad's embrace.

She pressed her palm against her butterfly necklace for good luck. Even though she knew she was doing the right thing, if her dad had any idea what she was hoping to achieve he'd be horrified. He still worried about her as if she were a child, and that was why she hadn't confided in him about her plans. About all the research she'd undertaken over the last eight years. The courses she'd studied on various psychic phenomena. She'd hated keeping it a secret from him, but he just wasn't logical when it came to some things. Ever since she could remember, his greatest fear was that Aurora might one day vanish into her mother's world, with no way of ever returning home. He'd never understand how *theoretically* confident she was of success.

It was much better that he didn't know. And afterward he wouldn't care that she'd put herself at what he considered an unnecessary risk.

The summer sun warmed her shoulders and the faint rustlings of the woodland and the indistinct humming of the bees sank into the beat of her heart, the fabric of her being. Without too much effort—after all, she'd had out-of-body experiences for all of her life—she slid into the astral planes.

So beautiful. For a lingering moment she soaked in the exquisite sense of tranquility before focusing on her physical body, immobile in the back meadow of her family's estate.

She could do this. For the sake of her mother, whose fragile sanity faded with every passing year, she needed to bring back proof that her treasured flower did exist. Because then, Aurora was convinced, her mum would remember the world where she had grown up really existed, and wasn't just some confused dream. She'd return to the fun-loving, irrepressible mum Aurora remembered from her childhood. The laughing, vibrant girl her dad had told her about. The one he had fallen in love with.

It would work. It had to.

Awe shivered through her as the vibrant landscape of the astral planes shimmered, as if a gossamer veil had fallen across the realm.

She focused her psychic energy on the flower and embraced her own transdimensional heritage. Her instincts were right. It would be enough to allow her to open a gateway from the dimension of her birth into the dimension where her mother had been born.

A spiderweb of glittering raindrops materialized in front of her, rapidly encompassing her entire field of vision. It pulsed, as if it was a living entity, and Aurora could feel herself being gently cocooned as the breathtaking web closed in around her.

It was happening. She'd not imagined it would be this easy. But there was no doubt, because the intricate latticework of raindrops was parting, and beyond would be her *mother's world.*

Excitement tingled, enhanced by a subtle vibration in the energy streams. But that was outside her glittering sphere. It had nothing to do with her. But before the thought had even fully formed her astral projection shuddered as the equivalent of a 747 jet thundered through the higher planes, shattering the glittering serenity. *Something was horribly wrong.*

Terror hummed through her as countless levels within the astral planes tumbled. Desperately she clawed her way back toward the physical world, staggered by the realization that even there the soul-wrenching shudders rocked the earth.

Was it an earthquake? In Ireland?

From a great distance she heard the frantic barking of her dogs, locked in their enclosure up by the house. Then her thoughts fractured, and the silent roar threatened to split her being irrevocably. She had the petrifying notion that the tenuous link between her spirit and body would unravel—that she'd be forever trapped in a shadowy purgatory of her own making.

She had to return. With one last desperate thrust of energy she propelled herself forward—and in that instance a blast of power so primal, so raw, smashed into her and sent her spiritually reeling.

Holy shit, what was that? The source didn't slice straight through her.

It enveloped her, an exhilarating fusion of the most fundamental elements of creation.

Diamond rainbows sparkled, obliterating everything. It was impossible while she remained separated from her physical body and yet she gasped, and something pounded in erratic disarray as if, incomprehensibly, she could feel her heartbeat.

Sensation ignited, and it didn't matter that she wasn't in her body because this wasn't in her body. It was *inside her consciousness*. Touching and claiming, and primitive lust erupted, enslaved, *consumed* her.

Exquisite ribbons of rapture embraced her, igniting a fiery maelstrom of need and desire. She writhed in uninhibited ecstasy, mindless, convulsing . . .

Falling . . .

She slammed back into her body with such force her ribs hurt, her head pounded and her limbs went numb. Shock hammered through her brain, clouding reason, distorting reality.

Oh god. Her astral projection had just come. And if the frustration thundering through her blood was anything to go by, she wasn't finished yet.

Everything hurt. She could hardly drag oxygen into her lungs. It was as if she was being crushed. *She was being crushed.*

Reality smashed through her stunned euphoric haze and terror returned, weaving through the lingering tendrils of unfulfilled lust. A heavy weight pinned her to the ground, from her ankles to her shoulders. A weight that was shaped like a hard, muscled body.

For a second she froze, her thoughts colliding in panic. Had someone attacked her while she'd been in trance? But that was impossible. She would have seen the intruder. She'd been looking at her body, and nobody else had been around.

And whoever it was, wasn't making any move on her. In fact . . . *was he dead?*

She wanted to keep her eyes closed forever in the hope she was having a horribly lucid dream, but the thought of cushioning a dead body was too much. Her eyelids opened in anxious fascination.

A muscled bronzed shoulder greeted her. Definitely male. His face was buried in the curve of her shoulder and neck, and a mass of tangled golden hair teased her cheek.

She hitched in a ragged breath, but not enough to clear the stupor that once again crawled through her brain. He wasn't dead. She could feel his heartbeat, and it was strong. Gingerly she raised her right arm, the one that wasn't pinned beneath him, and attempted to push him off her.

It was like trying to push against a mountain. A warm, living mountain, and with horrified disbelief she realized that her fingers were clinging to the taut flesh as if they were magnetized.

He didn't move, but something stirred. Fingers still glued to his shoulder, Aurora felt her face burn as the unmistakable length of his cock thickened and nudged against her tender core.

The insane urge to part her legs whispered through her mind and if it hadn't been for the fact it was physically impossible for her to move at all, she had the awful feeling she would have done just that.

Of course she wouldn't. *What was she thinking?* Clearly she was oxygen deprived. Her dry spell was catching up with her, and her unexpected thrills on the astral planes were still creating havoc with her libido. There was *no way* she wanted to shag this stranger. She didn't even know what he was doing there.

But she knew exactly what he was doing. His erection, even through his jeans or whatever he was wearing, was hard and demanding and angled across her swollen clit. A strangled groan escaped even as she dug her teeth into her lower lip and tried to block the spiraling need that claimed her womb.

She was being turned on by an unconscious man. It was sad and also, if she thought about it, slightly depraved, but she couldn't help it. He might be out cold, but his cock was the hottest thing she'd felt in years.

His naked chest crushed her and even though she was still wearing her tank top and shorts, her fevered mind imagined them away. Her fingers trailed across his exposed shoulder and hovered over the tempting tangle of golden hair.

This was madness. She needed to pull herself together. Perhaps she could wriggle free? But even as disjointed escape plans hammered through her mind, she wound a silken strand of his hair around her finger.

This couldn't be happening. Maybe she'd catapulted back into her body too quickly and this was all a hallucination? Did that mean that in reality she was lying unconscious on the ground? Was she seriously trying to convince herself that this was *all in her mind?*

His weight shifted; a slow realignment of heavy limbs as if, in the depths of his unconsciousness, he was slowly becoming aware of his surroundings. She froze, his hair still twisted around her finger in damning evidence, as his knees languidly eased her thighs apart.

Her heart thudded against her ribs and she tried to ignore the erotic tremors that claimed her sensitized clit. He wasn't doing anything on purpose. There was no need to get so excited.

But there was a great need for her to drag back control, to squash this crazy lust distorting reality and—

He lifted his head from her shoulder and looked down at her. And her tangled thoughts vanished. For one eternal moment an overwhelming sensation of déjà vu quivered through her. As if his perfectly sculpted face, enhanced by a sexy five o'clock shadow, was as familiar as her own reflection. Mesmerized she gazed into his astonishing eyes, a swirling kaleidoscope of blues, greens and silvers. She had never seen anything so captivatingly beautiful and yet threaded through the awe was a faint echo of haunting recognition.

She might have continued to stare into his eyes forever if he hadn't once again kneed her thighs farther apart. She gasped and deliberately broke the mesmeric contact as he settled himself more securely against her vulnerable pussy.

"What—?" Her voice was husky, a humiliating reminder of how horny she was for this complete stranger. Why wasn't she petrified? He could be a crazy ax murderer for all she knew. And yet fear was the last emotion scalding her blood. She glared at his jaw, but his jaw was a thing of masculine perfection and it didn't calm her skittering pulses in the least.

"Hmm?" The questioning rumble vibrated over her skin as he lowered his head and grazed his jaw along the curve of her cheek. Her mouth dried, throat closed and mind jellified.

For the life of her she couldn't remember what she'd wanted to ask him.

His warm breath caressed her face and the tip of his tongue flicked against her earlobe. An undignified squeak of protest— *more like mindless desire*—scorched her throat, and she felt his mouth curve into a smile of male satisfaction.

This was *crazy*. She clung desperately to that thought, the first sane one she'd had in ages. Sure, they were both aroused, but didn't this guy wonder what he was doing on top of her? Or how he'd even got there?

"What," she said again, "are you doing?"

His big body shook in silent laughter. Oh god. He was big all right. Her mind wandered south and mentally salivated over the hard length rammed securely against her damp channel.

Damp? She was more than damp. She was *wet*.

And she was still clinging to his hair. Mortified, she tugged her finger free and held her arm in the air, above their heads, in case she accidentally touched him and gave him . . . the wrong idea.

"What"—his whisper in her ear was seductively wicked— "would you like me to do?"

Decadent thoughts of dirty, uninhibited sex pounded through her mind. She didn't have the slightest doubt he could fulfill every fantasy she'd ever had, and then some.

Her body softened, opened, begged for more. She screwed her eyes shut, gritted her teeth and clawed desperately for a shred of sanity. What the hell had happened to her on the astral planes? Had she completely lost her mind?

"I meant," she said, realizing it was easier to articulate her thoughts when she wasn't actually looking at him. "What are you doing *here*?"

His teeth grazed her throat as if he thought she was joking. And then his fingers slowly raked through her hair until he held her in an unmistakable grip of possession.

"Look at me." It was a sexy command, his throaty whisper as erotic as if he'd accompanied his demand by stripping her naked. Instead of shocking her rigid, the thought entranced. She battled, in vain, to scrub the image from her mind.

But somehow she couldn't stop herself from looking at him.

He was breathtaking. Just as she'd always imagined a fallen angel must look like, radiating sex and sin from every pore. She wanted to bask in his radiance. *What she really needed was to get a grip.*

His gaze scorched her. The half-smile on his kissable lips conveyed he liked what he saw. Despite her good resolve her blood raced at that knowledge.

It was highly likely he was suffering from a concussion. Since when did guys like him ever want a girl like her?

Desperately, she dragged her scattered senses together. There had to be a perfectly logical explanation as to why he had suddenly appeared in her garden. Obviously, he had been astral projecting as well, and had got caught up in that weird disruption. Although that still didn't explain how he'd ended up *here* and not back from wherever he—

His mouth claimed hers, and wiped everything else from her mind.

Sensual and firm, he took instant advantage of her shock by sliding his tongue inside. Her arm dropped to his shoulder, her fingers clenched against rigid muscle, and his lips curved against hers in clear approval.

She melded to him, bending her knees so she could spread her thighs farther and he rocked against her, his cock so hard, so hot, she wondered how their clothes didn't incinerate.

His tongue teased hers, before he explored and plundered her willing mouth, causing whirlpools of arousal everywhere he touched. Feverishly her other hand gripped his biceps, as he braced his weight on that arm. Tremors of delight spiraled through her womb, tightening her need, at the leashed power beneath her exploring fingers.

He was magnificent. It was like exploring a sculpture of male perfection in the flesh. One hand tangled in his hair, the other clawed his straining shoulder while her tongue penetrated into his wickedly sensuous mouth.

He sucked on her, long and slow, and she'd never felt anything like it before in her life. A moan vibrated, echoing in their joined mouths, and it took her a moment to realize the sound came from her.

"That's it," he growled against her lips. "Don't hold back. I want to hear your screams, sweetheart. I want to hear how much you want me inside you."

His words inflamed, as vivid images flashed across her mind. She imagined screaming, could even *see* herself screaming, and her face burned. What was she thinking? She'd never been one to make much noise during sex. Maybe the odd gasp or sigh . . .

Sex.

Her breath brushed against his face, as he continued to look down at her with a blatantly possessive half-smile. He was so confident that her surrender was a foregone conclusion. As if there was no doubt that within minutes she'd be screaming mindlessly as she came around his violently thrusting cock.

To her horror, another passionate moan escaped. She clamped her lips together but it didn't make any difference. He grinned in triumph and traced one finger across the swell of her breast, circling her aching nipple.

She could hardly believe the way she was behaving. Anyone would think she was used to strange men dropping in on her with only one thought on their mind. But somehow that didn't seem very important, when all she wanted was to hold on to this golden vision and never let him go.

But it didn't matter what she wanted. As soon as he regained full use of his senses he'd be off. And her only chance to experience a wild, outrageous sexual encounter with a *complete stranger* would go with him.

Chapter Two

GABE had no idea what he was doing in a field. The last thing he remembered was picking up a quartet of females panting for a good time with a couple of archangels. He'd been at the glamour-shrouded club in Manhattan with Mephisto, his partner in hedonistic pleasure, and teleporting into the country hadn't been part of the plan. Damn, had Mephisto spiked their drinks? What other reason could there be for his inability to remember a simple thing like choosing one woman and bringing her here?

Wherever the hell *here* was?

Not that he was complaining. Not when the woman was so damn hot. Except he didn't recall seeing her at the club. Even inadvertently stoned he wouldn't have forgotten eyes as blue and deceptively innocent as hers.

"I think," she gasped, and he tweaked her erect nipple, to show her there was no need to think. Her eyes widened in apparent shock, but instead of using her delectable mouth on his, she hitched in an uneven breath. "I *think*," she repeated, sounding desperate, which only made him harder than ever, "there's been some sort of mistake."

She had a smattering of freckles across the bridge of her nose. For some reason he found them a turn-on.

"There's no mistake." A thought occurred to him. If she wasn't one of the four he'd spent half the night with, was it possible he'd grabbed her in error before leaving the club? That would account for why he didn't recognize her, and explain why she was acting so . . . oddly. "You're here because I wanted you. No other reason."

"No," she said as her fingers loosened from his hair and fell onto his shoulder. "I don't think so."

He rocked against her, slow and hard, and watched another blush sweep over her face. He couldn't recall the last time he'd seen a woman blush. They often became speechless or incoherent when he chose them, but since conversation was the last thing he was looking for when it came to a quick fuck that never bothered him.

In fact, it suited him fine.

He wound a silky length of chestnut hair around his finger. Copper highlights glinted in the sun and a faint hint of apples scented the air, momentarily distracting him from his single-minded purpose.

She washed her hair in apple-scented shampoo. Considering all the exotic fragrances in existence, none of which involved apples, he was vaguely unsure as to why he found the notion enticing.

But he did. He breathed in deep and this time it wasn't only apples he inhaled. It was the heady aroma of aroused woman.

That was more like it.

"Don't worry about it." His lips brushed against hers. Was it possible they hadn't even spoken in the club before he'd swept her away? No wonder she was convinced he'd got the wrong woman. "Everything's okay."

The strange amnesiac blank in his mind wasn't in the least bit okay, but he'd figure out the murky details later. Besides, that had nothing to do with the tempting female in his arms.

"But—" Her breathy whisper against his lips both aroused and astonished him. She was still talking? How could she even manage to articulate words when he was in the middle of *seducing* her? "It's not really okay."

She could say that again. He pulled back, just enough so he could look into her eyes and give her the full benefit of his archangelic radiance. He rarely resorted to such a blatant ploy but for fuck's sake he couldn't remember the last time a woman had uttered the word *but* when it came to having sex with him.

The hell he couldn't. He shoved the memory back into the black pit where all such memories festered.

Her beautiful blue eyes glittered. They were dark with lust, so that wasn't the problem. And if that wasn't the problem, what else could be?

"You're afraid someone might be watching?" That was possible. They could be anywhere. Again the question thudded through his mind. *Where was he?* "You want me to find us somewhere more secluded?"

She stared at him as if he'd just spoken in archaic Sumerian. Damned if he didn't find every odd look she gave him enchanting. At this rate he'd be in danger of coming before he even got her naked.

"What I mean . . . " She sounded as if every word was agony. He shifted his weight so his cock was more securely wedged against her welcoming pussy. Maybe inane chatter was her version of foreplay.

He preferred the more hands-on method. Tugging his finger from her hair he caressed the curve of her warm cheek, the angle of her jaw. Traced over her full lips and slid inside.

She choked, pushed at his finger with her tongue, and he grinned down at her. At least he'd managed to shut her up. And now they could get down to pleasure.

"Don't you find any of this just a bit *weird*?" Her fingernails dug into his shoulder, which was much more satisfying than her feathery touches from a minute ago. Except for the fact she wasn't doing it to arouse him. "I mean, you don't even know me."

"Sweetheart, if you'd just quit chatting I assure you I'll waste no time in getting to know you." He slid his hand under her tank top and cradled the curve of her waist. Naked, warm flesh. Nibbling kisses against her blessedly silent mouth, he palmed her lace-covered breast.

Exquisite.

She punched his shoulder. "But how did you get here?"

Once again he pulled back and stared down at her. He had the eeriest feeling she wasn't pretending ignorance or faking that edge of panic in her voice. But he couldn't believe anyone who frequented that Manhattan nightclub could be that innocent. It was *the* place to be seen this year for those vacuous, jet-setting universals seeking cheap thrills and cheaper sex on the primitive dive called Earth. Even if she was a pureblood mortal without any powers of her own she obviously existed in a social stratosphere that allowed her access to such a lifestyle.

He slowly tightened his hand around her luscious breast. Her eyes glazed, her lips parted and she gave a seductive little sigh.

"Don't you remember how I got here?" He would never confess he couldn't. But with a bit of luck she would fill in the blanks without even realizing it.

"Well, you . . . just kind of appeared from nowhere," she said.

He gritted his teeth against the rampaging lust and undertow of frustration that seethed through his blood. His loss of memory gnawed through him and it galled that he was hoping a mere mortal might be able to piece his recent actions together.

"You mean in the club?" He might as well give the impression he knew exactly how they'd both arrived here. "You don't remember us talking before I brought us here?" Not that talking was ever that high a priority when he hooked up with a female but he could gloss over details if it made her feel better.

"Club?" Wariness clouded her eyes. "I wasn't at any club. Were *you*?" She sounded astonished, as if the notion he might have been in a club was beyond her comprehension.

Gods, if he hadn't picked her up at the club where had she come from? Or was she also suffering from selective amnesia and genuinely couldn't remember what she'd been doing for the last few hours?

"Sure. The club in Manhattan." It wouldn't take a second to contact Mephisto and demand some answers. Problem was, amnesiac or not, this woman had snared his interest in a way few ever did. Crazy, but he realized he'd rather discover the truth from her than a distorted version from Mephisto. But since she still looked completely blank, as if she had never heard of Manhattan, he decided to elaborate. "Earth."

"Yes." Her voice was faint but relief washed through him. For a second there he'd imagined she didn't even know which planet she was on.

Did it really matter whether she remembered or not? He wanted her. She was willing. Afterward he'd take her back to the club and see if anyone knew her. Someone was bound to claim her.

But right now he intended to claim her for himself.

Chapter Three

AURORA struggled to think around the erotically charged lightning that stabbed from the tip of her nipple to the sensitive bud of her clit. The golden stranger still pinned her to the ground, his hand clasped possessively over her breast as if their incomprehensible conversation had never occurred.

How could he have been in a club in Manhattan? She had assumed he'd also been astral projecting when those strange vibrations had shattered the tranquility. That somehow it had catapulted both his spiritual and physical body from one point in the astral planes to another. She might not have ever come across something like that before but who knew what the side effects of such a disturbance might be?

But the reality appeared even more outrageous. Somehow it had transported this oblivious guy from a *club* halfway around the world and dumped him on top of her. A mortifying thought hit her. Had she, as impossible as it seemed, shared that spirit-shattering orgasm with him?

Why wasn't he completely freaked out? Anyone would think he was used to one moment being out clubbing and the next waking up on some random girl.

Maybe that was because he did often blackout and wake up on some random girl?

But if that was the reason he was so relaxed about his odd lapse of memory, why had he felt compelled to explain that the club was on Earth? Where else would it be?

"You tell me something." His voice slid through her like rich, warm chocolate, decadent and delicious. "How did *you* get here?"

She realized her tongue was lapping desperately at her lips, as if she was trying to taste the forbidden delight. God, how mortifying.

"I grew up here." The words were husky, inviting. He probably thought she was a total tart.

His mouth quirked as if her response amused him, and his thumb circled her nipple, a teasing caress. It was hard to focus on anything else. She curled her toes and forced herself not to squirm with mindless need.

"And where," he said, his incredible eyes snaring her sanity once again, "is here?"

His question sank into her fogged brain through the lust that threatened to completely consume her.

"Ireland." Her voice was breathless, partly with desire and partly with nerves at his reaction. What would he do now that he realized he wasn't even in America anymore, never mind New York?

His thumb paused in its relentless torture and for the first time she had the feeling he was looking at her—properly. She wasn't sure she liked the expression on his face. He not only looked as if he didn't believe her, it was as if he thought she was deliberately lying to him.

"Ireland?" His gaze roved over her face as if he was committing each feature to memory. And not in a good way. "You're not trying to tell me you're indigenous to *Ireland*?"

"Yes." She tried to ignore the glare of incredulity he arrowed her way. It was just a delayed reaction. "Where do you come from?" She couldn't work out whether he was British or American, and just to further complicate matters every now and then she caught an elusive hint of a strange, exotic accent.

He dragged his hand from her breast, leaving her cold and abandoned, and braced his weight on either side of her shoulders. He no longer looked in the least bit amused but whatever he was feeling hadn't yet affected his erection. It was as hard and distracting as ever.

"That," he said, sounding feral, "is irrelevant."

Obviously he'd imagined she was just another of his one-night stands. That was why he'd indulged in the mind-blowing foreplay. Because he'd had no idea of where he was or what had really happened.

Then again, neither did she.

"I know this is all a bit of a shock." Oh god, was she really trying to reassure him? She wouldn't mind a bit of reassurance herself. "Honestly, I have no idea how—"

He rolled onto his back, flung one arm across his eyes and swore. At least, she assumed he swore by the vehemence and the way he fisted his hands. The language was like nothing she'd ever heard before.

And yet she had the eeriest sensation that somehow . . . she had.

While he continued to growl in obvious frustration, Aurora pulled her rumpled tank top down and willed her hands to stop shaking. She was aroused, wet and had an amnesiac stranger to deal with. But at least she had some amazing raw material for future fantasies.

Her fingers curled around her necklace. She'd worn it constantly since having the piece specially commissioned five years ago, but for once its comforting familiarity didn't calm her nerves. It didn't calm her thundering heart, either.

She chanced another glance at the stranger and despite her faint annoyance with his attitude she couldn't drag her fascinated gaze away. His dark gold hair spilled over the grass, and while she'd always had a preference for blond guys there was something seriously riveting about this one. His body was all taut muscle and gleaming bronze flesh, like an athlete from ancient Greece. The zipper on his jeans was undone and although she tried not to stare at his black underwear, it was impossible not to. Because the silky material strained over his massive erection, and really where else could a girl look *but* there?

Her palms were sweaty, her chest constricted. She screwed her eyes shut for a moment before forcing herself to once again focus on his face. His arm was still flung across his eyes but at least he'd stopped growling. In fact, he was ominously quiet.

She pushed herself upright and gripped her fingers together on her lap. She was not disappointed that he'd so abruptly pushed away from her. The churning sensation in the pit of her stomach was . . . relief.

Now she could do what she should have done the moment he'd arrived. Offer him practical help.

"Do you want me to call the—" Hell, who exactly should she call in this kind of situation? There was no emergency service she knew of that dealt with whatever had occurred this morning. "Anyone?" she added, sounding completely lame.

His jaw tensed. Aurora pulled her iPhone from her shorts pocket, unlocked it and slid it across the grass to him.

"Maybe you'd rather call someone yourself?" *The U.S. Embassy, perhaps?*

"Go away." It was an autocratic command, as if he was used to issuing them and having them instantly obeyed. She didn't blame him for being pissed. She'd probably be exactly the same if their positions were reversed. Except there wasn't any need for him to be such an arse with her. It wasn't as if any of this was her fault.

Was it?

No. Definitely not. Whatever had happened to shake the astral planes had nothing to do with her. Since she'd turned eighteen, two years after her mum had begun to forget her past, Aurora's insubstantial desire to *do something* had gradually grown and solidified into an unshakeable quest. For the last eight years she'd researched meticulously and combined with her studies in biomedical science had concluded she stood a good chance of success. After all, it wasn't as if she was trying to access a purely theoretical world. Half of her DNA actually *originated* from that world.

"Well, I can't go away." She hoped she sounded calm and reasonable. "I'm staying here this weekend. This land belongs to my parents." There was no point becoming offended by his sudden display of arrogance. Or of allowing the insistent whisper in the back of her mind that *this was all completely insane* to gain the upper hand. Maybe that was part of the problem. Maybe she needed to take control of the situation instead of salivating over him like a complete nympho. "Would you like to come up to the house?"

He exhaled. Slowly, loudly and with the obvious intention of letting her know just how irritated he was. Without meaning to her glance slid to his crotch. He was still as aroused as ever. She really was a sad pervert.

"It's over. I'm not interested."

Despite her best intentions she couldn't resist another illicit glance. It was obvious that while his brain might want to pretend disinterest, judging by the bulge in his pants his cock had other ideas. *Had she really thought that?* So much for her attempts to take control of the situation. She bit her lip to stop herself from giggling. At least she hadn't said it out loud.

"I only meant if you wanted a cup of tea or—or something."

Gabe slid his arm over his forehead and glowered at the woman sitting cross-legged by his side. Her eyes were too bright, her cheeks were flushed and she had a half-smile on her face as if she found the situation hilarious.

Would she still find it hilarious if he pinned her to the ground, ripped off her clothes and fucked her so hard her brains ignited?

"I don't drink tea." He injected as much disgust into the words as he could. There was only one type of women he avoided. And they were the ones indigenous to Earth.

"Okay. I think we have whiskey, if you prefer."

For a second he just stared at her in disbelief. Why was she still sitting there, annoying him? He'd dismissed her three times. And she appeared not to realize. He shoved himself upright, ignored the unfulfilled throb between his thighs and caught sight of the cell phone she'd slid across the grass to him.

It was just an ordinary piece of human technology. Nothing special about it. He had a couple of cell phones himself. Yet he picked it up.

Lightning flashed through his arm, an electrical surge of energy that owed nothing to human engineers. And with the burning came the unmistakable image of Mephisto.

His grip tightened as disbelief hammered in his brain. What was this woman doing with something Mephisto had tampered with?

As if the contact had jarred his brain into gear, fragments of memory returned to him. Back at the club. He and Mephisto had got no further than planning their night's entertainment with those four willing females. Instead, Mephisto had pulled a bleeping iPhone from his pocket and scrutinized the screen.

And then, without a word of explanation, he'd teleported.

Gabe gritted his teeth. He vaguely recalled swallowing another tankard of brain-rot and then two of the quartet had lured him into a darkened nook. He remembered them feverishly pulling off his shirt, their gasps as they trailed their fingers over his chest—and then nothing else pushed through the impenetrable fog clouding his mind. That must've been the moment he'd blacked out.

And ended up here.

MEPHISTO, RENDERED INVISIBLE to the mortal realm by so many glamours his head ached, inched stealthily along the branch of the oak so he wouldn't miss a word of Gabe's response.

He couldn't imagine why Gabe wasn't enjoying those four girls they'd picked up. How the hell had he suddenly appeared from no-where? It was as if he had literally *fallen* from the sky. Whatever, he was the reason Mephisto was now choking on fucking glamours and hiding in a *tree*. The last thing he wanted was for the other archangel to catch a whiff of his presence in the troposphere.

Just moments ago Mephisto had been enjoying a front-row seat, right next to the oblivious Aurora as she entered the astral planes and attempted her insane experiment.

Of course he hadn't expected her to succeed. But still he'd turned up to watch the show. *And the crazy bitch had opened a rift.*

It wasn't often—make that never—that a mere mortal managed to stun him. But his hunch two years ago that this human would provide excellent entertainment at some point had paid off.

He'd first stumbled across her in London as she was leaving a college dedicated to psychic studies. Such places held a morbid fascination for him. He wasn't sure why, since the abilities of even the most psychically advanced humans was pitiful.

But for some reason, despite her not being his type or doing anything for his libido, he'd given her a second glance. And then he'd caught sight of the notes she was scribbling in her notebook as she leaned against the wall and was instantly intrigued.

They were not the normal observations of a student studying

advanced trance and channeling. She appeared to be putting her own unique spin on it all and his curiosity roused.

So he'd tapped into her cell phone—a stroke of genius in his opinion—that meant he could monitor her psychic fluctuations without exerting any unnecessary energy. And although he hadn't imagined for one second she'd get anywhere with her lofty plans to flout the laws of nature, her single-minded determination and bizarre convictions kept him hooked.

But before she could do anything else the astral planes began to tumble. He'd catapulted back into his physical body, settled back to watch the inevitable fallout—and instead had been nearly flattened by the improbable arrival of Gabe. *From nowhere.*

Unfortunately he didn't have the time to hang around and watch the finale. Aurora's inevitable fate he knew already. He was no longer interested in her. It was Gabe who now intrigued him. Because it was obvious the other archangel hadn't arrived voluntarily and who the hell possessed the power to transport an archangel against their will or knowledge?

Chapter Four

GABE tossed the phone back at the woman who caught it one-handed. He might still not be able to remember anything, but things were finally falling into place.

This was Mephisto's idea of a joke. And when Gabe caught up with him he was going to rip off his wings. Feather by fucking feather. Just because Mephisto was the oldest archangel in existence, the favorite of their bitch of a goddess and outranked any other archangel didn't give him the right to mess with Gabe.

He had no idea how the bastard had managed to knock him out and transport him here or even the point of the whole thing but he had a more pressing question right now.

"How long have you known Mephisto?"

Her eyes widened in apparent bemusement, as if his sudden change in topic had thrown her.

"I don't know anyone called Mephisto." She sounded so damn convincing he wanted to reach inside her mind and throttle her thought processes. Yet for some reason he couldn't fathom, he believed her. "Look, do you want me to take you to the hospital? Just so they can check that you don't have a concussion or something?"

With monumental effort he clawed through his mind, trying to recall the blank moments between seeing Mephisto vanish, and him waking up here. On top of this damn female and with an excruciating hard-on. Arousal was flooding every cell of his body as if he'd been nanoseconds from orgasm. And despite the last few minutes, he *still* had a hard-on of massive inconvenience.

Concussion wasn't the first word that sprang to mind.

"Do you have any idea?" he said, giving her a glare that in the past had caused mortals to collapse in terror. This infuriating female merely stared right back, as if mesmerized. For a split second he lost his train of thought. "Any idea how dangerous it is to become involved in things you know nothing about?"

Instead of wilting beneath his condemnation she stiffened, as if she took offense at his tone.

"I happen to know a great deal about it. More than you appear to, anyway."

He was so astounded that she was not only answering a rhetorical question, but contradicting him in the process, that he just sat there in silence as she continued to berate him. "Didn't you feel those weird vibrations? Don't you think that had something to do with all this?"

The words *weird vibrations* caused an eerie shudder of resonance along his spine but he ignored it. This primitive creature, who continued to pretend ignorance of his elevated status, was arguing with him.

His patience—not one of his few virtues in the first place—unraveled. If she refused to tell him what he wanted to know he'd find out by himself. With only a minimum amount of effort as befit her lowly perch on the evolutionary chain, he scanned the outer edges of her mind.

Instantly, psychic fire jabbed into his brain, so unexpected he recoiled. *She had rebuffed him.* It wasn't possible that she'd been aware of his intrusion. It had been so superficial as to be virtually nonexistent.

All of which was irrelevant. Her mind had not only refused him entry, but it had actively fought back.

"What did you just do?" Her tone was accusing but there was a thread of sheer astonishment in her voice, as if she couldn't quite believe her own question. "Did you try and get inside my *mind*?"

How did she know? Even the most psychically advanced humans were oblivious. It was only the primarily telepathic races that should've been able to pick up on such a mild scan.

He maintained eye contact, his irritation over the current situation fading into a reluctant fascination. "Do you have anything of interest inside your mind?"

Her lips parted in obvious disbelief that he hadn't instantly refuted her accusation. "I don't think that's really the point, is it?" she said, gripping her phone so tightly her knuckles turned white.

On the more civilized worlds uninvited psychic scanning was considered morally reprehensible. Since that ruled out the vast majority of planets in the universe, Gabe had never before been confronted by an irate victim.

Normally, they either had no idea of his intrusion or, in the cases where he really dug in deep, they were in no state to confront anything by the time he'd finished with them.

Briefly he considered a deeper penetration of this woman's mind. And then discarded it. Even a minor incursion could be fatal given the mental barriers she had in place. How had she managed to erect such a thing? Her protection would need years of training to perfect.

Which begged the question: Who had *taught* her?

And, probably more important, why?

"There must be something worth knowing inside your head." He was faintly shocked to realize he meant the words. He could barely recall the last time he'd been interested in what went on inside the skull of a female he wanted sexually. "Otherwise why bother with such a sophisticated defense system?"

Aurora realized her jaw was in danger of dropping yet again, and clenched her teeth as a preemptive measure. It was bad enough she hadn't imagined that sensual, silken touch on the outer edges of her mind. For a second she'd been so stunned by the contact she hadn't grasped its significance. Because, despite all the research she'd conducted and people she'd met over the last few years, not one of them had possessed the kind of telepathic ability she had inherited from her mother.

She had never shared such an intimate link with anyone but her mum. She had no idea how such a link would even *feel* with anyone else. And yet on a primal level her shocked suspicion had been absolute.

He had attempted to invade her mind.

Not that it made any difference. Psychic or not, he still had no idea how he'd ended up here.

With difficulty she relaxed her death grip on her cell phone and tried to make sense of his last obscure remark. *Defense system?*

"I have no idea what you're talking about," she said. It was a horrible cliché and the look on his face suggested he thought so too. "Just don't do it again, that's all."

His lips thinned, and for a moment she had the strangest compunction to apologize. After all, she had just insulted him. And she had no right questioning him really, did she?

Because he was . . . in the right.

The thought hovered in her mind, heavy and insistent. She frowned, felt her lips slowly part, felt the words forming on her tongue.

But she wasn't sorry. She hadn't insulted him. He might look like every girl's wet fantasy but that didn't give him the right to go around probing inside their minds.

At least, not in *her* mind.

She bit down hard on the tip of her tongue and the ridiculous urge to beg his forgiveness dissolved. If she didn't know better she'd think he was planting those thoughts in her head. Except she knew he wasn't because she couldn't feel his intrusion the way she had felt him before.

"You were saying?" His voice was low, smoky and wrapped around her in a sensual caress. His eyes enslaved her, beguiling her into their magical depths. The lust she had managed to dampen down once again surged through her veins.

He was gorgeous. He knew it and had no compunction in using it to his advantage. She hitched in a deep breath, tore her gaze from his and glared at her clenched hands. To her relief the hypnotic imperative to plaster her body against him and offer herself like a sacrificial slave crawled back into the depraved depths of her libido.

His sexual pull was frightening. Lethal. His past was probably littered with broken hearts and broken promises and if she didn't get rid of him soon she'd willingly be his next conquest.

She almost had been his next conquest. She couldn't quite figure out whether she was sorry or relieved she'd pulled back earlier. But no matter how much she still fancied him, the moment for mindless gratification had passed.

So long as she didn't look back into his eyes.

"I think we should go back to the house." She kept her gaze on her hands. "Then we can make plans on how you can get home."

He didn't reply. Didn't move. Eventually she couldn't stand it any longer and risked looking up at him. There was an odd expression on his face, as if he was attempting to process her words and finding it beyond him.

Somehow she couldn't imagine there was much he found beyond his capabilities.

Still he didn't respond. The silence stretched between them, taut and strangely brittle, as if the slightest wrong word might shatter the pervading peace.

"Don't you think so?" She tried to ignore it, but his silence was unnerving.

"I think," he said, looking at her as if she was a particularly exotic beetle he'd discovered crawling over his foot, "I could do with that whiskey."

"Right." Aurora refused to be insulted by the expression on his face. "Good idea." She could definitely do with a stiff drink or three, that was for sure. She grabbed the framed flower, pushed herself upright and mentally winced when her knees began to shake. She hoped he didn't notice. "Come on then."

He shot her a look that suggested he wasn't used to people telling him what to do. For a moment she thought he wasn't going to move, but then he expelled a pained breath and stood in a sensuous, graceful movement without needing to brace his weight on his hands at all.

Desire curled deep in her belly. Standing, she could admire his sculpted pecs and taut abdomen to their best advantage. As if fully aware of her furtive scrutiny he stretched, panther-like, biceps flexing as he linked his hands over his head. Dark gold hair dusted his chest, arrowing toward his unzipped jeans, and Aurora swallowed a groan of pure unadulterated lust.

He could probably taste the sexually charged pheromones radiating from her deprived body. But even that mortifying thought wasn't enough to stop her visual feasting.

The corner of his mouth quirked, as if he was fully aware of her regard, and he rolled his shoulders, muscles bunching and relaxing as if he was deliberately trying to tempt her.

Mindless gratification hovered on her immediate horizon, assuring her the moment could too easily be recaptured, and it was more than tempting. Mesmerized by the allure of his body she watched, helpless to tear her gaze away, as he turned to face the woodland that bordered the property.

Her ravenous gaze licked over his powerful shoulders and froze, unbelieving. Two deep gashes ran from his shoulder blades down the length of his back. Her breath stalled in her throat, unnoticed. *Good god, what the hell had happened to him?*

It looked as if an acid-drenched axe had sliced through to the bone, eating the flesh, distorting the muscle. Although the wounds were now healed and looked ancient, the passage of time hadn't disguised how horrific the injuries must have been, or how agonizing.

Slowly he turned toward her, and despite how she tried to hide it she knew the shock ricocheting through her blood was clearly reflected on her face.

He caught her gaze, held it and she watched his mesmeric eyes darken with comprehension. And then he took one stride toward her.

Chapter Five

GABE halted in front of the woman. She was no longer issuing orders as if she was his equal, or pretending disinterest when her arousal fragranced the air with devastating consequences for his libido. Instead, she looked as if she was about to faint.

He was used to mortals passing out in his presence. But usually they did that the second they met him, not twenty minutes later. Why would his scarred back cause her such trauma?

"You . . . Your . . ." She appeared incapable of coherent speech, but he had the strangest certainty it wasn't because he now scared her to death.

"Yes?" The word was pure ice. He couldn't figure out why her reaction affected him. He'd lived with his *disability* for millennia. It was who he was. And until now not a single mortal had ever dared to make even an oblique reference to his . . . lack.

She looked as if she wished she hadn't said anything. He would make her wish a great deal more than that before he'd finished with her.

"I'm sorry." The words tumbled out, and her blue eyes appealed to him for mercy. "It's just—you must have been very fortunate to survive such a terrible accident."

Fortunate and *survive* were not usually two words he associated with the horrifying circumstances surrounding the loss of his wings. He rolled his shoulders and could still feel, even after all this time, the phantom pull of muscles and feathers that had long since ceased to exist.

Bleak despair seeped from the fissures in his soul. He no longer possessed his wings but they would forever possess him; an intangible embrace as enduring as creation itself.

He shoved the memories deep into the abyss. After all these years it should have got easier to suppress the past. But it never had. He knew now it never would.

Deep in his heart he'd have it no other way. Because the alternative—*to forget*—chilled the essence of his being.

"Do you have any idea," he said, already knowing the answer, "what you're talking about?"

She blushed and looked suitably mortified. "No. I can't even imagine. I shouldn't have said anything." Before he could respond to her half-assed apology she looked up and their eyes meshed. "I do that. Speak before I think. Just ignore me."

He had every intention of ignoring her. But damn, her eyes were pretty.

"This way." She shot him a sideways glance as she clutched a silver frame to her breasts. Her copper-tinted hair was tousled, her eyes still captivatingly innocent. She barely reached his shoulder and her slender figure enhanced the inherent fragility of her species. He realized that far from ignoring her he could hardly take his eyes off her.

"So, um . . ." She was clearly still embarrassed by the way she'd drawn attention to his missing wings. Except, apparently, she didn't know the significance of his scars. "What's your name?"

For a second he thought he'd misheard her. In all his existence he couldn't recall a single time when he'd had to introduce himself. Damned if he'd start now.

"What's yours?" There was an edge in his voice. If he discovered this female was faking her innocence he'd take great pleasure in watching her brain leak out from her ears.

"Aurora Robinson." She shot him another glance, a questioning expression on her face. He ignored it. If she didn't know who he was, that wasn't his problem.

It was novel, though. He'd often had females whose names he never knew or would forget within moments of having them. Not once had the situation been reversed.

Yeah, it was a novel sensation. But he wasn't sure whether he liked it.

"You live here alone?" They were approaching a small stand of silver birches beyond which he caught glimpses of a stone-built farmhouse.

"No." He caught a thread of irritation in her voice, as if his refusal to answer her question grated on her nerves. "This is my family home. I already told you I'm just here for the weekend."

The house came fully into view, and some distance from it was an enclosure where two great wolfhounds, their bellies flattened to the ground, whined softly at their approach.

"Hey, boys." Alarm filled Aurora's voice as she took off toward them. It was a couple of seconds before he realized he'd been watching her butt as she jogged. "What's the matter?" Still clutching the silver frame in one hand, she unbolted the gate to the enclosure. The dogs didn't move and their dark eyes still riveted on him.

She crouched down, placed the frame on her knees and wrapped an arm around each dog. "Come on, guys, what's up?"

Gabe leaned against the gate jamb, crossed his arms and watched her fuss over the dogs. There was nothing special about her. And although her eyes were pretty and her hair glinted copper in the sun, as humans went she was completely average-looking.

Although, admittedly, the freckles across the bridge of her nose were enchanting, there was nothing outstanding in her physical appearance to account for why he was still here.

Why he still wanted her.

Must have something to do with the way she had blocked his psychic scan.

The dogs broke free from Aurora's arms and crawled on their bellies toward him. He saw Aurora's mouth open in astonishment as she toppled onto her butt, and he sent her a mocking half-smile as her dogs wrapped themselves around his calves.

At least her dogs recognized him. He had no idea why he found that notion darkly amusing.

Aurora huffed as she scrambled to her feet and flicked him a resentful glance. "What are you, a dog whisperer?"

"Among other things." It was odd, but seeing her so put out by her dogs' behavior had extinguished his lingering anger. Now all that remained was the lust, which hadn't diminished at all. "Are we having that whiskey or not?"

So what if she was indigenous to Earth? He would never see her again. And after he'd fucked her to their mutual satisfaction he'd find Mephisto and knock the shit out of him. .

Sounded like a plan. He gave Aurora the benefit of his archangelic smile, the one that could dazzle even the most jaded of demigoddesses. She squinted, as if the sun had temporarily blinded her, and stamped past him as if completely unaffected by his radiance.

He stared at her retreating back in disbelief. Had she just ignored him? How was that even possible? He turned and followed her through the back door and into the kitchen, the dogs on either side of him, their claws clattering on the flagstone floor.

"Make yourself at home." She jabbed a finger at the timber table and chairs in the center of the kitchen and refused to make eye contact. He considered her remark, decided it wasn't a demand and so hooked out a chair with his foot and sprawled on it.

"Whiskey." He accompanied his command with a smoldering gaze. Part of him couldn't understand why her belligerent attitude wasn't annoying him. Yet it wasn't. If anything the disagreeable frown she kept shooting his way made him harder than ever.

She put her silver frame on the workbench before turning to him. For a moment their eyes clashed and desire thudded in the air, hot and primal. He slid his hand over his thigh, a blatant invitation for her to join him. But instead of rushing to his side she folded her arms and stared at his naked chest. Within a second her gaze slid to the top of the table instead. He shifted on the chair and decided sitting had been a bad move.

"I'll get you a drink in a minute." Aurora took a deep breath and he watched her breasts swell beneath the thin fabric of her tank. He flexed his fingers, recalling the feel of her cradled in the palm of his hand.

The whiskey lost its enticement. He imagined bending her over the table, exposing her naked ass for his pleasure. Spreading her thighs and taking her from behind, while he raked his hand through her tangled chestnut hair. He could hear her erratic gasps of impending orgasm and could feel her wet sheath convulse around him. His cock was so damn hard it hurt.

"Come here." His whisper throbbed with promise and he hooked a finger in her direction so she was under no illusion as to what he wanted.

Aurora gritted her teeth and clenched her hands, fingernails digging into her palms. It would be so easy to just walk across the kitchen, plaster herself across his lap and let him seduce her knickers off.

That was exactly what she'd wanted in those hazy, lust-drenched seconds after she'd plummeted from the astral planes. If she was brutally honest she still wanted it.

But no way was she going to give it. Never in her life had she met such an arrogant, up-himself jerk. He didn't even have the common decency to look her in the eye when he spoke to her.

She conveniently ignored the times she'd given his crotch a furtive glance. She'd asked him a perfectly reasonable question, and he'd blanked her. Even after she'd told him her name, he hadn't bothered to reciprocate.

And if that wasn't bad enough, he'd then hypnotized her dogs. She shot them a black glare at their treachery but they still only had eyes for the golden one.

"I need to know," she said, focusing on the tabletop because despite her belated moral high ground, she had the despicable feeling that one look at his face would cause her principles to crumble. "What *exactly* you remember."

"I remember . . ." His voice was smoky with the promise of hedonistic delights. She swallowed a groan. She might not like him, but he wasn't making it easy for her to resist him. "That we haven't finished what we started, Aurora."

God, the way he said her name sent spirals of primal need through the core of her being. She resisted the urge to squirm, but it was a close thing. Instead she curled her toes, forced herself to remember he was . . . gorgeous . . . no, arrogant . . . and made the fatal error of looking up and catching his smoldering gaze.

For long seconds she remained captivated by the stunning beauty of his eyes. All she really wanted to do was drop to her knees, crawl across the floor and worship at his feet. She was vaguely aware he spread his thighs as if in invitation, and the imperative to go to him thudded with deafening insistence inside her mind.

She wrenched her mesmerized stare from his eyes to focus on his nose. *Which was also a thing of sculpted perfection.*

"Are you . . ." Her voice was raw and scraped her throat. She swallowed, tried once more. "Are you messing with my thoughts again?"

She didn't think he was. But he had to be. *She* would never imagine behaving in such a subservient way.

For a fleeting moment he looked nonplussed by her question. As if it was not only the last thing he had imagined her asking but also completely incomprehensible.

"Again?" He managed to sound offended. "I've never messed with your thoughts. Why should I?"

It would have been a fair question, if he hadn't tried to enter her head earlier. That had been unforgivable and if he did it once what was to stop him from doing it again. Maybe he had an entire arsenal of mind-probing techniques at his disposal?

The problem was, she believed him. Which meant the desire to prostrate herself before him came entirely from her own warped, frustrated psyche.

She squeezed her eyes shut and attempted to harness her scattered thoughts.

"Do you remember *anything?*" *Apart from how to use his cock.* She had no doubt he could remember how to use *that.* A hot flush crawled over her breasts and onto her face and a silent sigh echoed through her mind. It didn't matter whether she looked at him or not. She only had to think of him to think of sex.

"What's your obsession with remembering? Why does it matter?"

Her eyelids sprung open. He was still sprawled on the chair and he still looked like sin incarnate. And he didn't look even the least bit concerned by the previous events.

A shiver skittered over her arms as a chilling possibility surfaced.

"Has this happened to you before?" Her voice was barely above a whisper. But it made a kind of scary sense. She had assumed, when he told her about the club, that he'd been, well, clubbing. But maybe he'd consciously entered the astral planes in Manhattan with the express goal of physically ending up somewhere else?

Not Ireland, obviously. But although he'd been clearly shaken by that bit of news he wasn't that freaked out about it all. Was it possible he used a technique similar to the one she had intended to use to travel to her mother's homeland?

"Not that I remember." And then he grinned, as if he thought he'd just cracked the world's greatest joke.

She needed space. Away from him so she could think rationally without every single thought becoming drenched with sexual implications.

"Right." She swung on her heel and battled the urge to bury her face in her hands. "I'll get us something to drink. Won't be long."

Gabe watched her all but run from the kitchen, as if she feared he might try and stop her. His grin faded into a frown. She might be only an indigenous female of Earth but she was turning out to be one of the most puzzling women he'd ever met.

Desire heated her voice, lust darkened her eyes. Her body language told him she found him irresistible. And yet she resisted him.

It had been a while since a woman had offered him a challenge when it came to sex. He had to admit that this strange encounter, while frustrating, was also extraordinarily arousing.

He stood and strolled to the workbench where she'd left her silver frame. He picked it up and frowned at the pressed flower beneath the glass. Inexplicably a shudder inched along his spine. The flower was fragile and faded and something—something wasn't right about it.

Before he could scrutinize it further the dogs, both of which had followed him across the kitchen to lay at his feet, stiffened, their attention locked on the open kitchen door. And then, simultaneously, they leaped up, hackles raised, barking with such ferocity he reeled against the workbench and watched them hurtle into the hall.

Gabe dropped the frame onto the workbench and was at their heels as they skidded into a living room. Then he collided into their bodies as they came to a dead standstill.

Ancient horror hammered through his heart and spilled into his bloodstream. A jagged, violet fracture, like static lightning, split the room from ceiling to floor.

The Guardians were coming for Aurora. And she was standing in front of the violet fracture as if mesmerized.

"Aurora." His voice was harsh. "Get away from there." Even as he spoke the imperative to leave thundered through his brain. What was happening here had nothing to do with him. It was none of his concern.

It didn't matter if Aurora ran. The Guardians had singled her out. She would be captured. She would be taken.

He couldn't interfere. It was against ancient protocols. But still he couldn't leave.

She looked at him, and he saw raw terror clouding her eyes. "Keep back." Her voice cracked with fear and her arm swung out, hitting his chest, an unmistakable gesture of protection.

For a second his entire focus zeroed in on her. He forgot about the dark energy seeping from the fracture, forgot about its implications, forgot everything but the fact Aurora had just attempted to push him away from the face of danger.

No one pushed him from the face of danger. No one imagined, let alone put into practice, the outrageous assumption they had the ability to protect him.

She didn't know who he was. Equally, she could have no idea what nightmare waited for her once she entered the Guardians domain. Revulsion curdled his gut and he gripped her arm and pulled her around to face him.

"Don't." She pushed against him, eyes wild, breath erratic. "Let me go."

In his peripheral vision he saw the loathsome figures appear within the glowing violet cloud. He knew the kind of things the Guardians would do to her to satisfy their sick craving to soak in a mortal's terror. Their species went back a billion years, to the sunrise of time itself, and their hatred of any other form of life that had evolved after them was absolute. Two million years ago the Alpha Immortals, ancestors of every immortal alive today, had emerged from the fallout of a supernova. Within a million years they had banished the marauding Guardians to the outer edges of creation, but still the creatures abducted innocent victims to feed their perverted addiction. Disgust gripped his stomach, and an ancient, long-buried instinct rose.

He wrapped his arms around her, held her head securely against his shoulder so she couldn't move a muscle, and without even a second's hesitation took her to the safest place on Earth.

His sanctuary.

Chapter Six

WHAT was he doing? Aurora tried to move her head, tried to see what had happened to that terrifying streak of lightning. But his fingers bit into her skull, keeping her plastered against his shoulder and not only could she not move, she could hardly breathe.

Then she forgot about breathing, forgot about the violet lightning as a whiplash of white fire streaked through her brain, her lungs, her heart. Instinctively she tried to curl into a ball but still he held her in an iron grip, even as a scream of primal terror locked in her throat.

And as suddenly as it began, the horrifying sensation of her every atom flying apart ceased.

She realized her nails were digging into his naked flesh, that her mouth was squashed against his shoulder. The entire length of her body molded his and the crazy thought drifted through her mind that she should stay here, trapped in his arms, because only here was she . . . safe.

Gingerly she unhooked her nails and saw the crescents gouged into his flesh. She pushed at his chest and lifted her head. He didn't try and stop her and as she stumbled backward, nausea churned and sweat beaded her skin.

No way was she going to throw up in front of him. She swallowed, tried to focus on his face but everything was blurred as if she'd been plunged under murky water.

"Are you okay?" He didn't sound concerned. He sounded irritated. She let out a shaky breath, tried to focus once again. It was the eeriest sensation but she could've sworn they were no longer in her parents' living room.

"I don't feel so good." A sluggish recollection crawled across her mind of violet lightning that had suddenly appeared in front of her.

He muttered under his breath in that same strange language he'd used before. "You'd better sit down." He took her arm and propelled her sideways and her brain finally reconnected with her vision.

"What the *fuck*?" Her heart kicked against her ribs in sudden panic as she stared, uncomprehending, at the smooth stone floor. Where were the faded, antiquated rugs that had been in her family for countless generations?

"Just sit down before you fall down." He pushed her, none too gently, onto a timber chair.

She sat, but only because her legs threatened to buckle. She gripped the sides of the chair and risked glancing up. They were in a kitchen, but it wasn't her kitchen. It was large, square and constructed of polished stone, and through the vast expanse of glass windows was a lush forest.

Her stomach heaved and she clamped her teeth together before finally looking in *his* direction.

His arms were folded and he was glaring at her as if this was all her fault. A shiver raced over her arms, cooling the sweat, increasing the nausea. *Was this all her fault?* And what, in any case, *was* all this?

Her chest tightened and it became hard to draw in a breath. She knew on some fundamental level she was in danger of tumbling into severe shock but couldn't seem to get a grip. Because there was nothing to grip on to. Because none of this made sense.

"Drink." It was a harsh command and she was aware of a strong hand holding the back of her head and a crystal glass pushed against her lips. Sparkling cold water trickled down her throat and she saw rainbows dance across the ceiling as sunlight caught the crystal facets of the glass.

She choked, pushed his arm away and wiped her mouth with the back of her hand. Either she was in the middle of the most lucid dream she'd ever experienced or this was really happening. And although she much preferred the dream scenario she had a terrible feeling this was anything but.

"What did you do?" She wanted to sound tough, but her voice wobbled. "How did I get here? Did you pull me through the astral planes?" He must have done. Although how he'd managed such a thing she couldn't imagine. Besides, why couldn't she remember the journey? And why had she felt as if every atom of her body had shivered on the edge of destruction?

He placed the glass on the stone workbench with great precision, and she got the impression that in reality he would love nothing better than to shatter both. Then he looked at her as if he'd never even heard of the astral planes, much less actually ascended to them.

"The astral planes?" His tone confirmed his expression. "Of course I didn't. This is where I live."

Aurora risked another glance around the kitchen and the forest skimmed her peripheral vision. Should she assume they were now in America? If so, they certainly weren't in Manhattan.

She wasn't going to panic. There was probably a very simple explanation for her current situation and it had nothing to do with her having lost her mind.

So he hadn't pulled her through the astral planes. But somehow he had transported her from Ireland. She knew it wasn't impossible. Her own mother had once done a similar thing on the night she'd walked into her father's arms. But they'd had a prior psychic connection, years of shared dreams and linked visions. They were already, in many ways, irrevocably entwined together.

And, of course, her mother hadn't physically traveled miles across the world. She had merely taken one step that had propelled her from her own dimension into this one.

Aurora had grown up with that knowledge. It was familiar, no matter how improbable anyone else might think it. But the thought of being catapulted halfway around the world within a couple of seconds was seriously . . . terrifying.

She struggled against the overwhelming urge to curl into a ball and close her eyes. Denial wasn't going to make any of this go away. Information, after all, was power.

"Yes, but how did we actually *get* here?" *Did she really want to know?*

For a moment she didn't think he was going to answer her. Then he exhaled an impatient breath. Anyone would think he found her questions completely unnecessary.

"Teleportation." He sounded deadly serious and her instinctive response to scoff shriveled in her throat. "Your body dematerialized in Ireland and instantaneously rematerialized here. But don't worry. It's unlikely you mislaid any vital fragments en route."

Teleportation? Was *that* how he'd landed on top of her today?

"And where exactly is your home?" Was that really her voice? She sounded eerily calm. He'd never guess how close she was to sliding off the chair and hiding under the table.

"Somewhere you'd have no hope of finding on any godsforsaken maps of your world." He sounded like that fact gave him a great deal of grim pleasure.

She wiped her sweaty palms on her shorts and tried to ignore the erratic pounding of her heart. She wasn't going to fall apart. That wouldn't clarify her current situation or help her get back home.

"And why," she said, as if she was perfectly used to teleporting as a means of transportation, "did you do that?"

Gabe stared at Aurora as disbelief crawled along his spine. Why wasn't she incoherent with fear? He'd just teleported her thousands of miles across the ocean and she was acting as if they'd just strolled across the street.

He wasn't sure why her serene attitude irked him, but it did.

"Because." His voice was savage. "I had the crazy urge to save your ass."

Her eyes glazed as if she was trying to make sense of his remark. "Save my ass?" She sounded confused but before he could enlighten her any further, her eyes widened in sudden recollection. "From that violet lightning, you mean?"

And still she kept on with the questions. He couldn't recall the last time a mortal had fired so many questions at him without his express permission. Did she *still* have no idea with whom she was dealing?

"From the Guardians." His revulsion for the creatures soaked every word, but Aurora's expression didn't alter. She clearly didn't have a clue who the Guardians were. "That *violet lightning* as you call it is their method of transportation between their world and this."

By rights Aurora should now gasp in shock and perhaps collapse onto her knees and grovel at his feet. He'd know what to do with her then. Sweep her into his arms, comfort her and screw her senseless.

And once that was done the burn in his blood would subside and he could work out, in a cold, logical manner, what he was going to do with her. Instead of which every time he looked at her all he could imagine was how she would feel and how she would taste as she wrapped her legs around him.

Her lips parted in obvious shock. She was in the perfect position to take him into her mouth. The realization he couldn't stop thinking about sex, even when he'd just broken one of the oldest protocols by rescuing her, caused his mood to degenerate further.

"You mean," she said, sounding torn between fascination and disbelief, "they come from another dimension?"

She was asking all the wrong questions. She was indigenous to Earth and so far they hadn't attained the technology to do anything more than a tentative prod beyond their own solar system. They had no conception of the life that seethed in the universe and would certainly burst a collective artery if they ever discovered their world was a popular destination for degenerates who enjoyed sporting with primitives.

As a species they certainly weren't ready to discover what archaic creatures survived in the vast expanses of space between galaxies. The merciless Guardians, who had retreated into the inhospitable Dark Matter and created their immense domains, aka *the Voids*, countless millennia ago. "Of course they don't come from another dimension." *What had given her that idea?* "Trust me. You don't want to fall into their clutches."

For a moment she looked as if she was about to finally succumb to delayed terror and pass out. But then she gripped her fingers together and although he didn't want to feel anything but irritation at his rash rescue, reluctant admiration for her sheer force of will uncoiled in his chest.

"Don't worry." At least he could reassure her on one thing. "They can't get to you here. It's physically impossible for them to penetrate my island."

Instead of appearing soothed, Aurora's eyes flashed with fear and she stiffened in the chair as if he'd just delivered devastating news. "They wanted *me*?" She sounded horrified, and he realized that hadn't occurred to her until now. Shit. By attempting to reassure her he'd only managed to panic her further. "But why?"

Ancient images flashed through his brain, meshed with ageless rumor and eternal speculation. He could tell her exactly what the Guardians wanted her for. They would drag her to their torture chambers and subject her to any number of their so-called experiments. And as for the why . . .

He discovered he couldn't do it. Why frighten her more than she was already? Just because he didn't normally care about shredding a mortal's frail sensibilities when it suited him was neither here nor there.

Aurora had tried to save him from the Guardians, even though she hadn't known what they were. Even if her attempts were feeble in the extreme and doomed to dismal failure, it didn't change the fact she had *tried*.

Why hadn't he left her the second he'd discovered she was indigenous to Earth? Then he wouldn't be in the middle of this messy moral dilemma that rocked his necrotic soul.

He didn't do soul searching. He didn't do charity work. And he wasn't about to start now.

But still he couldn't tell her the full truth.

"How should I know? They enjoy abducting mortals and . . . playing with them."

She stared at him as if he was her worst nightmare and he had the unbelievable urge to drop his gaze. As if he was somehow in the wrong. When all he'd done was save her from a fate more horrific than her mind could comprehend.

"Mortals?" There was an unmistakable wobble in her voice. "Are you trying to tell me that the Guardians aren't even human?"

"Human?" If her question hadn't been so naively pathetic he would have laughed. Except he couldn't laugh, not when she continued to gaze at him with those enchantingly innocent blue eyes. Because her ignorance wasn't amusing. It was terrifying. "No. They're not human."

What little color that remained in her cheeks faded. It was painfully obvious that until this moment the conception of alien life had never truly registered.

"But why did they come after *me*? Is it because of something I did?" She sounded horrified. Did she really believe she was capable of doing anything to invoke the legal strictures of the Guardians?

"Doubtful." Make that impossible. No way could Aurora have done anything to warrant the Guardians unleashing their own brand of justice on her.

"So it was just totally random that they appeared today?" He caught a faint hint of desperation in her voice, as if despite his reassurance she still harbored the suspicion that she was responsible for the Guardians' arrival.

"The Guardians," he said, even as a section of his mind demanded to know why he was indulging Aurora by answering her incessant questions, "are totally random bastards. They would have turned up today whatever you were or weren't doing."

That was true enough. And then a thought stabbed through his brain. *Had their appearance in Aurora's life anything to do with him and Mephisto?*

The possibility gnawed. It was unlikely. Through longstanding mutual animosity and ancient protocols, archangels and the Guardians avoided each other's presence. But if Mephisto's interference had in some incomprehensible way exposed Aurora to the Guardians' attention then he was doubly justified in snatching her from their fetid jaws.

"How do you know that?"

"What?" He frowned at her, his mind still working on the possibility his inexplicable arrival in Aurora's life was somehow connected to the Guardians' appearance. Although he was certain there was no connection, a fragment of doubt refused to die. And with the doubt came, of all things, *guilt*.

Over a human.

"How do you know so much about them? I've never even heard of them."

Irritation spiked and he welcomed it, nurtured it, because it helped to slaughter the despicable tendrils of guilt that insisted on weaving through his brain. Didn't she ever shut up? Why wasn't his word that she needed to be saved from the Guardians enough for her?

He'd done nothing but answer her incessant questions since the moment they had met. He, the Archangel Gabriel, who answered to *no one*.

The silence screeched between them. Her fingers fidgeted, she crossed and uncrossed her ankles and a couple of times the tip of her tongue peeked between her lips.

He realized he was staring at her lips. Waiting for the third time.

Fuck. He didn't do waiting. Not when it came to women and sex. And he'd be damned if he'd wait much longer for Aurora. She'd wanted him from the second they'd met. The sooner he had her, the sooner he'd be able to turn his mind to sorting out this mess.

"Okay." She shot him an odd look, as if finally realizing he no longer intended to satisfy her insatiable curiosity. He drew in a deep breath. The situation wouldn't be intolerable. Now she understood the need to hold her tongue. "So who are you, exactly?"

Or not. Briefly he considered ignoring her question, as he had ignored her previous question, but guilt still crouched in a dark corner of his mind and it galled. She wanted the truth? He'd give her the truth.

"Your savior." Each word dripped with derision. Not that he expected Aurora to appreciate the irony of his comment. When was the last time he'd been anyone's savior without a hefty price tag attached for his services?

For a moment she just continued to stare at him and he narrowed his eyes, daring her to pass comment on his remark. The silence extended, fraught with words unsaid, and his taut muscles began to relax. This uncomfortable arrangement would work, so long as she didn't keep firing endless questions his way. Then she blinked, breaking eye contact, and pushed herself to her feet.

"And how long do you think I'll need to stay here before it's safe to go back?"

"Go back?" After everything he'd just told her, her first thought was how soon she could go back?

"Yes." She flattened one hand on the table, as if she still needed support. "I mean, do you think the Guardians have gone now? Is it safe for me to go home yet?"

He had no idea how long the Guardians would wait for her. It depended how much they wanted her. One thing was for sure though. They'd be mad as hell that an archangel had snatched their prey from right under their nonexistent noses.

That alone could make them more tenacious in their desire for this particular human.

Curse the gods. This was his sanctuary, his bolthole, the headquarters for his black ops ventures. He'd never brought a mortal here. The thought had never crossed his mind. But because of one unguarded second Aurora Robinson was not only here—she could well be here for *weeks*.

It was a nightmarish prospect. There was a world of difference between sharing a few pleasurable hours with a desirable female and having that female intrude into his personal existence. Especially when she did nothing with her mouth but talk.

And he had no one but himself to blame.

But instead of thanking him, instead of showing due gratitude for the great sacrifice he was making to ensure her continued safety, all Aurora wanted to know was how soon she could leave.

It was obvious she had no intention of shutting up. He'd seduce her and exhaust her so thoroughly her brain would require all its power to maintain basic life functions. She'd have no energy left to think of questioning him again.

"Try and understand." The words were as much for his benefit as hers. Hammering home the full implication of his unthinking action. "You're not going back, Aurora. You're here until I deem it safe for you to return to your life."

Chapter Seven

AURORA stared up at him, maintaining eye contact. She would *not* allow panic to distract her. She was *not* losing her mind.

"And when might that be?" All things considered she sounded amazingly calm. They might have been discussing the local train timetable.

Once again he didn't answer her. But the heat of his gaze seared her skin and her uneven breath had nothing to do with her current situation and everything to do with the sinfully sexy bastard in front of her.

Because he was being a total bastard. Why was he acting as if she had no right to ask where she was? And even when he answered her it was as if he was doing her a huge favor.

Maybe he'd made all that stuff up about the Guardians. How did he know so much about them? But even as the thought slid into her mind, it refused to take hold. Because in her gut she believed every word he'd said.

"Is there some way of finding out how long the Guardians will hang around?" No way did she want to return if they—whatever exactly they were—were still waiting for her. But surely they wouldn't wait for long.

Would they?

One thing was for sure. She couldn't stay here indefinitely. Her mother needed daily contact with her—by phone, email or text, anything. And if she didn't go and visit at least every other weekend, her mum's confusion magnified. Her dad said she was her mum's touchstone, her last tenuous link to reality. If Aurora disappeared without a word how would that affect her mother? She didn't even want to imagine.

There had to be another way of avoiding the Guardians.

She stepped toward him and caught a flash of satisfaction in his eyes, as if finally she was doing something of which he approved. Her glance skated over his chest and, as if drawn by an invisible thread, tugged lower.

God. He was becoming aroused again. And she couldn't tear her fascinated gaze away as the silk tented through his unbuttoned jeans with provocative invitation.

Her fingers tingled with the need to touch. Heat seared her cheeks, penetrated her brain. It didn't matter where they were or what danger she might be in. She still found him bloody irresistible.

But she would resist. She had to. Because she had the feeling being with him would be so damn fabulous she could end up forgetting her own name. Never mind anything else.

He still didn't answer her. Maybe he just didn't know the answers. Why couldn't he simply tell her that?

"I need to go home as soon as possible. You can understand that, can't you?" She risked glancing up and caught a glint of incredulity in his eyes, as if her remark had caught him completely off-guard. "It's not that I don't appreciate what you did." She didn't want him to think she was being ungrateful. But the point was if she was safe from the Guardians here then all he had to do was explain how that worked and then she could ensure she took the same precautions. "But I just—"

Without a word he turned on his heel and stalked from the kitchen. Aurora stared after him, bemused. What was that all about? Was he the kind of guy who didn't like to be thanked?

Well, even though he did have a bit of an attitude problem he deserved to be thanked for what he'd done, so she followed him. A wide, stone-tiled hallway greeted her and he was halfway along it, making his way toward the simple stone staircase.

"Hey." She waited a couple of seconds but he didn't pause, didn't glance back at her. "Where are you going? I'm in the middle of talking to you."

He paused then, and she waited for him to turn around. But he didn't. A flicker of trepidation trickled along her spine at his rigid stance. What was the matter with him? Now she thought about it he didn't give the impression of someone who was uncomfortable with being thanked. Anyone would think her perfectly reasonable remark had infuriated him.

"It's kind of you to offer to put me up for a while." Well, it was. Even if the circumstances surrounding his offer were completely crazy. "But I can't stay. I have commitments and in any case my m—"

Slowly he turned and for some reason that was enough to dry the rest of her words in her throat.

"Be silent." His voice was low, even, and yet she flinched as if he had roared the words inside her brain. "Stop questioning my every command."

His every *what*?

"Command?" Had she misunderstood? "Your every *command*?"

"You'll stay here until I say otherwise. There's nothing to discuss."

Was he for *real*? "What century are you from? You can't go around giving me orders like that. If I want to leave here I will."

"No," he said, his gaze scorching her. "You won't."

For a moment words failed her as she stared into his smoldering eyes. The insubstantial desire to agree with him floated through her mind. It would make everything so much easier. And, after all, what else could she do?

She tore her gaze free and glared at his rigid jaw. As if surfacing through a cloudy pool her thoughts swirled back into focus. Sure, she hadn't a clue where she was and on top of that she didn't have any money, let alone her passport, on her.

But right now that didn't matter.

"You can't keep me here against my will."

Finally he took a step toward her. She only just stopped herself from taking a step back to compensate.

"I can do," he said, his voice ominously quiet, "whatever I please."

It was a blatant threat and all things considered she knew she should have been shivering with terror.

Except, bizarrely, his threat didn't terrify her. It annoyed her. Who did he think he was, issuing orders and throwing his weight around as if he was some sixteenth-century royal dictator?

She folded her arms and once again risked looking into his eyes. "Don't count on it."

His pupils expanded; a heady combination of lust and rage and again she stared, mesmerized, and all but forgot why she was mad with him.

"If I want your opinion I'll ask for it." He flicked a scorching glance over her, branding her flesh and heating her blood. "I suggest you don't hold your breath."

His insult shouldn't have bothered her at all. She hardly knew him. But his words rammed home the indisputable fact that while he wouldn't hesitate to sleep with her he had no interest whatsoever in her as a *person*.

Fine. She was only interested in *him* as a sex object because his personality could sure do with some major readjustment. Except it wasn't fine. And she couldn't think of a single thing to say in response that wouldn't let him know how much his caustic remark had hurt.

The resulting silence thundered in her ears. After a moment, when it appeared he'd been waiting to see if she had any comeback to his comment, his stony expression softened. Incredulous disgust curdled her stomach as she realized how easy it was for him to demolish her self-righteous indignation with nothing more than a seductive glance.

"Follow me. I'll show you to my suite."

Where, no doubt, he expected to seduce her into eternal compliance. As if that was already a foregone conclusion he took another step toward her. This time there was no inherent menace in his approach. This time he exuded raw, sensual desire.

"You have my permission to enter any room you like, apart from my office." He sounded as if he was bestowing a great honor. Aurora gritted her teeth. She wouldn't give him the satisfaction of responding, the arrogant jerk.

Another fraught silence suspended between them. It was clear he expected some kind of response and the slight narrowing of his eyes suggested he couldn't understand her prolonged muteness.

"Aurora." His voice was no longer as hard as granite. It purred through her mind, a sensual caress, and she marveled at his sheer, unabashed nerve. "Speak to me."

Oh, so now he wanted her to speak? When it suited him?

"I have nothing to say to you." Her voice wasn't as frosty as she'd like, but it would have to do. "Except for this. If you think I'm going to share your bed you're mad. Just because you saved *my ass* doesn't give you rights over any part of my body. Are we clear on that?"

His jaw visibly tensed and there was no mistaking the look of shock that flashed across his features. As if she had just accused him of something not only despicable but also, until this moment, something he hadn't even contemplated.

With a sense of surreal disbelief she realized he was offended by her remark. After everything he'd just said to her he had the nerve to take offense when she retaliated?

She waited for his cutting reply. It didn't come. Uneasily she realized that she'd completely misinterpreted his offer. After all, the chemistry had sizzled between them from the second they had met. It had nothing to do with him rescuing her and expecting sex as payment.

Not that she'd meant that. He must know that wasn't what she'd meant? Even if her words had inferred *exactly* that?

She glared at him. How had he managed to make her feel guilty? He needed to know she wouldn't put up with his medieval attitude. But she hadn't meant to accuse him of something that, in her heart, she knew he would never demand.

But how did she know that? How could she be so sure?

Before she could sort out her tangled thoughts he turned his back on her, climbed the stairs and disappeared around the corner.

Chapter Eight

GABE stormed into his suite, slammed the doors with such force the timber frame splintered and went out onto the expansive balcony. He stood at the very edge and glared at the subtropical forest that surrounded his villa, but saw only the disdainful expression on Aurora's face as she had accused him of expecting her to become his—what, his *sex slave*?

Was that what she really thought?

He'd sunk to the depths of depravity in his time. Had cohabited with the dredges of the universe and indulged in a multitude of drug-induced crimes across countless galaxies. But never had he come close to extorting sex for services rendered.

Deep in the ruined tangle of muscle and sinew that gouged his back, he could feel the ancient tug. He rolled his shoulders, flexed his pectorals, tried not to let the black anguish overtake him.

But the ache permeated his being, a constant physical reminder of all he had lost. Once, he hadn't cared. Had welcomed his deformity, flaunted his scars, taken a twisted sense of satisfaction in the fact he no longer possessed that which defined his species.

It hadn't lasted long. A few insane decades at most. And then reality had crashed through his haze of guilt and grief. The reality that he would never again experience the exhilarating freedom of soaring through the skies.

Eventually he'd learned to live with it.

His hands fisted, jaw tensed. Adrenaline pumped through his arteries, feeding the rage, stoking the lust that refused to subside. Every cell in his body screamed for release, to know once again the power and ecstasy of spreading his wings and owning the heavens.

Air hissed between his clenched teeth and he wheeled around, glared at his coolly elegant bedroom. Only two things could take the edge off this frenzied fire in his blood. Fighting or fucking. Right now, he didn't care which it was so long as it left him incapable, for a few blessed hours, of coherent thought.

Aurora. Her face materialized in his mind. How dare she level such base accusations at him? But even as the thought hammered through his brain, the vision of taking her while fury sizzled between them caused his cock to harden with shocking force.

She could protest all she liked. The lust between them had nothing to do with him having saved her from the Guardians. Her body wanted his and within moments he could have her writhing in mindless pleasure.

And afterward she would be sated and pliant and would finally know her place.

His blood thundered at the enticing image of Aurora on her knees, looking up at him with adoration and the respect that had so far been entirely lacking.

He marched into his dressing room and grabbed a black shirt from the timber closets built into the walls.

It was galling to know that even now he still wanted her. But he'd be damned if he was going to pursue her like a lust-struck mortal. Sooner or later she'd succumb to the desire in her blood and *she* would come to *him*.

In the meantime he intended to find a couple of willing females and fuck their primitive brains out.

AURORA HOVERED AT the bottom of the stairs, but as the minutes slid by he still didn't reappear. What was he doing?

Waiting for an apology?

She could swallow her pride enough to say she was sorry for accusing him of expecting sex as payment for having rescued her. It was a stupid notion in any case. He knew full well she'd wanted him from the minute he'd landed on top of her.

But she'd also make it clear that she wanted some answers. Make that a lot of answers. Because by god, she had a lot of questions.

She made her way up the stairs. The stone was worn, as if they had endured the steps of thousands over the centuries. She glanced over her shoulder and paused for a second to admire the sheer simplicity of the hallway and the endless windows with their breathtaking views. He apparently lived in paradise.

Upstairs were five timber doors—one to her left, an enormous double one directly ahead and two on the right.

"Hello?"

Silence greeted her. Heart hammering, she gingerly pushed open the first door on her right.

The room was completely empty. She tried the second door, with the same result.

The doors ahead beckoned. So she tried the one on her left.

It was obviously his office. The one he had forbidden her to enter. She nearly walked straight in, just to prove she could, but decided it wouldn't help her attempt at apologizing if he suddenly emerged onto the landing and caught her.

She eyed the last doors. They must have been about ten-feet high and six feet across and if she didn't know better she'd think he was trying to compensate for something.

"I know you're in there." She tried to make her voice sound commanding but wasn't at all sure she'd succeeded. "Can you come out so we can talk?" Because she really didn't want to have a discussion in his bedroom. It would be too distracting.

More silence. He obviously wanted her to grovel. He was going to be disappointed.

"I didn't mean what I said just now." *Was he listening?* "I'm just—look, do you think you could come out because I feel like an idiot talking to your door."

The silence became oppressive and unease knotted her stomach. Before she could stop to think of the possible consequences she pushed open the doors.

His bedroom suite was magnificent in its simplicity. The bed dominated, a massive timber four-poster, so huge it could easily accommodate six people. *And it probably did.* She scowled, dragged her gaze away and then stared in reluctant awe at the fabulous view through the open double doors.

Slowly she made her way toward the balcony and then stopped at the doorway, senses reeling. The balcony extended the length of the villa and was just as wide. *But there was no safety barrier.* Even from where she stood it was enough to give her a whisper of vertigo.

She swung around and stepped back into his bedroom. A carved archway led to another room. His bathroom? She decided she didn't care. Because it was glaringly obvious he wasn't here.

Her good intentions to apologize and have a rational conversation with him evaporated. The bastard had *teleported*, leaving her up the creek.

She swung on her heel and marched back down the stairs. She might not possess the technology he did in order to teleport but she wasn't as stranded as he imagined.

She *would* escape. And he would be . . . astounded.

GABE RETURNED TO the club in Manhattan. It was a long shot, but Mephisto might still be there. But after scanning the darkened interior and asking the bartender it became clear he wasn't. And hadn't been since earlier that morning, around the time when Gabe had unceremoniously landed on top of Aurora.

He shoved her from his mind. He'd come here to forget about her. It wouldn't be hard. He glanced around, his interest no longer in discovering Mephisto's whereabouts, and a pair of identical redheads caught his eye. When they realized his glance didn't immediately pass over them, they clutched each other and dissolved into giggles.

They'd do. He took a step toward them.

"My Lord Gabriel."

The voice directly behind him brought him up short. He swung around and glared at the tall male who eyed him fearlessly. "I'm busy." Gabe turned away. The male didn't back away, didn't apologize. What the fuck was wrong with mortals today?

"A moment of your time, my lord. That's all I ask."

"Not now."

The male gripped his upper arm. "I've been searching for you for the last three Medan moon cycles."

Gabe looked him in the eyes, then deliberately dropped his gaze to his upper arm. The male didn't let go. It was a measure of his desperation, but Gabe didn't give a shit about his desperation. The man had about three seconds before he lost that hand for good.

Finally the male appeared to realize his near-fatal error and slowly freed him. "Forgive me." He bowed his head in respect, this time keeping his eyes trained on the floor. "Lord Gabriel, you're the only one who can help me. I beg you to consider my request."

There was a protocol to be followed for anyone who wanted to approach him with regard to requesting his services. Being accosted in a club, in full view of dozens of pairs of curious eyes, wasn't an intelligent move for someone hoping to win his favor.

There were other appropriate channels. Generally he preferred to conduct business on a suitably remote and inhospitable planet. But it had been weeks since he'd finished his last assignment. Maybe this man could offer him something of interest. Something he could focus on other than the annoying presence of Aurora on his island.

He swerved into a darkened alcove where a couple was entwined. For some crazy reason they reminded him of Aurora's accusation and his banked rage flared once again. "Move it."

After a startled glance in his direction, the couple leaped to their feet and sidled past him in clear relief he hadn't accompanied his demand with a couple of thunderbolts.

He sprawled on the seat and propped one booted foot on the table. Without waiting to be invited the male sat opposite.

"My name is Jaylar. I come from the planet Medana, in a solar system in the Beta Spiral of Andromeda," he said without preamble. "My daughter, Evalyne, is missing. We believe she's been taken off the planet."

"Maybe she just took off by herself." He had no time for over-protective fathers. Or possessive lovers. Not to mention ex-lovers. They all tried it on with him, thinking he'd make an exception.

He never did.

"You misunderstand, Lord Gabriel." Jaylar swallowed, clearly struggling with emotion. Gabe flicked his glance around the club to give him a moment to compose himself. "Although the blood of the gods flows in my veins, my lineage is diluted and Evalyne's mother is a pureblood mortal. Evalyne didn't inherit my ability to teleport. She's never left Medana in her life."

Gabe rapped his fingers on his thigh. "So she found herself a lover who could give her something she lacked." He shoved his foot from the table and prepared to leave. This was a waste of time. "I don't track runaway lovers."

Jaylar leaned across the table. His eyes glowed with a hint of madness. "She's four years old, Lord Gabriel."

Four years old. An ancient ache reawakened deep in his chest and he smothered the urge to sigh in defeat. Of course he would take on the mission. A four-year-old child. A female at that. How could he not?

He kept his expression impassive. To allow the slightest inclination of his personal feelings to show would be suicidal. He'd be inundated by frantic parents searching for missing offspring, whereas at the moment only those on the verge of insanity dared approach him with such requests.

After all, the Archangel Gabriel wasn't known for his benevolence or sense of empathy. He took on assignments only if they appealed to his warped sense of adventure, not because he cared whether the perpetrator deserved to be hunted or not.

If the potential adrenaline rush was high enough, he considered the request. In return he demanded the client's soul. Rumor had it he claimed their life as well.

Either way, it was a fair price for hiring the services of an archangel. Even if the rumors were little more than a smokescreen for what he really exacted as payment.

He slung his arm over the back of the seat, rapped his fingers on the leather upholstery. "Give me the details. I'll let you know what I decide."

Jaylar slid a small package across the table. "We'll pay anything. My life is yours. My wife wants you to know——"

"Stop." Gabe picked up the package. It felt like a disc. "I'm not interested in anything your wife has to say. I don't work for pure-blood mortals." Mainly because the vast majority wouldn't have the first clue he existed or if they did, how to contact him.

And he wasn't interested in anything Jaylar's wife had to say because her husband had already given him all the information he needed.

Jaylar's jaw tensed as if in offense but he said nothing. Gabe dropped the disc into his shirt pocket. "I require access so I can contact you at any time."

Jaylar jerked his head in assent for the mind probe. It took a few fleeting seconds for Gabe to gather the information he required in order to initiate a telepathic link in case of emergency.

He stood, ending the interview. "I'll be in touch."

Jaylar also stood. "How long before you decide? Is there a way I can contact you in the meantime?"

Gabe shot Jaylar a smoking glare. "When I've had time to access the information, I'll let you know whether the assignment appeals."

Jaylar's hands fisted, but he didn't say a word.

"And no, you can't contact me. The link is strictly one way."

Gabe strode from the darkened alcove, temper simmering deep in his chest, blood thrumming dangerously through his veins. The man might be of paramount importance on his own world due to the trickle of gods' blood in his veins. But such a diluted heritage meant nothing to Gabe. For daring to question him he should have thrown the disc back into Jaylar's face. Should have refused the assignment without a second's hesitation.

And had it been any other assignment, no matter how intriguing it had sounded, he would have done just that.

But a child was involved. He already knew he was going to take on the case.

The music thundered, the floor vibrated and the infrared lighting streaked across the club's dance floor. It matched his mood exactly. But then Aurora's blue eyes, pert nose and those enchanting freckles swam into his mind, and the rage coalesced into brutal lust.

He bared his teeth, hardly noticed how the crowd parted before him. It was intolerable that a woman—a mortal—possessed the ability to invade his mind and arouse him to such a degree that it interfered with his thought processes.

"My Lord Gabriel?" The seductive gasp wrenched him from a satisfying vision of feeding Aurora his cock, inch by inch. That would shut up her incessant questioning.

He glowered down at the voice and realized the two redheads from earlier were gazing up at him in reverential wonder. Although clearly the expression on his face wasn't what they'd been expecting. Already their smiles of adoration were fading and trepidation replaced the desire in their eyes.

"Yes?" He sounded feral. He damn well felt feral. These two had better be up for a few hours of raw uninhibited fucking.

"We thought—I mean, we wondered . . . " The first one stumbled to a halt and shot her fellow redhead a desperate glance.

"My Lord," the second one said, her voice breathless and sexy. With great effort he forced the frown from his face. Instantly both females edged closer to him, as if unable to help themselves. "My sister and I are celebrating our coming of age." She gave him a smoldering look from beneath the heavy veil of her silver-tipped eyelashes. "We'd be honored if you'd join us in our suite for a private . . . party."

Chapter Nine

AURORA returned to the kitchen, slid open the door and reeled back in shock as the humidity hit her. It had never occurred to her the villa was air-conditioned.

As far as she could make out she was entirely surrounded by lush rainforest. The sky was azure, the air was filled with the call of exotic songbirds and she had the uncanny sensation that the forest had momentarily stilled at her appearance. That it was . . . watching her.

She wiped her sweaty palms on her shorts and took a couple of steps across the stone terrace. Massive urns decorated the terrace with vibrant blooms spilling over their edges and tumbling across the ground. By the look of things she was somewhere in the subtropics.

There was one way to find out for sure. She'd check the GPS app on her phone.

And wasn't that just typical? There was no signal. She shoved the phone back in her pocket and eyed the baleful forest. As much as she wanted to explore further—for all she knew there could be a major town within easy walking distance—she had the strongest conviction she was entirely alone. And in any case she had no idea what wildlife might inhabit that forest.

Back in the kitchen she pulled one of the cushions from a chair and tossed it onto the floor before sitting crossed-legged on top of it. Despite how much she wanted to continue her attempt to enter her mother's dimension, she knew it was too dangerous. But even though she'd spent the last eight years working toward the moment when she could cross dimensions, she'd also studied the viability of using those same psychic abilities to travel *without breaching dimensions.*

Her first thought after knowing Gabe had left her had been to put her theory into practice and find her way home. But now that she'd calmed down, she knew that was just as irresponsible as continuing with her original plan. Suppose the Guardians were still there, waiting for her?

It galled knowing that she couldn't shock Gabe by disappearing without a trace but she'd still enter the astral planes. It always soothed her and she often had the most amazing ideas while there.

Such as eight years ago, when it had first occurred to her to try and open that elusive gateway between dimensions.

With a bit of luck she'd have another brilliant idea that would help with her current situation. Although if she was honest the whole *crossing dimensions* plan hadn't exactly lived up to her expectations, had it?

She pushed that unsavory thought from her mind and prepared to slip into trance. Unease flickered through the outer edges of her consciousness. *What was going on?* She could almost see the astral planes, could almost feel the heavenly beauty but she couldn't reach them. Couldn't enter them.

It was as if she and the astral planes were two negative forces of magnetism, and no matter how hard she pushed her spiritual essence simply slid away, impotent.

Heart pounding, she glanced wildly around the kitchen. Ever since she had been a small child she'd been able to astral project. Her parents had taught her the ground rules of safety, as soon as they'd realized what she was doing. Never in her life had she been refused entry to those glittering peaceful realms.

Until now. The truth punched through her gut, a physical pain. Some kind of psychic barrier glimmered, like a sphere of water, allowing her to see but not touch the higher planes. Renewed panic gushed through her bloodstream.

What was going on? Where had he taken her, where even something as fundamental as ascending into trance was now beyond her abilities?

She was somewhere she'd never imagined could exist because it didn't matter where you were. Access to the astral planes was universal. It wasn't theoretical, it just *was*.

But all the facts in the world didn't mean shit. Because *this* was her reality.

And she couldn't leave it.

GABE LAY ON the rumpled bed in the room the twins had reserved in one of the luxurious hotels in Times Square. They'd driven him mad within forty seconds with their constant giggles and breathless exclamations; from their admiration of his archangelic presence to the strangeness of the city to the sheer *naughtiness* that they were slumming it up on planet Earth.

They'd only quit when he palmed the top of the noisiest female's head and pushed her to her knees. Then they got the message he was with them for one thing only and it wasn't conversation.

Resting his head on his forearm he stared up at the ceiling. The fingers of his other hand idly tangled in the long hair of the redhead who was busy worshipping his nipples. Another mouth worked his cock and Gabe couldn't muster the enthusiasm to watch either.

He tightened his grip in her hair, hauled her up and stared into her lust-glazed eyes. They weren't blue.

"My lord?" Her hands flattened onto his chest for support. "Shall I do something else?"

Her sister released him to wriggle further up his thighs. Two identical, beautiful faces gazed at him in reverential awe, both willing and desperate to sate his every desire.

And all he wanted was for Aurora to be in their place. Sucking his cock; biting his nipples; sliding her body over his and looking at him as if he was all that mattered in her sorry existence.

A growl rasped his throat and he tossed the nearest girl onto the bed, face first, her luscious ass displayed to view. Aurora would do all those things and more, but first she would apologize. First she would learn her place.

He gripped her hips, heaved her upward. Oh yeah, Aurora would learn her place and she would revel in it, mindless with delirium, and he would fuck her so damn hard she wouldn't even be able to leave the bed after he'd finished with her.

The other redhead wrapped herself around his thighs, her fingers reaching for his cock. Shock slammed through him and for a moment he froze as reality readjusted.

He didn't fucking believe it. He'd been fantasizing about Aurora. Had all but thrust into this willing female—*believing she was Aurora.*

If that wasn't bad enough his cock instantly lost all interest in proceeding. He loomed over the quivering redhead and cursed violently in his head but it made no difference. And if he didn't do something about it within the next couple of seconds his reputation was in tatters.

Incendiary with frustrated rage he slid into the female's unprotected and unknowing mind. He found her center of pleasure and with barely a psychic touch catapulted her into paroxysms of uninhibited orgasm. A moment later, after repeating the maneuver with her sister, both females lay on the bed, clutching each other, their bodies convulsing with mindless delight.

With a shudder Gabe shoved himself from the bed, grabbed his pants and pulled them on. It was undignified to resort to such base tactics and he'd never needed to before now. But better this than risk a rumor that he was impotent.

Another shudder rocked through him, and his mind filled once again with the tempting image of Aurora.

That damn human. She was corrupting his reason. He would obviously be plagued by her until he'd had her, and if that meant taking her before she'd begged his forgiveness then so be it. At least afterward he'd no longer be rabid with this crazy, debasing need.

HIS VILLA WAS dark and silent as he teleported directly into the kitchen. He flicked on the light and it spilled out into the hallway, illuminating dark corners and enhancing shadows. Frowning he went into the living area beyond the kitchen and instantly the scent of fear enveloped his senses in a damp, fetid wave.

His heart jackknifed, although he couldn't think why. Aurora was in no danger here. Nothing could touch her inside the villa. But still his heart thundered and only when he saw her huddled on one of the low, wide sofas did his breath release in a soundless sigh.

She was there. Of course she was. Where else could she be?

Slowly he crossed the floor and stood looking down at her. In the muted light she looked so vulnerable. As if the slightest harsh word from an archangel would send her tumbling into insanity.

He crouched down and gently brushed errant strands of hair from her face. Her skin was warm, damp. Had she been crying?

Forearms resting across his thighs he continued to frown down at her. The scorching anger that had driven him from here, that had sustained him through the following hours and then shamed him just moments ago, faded. She had no idea who he was. It was unreasonable to expect her to show him the respect his rank demanded when she remained ignorant of his heritage. He should have explained instead of allowing her to goad him with her words.

She was only human. He couldn't quite fathom why he'd allowed her remarks to infuriate him to such a degree. And sure, she was here on his island and that was going to be a massive pain in the ass, but it wouldn't be that long before the Guardians gave up and looked elsewhere for their depraved fun.

With a few ground rules he could put up with her for a few weeks. Months, even.

Her eyelids flew open and at the same instant the fear he could taste emanating from her escalated. She was terrified. What had happened while he'd been gone? Or was this simply a delayed reaction—the reaction he'd expected but not received from her after they'd arrived here?

"It's okay." He cradled her face, stroked the pad of his thumb across her heated cheek. She didn't move, didn't respond, just continued to stare at him as if he was something that had crawled out of her darkest nightmare.

His fingers slid into her hair, a touch of blatant possession. By natural order of the vast gulf that separated their species she should fear him. And yet, oddly, he didn't want her to.

He leaned in closer. The hint of apples that had so tantalized him earlier had vanished, eradicated beneath sweat and fear. But still he found her irresistible.

"Aurora." His voice was husky, persuasive. He would show her there was no need for her to cower before him. In his bed, in his arms, she could be as wild as any proud demi-goddess he'd laid. "I forgive you."

She sank against the back of the sofa in silent invitation. His blood thundered in his arteries, cock strained against his pants, and even though she could do with a damn good shower he couldn't wait.

They could shower afterward.

He eased onto the sofa, wrapped his hand around the back of her neck. She gasped, and before he could claim her breath as his own she curled her fingers around his wrist and dug her nails in.

An appreciative growl rasped his throat. That was better. He resisted her efforts to drag his hand from her neck and grinned down at her. Already her terror was fading and another far more satisfying pheromone spiked the heated air.

"Fight all you like. You're not going anywhere."

Her nails scored his forearm with so much force the scent of blood mingled with the heady lust. Air hissed between his teeth and with his free hand he gripped her wrist and pinned her arm above her head.

"Get off me." She glared up at him, breasts heaving just inches from his chest, desire snaking through every word. "You bastard! Where the hell am I?"

Her disrespect, far from enraging him, tightened the need in his gut, heightened the throb in his temples. He threaded his fingers through hers, palm to palm, her hand so small and fragile it caused a strange ache in the center of his chest.

"You're where you belong." The words were little more than a growl and to reinforce her position he dragged his hand from the back of her neck, curled his fingers around the top of her tank and ripped the material in two.

Her entire body quivered beneath him and her free hand suddenly gripped his throat. It didn't hurt. She was incapable of hurting him. But it was *surprising*.

"I don't belong here." Her fingers dug in deeper, and his cock thickened in instant response. He leaned toward her, a blatant invitation to continue and, of course, she immediately stopped.

"You belong"—damn, it was harder to speak than he thought—"wherever I say you do."

Her hand slid from his throat in an agonizing caress to cup his jaw. Her nails speared his flesh. "You abducted me."

"I saved you." It shouldn't matter what she said, but *abducted?*

She panted into his face, and her fingers trapped between his curled into his knuckles. "And dumped me somewhere that shouldn't even *exist?*"

He pushed her ruined top off her shoulder, traced his finger along the lacy edge of her bra. He never took his eyes from hers.

"You can put it down to my benevolent nature." And if she believed that she'd believe anything.

She gripped his hair and he stifled a groan as pinpricks of fire stabbed into his brain. They clearly weren't compatible when it came to conversation but he had every conviction they'd be explosive in the sack.

"You still haven't even told me your *name.*"

He tugged the lacy cup from her luscious breast. Her erect nipple taunted him, dark and inviting in the shadows that surrounded them. "Gabe," he said, hardly aware he had even spoken.

"Are you going to let me go?" Her fingers convulsed, a brutal caress, and he obliged her by lowering his head.

"No." He flicked his tongue over her nipple, then sucked her into his mouth. Hard. She reared into him, erratic gasps fanning his forehead, and dug her fingers farther into his scalp.

"So I'm your prisoner?" Her breathless accusation grazed his flesh and he dragged his teeth over her succulent nipple. Didn't she *ever* shut up?

"Yes." The word was feral. Since when had he treated her like a prisoner? He released her trapped hand, gripped her bra and ripped the offending material from her breasts. A delicate chain glinted around the base of her throat, somehow enhancing her innate fragility.

"You can't"—her hand clamped over his shoulder but she didn't try and push him away—"keep me here forever."

He rolled on top of her, kneed her thighs apart and jammed the length of his erection against her damp core. Bracing his weight on his hands either side of her shoulders, he glared down at her, his unbuttoned shirt baring his chest.

Her hair was tangled, her clothes in shreds and her naked breasts tempted him more than they had any right to.

He had no intention of keeping her forever. The minute he was sure it was safe for her to return to Ireland was the last minute she would spend on his island.

But no mortal told him what he could or couldn't do.

"Watch me."

Her ragged breath caressed his jaw; her fingers tangled in his hair and dug into his shoulder. Damn her for arousing him with every move she made.

"What is this place?" She hitched in another breath, her nipples grazing his chest in an erotic kiss. "Are you some kind of crazy scientist conducting illegal experiments?"

He dragged his mesmerized gaze from where their bodies meshed and glowered at her. His frantic libido urged him to ignore her ludicrous statement. It would take no effort to strip her shorts away, to free his cock and thrust into her tight embrace. She was wet, she was ready and no matter what crazy shit she insisted on talking about he knew, without doubt, she wanted him.

"What?" The word jerked from him without his permission. "Do I *look* like a crazy scientist?"

Her hands slid downward until they were flattened against his naked chest. He'd not felt anything so damned seductive in millennia.

"You've mastered teleportation." The tips of her fingernails grazed his flesh, as if she couldn't decide whether to caress him or gouge him. "And exactly what kind of security system have you set up here? Because I've never come across anything like it before in my life."

Through the layers of frustration and incredulity one coherent thought clarified. He was on the edge of sexual combustion and all she could talk about was his fucking *security system*.

"I already told you." *Had* he told her about the force field that enclosed the island? "It keeps the Guardians out." And had the added benefit of concealing the island from human prying without the need for constant glamours.

"And keeps me *in*." Her voice was accusing but her fingers caressed his chest, a featherlight touch that drove him mad with elusive promise.

"Of course it doesn't." It was a damn effort to process her random comments, to articulate intelligent responses. "You can travel through it as easily as I can."

"No I—" She cut herself off and her eyes widened. "You mean I can *physically* just walk out of here?"

Fury scalded his senses even as utter disbelief hammered through his brain. She was talking about leaving *again*? When he was as hard as a rock and they were seconds from screwing?

His hands fisted into the cushions of the sofa. She looked up at him, the picture of sultry innocence, as if she had not the slightest clue of the lust that raged between them. Couldn't she feel the extent of his erection between her thighs? Was she was completely unaware of how her arousal scented the air?

"We're on an island in the middle of the Bermuda Triangle." His voice was harsh. "I'd like to see you try and walk out of that." When she opened her mouth to argue that point as well, he bared his teeth in a savage snarl. "And believe me, Aurora, nobody will ever be able to find you unless I allow them to."

Chapter Ten

IN the back of her desire-drenched mind, Aurora knew that she should shove Gabe onto the floor and regain a modicum of self-respect. But despite his breathtaking arrogance and Neanderthal tendencies *and* the humiliating fact she could detect feminine perfume clinging to his clothes, her fingers refused to cooperate.

Her hands remained plastered against his chest as if they were welded to his iron-hard pecs. And no matter how hard she tried to break eye contact, his intense glare mesmerized her.

"How do you know that?" If only she sounded more in control. If only every breath she took wasn't filled with the scent of his raw masculinity. "Make a habit of abducting potential subjects and hiding them on your island?"

He gave her a feral grin and looked as if he'd like nothing more than to sink his teeth into her carotid artery. The image was shockingly arousing, and without conscious thought she rubbed her palms against the seductive dusting of hair across his sculpted chest.

"That's right." He rammed his erection against her sensitized flesh and the air punched from her lungs.

"You . . ." She had no idea what she'd been about to say and it didn't matter because he slammed down onto her, crushing her hands between their near-naked bodies.

It would be so easy to push her questions and concerns aside. So easy to lift her mouth to his, to wrap her legs around his thighs, to let the desire overpower her myriad worries.

He expected her to. She writhed in frustrated need as his hand skimmed her waist, wrenched the button from her shorts and slid inside. His breath hissed against her open mouth as his finger circled her swollen clit, the pressure just enough to send shockwaves splintering through her womb, to have her panting mindlessly for more.

"Better." He smiled in blatant triumph, as if her imminent surrender was exactly what he expected, and as his finger slid inside her wet channel a moan of pure need rasped her throat.

She wanted him with a desperation that shocked her, but even as the need pounded, even as he slid a second finger inside her, a silvery thread of sanity glinted.

She couldn't let him deflect her questions with sex. If Gabe believed she was completely in his sexual thrall, he would never tell her anything.

"Wait." She pushed against his chest. He growled against the curve of her neck and continued to torture her, his fingers inside her and his thumb tracing with exquisite expertise against her vulnerable clit.

"No. Stop talking." His voice was raw with lust but it was a command nevertheless. She squirmed, clutched his chest. Why was she trying to resist him? He was irresistible. She wanted him and that was . . . enough.

"*Gabe.*"

He reared up, just enough so he could look at her, and even in the gloom she could see the flash of disbelief in his eyes. As if her continued resistance to his undoubted charms staggered him.

Thank god he had no idea just how hard she found it to . . . resist his charms.

"I need to know . . ." What did she need to know? All she knew was how much she wanted him. "How I can contact—"

He bared his teeth and practically snarled. "You don't *need* to know anything. Is that clear?"

It was clear he was on the edge. The thought hammered through her brain, igniting what remained of her good sense. But still she couldn't let it go. If she had to remain here for a while that was one thing. But she couldn't disappear without a word. She had to let her mother know that everything was okay.

She dug her nails into his rock-hard muscle. He aroused and infuriated her in equal measure, and the combination was potent and primal. She wasn't sure whether she wanted to punch his face or screw him senseless.

Of course she knew. She wanted to do both. Simultaneously.

"Don't treat me like an idiot." If he didn't answer her soon she was going to forget why her questions were so important. *And they were important.* "Just tell me how I can get through your security shields." *And for god's sake, hurry up.* She couldn't hold him off much longer. Didn't *want* to. Shit, maybe they could just have this conversation afterward, when her mind was clear?

With a violent curse in that strange language he'd used before, he pushed himself off her. Staggered by his sudden departure she stared up at him as he stood by the side of the sofa, his bare chest heaving with exertion, the breath hissing between his clenched teeth.

He looked magnificent, like an untamed barbarian from the dawn of time. The image burned into her brain, inflaming her blood and incinerating the last lingering remnants of good sense she retained.

Her limbs were heavy, uncoordinated, but she struggled to sit up and slide her legs off the sofa. She needed his arms around her, needed to feel his body against hers. *Needed* this ravening desire to be sated before she tumbled into madness.

"Three ground rules." His voice was pure controlled fury. "Don't give me orders. Stay out of my way. And"—he paused for a heartbeat and his condemning glance seared her from the top of her head to the soles of her feet—"for gods' sakes, clean yourself up."

GABE LEANED BACK in his chair and stared at the ceiling of his office. After sifting through the intel on the disc Jaylar had given him he'd sent a telepathic message to the man informing him he would take the case. The holographic images of the dark-haired little girl imprinted on his brain and churned up long-buried memories of another small girl; a child who had once cradled his heart in her tiny hands.

He squeezed his eyes shut, forced the ancient memory back into the shadowy corners of his shredded soul. *His precious Helena.* He would never forget and he would never forgive. But vengeance had corroded him long ago and now there was nothing left but an echo of guilt and loss and an elusive whisper of the love that had once embraced his life.

Slowly he flexed his fingers, forced his eyes open. The interminability of his existence stretched out before him, a bleak desert of meaningless interactions. If he hadn't had his missions to occupy his mind over millennia he would have sunk into oblivion long ago.

The silence wrapped around him, a soothing cocoon. Brooding, he stared through the window as the moonlight turned the forest into a silvery mirage. He had spent nights without number doing just this. But tonight, instead of the solitude numbing his fractured psyche it only served to reinforce the knowledge that he was *not* alone.

How much longer was Aurora going to take? After he'd directed her to his bathroom—since it was the only damn bathroom in the villa—she'd flounced through his bedroom as if she were an Alpha goddess. Never mind that her clothes were in tatters and her hair was a tangled mess, or that she'd left him so fucking hard he could barely walk upright.

Stay out of his way? That was a joke. How did he think that was going to work when he had no intention of allowing her to leave his island until he was sure she'd be safe? When there was only one bedroom? When, in reality, he had no inclination whatsoever of having Aurora under his roof without also having her in his bed?

As if his thoughts had summoned her, he heard his bedroom door open and with a flicker of disgust acknowledged the anticipation that fired his blood. He continued to stare through the window and deliberately didn't turn when he saw her reflected presence hovering at the open door of his office.

Let her wait.

And within a couple of seconds he was the one who could no longer wait. He turned, and swallowed the groan that threatened to disgrace him.

She was wearing the shirt he'd left out for her. Only now did he realize, with self-derision, that the shirt was blue. To match her eyes. And far from hiding her tempting curves she'd folded her arms and caused the soft cotton to hug her breasts and skim her thighs. Her hair was still damp and curled into enticing tendrils over her shoulders, and she was glaring at him as if she'd like nothing better than to gouge out his eyes.

"Well?" Her voice was sharp, disagreeable, and he couldn't remember the last time a mortal had ever used such a tone with him. "I don't know about you but I've had a really long day and I'm starving."

Shit. It hadn't occurred to him that Aurora wouldn't simply help herself to whatever was in the kitchen. It was well stocked with non-perishables. And although he didn't like the way she was looking at him or the way she addressed him he had to agree. It had been a hell of a long day for her.

The realization did nothing to improve his mood.

"Everything you need is downstairs. There was no need to starve yourself to try and prove a point."

"Oh, I don't think *I'm* the one trying to prove a point here, do you?"

For a second he stared at her, speechless at her nerve. It had been a long time since he'd put himself out to aid a mortal, especially a human indigenous to Earth, and this was the reason why.

Because they were ungrateful, selfish and egocentric.

By rights Aurora should be worshipping at his feet. But instead she behaved as if he was the one in the wrong. The overwhelming urge to show her exactly who and what he was flooded his senses, to watch the shock ricochet through her as she struggled to comprehend, and yet he had the resigned conviction that the moment had passed.

He was condemned to share his sanctuary for the next who knew how many nights with a woman determined to make him continually regret his uncharacteristic gesture of benevolence.

"I have nothing to prove to you." He stood up and didn't miss the way her eyes darkened at his approach. She wanted him. But still she denied him. He didn't understand it and, despite his best intentions to ignore everything about Aurora Robinson, her stubbornness was seriously pissing him off.

He'd never had to beg a woman for sex and he certainly wasn't starting now. Usually the problem was avoiding females who wanted him but did nothing for his libido.

This was a first. *Almost a first.* The ancient memory drifted in his mind and he shoved it brutally back into the shadows where it belonged.

"Really?" Her voice was scathing as she hastily backed away from the door. He took grim satisfaction from the knowledge his closeness unnerved her. "Because I'm starting to think that whole Guardians stuff is a load of old rubbish you made up to justify your actions."

She stood barely an arm's length from him, glaring at him as if she couldn't decide whether she wanted to knee him in the balls or tackle him to the floor for another reason entirely. And right now it didn't matter. How *dare* she suggest he had orchestrated the Guardians' arrival for his own purposes?

He rolled his shoulders and craved to feel, just one last time, the exquisite euphoria of unfurling his wings. Of rendering Aurora inarticulate with awe.

"If there's one thing you should know about me." He waited until she stopped fidgeting and once again, with obvious reluctance, looked him in the eyes. "It's this. I have no need to ever justify my actions to anyone. Least of all to you."

AURORA SPLAYED HER fingers against the curved edges of the sink in the kitchen and took another deep breath. Five minutes ago, after telling her exactly how little he thought of her, Gabe had stalked down the stairs and by the time she'd recovered her wits enough to follow him, he'd vanished.

Once again leaving her alone in his villa.

Her stomach growled but the thought of eating caused nausea to rise. God, what was she going to do?

Slowly she turned around and leaned back against the work-bench. Despite her cheap shot, she didn't believe for a second Gabe had anything to do with that violet lightning that had appeared in her parents' living room. She didn't believe he was a serial kidnapper, either.

He'd abducted her not because he was a mad scientist who collected victims in order to experiment on them, but because he genuinely thought she was in danger from the Guardians. And he was keeping her because he thought she was still in danger.

Logically, she understood that. Accepted that. The trouble was he managed to stir up a sizzling whirlpool of emotions whenever he looked at her, never mind touched her, that caused cold logic to fail every time. But what really burned her pride was how he'd virtually told her she stank seconds after trying to seduce her.

Fine. If he was incapable of conducting a civilized conversation then she'd find the answers she needed by herself. Damn his orders. She'd search his office. There was sure to be some way of contacting the outside world. And with luck she'd discover the secret of his mysterious security shields. Because if there was a way to replicate them, then surely there should be some way of adapting the technology so that *she* could use it to repel the Guardians?

And then she could go home to Ireland. To her family.

Chapter Eleven

AURORA stood outside Gabe's office and glanced over her shoulder, guilt nibbling deep in her gut. She didn't know why she felt guilty. It wasn't as if she intended to steal anything.

If he'd just answered her questions she wouldn't have dreamed of invading his privacy. But since she had no intention of sitting on her backside, chewing her fingernails until he deigned to return, then she'd raid everything she could until she found out what she needed to know.

She sat on the huge swivel chair, the leather worn and somehow comforting. His timber desk was massive, curved and worryingly tidy. There wasn't even a laptop. And while she knew it had been a long shot, she'd harbored a hope he might have left his laptop on. Then she could send her parents an email telling them not to worry about her. She glanced at the windows, where the forest was a stark silhouette by the light of the moon, and then looked back at the filing cabinet beneath one end of the desk.

Rifling through stuff on his desk was one thing. But actually opening drawers and rummaging was something else. She knew she was being ridiculous in her distinction but couldn't help it. And so before she could freak herself out anymore with her warped perception of morality she pulled open the top drawer.

She wasn't sure what she expected to see but it certainly wasn't a small pile of seashells. They were nothing special, quite ordinary. And yet they sent shivers racing along her arms, as if they were somehow . . . significant. The only other item was a photo frame.

A sense of foreboding inched along her spine. There was nothing in here that could help her. This was intimate, private, and she had no right poking through such personal things.

But still her hand reached out. Still her fingers curled around the frame. It felt as if the front was edged in similar shells and another ripple of doubt claimed her.

For a few agonizing seconds she hesitated and then, deliberately recalling the way Gabe both ignored her questions and insulted her, she tightened her grip and pulled the frame out of the drawer.

Disbelief slammed through her, punching the air from her lungs. She dropped the frame onto the desk and keeled forward, her mind reeling.

It was Gabe. She clung onto that irrefutable fact. She'd recognize his golden hair, his impossibly fabulous eyes and distinctive beauty anywhere. But even as her chest contracted with disbelieving panic, she couldn't block out the rest of the picture.

This Gabe had wings. Wings the color of clotted cream, with delicate streaks of pale gold glinting through them. Heavenly highlights brushed each individual feather.

Wings. *The man had wings.*

They were folded behind his back but were clear enough. He had one arm around a black-haired woman who was laughing up at him, and in his other he held a small child whose tiny hand was entangled in his hair.

Gabe was laughing too. As if he hadn't a care in the world.

And he had fucking wings.

She collapsed facedown on the desk. One word pounded through her brain but that was crazy. Impossible. He couldn't be.

There were no such things as angels.

Squeezing her eyes shut, all she could see were the horrific scars on his back. *Exactly where wings would be.*

She ignored the wild staccato of her heart and forced herself to look again at the picture. In case she'd been hallucinating. But the evidence was there in the incredibly lifelike painting. Happiness radiated from the three of them, so real and uninhibited she could almost feel the emotion spilling into the stark, silent room.

And there was more than happiness. Love saturated this scene, as if it was a living entity and not confined to the boundaries of the frame. Their love glowed from their eyes, spun a magical web around them both that encompassed and illuminated the child.

Their child. Had to be. There was no doubt in Aurora's mind whose daughter she was, even without the additional clues of the little girl's golden hair and silver-and-blue-streaked green eyes.

Gabe had a family. He was an *angel* and he had a family.

She had almost had sex with an angel.

Her stomach churned and she pushed herself from the desk and slumped against the back of the leather chair. For all her life she'd been aware there was more to the world than science could prove. She believed in an alternate dimension because it was part of her heritage. She knew it was possible to travel through those dimensions.

She accepted the reality of telepathy since she and her mother had shared that special bond until a few years ago. But angels, like fairies and unicorns, belonged in the realms of fantasy.

Clearly, she had just entered that realm.

No wonder he was so arrogant. No wonder he considered her questions beneath his dignity to answer. *He was an immortal.*

And he lived on an island in the middle of the Bermuda Triangle.

As if drawn by an invisible thread she once again gazed at the exquisitely rendered painting. It was so realistic, like she was looking out of a window at a real scene. In the background there was a stone villa and she frowned, caught by its odd familiarity. And then it hit her.

It looked like the villa she was in right now.

Her heart jackknifed, the pain more than merely physical although she couldn't think why. He'd brought her to his family home? And then tried to *seduce* her? What kind of morals did angels have? Weren't they supposed to be good and holy and radiate a heavenly benevolence?

It hardly mattered what the myths and legends said about them. Because Gabe appeared to be the reality, and he behaved more like a testosterone-fueled demon than any angel in the fairy tales she'd read as a child.

She looked at the woman with her lavish earrings, jewel-threaded hair and bangle-adorned arms. And then at the child, her waist-length hair a mass of untidy ringlets. Neither had wings. Was the woman not an angel? What did that make the child? Elusive fragments spun through her mind but before she could grasp their significance, her tired gaze caught on a gold chain that glinted around the little girl's throat.

Disbelief stabbed through her. *It couldn't be.* But, suspended from the delicate chain, a shockingly familiar butterfly sparkled, and gold dust and minuscule rainbows were trapped in the tiny, flawless wings.

It was identical to the necklace she had worn for the last five years.

The necklace that had haunted her dreams for as long as she could remember. Recurring, endless dreams of rainbows and gold dust and magnificent jewel-like butterfly wings had been her nightly companion as a child. And as an adult she had sought to capture the dream, to make it a reality. To her dad's horror she'd used a good chunk of her grandmother's inheritance to commission the piece from one of the top London jewelers.

She'd never seen anything similar to it before. Yet here, in an angel's treasured painting, was her beloved butterfly necklace's twin.

It couldn't be coincidence. There had to be a connection even if for the life of her she couldn't imagine what.

Besides, it was a lot easier to focus on that than the mind-shattering reality that she'd been saved by an *angel*.

Chapter Twelve

ETA Hyperium was a shithole. And that was an understatement. But since it was the hub of the slave trade for the technologically advanced mortals of the Sextans Galaxy, it was never going to be anything else. Even the weather had given up millennia ago and now the surface was a bleak landscape of withered trees and stunted wildlife that scavenged beneath the dying red sun.

Gabe materialized in a dark corner of the vast lot outside the major auction block. He could've arrived directly inside but he didn't want to draw any unnecessary attention to himself. The place might look as if it was decrepit but that façade concealed phenomenal security. And although the owner knew damn well who and what he was, Gabe had no inclination for the general clientele to guess.

His cover as a megalomaniac half-blood demon always worked, and he shouldered his way inside. No one would assume he was an undercover archangel. Not in this savage sector of the universe.

Thick, noxious smoke offended his senses, melded with the scent of greed, depravity and prohibitively expensive alcohol. The auction parlors were separate from this main drinking den, accessible only by going through another rigorous security check, and the lighting was dimmed as if that might disguise the nature of the place. He swept his glance around the crowded tables, searching for his contact, Eblis.

A hand slammed onto his shoulder. "Hey, Gabe. Been a while."

Gabe turned. "Got a minute?"

Eblis rippled his pearlescent wings and lesser patrons scattered hastily out of the way. No one wanted to draw Eblis's attention toward them. Not only was he one of the most feared slave traders in the Sector, he also happened to be one of the most powerful demons in existence.

He was also the sole owner of this complex, but that was something very few were aware of.

Eblis jerked his head and they approached a crowded table. The muscled occupants fled before the demon had to utter a word.

"So what's the deal?" Eblis undulated his wings as they sat down and indicated with a flick of his finger to a half-naked waiter they required drinks. "Found a way to get back at her Celestial bitch-fuck?"

"Not yet." Gabe relaxed against the circular sofa and hooked his arm over its back. If there was one species in Creation who had cause to loathe his goddess even more than the archangels, it was the demons. But much as he usually enjoyed countless hours getting drunk with Eblis and sharing visions of agonizing ends for that particular Alpha Immortal, tonight he just needed info because he had to get back to Aurora.

Huh. What?

The hell he did. He needed to get the info, and then he and Eblis could find a few females and he would finally be rid of the scorching need burning his blood.

"You here for business or pleasure?"

Despite his best efforts Aurora's blue eyes invaded his mind. Fury, *disbelief*, at her continued rebuffs and incessant demands thundered through his brain and frustrated desire pounded the length of his cock. He had no intention of returning to her until he'd been well and truly laid. "Both."

"Spill."

"Heard of any child slaves from the Andromeda Galaxies being traded recently?"

Their drinks arrived, the sizzling alcohol so potent one sniff of its fumes was enough to send weak-minded mortals comatose. Eblis drained half his tankard before smashing it down onto the table.

"None of these Sextans bastards can reach the Andromedas, Gabe. They can't get anywhere without their crazy little spaceships. You know that. They couldn't even get to the Milky Way and that's their closest neighbor."

"You get the occasional trader who can cross galaxies." He paused for effect. "Foreign slaves always ratchet up the price."

Eblis didn't argue. He didn't have to. They both knew that slaves who originated outside the Sextans Galaxy were smuggled in by the unscrupulous who weren't restricted to spaceship travel. They were descendants of gods and demons, who had inherited their immortal ancestors' ability of interstellar teleportation. And Eblis allowed it, so long as he received a hefty profit of any sale.

"Got details?"

Gabe showed him an image of Evalyne.

"She's a native of Medana." He placed the small star map globe on the table and opened the holographic image of the Beta Spiral of Andromeda. Medana was, after all, an insignificant little planet hidden within an obscure solar system. He didn't expect the demon to know the place offhand.

Eblis shifted, his feathers ruffling in a nonexistent breeze, and Gabe zoomed in further, suns and planets and moons shooting by until the six-planet solar system of Evalyne's birth hovered above the table.

"I recognize this system." Eblis raised an eyebrow and glanced through the planet at Gabe. "Saw some pirates from the Fornax Galaxy plotting the chart about, what, three months ago."

AURORA JERKED AWAKE, her heart pounding. She hadn't meant to fall asleep. She'd intended to wait up for Gabe's return and then ask him, outright, whether he really was an angel. Even in her own head it sounded like a ludicrous question but she'd seen the evidence. She was *not* going mad, no matter how outrageous everything appeared.

Still curled up on the sofa, she squinted at the glass doors. Dawn had broken and, for a second, as her eyes adjusted to the gloom, she thought she saw the outline of a shadow peering in at her. Her mouth dried as the suspicion coalesced into certainty.

Someone was watching her.

As if her thought acted as a trigger a pale beam of light illuminated right outside the doors. And the shadow solidified into a huge male shape. And god almighty *he had wings.*

Paralyzed with terror she could only stare at the stranger who was looking directly at her, his evil grin seeming to bore into the center of her brain. Then he raised his hand and knocked on the glass, and her petrifaction shattered.

She swung her legs off the sofa, never taking her mesmerized gaze from him. He appeared to be dressed in black leather and if it weren't for the *wings* he'd look exactly like a stereotypical drop-dead gorgeous Italian heartbreaker.

Before she quite realized she'd even moved she was standing in front of him, with only the glass separating them. She flapped her hand at him. If he thought she was letting him in, he was insane.

"Open up, Aurora." He sounded as if her theatrics amused him. And how did he know her name? "Gabe's told me all about you."

Her question now answered, she hovered uncertainty. There was no reason to doubt he was telling her the truth and yet every nerve she possessed screamed at her to retreat.

But suppose Gabe had sent this . . . *angel* to make sure she was okay? Perhaps he was some kind of servant and was going to take her to his master?

And in the end did it really matter if she opened the door or not? If he wanted to get in there was nothing stopping him from smashing the glass.

Only as she slid open the door did she realize there were no locks in any case.

He strode inside, a darkly majestic presence, and she stumbled back a step as a truly awful thought hit her. Suppose, like a vampire, he had to be invited in? And suppose, like a vampire, he now intended to end her life?

"Who are you, then?" Panic made her sound belligerent. But that was probably better than collapsing into a terrified heap at his feet. "One of Gabe's minions?"

The leer on his face froze, as if she had just leveled an unimaginable insult his way. And even though he didn't move toward her she retreated another step, unnerved by the palpable wave of malignancy that pulsed in the air between them. He didn't respond, at least not verbally, but as his black eyes narrowed a knife's edge of burning pain slid into her brain.

She clutched her head, fury swamping the encroaching fear. She didn't care if he was an angel, a demon or figment of her imagination. He had no right to invade her mind. "Get the fuck out of my head."

Mephisto was so astounded at being unable to penetrate the

outer layers of Aurora's mind that he scarcely acknowledged her insolence. Sure, it would take no effort to smash her psychic barriers and have a leisurely wander through her memories. The only thing stopping him was Gabe.

Yesterday, after Mephisto had watched Aurora ascend into the astral planes and then witnessed Gabe's inexplicable arrival, he'd assumed Gabe had left the human on Earth. But a half hour ago he'd discovered, from fellow archangel Zadkiel who had just received an irate visit from Gabe, that Gabe had done no such thing.

Apparently, Gabe had temporarily lost his mind and when the Guardians had come looking for Aurora, instead of leaving her to her fate he'd *rescued* her.

It was ironic that the only reason why Mephisto had missed Gabe make a total fool of himself was because he'd had to attend the centennial meeting with the Guardian elite. It was a mind-numbingly repetitive duty but absolutely essential in order to yet again ratify the terms of peace between all sentient beings in the universe—and the Guardians.

It was also off the record. Not even his fellow archangels knew of his diplomatic ties with the Guardians and that was the way Mephisto wanted it to stay. The treaty had been hammered out eons before he'd been created and a lot of the clauses were morally repugnant. But at least they served to muzzle the Guardians' otherwise insatiable urge to annihilate all forms of existence that didn't conform to their own.

If Gabe had gone to so much trouble to keep her from the Guardians' clutches there was no way he'd ignore it if Mephisto shredded his pet's cortex.

Even if she did deserve it.

And how had she repelled his probe? Since when did humans possess such psychic control? Maybe that was the reason Gabe had given protocol the finger. Because it was definitely worth investigating.

At no point during the last couple of years had it occurred to him she might have something of such interest lurking between her ears. He'd only been interested in the outcome of her theories.

Aurora glared at him as if his presence no longer awed and terrified. He unfurled his wings and shimmered his magnificent feathers but if anything the look on her face darkened even further.

"I see you've managed to drive your lord and master elsewhere." He folded his wings since the display hadn't reduced Aurora into a quivering heap at his feet, although he still wasn't sure why. Most primitives either prostrated themselves or devolved into stuttering imbeciles at such a glorious sight. "Got tired of your acid tongue already, has he?"

"Oh." She flicked her glance over him as if he was some kind of gargoyle. "I doubt *that*."

Mephisto smothered the flare of irritation. It was rare for a mortal to rub his feathers up the wrong way but Aurora was doing a damn fine job of it.

Zad had told him Gabe had been en-route to visit their disreputable cousin on Eta Hyperium. There were only two reasons why anyone would willingly go to Eta Hyperium and since Gabe had no need of slaves that left the other option. Very dirty sex.

Up until a moment ago, Mephisto hadn't decided whether it would be worth his while taking Aurora to that shitty little planet. But she was so damned annoying it would serve her right if she saw what Gabe got up to when he wasn't rescuing her from the outcome of her ignorance.

He offered her a mocking smile. As he intended, she visibly bristled with offense. "Would you like to know where he's gone?"

He could feel tension radiating from her. It was obvious she was dying to know where Gabe had gone, and equally obvious she hated the fact that Mephisto held the answer. Finally her curiosity won. "Did Gabe send you to check up on me?"

It irritated the hell out of him that she kept inferring he was somehow under Gabe's jurisdiction. "What do you think?"

"I don't know." She glanced at his wings as if she couldn't quite believe their magnificence. "Who *are* you?"

His headache resurfaced. It was always painful communicating with obliviously ignorant mortals. "You, human, may address me as the Lord Mephisto."

She hunched her shoulders and eyed him as if trying to work out his ulterior motives. Her fingers curled around a necklace that was hidden beneath Gabe's shirt as if it was some kind of talisman. "Mephisto?" She sounded as if she was talking to herself. She'd better be. No mortal addressed him so casually and survived to repeat their error. "Are you able to take me to Gabe?"

He only just managed to hide his shock. She *wanted* him to take her to Gabe? He'd been preparing a strategy to persuade her to go with him. That way Gabe couldn't accuse him of abduction, but if she was willing to trust him without him having to make any effort then that was fine by him. "Since you asked so nicely." Sarcasm dripped from every word but if Aurora noticed she chose to ignore it.

"All right then." She sounded as if she was the one doing *him* a favor.

"In that case you need to change." He slung the bundle he'd collected from his palace at her feet, immensely satisfied by his choice. In fact if he'd known how belligerent she was he would have chosen something even less concealing.

She prodded the outfit with her toes and he watched her expression slide from uncertainty into shocked disbelief. "I'm not wearing any of that. Are you *mad*?"

Did she talk this way to Gabe? He couldn't begin to fathom it.

"Babe, where we're going you'll stick out like a virgin sacrifice wearing Gabe's shirt." *Had Gabe actually given her his own shirt to wear?* "Trust me, in the leathers you'll blend into the wall."

AURORA STARED AT her reflection in Gabe's bathroom mirrors, seeing but not quite believing. If the outfit had looked outrageous when she'd picked it up, it now looked completely disgusting.

She could cope with the black fishnet stockings and six-inch stilettos. She could even accept the crotchless G-string since the scarlet micro-mini leather skirt just about covered her bottom.

But what she really couldn't stomach was the skimpy leather top that not only barely covered her assets but had strategic slashes that showed off her nipples.

What sort of place was Eta Hyperium if this kind of gear was standard?

Face burning, she pulled Gabe's shirt back on and then tottered unsteadily back to his bedroom. Much as she'd like to kick up a fuss it really wasn't worth it. She wanted Gabe to know he couldn't just disappear whenever they had a disagreement and then expect her to wait without complaint until his return. But unfortunately for that she needed Mephisto's assistance.

She pulled up short. Mephisto was standing in the center of the bedroom and for a split second she saw his eyes narrow as he swept his gaze over her. She straightened her spine, preparing to do battle, but he didn't remark on the shirt. Instead he strolled toward her and wrapped his wings around her.

Engulfed in darkness she stiffened in shock as softness and strength and unimaginable power thrummed through every feather. *Angel's wings.* She heard him tell her to hold on, felt his arm wind around her in a crushing grip and then she couldn't think anymore as her atoms exploded.

HER FEET LANDED on solid ground, her stomach a second or so later. She kept her eyes screwed shut and tried not to fall apart at the realization she had just . . . teleported.

There was nothing to panic about. She had already teleported once with Gabe. The only difference being *then* she'd had no idea.

She forced her eyes open and unpeeled herself from Mephisto but he didn't get the hint. His arm remained like an iron band around her waist and one immensely strong wing encased her in an altogether too possessive manner. All she could see, over the top of his midnight feathers, was that they were passing through a complex security system, in a strangely dilapidated-looking foyer.

She struggled and his wing slid down her body, sending shudders over her skin. With a gasp she clapped one hand to her chest, and her worse fears were realized.

"What did you do with the shirt?" *And her necklace.* The panic threatened to send her over the precipice. She dug her fingernails into the palm of her hand and forced herself to focus on the reality. No matter how crazy that reality was.

"Gone." The palm of his hand splayed across her naked belly, his fingers far too close to the apex of her thighs. "Think yourself lucky I allowed you to keep the leather on for daring to disobey me."

What had he done with her necklace? It was an incredible, tenuous link between her and Gabe and how was she supposed to convince Gabe of its existence if this egotistical dickhead had *destroyed* it?

"Where's my necklace?" She hoped he couldn't hear the panic edging her voice.

"Didn't go with the look, babe." He managed to sound both bored and amused, an infuriating combination. If that wasn't bad enough his wing glided lower, still concealing her breasts but curling around her thighs in blatant possession. She gritted her teeth and glared around the darkened club. If it was a club. Strange incenses prickled her nose but even the gloomy interior didn't disguise one thing.

Despite the outlandish costumes worn by the other beings in this place, the only ones displaying as much flesh as her looked as if they worked here. And judging by the spiked collars around their necks and the way patrons touched and fondled them, they weren't employed merely to serve the drinks and nibbles.

They *were* the drinks and nibbles.

He'd brought her to a bloody sex club. Had Gabe stormed off in the middle of seducing her to go to a *sex club*? Mortification and injured pride burned her blood, and only when Mephisto's relentless grip on her tightened did a terrifying possibility enter her mind.

She'd been so desperate to prove to Gabe that she wasn't entirely at his mercy. That she wouldn't put up with his moods or having her questions ignored. Using Mephisto had seemed like a good idea at the time. But only now did it occur to her that just because Gabe knew Mephisto didn't mean Mephisto could be trusted to keep his word. Maybe he never intended to take her to Gabe at all. Had Mephisto brought her here to *sell* her?

"Hey, Gabe," Mephisto said, and Aurora stumbled as her thoughts tumbled in erratic disarray. Gabe *was* here? Well thank god for that. He was an arrogant bastard for sure but compared to Mephisto—no, there *was* no comparison. Because despite Gabe's attitude he definitely had a core of decency.

And then she caught sight of him. Sprawled on a sofa, completely ignoring her predicament, his entire attention was focused on a pair of near-naked females who were going at it on the table in front of him.

Chapter Thirteen

GABE mentally rolled his eyes. He'd spent hours looking forward to finding Mephisto and kicking his ass, but four tankards of brain-rot with Eblis had mellowed his mood. The last place he'd expected the other archangel to appear was here, and he flicked Eblis a glance to see how he was taking the intrusion. Eblis and Mephisto loathed each other and it had everything to do with the fact that Mephisto was the first archangel their goddess had created after rejecting her flawed first children.

The demons.

Eblis, surprisingly, didn't look infuriated at how Mephisto had hoodwinked security. Bizarrely, he looked enchanted.

That was a first. Before turning to see what miracle Mephisto had wrought to extract such an expression from Eblis, Gabe gave the entangled females an appreciative glance. Neither had blue eyes, chestnut hair or freckles across their noses but, more important, they didn't use their mouths to fire incessant questions his way.

He had every intention of sampling those mouths later. And this time he'd allow no image of an irritating human from Earth to interfere with his long overdue pleasure.

Finally he slung Mephisto a glance. *And saw Aurora.*

The buzz of background conversation dimmed as he focused on the pair of them. His heart rate accelerated, gut tightened and every muscle tensed as adrenaline spiked and flooded through cells and synapses.

Aurora was with Mephisto, who had his wing around her in a blatant gesture of possession. White rage sizzled through Gabe's arteries, disbelief and sheer unadulterated *envy* that Mephisto, the bastard, retained the ability to wrap Aurora in his wings at all.

And he had no right.

"What the hell?" He shoved the table back with his boot, sending the entertainment sprawling across the floor. Mephisto shot him a grin and slid his cursed wing over Aurora's body and his heart jackknifed.

What in the gods' names was she wearing?

Mesmerized he stared at her exposed nipples peeking through the slashes in the scarlet leather. They were dark and erect and enticing and without conscious thought he surged to his feet, blood pounding and arrowing directly to his damn cock.

"Not bad," Mephisto said, and as his wing trailed lower Gabe saw how his hand virtually cradled her sex. *And she let him.* "For a mortal indigenous to Earth."

"Earth?" Eblis sounded enthralled. "You brought me a human from *Earth?*"

Gabe felt ancient muscles flex and contract as phantom wings attempted to unfurl with outrage. He had possessed his wings for only a fraction of his long existence yet they were a part of him still. A part of him forever. And right now he would give almost anything to possess them once again, to match Mephisto wingspan to wingspan and prove to creation that he was *once again whole.*

"Take your fucking hands off her."

The words were barely audible but thundered through his brain and directly into Mephisto's. For a fleeting second he saw surprise—shock?—flare in Mephisto's eyes as if Gabe's response had exceeded his expectations.

Then Mephisto drew back his wing with a flourish, exposing Aurora to half the depraved clientele of the club, and shoved her forward. She tottered on the spindly black stilettos and as he grabbed her wrist before she ended up on the floor he ran his scorching glance over her fishnet-clad legs. Lacy scarlet suspenders decorated her thighs and his shaft thickened in primitive response.

"You're welcome to her." From the corner of his eye he saw Mephisto fold his arms. "She might be a reasonable lay, Gabe, but fuck me she's a disrespectful bitch. She's in need of some serious discipline. Sure you don't want any help? I could give you a few pointers."

It shouldn't matter if Mephisto had just had sex with Aurora. Except it did.

Mephisto had no right to touch Aurora. Because she belonged to *him*.

He shoved her onto the sofa and took one step toward Mephisto. "Not your problem. You understand?"

"Jealous, Gabe?" Mephisto's voice was mocking and it was the final straw that sent him over the edge. He grabbed Mephisto's throat, shoved him up against the wall and grunted when Mephisto slammed a heavy fist into his ribs.

Rigid with shock, Aurora kept her knees glued together and her folded arms plastered across her exposed breasts. In mounting stupefaction she watched Gabe and the dark-winged devil knock lumps of stone from the wall and nobody attempted to stop them.

She glanced at the massive man next to her and then couldn't look away. He had wings, too. She hadn't noticed before. He grinned at her and she mentally recoiled.

This was only one reality. Gabe had pulled her into his world, but it didn't make her own world any less real. And no matter what happened she would never forget her real home. And somehow she would find a way to return there.

She gripped her wavering courage, ignored the stranger's now plainly lascivious smile and lurched to her feet.

Acutely aware they were the center of attention, she thumped Gabe's biceps while at the same time keeping her other arm wrapped around her chest.

"Will you just stop it?" She sounded on the verge of hysteria. Probably because she was. "What's the *matter* with you?" If anyone should be raging it should be her.

Simultaneously they both turned and looked at her as if she was an insect who'd suddenly discovered the power of speech. With a stab of shock she realized it was quite likely they *did* regard her as little better than an insect. She resisted the desire to slink back to the sofa and instead glowered back at Gabe.

"Sit down." Gabe sounded as if he was hanging onto the remnants of his temper by sheer force of will. "You're making an exhibition of yourself."

The sheer nerve of his comment should have infuriated her. But instead she had the awful urge to laugh. And if she started laughing she had the feeling she might never stop.

"I'm not the one behaving like a testosterone-stuffed adolescent." Mephisto choked. If only he *would*.

"No." Gabe looked at her as if he wished he'd never laid eyes on her. "But you are the one showing off your naked ass to half the perverted bastards in this place."

Talk about a cheap shot. Only the fact she didn't want to draw any more attention to the shortness of her skirt prevented her from tugging at the hem. It didn't help that she couldn't unfold her arm from across her exposed breasts, either.

"This outfit," she said with as much dignity as her simmering indignation allowed, "wasn't my idea."

"Park your asses, archangels," the winged stranger said from behind her. "Although the human can remain standing. I like the view."

Aurora didn't even have time to whirl around before Gabe grabbed her shoulders and forcibly shoved her down on the sofa. He then planted himself between her and Mephisto and slammed his booted foot on the table as two waiters placed steaming tankards before them. Obviously *she* wasn't considered important enough to serve, but to hell with that. She was parched. Keeping one arm firmly across her chest she gingerly reached out for the tankard in front of Gabe.

He wrapped his hand around her wrist and pushed her arm back. "Drink that and die."

It was hard to be assertive when she had to remember to keep her knees together and her nipples undercover. She refolded her arms and cradled her abused wrist under her armpit.

"Fine." Her voice sounded brittle. She couldn't quite believe she was arguing with an angel in a sex club on an obscure planet she'd never even heard of. Yet somehow she still had difficulty believing Gabe really was an angel. *What had happened to his wings?*

Mephisto leaned forward so he was leering right at her.

"Here, help yourself to mine." With one finger he slid his tankard across the table. She'd sooner drink arsenic than anything he offered her.

"Back off." Although he spoke to Mephisto, Gabe didn't take his smoldering gaze from her. "I mean it, Aurora. This stuff will kill you."

"Shit, Gabe, you're no fun." Mephisto grabbed his tankard and drained it and Aurora seethed in silent injustice. How was she supposed to have known it was lethal for mere mortals?

"Are all the females like this on Earth now?" The winged

stranger—was he another angel?—sounded enthralled at the notion. "Think it's time I took a vacation there if so."

Gabe jerked his head at a waiter and ordered a jug of water that appeared with dizzying speed. Clearly, no one wanted to get on the wrong side of a pissed-off angel.

"The humans of Earth," Gabe said, "are the same as they've always been." It was obvious his comment was anything but complimentary.

"Maybe you're just jaded. Because she's like no human from Earth I can remember." The stranger slung his arm over the back of the sofa and scrutinized her as if she was a slab of meat. Prickles of alarm raced over her vast expanse of exposed flesh and despite her best intentions she flashed Gabe a horrified glance. He didn't appear to notice.

"Anomalies crop up everywhere." He sounded as if he was talking about a freaky mutation. And since she'd always harbored a deep-rooted fear of being an anomaly of nature his remark seared through her heart like a branding iron.

"I am *not* a freak of nature." Yet she'd never felt more like one. Her flesh burned with mortification and her brain pounded from the affects of the polluted atmosphere. She wanted nothing more than to make a grand exit but since that was impossible she stiffened her spine until she thought it would splinter under the pressure.

"Did I tell you, I'm opening a new fetish club?" the stranger said. "Catering to the seriously depraved. I could market humans with this attitude in ways you couldn't imagine. Where exactly did you find her? I feel a hunt coming on."

Breathe. Her panicked mind issued the command before her brain seized up altogether. Gabe wasn't going to hand her over to this . . . slave trader.

"It pains me to admit," Mephisto said, "but for once I agree with our vulgar relative. How *did* you find this one, Gabe?"

"You tell me." Gabe sounded calm. Indifferent, even, but she could feel raw tension spiking from him, sizzling in the heavy air between them. "She was your plaything before mine."

"The hell I was." Aurora glared at Gabe and couldn't figure out whether she was more offended by his assumption that she'd associated with Mephisto before him, or the fact he didn't appear to care if she had. "I only met him tonight when he turned up at your place looking like a made-over Satan."

She heard the stranger snort with apparent amusement, but both Gabe and Mephisto looked anything but.

"One more word," Mephisto said, and for once he sounded deadly serious. "And I'll rip out your tongue." He slung a glance at Gabe. "The noise that comes out of her mouth gives me a headache. She'd be a lot more attractive mute."

"Maybe she does other things with her tongue to make up for the vocals." The winged stranger wound a length of her hair around his finger and she jolted back, heart hammering against her ribs. "Wouldn't mind finding out. You up for a bit of a trade, Gabe? I won't damage the goods."

Freezing terror slammed through her heart as the full force of her circumstances exploded in her mind. She was no longer on Earth. She had no idea of the laws, if any, that governed these angels— *demons?* They behaved more like gangsters than anything with a heavenly connection and their power appeared absolute.

Her hands were clammy and insanity whispered through the outer edges of her mind. The cloudy atmosphere closed in on her, oppressive and alien and a terrifying yet comforting certainty drenched her. She was going to faint. And then she was going to die.

Chapter Fourteen

SEEING the demon touch Aurora as if she was displayed on an auction block caused Gabe's blood to boil and it took more self-control than he'd exerted in a long time not to leap to his feet and catapult Eblis across the club.

He shouldn't care what Eblis said or did. It meant nothing. And yet he couldn't let it slide.

"This female isn't for sale or hire, Eblis." He glanced at the demon's fingers that were still entwined in her hair. "Remember that."

Eblis tugged his fingers free, apparently unconcerned that Gabe had declared territorial rights within the boundaries of his own club.

"You've taken this female under your wing?"

From anyone else Gabe would've taken issue with the jibe. Except, coming from Eblis, it wasn't a jibe. The ironic truth was, despite how millennia ago the archangels had rejected their goddess as utterly as she had once rejected the demons, if Gabe still possessed his wings he and Eblis would still be blood enemies. Yet the loss of the one thing that defined both archangels and demons had been the catalyst for this unlikely friendship.

"She's mine." Since those words were tantamount to ownership he knew Eblis—and even Mephisto—would no longer consider Aurora fair game.

"Hey, that's good by me." Eblis snapped his fingers for more drinks. "I've no desire to plow in your property. You should've said something."

A shudder rippled over Aurora, and Gabe waited for her outburst. He couldn't believe she'd let that remark go uncontested. But still she didn't utter a word, and irritation spiked.

So now she was giving him the silent treatment? What game was she playing? He gripped her jaw and forced her to look at him. And saw her eyes.

They were glazed, out of focus. As if she was slipping into shock. After everything that had happened, she was slipping into shock *now*? It didn't make any sense to him, but one thing was sure. Her terror was real. With a muttered curse he poured her some water and forced a few drops between her lips.

"Hell, Gabe. I would never have touched her if I'd known." Insincerity dripped from every word Mephisto uttered. "You *really* should have said."

"I'm saying it now." To reinforce his words, Gabe slung his arm around Aurora's shoulders and pinned her to his side. She was annoying, disrespectful and drove him mad with her endless questions. But, bizarrely, he'd much rather face all those unpleasant aspects of her personality than this unnatural stillness.

"If you want to keep her safe from the Guardians when she's not on your island," Mephisto said, "you'll have to make it official."

So Aurora had told Mephisto about the Guardians. He didn't know why that irked, but it did. *What else had she told him?*

To keep her safe from the Guardians all he had to do was take her back to his sanctuary. They couldn't touch her there. But without his personal protection any passing immortal who took a fancy to her could take their chances.

Fuck that for a scenario.

He'd never given his protection to a mortal. But he knew all about the ostentatious ritual involved. How the mortal had to go through a complicated cleansing ceremony and the oath of allegiance and obedience they had to give to their immortal protector. And, of course, how it all had to be undertaken on ancient, sacred ground on the night of a full moon.

Apart from the fact he couldn't see Aurora either prostrating herself at his feet or swearing undying obedience to his every command, there was really only one aspect of the whole thing that was essential.

He held out his hand, palm up, to Mephisto. The other archangel raised his eyebrows but didn't make any comment as he handed over his ceremonial athame.

"Give me your hand," he said to Aurora but she appeared frozen, so he released his hold around her shoulders and manacled her wrist with his thumb and forefinger. Ancient ritual dictated the lucky recipient of an immortal's favor should smear their naked body with their mixed blood. If it wasn't for the fact the ceremony predated Mephisto's existence by several millennia Gabe would've been inclined to think the whole performance originated from Mephisto's warped imagination.

For one agonizing second, as the tip of the blade touched his skin, he hesitated. Logically he knew he was doing this only to ensure Aurora's safety. But still, he couldn't help the splinter of guilt that burned through his heart. As if by participating in such an ancient ritual he was somehow betraying the memory of his long lost love.

Never had he imagined being in this position. But Mephisto's mocking words had forced him to face another stark fact. If he didn't go through with it, how would he know for sure, after he returned Aurora home, that the Guardians wouldn't one day find her again? He sliced open his palm and before Aurora could move he drew the blade across her palm as well. She flinched and shot him a look of shocked incredulity.

"What the hell?" Her voice was barely audible, as if she was having trouble locating it. He loosened his grip around her wrist and pressed their bloodied palms together.

"This human from Earth, Aurora Robinson, is under my protection." And that was it. All it took was the immortal pledge and a drop of immortal blood and Aurora was his. He saw Mephisto narrow his eyes, obviously checking her aura. He didn't bother checking it himself. He waited until Mephisto once again looked his way. "You clear on that?"

"Right." Mephisto was frowning and surprisingly made no further comment on the pledge, as if something had distracted him. "So are you dumping her back in Ireland?"

It was the logical thing to do. Now that he'd extended his official protection the Guardians couldn't touch her, no matter where in the universe she was.

Something dark and deadly coiled deep in his gut. Aurora now belonged to him and he'd damn well keep her until he tired of her and only then would he let her return home. "When I'm ready."

Aurora pulled her hand free and looked at her palm. The wound was already healing, due to the immortal properties of his blood, but she didn't seem to find it strange.

"The Guardians can't get me anymore?" Her voice was husky and although he knew it was because she was recovering from whatever had almost sent her over the edge, it still managed to arouse him. He'd got the intel he needed. He'd take her back and this time nothing would stop him from finally having her.

"That's right. They can't touch you without incurring the wrath of the Immortals."

She didn't look suitably awed that he'd bestowed such rarely given protection her way. Instead she refused to maintain eye contact and glanced around the club in an oddly furtive manner. As if she was scoping out the place for alternative exits.

No chance.

"I really need to use the bathroom." Her voice was little more than a whisper. He almost told her not to bother, that they were leaving. Then again, once he wrapped his arms around her and took her back to his island he didn't intend letting go until he'd slaked this insane desire.

He looked at Eblis, who jerked his head at a nearby slave.

"Take this human to the restroom. She's valuable, you understand?"

The slave, a seven-foot muscular eunuch from one of the less civilized planets in Sextans, bowed. Gabe felt Aurora recoil.

"I don't need an escort." She sounded outraged. Didn't she realize that walking through this club, dressed as she was, was asking for trouble? Not everyone here could read auras and therefore know she belonged to him.

"Would you rather I took you?" He saw the scandalized glance Eblis shot his way but ignored it. If he wanted to play bodyguard he damn well would.

She pushed herself up and slung him a glare that should have irritated him after everything he'd just done for her, but instead caused his blood to heat further. He'd give her five minutes. And then they were leaving whether she was ready or not.

"No, thank you." Her voice was clipped and she edged past Eblis, who leered with appreciation at her cute ass. "I'm sure I can manage." She then tottered on her astronomically high heels after the slave. Her jaw angled proudly and her arms were still plastered across her breasts.

Damn leather outfit. Mephisto was a perv. What was he trying to prove by making her dress like one of his sacrificial whores? Gabe shifted on the seat as arousal thundered through his groin. On Aurora, the outfit was the sexiest thing he'd seen in centuries. He couldn't wait to rip it off her.

"Interesting." Mephisto hooked one booted foot across his knee. "Never thought I'd see the day when another woman had you by the balls, Gabe."

At any other time he would've slung Mephisto across the club for daring to raise the past. But right now he was more interested in seeing whether Aurora made it across the floor without falling off her heels and breaking her ankles.

But damn, the glimpses of her rounded ass she displayed with every exaggerated step she took were pure exquisite torture.

"Cut the crap." Eblis gave Mephisto a filthy look that could reduce lesser beings to puddles of slime. "Since you didn't come bearing gifts, what the fuck are you doing here?"

"Just delivering Gabe's investment." Mephisto ruffled his feathers. "Went to so much trouble over her, I didn't think he'd want to leave her in my capable hands for longer than necessary."

Air hissed between Gabe's teeth and as Aurora finally disappeared from view he turned to the other archangel. "Shut the fuck up. Whatever interest you had in Aurora before stops right now." And at the first opportunity he was going to smash her damn cell phone Mephisto had inexplicably tampered with.

Mephisto shrugged, but his eyes gleamed with unholy glee. "Fine by me. I have no perverted desire to be lumbered with a human who's obsessed with interdimensional travel."

"What shit are you on, Mephisto?" Eblis sounded disgusted but also . . . intrigued.

"She's not obsessed with interdimensional travel." Gabe wasn't sure why Mephisto's accusation irritated him so much, but it did.

"You sure about that?" Mephisto said. "What do you think she was doing on the astral planes the moment before you arrived on her land, Gabe?"

An unwelcome memory stirred. When he had taken her to his island the first thing she'd asked was if he'd pulled her through the astral planes. And then she'd asked if the Guardians came from *another* dimension.

Was Mephisto suggesting Aurora had attempted inter-dimensional travel while she was on the *astral planes?* It didn't even make any sense. Assuming someone was crazy enough to try and breach dimensions in the first place, why would they want to without their physical body?

Mephisto lied as effortlessly as he breathed. But Gabe had the uncanny certainty that he wasn't lying this time.

"How do you know all this?" The words grated his throat and he glared across the club in the direction Aurora had taken.

"I've been tracking her for the last couple of mortal years," Mephisto said. "Through her cell phone."

"So that's why the Guardians are after her." Eblis sounded fascinated.

"The second she breached dimensions," Mephisto said, "she gave them the perfect excuse to hunt her across the universe."

Fury erupted and Gabe shot to his feet, adrenaline pumping with murderous intent. He'd given Aurora his protection *and it meant nothing*. If she had breached dimensions she had given the Guardians, the self-appointed keepers of laws so ancient their reasoning was lost to the fog of time, carte blanche to exact retribution and his protection was void. She would only be safe from the Guardians within the protective barrier of his island.

Only the beloveds of Immortals were immune from the Guardians' grasping claws, no matter what the provocation. Unlike be-stowing protection, that inevitably created a status of one-sided dependency, a beloved was their Immortal's equal. There was no need for archaic rituals or a blood exchange. It was love that granted the same immunity. And Aurora wasn't and would never be his beloved.

"You bastard." He glowered at Mephisto, who remained reclining on the sofa as if he was enjoying rare entertainment. He'd known from the start a pledge of protection was meaningless.

"So what's your next move, Gabe? Taking her back or leaving her here? I bet Eblis could sell her no problem before the Guardians come knocking again."

All Gabe's half-baked plans of how he could put up with Aurora for a few weeks—months, even—so long as she agreed to a few ground rules disintegrated. The Guardians hadn't randomly picked on her for one of their distasteful abductions. They wouldn't move onto another victim when they got tired of looking for her. They would hunt her down until they found her because they were vindictive, tenacious fuckers. The moment she stepped outside the protective barrier of his island she was vulnerable.

Unless he wanted to take responsibility for Aurora experiencing the Guardians' unimaginable version of justice then leaving her *anywhere* wasn't even an option.

"Tell me one thing." Not that he expected Mephisto to but he had to ask because the blank fragment in his mind was eating him alive. "How did you wipe my memory of leaving Manhattan and arriving in Ireland?"

Confusion glinted in Mephisto's eyes for one fleeting microsecond but it was enough. Gabe's unexpected transportation had nothing to do with the other archangel and more than that—Mephisto had no idea how it had happened, either.

"I never," Mephisto said, "share the secrets of my success."

Gabe swung around, kicked the table from his path and stormed through the motley crowd. He'd always been so convinced Mephisto was the one behind his arrival in Aurora's life that he'd not considered any other possibility. *What other possibility could there be?* But if Mephisto hadn't dumped him in Ireland then who—or what—had?

The eunuch was standing guard outside the bathroom door but instantly stepped aside at Gabe's approach. He shoved open the door, dislodging the spindly chair that Aurora had obviously used as a puny barrier, and saw her sitting cross-legged on the floor of the gaudily mirrored powder room.

Her eyes were closed, her breathing so shallow as to be all but nonexistent. She didn't stir at his entrance, and appeared oblivious when he kicked the door shut and it was then the truth hit him.

She was ascending into trance. Entering the astral planes. And although he couldn't fathom why she'd want to do such a thing now, he'd be damned if he was going to hang around and wait for her to return in her own sweet time.

He crouched, gripped her shoulders and glared into her calm face.

"Get the hell back here, Aurora, or I swear I'll follow and flay your soul until you scream for mercy."

Chapter Fifteen

HE followed her anyway because the chances of Aurora obeying him without question were remote. As soon as he entered the astral planes instead of the tranquil realm he recalled from millennia ago, echoes of chaos vibrated. Unnatural, unprecedented, but he didn't have time to wonder, didn't have time to investigate. Because Aurora was before him, glowing with pure energy, and before she had time to do any other godsdamned stupid thing he smothered her with his spiritual essence, intending to catapult them both back into their physical bodies.

In that second as they merged an overwhelming sensation of déjà vu rippled through him, body and soul. An unsettling, impossible certainty that he had been here before, done this before, with Aurora. And when his cock thickened, when his blood thundered he was so infuriated at how easily she could arouse him that he slung her from him and they collided on the cold tiled floor of the bathroom.

Panting, Aurora faced him on her hands and knees, her hair

tumbling over her shoulders. She looked feral and furious and infinitely fuckable.

"You could've killed me doing that."

Right now, he didn't much care if he had. "What the hell do you think you were doing?" He knew what she thought she was doing. Escaping. But her logic made no sense. Sooner or later she would have needed to return to her physical body.

"What do you think I was doing?" She bared her teeth like a rabid dog. His hands fisted on the scratched floor. Her subservience, such as it was, hadn't lasted long. "Getting away from *you.*"

"You thought I wouldn't be able to follow you? Bring you back?" He leaned closer until their erratic breath mingled. "What was your plan? To stay in the astral planes indefinitely? What about your body? Hadn't thought that far ahead, had you?"

Something flashed in her eyes, something angry and proud and he had the strangest sense that whatever she had planned, she imagined she'd solved the problem of her soul and body's division.

"I knew exactly what I was doing."

She no longer smelled of apples. Her scent was of him, his soaps and shampoo. He drew in a deep breath, savoring, and the evocative flavor of supple leather and sensual woman mingled with erotic enticement.

He would not be distracted. He would discover her truth. But damn, it was hard to concentrate.

"That's a matter of opinion." He glared into her flushed face, her over-bright eyes, and struggled to comprehend how this fragile human could possibly have committed the crime Mephisto accused her of. "Tell me what you were doing in the seconds before I awoke on your land."

For a second, confusion clouded her eyes, as if his shift in focus made no sense to her. But it was gone in an instant and she lifted her chin in a defiant gesture. As if his demand was unreasonable.

"I was meditating."

Suddenly aware he was on all fours, he reared up onto his knees. She followed, a mirror image, but had to crane her neck to maintain eye contact. The creamy swell of her breasts was barely contained within the tight scarlet leather, and her erect nipples goaded him with blatant invitation.

"Meditating?" His voice was harsh and he dragged his mesmerized gaze up to her face. "Is that what you call it? How about we go for the truth? You were screwing with the laws of nature and thought you'd get away with it."

"I *wasn't*—"

He gripped her shoulders and whatever other lies she'd planned on spewing vanished into a seductive gasp. She smashed her palms against his chest then curled her fingers so her nails dug through his shirt and into his flesh.

"You weren't attempting to breach dimensions?" Mephisto had to be mistaken. There was a reasonable explanation for whatever she'd been doing.

She hitched in a shallow breath but he refused to be enticed by the way her breasts quivered. Refused to acknowledge how she palmed his nipples or the fact her eyes were so dark the blue was all but obliterated.

Refused to respond to the lust thundering through his veins. And failed on all counts.

"Yes." She sounded defensive and for a second he simply stared at her, uncomprehending. Had she just admitted her guilt? Did she imagine it was a minor misdemeanor instead of a major infraction of universal proportions? "But you don't understand. The thing is—"

"I don't understand?" One hand wrapped around her throat and her pulse skittered against his fingers, erratic and sensuous. He plunged his other hand through her hair, grasped the back of her head. Her lips parted but she didn't attempt to escape. "You breach dimensions and then have the audacity to try and seduce *me*."

Her fingers clawed along his throat and whether by accident or design the movement brought her up against his body. He tightened his grip in her hair and his other hand molded the curve of her breast and cupped her succulent nipple in the palm of his hand.

"You were the one with the hard-on." She sounded torn between disgust and desire. "Didn't see you trying to fight me off."

He pinched her nipple between thumb and forefinger and her eyes widened, but she didn't retreat. Instead she dug her nails into his neck and the pain was sharp and erotic and sent splinters of fire ricocheting straight to his groin.

"How did I end up in Ireland?" He growled the question, hating to ask a human such a thing but needing to know whether Aurora—unimaginable as it was—was responsible.

She slid her fingers into his hair, tugged viciously. A primitive groan tore his throat and he tweaked her irresistible nipple in retaliation.

"I don't know," she gasped as she writhed in his merciless grip. "You just suddenly *appeared*."

He dragged his fingers through her hair, tugging on tangles, watching her face, daring her to complain. "I could enter your mind, tear it apart." His hand slid down her back, tracing her spine. "Find everything there is to know about you. Is that what you want?"

"What are you?" She tore into his skull and involuntarily he gritted his teeth and gripped the tempting curve of her ass. *Was she naked beneath this minuscule skirt?* "A demon?" And then she hissed in apparent outrage as he gripped harder, parting her butt cheek. Fuck, but he wanted to see her smooth, rounded ass framed in this decadent scarlet leather.

"Try again."

"You don't act like an *angel*."

He offered her a feral grin, abandoned her breast and molded the curves of her body before lifting her skirt and pressing his hand against the small of her back. A slender leather thong whispered against his flesh. *Not naked.* The knowledge didn't diminish his erection at all.

"That's because I'm an archangel, sweetheart." He slid his thumb beneath the slip of leather and tugged, so it tightened against her sensitive pussy. She stumbled against him, shock radiating, but whether that was because of his action or revelation he didn't know.

Didn't care.

"Archangel?" Her voice was husky, awed. She even stopped gouging his skull. "The Archangel *Gabriel*?" For a second he thought she sounded disbelieving, but clearly lust was interfering with his brain processes.

"That's right." And if she fainted with shock *now* he was going to be seriously pissed.

Desire-glazed blue eyes gazed up at him and her hands dropped to his shoulders. Her lips parted but no question followed, only the ragged sound of her breath. He lowered his head to savor that mouth, to taste and plunder as he took them back to his island. And then she spoke. "What happened to your wings?"

She dared to ask about his wings? Ancient rage collided with his lust. She had no right to question him on anything—but least of all on that.

"Don't you ever," he snarled, clamping his hands on her hips, "dare bring that up again."

Her eyes widened, as if he had just said something outrageous. Then she thumped his chest with both hands and that was so unexpected she managed to give herself leverage to twist sideways and out of his grip.

"Get out of here." She'd fallen onto her hands again, and shot him a look of loathing over her shoulder as she attempted to crawl away. "I want to—"

He gripped her hips, pulled her back, the image of her ass peeking from beneath the ragged hem of the skirt burning his retinas.

"What do you want?" Brutally he jammed her against the rigid length of his erection. "This?"

"Let go of me." She wriggled from her waist, her hips swiveling and his cock welcomed the torturous friction. "You bastard. You can't treat me like this."

He wound one arm around her waist, effectively holding her captive. He ran his other hand up the length of her back and pushed her hair over her shoulder. Leaning over her he grazed his teeth against the vulnerable curve of her neck and smiled with grim satisfaction at the tremors that attacked her silky-soft skin.

"I can do whatever the hell I please."

She continued to glare at him, her eyes dark with renewed desire and simmering fury. No hint of fear tainted the air, no terror that her life hung in the balance. No lingering tendril of awe.

Just raw lust. He could see she hated how much her body wanted him. At least they were equal in that because he was incensed by how desperately he craved this primitive joining.

Her uneven breath fanned his face. She stopped wiggling, as if realizing every move she made did nothing but increase the scorching need between them.

"What does that make *you*, then?"

He lowered his head and nipped her succulent flesh between his teeth. She gasped in shock, jerked back against him and didn't immediately pull away.

Too late now. His arm tightened around her waist as he savored the taste of her on his tongue, between his lips. She moaned in sensual defeat as he marked her in a primal gesture of possession, as his mouth claimed the curve of her neck.

"Told you once. Your savior." His mocking response against her ear caused her to shiver and she bucked, as if trying to throw him off. "Stop fighting it. You want this as much as I do."

"You arrogant"—she appeared to be struggling for an adequate insult and he sucked her earlobe into his mouth, toying with her crystal stud with his tongue—"*archangel.*"

Still holding her securely in one arm, his other hand skimmed her waist, hips and naked silken thighs. In his mind's eye he saw the slutty scarlet garters she wore and the lace burned his fingers.

"You want me to stop?" He growled the words against her ear as he slid his hand between her thighs to cup her sex. *Gods.* The strip of leather, far from impeding his access, was crotchless.

Pure lust stabbed through his groin, a ferocious primal imperative to take and conquer. She was hot, wet and bucked helplessly as he stroked his fingers over her swollen clit.

"Yes. *Yes,*" she panted, squirming in his arm. She was no longer looking at him. Her head dipped, her hair spread across her shoulders and her butt rubbed against his cock in delirious abandon.

He slid one finger inside and she clenched her muscles, entrapping him in a silken cocoon. He gritted his teeth, closed his eyes and breathed in her evocative, erotic scent.

"Why?" His voice was hoarse, and he slid a second finger into her. Gods, this was torture. He could taste her impending orgasm, could feel the erratic thunder of her heart against his arm. And still she denied her need.

"Because . . . you're . . ." She appeared to lose her train of thought as tremors licked through her. He stopped circling her clit, slowly withdrew his exploring fingers. "A *bastard.*"

He slid his fingers, coated in her juices, over her soft curls. Back and forth. Enough to tantalize, not enough to send her over the edge.

"So what?" He dragged his gaze down her back and focused on

where her ass wedged against his groin. "It doesn't matter what you think of me. It doesn't matter what I think of you. *This* has nothing to do with any of that."

Her head swung up, then fell again as if the effort was too great. "It does matter."

Still stroking her sex he cradled her breast in his other hand, flicking his thumb over her erect nipple. Choked moans spilled from her lips and liquid heat spilled over his teasing fingers. Blood thundered in his temples, his vision blurred and Aurora's powerful arousal tormented him with every rasping breath he took.

"Don't you want my cock inside you? Fucking you as you've never been fucked before?" Damn her, why did she resist? This need had throbbed between them from the moment they'd met. Why did she have to complicate a perfectly simple act?

"Yes." It tore from her throat as if against her will.

With a primal hiss, Gabe wrenched his pants open. He rose on his knees, gripped her hips and angled her for his viewing pleasure. Her rounded ass tempted him, framed in tattered red leather, and her gleaming pussy mesmerized him. "It's just a fuck, Aurora." He scarcely recognized his own voice. "Get it out our system. Just one godsdamn fuck."

Chapter Sixteen

THROUGH the thunder that pounded in his head he heard Aurora's hiss of outrage, felt the renewed wave of fury radiate from her. But it didn't matter. Nothing mattered but slaking this damn need and then they'd both be able to think clearly.

At least, he would.

His cock nudged her wet slit and she bucked, as if in shock, but she didn't squirm away, didn't tell him to go to hell. Her heat scorched, and while an inexplicable whisper in his mind craved to prolong this moment, to savor and cherish the first time he entered her tempting body, the moment for tender foreplay had long passed.

He thrust into her and an agonized groan tore from his throat as her tight sheath expanded around him. She fell forward, cradling her head on her arms, and he heard her staggered gasps of shock.

Damn, she felt good. Hot and wet and so fucking tight around him he could hardly breathe. Hardly think. He pulled out, an excruciating drag of flesh against flesh, and stared, mesmerized, at the sight of his cock invading her irresistible pussy.

She quivered and it was too much. He slid into her again and her embrace was silken fire, licking over and into his cock, igniting his blood and infecting his sanity. He palmed her ass, and as she bucked against his thrust the view and friction was so erotic another low growl burned his throat.

He reached around, found her sensitized clit and tortured her as she tortured him. Her thrusts matched his, a frenzied maelstrom of mindless lust and ragged breaths. She choked on her incoherent words, squeezed him tight and convulsed in waves of raw, uninhibited pleasure.

And tipped him over the edge. He gripped her thigh and pumped into her, hot and furious and it was so fucking good, felt so fucking right to fill her with his seed, hear her erratic gasps, and feel her body tremble at his onslaught.

He collapsed, bracing his weight on his hands as he knelt over her, still inside her, entrapping her and inhaling her evocative scent of sex and satiation. Satisfaction hummed in his blood but it was a fleeting satisfaction as, captured by her silken heat, his cock remained as hard as ever. Deep in his mind a warning stirred but he couldn't think why. Couldn't *think*. Because he needed her again, wanted her again, and there was no reason why he couldn't—

She suddenly severed their connection by sprawling onto the floor. *Well, hell.* They were still in Eblis's club. The realization that he'd forgotten their surroundings stunned him. He reached down and brushed the tangled hair from her face. Her mouth was open and she was sucking in oxygen as if she'd almost drowned. Her cheeks were flushed and she didn't turn to look at him.

"Hey." His voice was raw. "Aurora."

Her eyelashes flickered open, as if it took great effort. He shifted so he knelt next to her and could see her face properly. Still cushioning her head on her arms, she gave him an exhausted glance before dropping her gaze to his groin.

His body's response was so obvious she might just as well have reached out and gripped him. He wanted and intended her to, but not here. They'd done seedy. Now he wanted her back at his villa so they could take their time.

"Finished?" Her voice was breathless, but that didn't disguise the disgust. "Is that it now?"

Irritation slashed through the post-sex euphoria that had temporarily eased his rage. "Do I look finished?" The irritation mounted when she turned her blue gaze up to him and he saw the rage reflected. *What the hell was she mad about?*

"You tell me." She pushed herself upright and winced, biting her lip, as if every move drove broken glass through her bones. "It was just one goddamn *fuck* after all. Nothing special."

Blood pounded against his temples as he stared at her in mute disbelief. It might not have been one of his finest moments, but how could she sit there and say it had been *nothing special for her*?

"That remark might carry more weight"—he injected as much derision in his voice as possible, although he was still reeling from her sheer nerve—"if your orgasm hadn't damn near fried your brains."

Her face heated and eyes sparkled with fury. Fascination threaded through his anger, and that just made him madder than ever. But still he couldn't tear his gaze away from her.

"That doesn't mean a lot." In his peripheral vision he saw the way she fisted her hands in her lap, as if she'd love nothing better than to punch him in the balls. "I wouldn't be surprised if you just poked a mental probe in to do all the work for you."

He'd lost count long ago of how many females he'd taken. Few were memorable. But no matter how good or indifferent the sex had been from his viewpoint it was always spectacular from theirs. How could it not? Their libidos were already sizzling before he even touched them, simply by virtue of who he was.

Bedding an archangel was, he'd discovered in his far distant youth, a powerful aphrodisiac on its own for pure mortals.

No one, mortal or otherwise, had ever accused him of short-circuiting their brains in order to bring about climax. That Aurora had even considered such a thing, never mind had actually spelled it out with insulting disregard, astounded him.

And then the unwelcome image of a pair of redheads spiked the outer reaches of his mind. It was like a frigid slap across his testicles, except instead of diminishing the rabid lust that polluted his reason, it escalated.

"Not my problem if your sexual hang-ups can't cope with the reality." He realized he was glaring but couldn't stop himself. How did this woman manage to rile him so easily? "Get used to it." Because before he'd finished with her she would be under no illusion that he needed to *cheat* before she fell apart with mindless delirium.

"Get used to it?" Her mocking echo caused his phantom feathers to bristle with offense. "Why? We've done it once, got it out of our system. That was the deal, right?"

The deal? Her belligerent demand thundered in his brain and then, finally, the reason for the faint warning bells in his mind smashed through his consciousness.

He wasn't supposed to want her again. Not instantly, anyway. Fuck, when had he ever wanted to go a second round with the same female without so much as an alcohol break?

Why hadn't his brain cleared?

He was the Archangel Gabriel and he was on his knees in a shitty bathroom attempting to reason with a shrew of a human. A human he'd just fucked. By rights she was the one who should be on her knees before him, worshipping at his feet, mindless with gratitude at the honor he'd tossed her way.

For one shocking moment words entirely eluded him.

"Well?" She shifted gingerly, as if her ass hurt to sit on. "You got what you wanted, didn't you? So now you can let me go."

"Don't try that one." He was torn between shoving his unabashed erection back inside his pants or down Aurora's throat. "You were all but begging for it back in Ireland."

She snarled and yet again fascination with her extraordinary responses flooded his senses. Not even the few minor goddesses he'd laid had displayed such breathtaking arrogance. And at least in their cases they'd have reason for it. Aurora, with her heritage, had none.

"All right." Somehow she managed to grind the words between her teeth. "So I did want you. And now I've paid the price. So we're even."

Even? If he didn't have the urge to throttle her, he would've laughed. *Even?* She wasn't even close.

Apparently she wasn't finished, either.

"And now you can take me home."

Frustration ripped through him, a dangerous addition to the lust and fury that already warred for dominance. They were back to where they'd started and the only possible solution to her predicament condemned them both.

"How many times do I have to repeat myself?" *Probably ten times a day for the next sixty years.* "You go back and the Guardians will take you. And I'll tell you this—vivisection will be the least of your worries then."

For a moment sheer terror flashed over her face, but she wrapped her arms around her waist, apparently forgetting about her exposed nipples, and collected herself. Despite his personal feelings he couldn't deny the stir of grudging respect.

"But they're not after me anymore. I'm safe now."

"What?"

She gnawed her lip for a second as if reluctant to continue. He found that hard to believe. She didn't normally have that problem.

"You gave me your protection." She shot him a look as if she couldn't decide whether she should be grateful or insulted by his protection. "And now the Guardians can't touch me."

"Yeah, about that." He leaned into her space, daring her to retreat. To her credit she didn't. And still her blue eyes threatened to deceive him with their innocence. "You managed to negate my protection the second you *breached dimensions.*"

Aurora glared into Gabe's eyes and told herself he was lying. Except deep in her heart she knew he wasn't.

She'd succeeded in the first part of her plan. And the consequences of that one act were so devastating it looked like she was going to pay the price for the rest of her life.

There was a time for bravado and there was a time for humility. And as much as she wanted right now to tell Gabe exactly what she thought of him, he was also the only one who might—*could*— help her.

"I didn't know I was breaking some sort of cosmic law." She struggled to keep her voice even, but it was impossible. No matter how she tried to block the memories from her mind, her body still quivered with despicable shocked pleasure in the aftermath of her shattering orgasm.

Her uninhibited response to Gabe's brutal seduction infuriated her pride, but she'd deal with that later. Right now she had to convince this arrogant *archangel* that he needed to intercede with the Guardians on her behalf.

She tried to avert her gaze as Gabe shoved his erection back into his pants. Just looking at it caused renewed tremors to flutter in her womb. He'd thrust so deep and hard, taken her with such force and disregard she'd wanted to kill him. Except coherent thought had fled within a second as her body ignited into a million fiery whirlpools. She might want to delude herself the sex had been mediocre, but she had the horrible suspicion he was as aware as she was that it had damn well nearly incinerated her sanity. She tensed her sore muscles in a pathetic attempt to reassert control. And only managed to stoke the glowing embers higher.

"Now you do know." He sounded rabid as he attempted to close his pants. That had to hurt. She hoped it did. *Only a goddamn fuck? Get it out of their system?* What did he think she was, a space whore?

The thought punched through her mind with numbing implication, and finally she managed to drag her gaze up from his crotch to his face. His eyes were narrowed, his mouth grim, and a palpable sense of dark menace pulsed in the air between them. Yet still her heart jolted in her chest. Because despite how much she hated this entire situation she still wanted him.

"What about god?" *Make that God with a capital G.* "Couldn't he help?" The words rushed from her as he lurched to his feet in an oddly ungraceful manner. Probably because he'd drank too much. *Bastard.* Not that it had affected his performance so far as she could see.

"Which god are you thinking of?" He glowered down at her from a great height, and it was easy to imagine he himself was an ancient god of Greek myth. "I'll see if he's available for a consultation." Sarcasm dripped from every syllable.

Gritting her teeth against her abused muscles, she pushed herself up and tried not to stagger on the spindly heels. Belatedly, she remembered the disgusting state of her attire and although it was a redundant gesture, given their recent encounter, she once again wrapped her arms around her exposed breasts.

"Your god." Considering she now had no option but to believe in angels, she supposed it wasn't that much of a stretch to accept the existence of countless gods, either. Maybe there really were unicorns, too.

"My goddess," Gabe said with obvious satisfaction, "would crush you to dust before lowering herself to listen to your complaints."

Goddess. Right. An odd rushing noise filled her ears, and her head felt oddly light like she'd had too much whiskey.

"What about a holy tribunal? Court of Appeal?" She blinked, trying to clear her vision, but the room spun and still Gabe looked strangely fuzzy around the edges. "Don't I even get a fair trial?"

"There's nothing fair about it. What gave you that idea?"

A phantom fist tightened around her heart.

"But you're an archangel. You stand at the left hand of God." Panic hitched higher. "Goddess." Somehow it didn't sound the same, but what did specifics matter if it got the job done? "I mean, your goddess is the highest power, right?"

He bared his teeth in a parody of a smile. "She's always liked to think so." His tone suggested he didn't share that view. In fact, he sounded as if he didn't think much of her at all.

That couldn't be right. Even if it was a goddess and not a god who'd created the angels, surely the rest of the legends—ancient history—hadn't got it all wrong? Weren't angels supposed to adore their Maker? Do anything for him—or *her*?

Terror made her reckless. She stepped forward, curled her hand around his biceps and peered up at him. There was nothing soft or gentle in the glare he arrowed back at her. No hint of empathy for her plight or indication he even gave a damn.

But he'd saved her once. She had to remember that. Had to try and appeal to his sense of honor no matter how hard it was to admit to herself that he possessed such a thing.

"Could you plead my case with her? If you tell her the reasons why, I'm sure she'd—"

"Throw you to the Guardians herself. Yes, she would." He gripped her shoulders and gave her a shake that was so unexpected she clutched wildly at him before she fell off her hated heels. "Get this in your head, Aurora. I haven't seen her for millennia. And if I ever come face-to-face with the bitch again, the last thing I plan on doing is appealing to her nonexistent compassionate nature."

Two things slammed into her panicking brain. Gabe wasn't going to help her. And he was *thousands of years old.*

He was an archangel. He was an immortal. She'd already faced that. But she hadn't really considered it. Hadn't comprehended just how ancient he truly was. And even now she struggled to comprehend because he looked like a human—hot as hell, for sure, but still a human—and far from looking like a legend from antiquity he looked as if he'd yet to celebrate his thirtieth birthday.

Her eyes stung and she blinked rapidly, trying to dispel the violet streaks that invaded her vision. But like the aftereffects of a camera flash they remained imprinted on her eyelids.

She widened her eyes as she realized she wasn't hallucinating. The violet lightning splintered directly behind Gabe's head, and long silvery fingers pushed through the fracture. *The Guardians.*

Time froze as the violet shard expanded as if it were a door that had been violently flung open. Even as her fingers instinctively clutched Gabe's arms, a small gray alien with a huge dome head and reflective almond eyes stepped through the chasm.

An alien. The Guardians were gray aliens.

Gabe stiffened, glanced over his shoulder and hissed words in that ancient language he favored. Before she had time to even suck in a second petrified breath, he wrapped his arms around her and the seedy bathroom vanished as he teleported them out of there.

Chapter Seventeen

AURORA reeled and only the fact Gabe's arms still crushed her shoulder blades prevented her from toppling off her stilettos. Slowly he loosened his grip and she stumbled backward, livid to realize they were back in his bedroom.

"Don't touch me." She flapped her hand at him even though he hadn't moved toward her. "I'd rather kill you than have sex with you again." *Gray aliens were real; and they were more than anyone had ever imagined.*

"Now that," Gabe said, his gaze drilling into her like kaleidoscopic lasers, "is something I'd like to see."

She had the feeling he was mocking her, But what did that matter after what she'd just found out?

"The Guardians . . ." The words tangled on her tongue because they conjured up something warrior-like, magnificent—even if they were the bad guys. She'd never seen or imagined anything less *Guardian-like* in her life. "Why didn't you tell me what they really were?" The panic slammed against her chest. *Or was that her heart?* "They're not even human."

"I told you they weren't human." He sounded infuriatingly calm. "*I'm* not human, either."

"You look human." Even as she shot the words at him she knew her logic was badly flawed. But she didn't care. Gabe might be an archangel but he looked like a man. She could talk to him, reason with him and argue with him. For the life of her she couldn't imagine doing any of those things with the Guardians.

And wasn't that what Gabe had been telling her all along?

"Only," Gabe said, "superficially."

In this case, superficially worked for her. "They're *aliens*." But even saying the word aloud didn't lessen the disbelief. Bemused, she watched Gabe begin to undo the buttons of his shirt. *Why was he taking off his shirt?* For some inane reason, flashes of old fifties sci-fi movies tumbled through her mind. "Don't they have flying saucers?"

"A quaint misconception." She stared in fascinated disbelief as he tossed his shirt across the floor, exposing his magnificent torso. "They've never needed that kind of technology. We assume the energy they harvest from the Dark Matter they inhabit provides them with their version of teleportation."

She'd read up on Dark Matter during her research but it was more a case of what science concluded it *wasn't*, rather than reliable data of what it *was*.

Probably just as well. How would people react if they discovered the universe was policed by gray aliens that lived in vast expanses of mysterious dark space that even, by the sound of it, archangels didn't fully understand?

A scary urge to giggle bubbled inside her chest. The *Twilight Zone* was real, and she was right in the middle of it. "So that violet lightning. That's just—what?"

"Think of it as an interstellar elevator." He ran a leisurely glance from the top of her head to her aching feet. It was blatantly sexual, and with a jolt she remembered the slutty outfit she wore that exposed more than it concealed. "Except when you enter the fracture you arrive at your destination instantaneously."

A shudder crawled along her spine. Twice she'd looked into that fracture. Twice she'd escaped. Within the space of a couple of days she'd breached dimensions, hooked up with an archangel, met a demon and traveled by teleportation. But the knowledge that gray aliens existed threatened to tip her over the edge. "I— You—" She didn't know what she wanted to say but it didn't matter, because her brain refused to engage with her tongue in any case. She pressed her hands against her chest, as if that might help slow her galloping heart.

"I know. You'd rather kill me than have sex with me."

"What?" Distracted by his bizarre comment the terror of the Guardians receded. "Why would I want to kill you?"

"Beats me." The smile he leveled her way sizzled with sin. She forgot how to breathe, but it had nothing to do with vindictive aliens. "I think sex would be far more satisfying for both of us."

A dim memory surfaced. She'd threatened to kill him if he touched her. Was she *insane?* She only had to look at him and she wanted to touch him. In fact, she couldn't think of anything she wanted more right now than to fall against his gorgeously bronzed chest and feel his arms around her. Since she didn't trust herself to do just that, she staggered back a step and came up against the side of the bed. "How could I kill you? I thought you were immortal."

He shrugged, and his muscles flexed in breathtaking harmony.

"Compared to a human's lifespan. Not compared to, for example, a member of the Alpha Pantheon."

"So you really can die?" The notion was astonishing and yet his example made perfect sense. After all, to a butterfly a human would appear immortal.

"Everything ends eventually." Finally he took a step toward her, but still didn't touch her. "Is this your strategy? An attempt to talk me to death? Because it won't work."

She didn't want it to work. She wanted to wrap her arms around him, hold him close, breathe in his scent and drag her fingers through his hair. The image was so visceral it was a shock to realize that, in reality, they weren't even touching.

She reared back, forgetting she was already pinned against the bed, and lost her balance. Before she could push herself off the bed he trapped her between his hard thighs. And there was no need to imagine inhaling his scent because its evocative promise tantalized her with every ragged breath she took.

She was far too close to his groin. If he wasn't still wearing his pants she'd likely be—

She let out a pitiful groan and fell back, bracing her weight on her hands. The action thrust her breasts forward and she probably looked as if she was giving him a blatant come-hither invitation. But at least now she was no longer mere inches from the hypnotic bulge in his pants.

Briefly she squeezed her eyes shut before forcing herself to look up into his face. He wore a self-satisfied smile as if he knew exactly what had just crawled through her mind.

"Is that all you ever think about?" The accusation would have sounded better if her voice didn't drip with lust. She plowed on regardless. "Sex?"

He leaned forward until she had the choice of meeting his mouth with hers or lying flat on the bed. It immediately became apparent her mouth held no interest for him as he flattened his chest against her breasts in order to push her back. So much for choice.

With his hands on either side of her shoulders, her nipples strained against the delicious friction of his naked chest. God, how degrading. *She* was the one who couldn't stop thinking of sex.

"When I'm with you?" His breath whispered across her parted lips. "Yes."

Her legs were trapped between his muscular thighs, his cock nudged securely against her damp core, and they were plastered together from groin to chest. Yet he didn't crush her with the full extent of his weight—just enough so she couldn't escape.

Not that she wanted to escape.

"Just another notch on your bedpost." She dug her fingers into the cool cotton of his sheets to stop herself from raking them through his hair.

"Something like that."

It shouldn't hurt, but it did. But she'd never been just a notch on anyone's bedpost before. Then again, Gabe wasn't just anyone. He was an archangel. She didn't even want to imagine how many women he'd had in the past.

"What happened to just one—" The word lodged in her throat as Gabe trailed his fingers along the length of her arm, over her hip, and unhooked one of her suspenders. Somehow she couldn't say *fuck* when his lips were all but touching hers. "Time," she substituted, feeling ridiculous but relieved that he didn't laugh at her belated show of prudery. "You said it would get me out of your system." She hadn't forgiven him for that. She'd never forgive him for that. But the anger she should be feeling at the memory stood no chance against the molten desire that seethed in her veins.

He unhooked a second suspender and slid under her thigh to tackle a third. It was shockingly erotic.

"It didn't." No attempt at flattery, just that stark response. He shifted his weight and began to work on her other stocking. "That's why I'm still here."

"Big of you." The words grated between her teeth. Her temper didn't improve when Gabe flashed her a wicked smile and deliberately ground his erect cock against the crotchless G-string.

"You can't tell me you don't want me again." He sounded so sure of himself. So damn smug. It didn't help that she couldn't breathe properly. Her heart hammered like a thing possessed and she was already so wet he had to feel her even through his pants.

She squirmed, but since his thighs were as unmoving as granite all she succeeded in doing was agitating her sensitive clit against his rigid length.

More furious with herself than him, she punched him just above his heart. He retaliated by rolling her stocking over her thigh.

"What the hell," she gasped, "do you think you're doing?"

He pinned her to the bed with one arm across her chest while he stripped the stocking off her foot, the shoe tumbling to the floor.

"I don't want you looking like Mephisto's whore any more."

She forgot to punch him again. "Mephisto's *what*?" Was he suggesting that's what she was? Even after she'd told him she had never met the egocentric bastard before today?

He peeled the other stocking from her before she quite realized. He no longer looked amused, either. "Don't ever get dressed up for him again."

She grabbed his throat and sank her nails into him. "Or what?" She glared into his eyes and dug in deeper. It wasn't as if she could really hurt him.

He gripped her wrist and forced her arm above her head. Her other arm was still trapped beneath his body and she couldn't move a muscle although every nerve she possessed screamed in fiery torment.

"Or I'll have to tether you until you learn your place."

She huffed out a breathless laugh of derision. "I'd like to see you try." God, she hoped he couldn't guess just how much she'd like to see him try. She still retained a tiny sliver of pride, after all.

"That can be arranged." Without breaking his hypnotic gaze he slid something oddly abrasive around her entrapped wrist. Shock punched through her and shivered in the pit of her belly. *He'd taken up her dare.*

"What?" She squirmed, twisting her head, trying to see exactly what he was doing. "Oh my god, are you using those *stockings?*"

He tightened the knot around her wrist and tugged as if testing its strength. Then he wrapped his other arm around her waist and heaved her further onto the bed. She managed to dig the nails of her free hand into his shoulder, and his warm flesh sent tremors of pure desire sizzling along her sensitized nerves.

"Might as well get some more use from them before I burn them." He leaned over her, apparently unconcerned when her nails scored across his chest, and although she couldn't see what he was doing it was blindingly obvious.

She doubled her efforts at escaping his grip, her heart galloping and breath rasping in her lungs. She might as well have tried to fight a mountain, and within seconds he pulled back, straddled her hips and gave her a smile of pure masculine triumph.

Her arm was pulled taut above her head and he had clearly fastened the end of the stocking to the foot of his bed. She wasn't sure whether to melt in a puddle of mindless lust or poke out his glorious eyes.

"Like being in control, don't you?"

"Always."

"Is that your thing? Tying up women with their stockings?" Even as she spoke he was wrapping the second length of fishnet around her wrist in a leisurely manner as if he had all the time in the world. As if he wasn't on the point of spontaneously combusting if they didn't have sex right now.

Or maybe that was just her.

"I wouldn't say it's my *thing.*" The corner of his mouth quirked as if he found her question quaint instead of sexy.

Not that sexy had been her intention.

"Although it's the first time I've used the woman's own stockings on her."

Now both arms were stretched above her head and she'd never felt so wantonly vulnerable in her life. She curled her toes to try and focus. If Gabe wasn't on the edge then she'd be damned if she'd let him know how close she was.

And then his words tumbled into some form of coherence. He might have done all this before, but she was the first he'd used *stockings* with. It was sad to find that so arousing but she did because it meant this was new for him, too. Even if only by the tiniest of detail.

"I suppose you have handcuffs and ropes and . . . things in your bedside drawer." The words spilled from her lips in a crazy torrent as Gabe stood and began to peel off his pants. She crossed her ankles in a vain attempt to control her body's reaction to the sight. It didn't work.

He kicked his pants aside and hooked his thumbs into the midnight boxers that did nothing to disguise the mesmerizing extent of his erection.

"No, but if ropes and handcuffs are your *thing* I'll see what I can do."

Spellbound, she couldn't drag her fascinated gaze from his groin. She knew she was practically salivating, knew Gabe's ego was probably inflating to impossible proportions because of her fascination. But she couldn't help herself. How much longer was he just going to stand there, tormenting her? Why wouldn't he rip off his boxers and finish what he'd started?

"So what do you usually use then?" Oh god, he was finally inching his boxers over his hips. Her mouth dried, lungs seized up and her fingers clenched and unclenched in a futile attempt to reach out and touch.

"Whatever comes to hand." The grin he arrowed her way was evil incarnate. "I can improvise if pushed."

She tugged on her restraints. "I noticed. I suppose you've had a lot of practice doing that here—secluded island, no interruptions . . ."

A shadow darkened his eyes as if her comment was unexpected.

"No." He sounded oddly reluctant. "Not here. I don't bring women here."

Before she could make any sense of that he turned and marched from the room. He had a perfectly proportioned butt, tight and sexy, and his powerful bronzed legs were a sculptor's delight. She let a muffled sigh escape as he disappeared through the doors.

Then she stiffened as the realization hit. He'd walked out on her. What was she supposed to do now? *What had she talked herself into?*

Chapter Eighteen

AND then he was back, striding toward her across the room, his gaze as intense and his body as irresistible as ever. Her lips parted in a soundless question. *Where did you go?* But the words floated in a haze as the answer hovered on the horizon.

He'd probably just taken care of protection. But even as the thought whispered through her mind, even as her drugged gaze slipped to his groin, doubt scraped along her senses in discordant unease.

His glorious erection remained unsheathed. And a wicked-looking dagger glinted in his hand.

Her heart pounded and she reared off the bed, struggling futilely against her restraints. He stood over her like a conquering barbarian: naked, aroused and *holding a deadly dagger*.

He straddled her with ease, despite her flailing legs, and sat on her thighs. The weight was enough to immobilize her but not enough to hurt. It was also, infuriatingly, more than enough to cause renewed tremors of desire to spiral through her sensitized core.

"Miss me?" He brushed her hair from her face. She wanted to swipe his hand away. She wanted to wrap her legs around his waist. Most of all she wanted this crazy lust vanquished so she could once again think clearly.

"Untie me." Her voice was raw. The thought of bondage might have been exciting, but in reality the loss of mobility was . . . frightening.

"I will." His finger trailed along her face, over her throat and traced the frayed edge of her tiny leather top. Then he raised the dagger. "Trust me."

Was that a question or a demand? She stared, hypnotized, as he lowered the dagger to her breasts and a whimper escaped. Shouldn't she be terrified?

But it wasn't terror that caused her ragged breathing or liquid heat to bloom between her thighs. Because despite how she'd changed her mind over the whole bondage idea the last thing she wanted was for Gabe to stop . . . whatever he was doing.

"Aurora." He savored her name as if it was an exotic treat. "Do you trust me?"

It was a question. She struggled to remember all the reasons why Gabe was the last person in the world she should trust. And couldn't.

And it didn't matter. Because no matter how bizarre the conviction, deep in the fundamental essence of her psyche, she did trust him.

"Yes." It was surrender, yet felt like a benediction. As if, against all perceptions, it was not Gabe who held ultimate power in this game.

Something flickered in his eyes, an emotion too fleeting to comprehend, but she had the strangest sensation that he hadn't expected her unhesitating acceptance. He didn't say anything, didn't break eye contact, but she felt the tip of the blade slice through the leather as if it were silk.

He peeled the severed leather over her breasts, leaving her exposed to his gaze. But still he looked into her eyes, and despite the fact she was tethered to his bed and that he pinned her beneath his powerful body, it was the mesmeric beauty of his irises that held her truly captive.

"If I didn't know better, I'd imagine your silence was due to reverential awe at the skill of my magnificent dagger." His voice was smoky and curled around her senses like a potent aphrodisiac.

Her mouth was dry and the echo of her heart fluttered erratically in her throat. It was hard to breathe, impossible to think, but still a breathless laugh escaped.

"Your dagger is pretty"—she momentarily lost her train of thought as he leaned forward so his erection teased the swollen lips of her pussy—"big. *Amazing*," she corrected hastily as he began to grin, and then realized that wasn't the right word either. "Egotistical," she sighed, and stirred restlessly beneath his imprisoning weight.

The tip of his nose brushed hers. A featherlight touch, hardly a touch at all, and yet the pit of her stomach knotted with an absurd pleasure that bordered on pain.

"How gratifying to know my weapon meets with your approval."

His breath against her mouth was an erotic caress. She wanted to spear her fingers through his hair, wind her arms around his shoulders and drag him onto her ready body. But still he maintained a whisper of distance between his chest and her aching breasts. And there was nothing she could do because she was . . . tethered.

A delicious shiver raced over her arms, across her breasts and circled her nipples. His eyes darkened, as if he could sense the shift in her arousal, and then he sucked one ripe nipple into his mouth.

She clenched her fists and arched her back in a futile effort to assert control. He cupped her breast, held her firm and suckled hard, and spirals of agonizing pleasure ignited between her erect nipple and sensitized clit.

He transferred his attention to her other breast, licking and sucking and dragging his teeth across her flesh. The sensual onslaught was like nothing she'd experienced or had dreamed before. His fingers stroked and caressed and his mouth and tongue were instruments of sweet torture.

"Killing me," she managed to gasp as she clung onto the fishnets as if they were an anchor to sanity.

Gabe raised his head, his jaw still grazing her tender flesh. "Thought that was your plan for me." His voice rasped and he sent her another one of his sinful smiles. "Don't die yet. I haven't finished." He inched farther down her body, and she felt the tip of the dagger slice through the skirt before he flung the ruined garment onto the floor.

He rose to his knees and she saw him looking at her, but right now she didn't care how cheap and nasty the crotchless G-string was. Because the expression on Gabe's face caused a fierce pain in her heart as the knowledge punched through her that he found her *irresistible.*

An archangel.

Another ragged gasp escaped and between her thighs wet heat trickled. She knew the G-string covered next to nothing. Knew Gabe must see how desperately aroused she was. And still she didn't care.

"I will die," she croaked, tugging mindlessly on her restraints, "if you don't hurry up."

Without taking his gaze from her wantonly exposed crotch he slowly peeled the G-string over her hips, then in one swift glint of metal the last of the leather ripped from her body.

"I don't do *hurry up.*" But even as he spoke he roughly kneed her thighs apart, the savage gleam in his eyes denying his words.

Legs free at last, Aurora wrapped herself around him, rising off the bed to plaster her groin against his rigid cock. God, it felt so good and she squirmed helplessly, frantic with need, mindless with primal lust. He let out a hiss and his hands smashed down on either side of her head, bracing his weight. His tangled hair framed his face, his tautly muscled shoulders filled her world and the head of his erection nudged her swollen clit.

"Archangel." Barely aware she'd spoken aloud, the evocative image spilled through her mind. "Gabriel." She dragged out each syllable, savoring the taste of his name on her tongue.

He growled a curse in his own language—surely it was a curse by the wild look in his eyes—and slid the head of his cock over her wet slit. The exquisite pressure teased and probed but did not penetrate, no matter how she squirmed.

"You want something, Aurora?" He panted into her face, looking nothing like an archangel and every inch a hedonistic demon of pleasure.

"Yes." Her fingers clawed in useless frustration and she glared up at him. "*Yes.*"

"What is it you want?" Again he dragged his engorged shaft across her sensitized lips and her womb quivered with agonizing anticipation. "My cock inside you? Is that what you want?"

She dug her heels into his butt, her muscles straining with the effort of bending him to her will. But he was as hard as iron and as immovable as a mountain.

"Yes." God, had she screamed? And did she even care?

His mouth all but touched hers, their erratic breath mingling, their gazes meshed as one.

"Tell me. Say the words." It was a growl, an erotic command, and primal need scalded her blood. She'd never articulated her desires before. But the thought of doing so now, to Gabe, was overwhelmingly seductive.

"I want your cock inside me."

His eyes glittered with heightened lust and raw power sizzled through her veins. She'd never imagined saying such a thing could be so . . . liberating.

"And?" He sounded rabid and she stared up at him, uncomprehending. "What else do you want me to do, Aurora? Tell me."

She flicked the tip of her tongue over her dry lips and saw how he watched, hypnotized.

"I want you to . . ." The word lodged in her throat, a crazy inhibition that had no place in a world inhabited by angels and demons and cold-hearted goddesses. "Fuck me. Hard and fast and I want it *now*."

He thrust into her so *hard* and *fast* the breath stalled in her lungs and she wheezed incoherently, fingers clenching and toes curling. Sensation consumed her, a pulsing maelstrom of friction and flesh and harsh, hot breaths. His brutal possession enslaved her body and shattered her mind, as his cock invaded her willing sheath and his balls slammed against her tender flesh.

"Damn." His intense gaze scorched as he panted against her lips. "You're a good fuck, Aurora. You're so tight and hot. It's fucking insane."

Words hammered in her mind but she'd forgotten how to speak, forgotten how to think. All that mattered was the man, *the archangel*, between her thighs, who looked at her with such focused intensity and who *fucked* her as if the world was about to end.

And then the world did end. In a cascading torrent of pure sensation that consumed and ignited in simultaneous delirium. And without even realizing it, she wrapped her arms around his shoulders and held on tight as he rammed into her and came with ecstatic abandon.

Chapter Nineteen

EYES closed, breath scorching his lungs, Gabe's muscles slowly relaxed. Aurora was soft and warm beneath him, her arms still clasped around his shoulders, and it felt oddly right.

Idly, he played with her hair, enjoying the feel of her heart hammering against his chest, the uneven gasps of breath against his throat and the tremors that raced through her body at satisfyingly frequent intervals. He breathed in deep, savoring the scent of woman, of sex and the unique flavor that was Aurora and waited for the inevitable fissure of disconnection. But the usual disinterest to prolong any kind of contact after orgasm didn't wash through him. No overpowering need to untangle limbs and sink into his own private space thudded through the post-euphoric haze. And his cock, still buried inside her tight cleft, stirred. Again.

He should have known once—twice—would never be enough to sate the madness in his blood when it came to Aurora. She aggravated him too much, fascinated him too much to be cleansed from his system so easily.

But that still didn't answer the fundamental question of why he continued to lie here, in the aftermath. He was content to wind her hair around his finger, breathe in her evocative scent and enjoy how she clung to him as her erratic breaths gradually calmed.

"You untied me." She sounded drowsy, sated and slightly surprised. As if she hadn't expected him to cut her loose in the moments before they'd come.

He didn't know why he had. It had been an instinctive action. Certainly had nothing to do with wanting to feel her arms around him because why would he want that?

Her fingers caressed his shoulders, perilously close to where his wings had once been. Females without number had touched, kissed and licked him there. But they ultimately ignored the question as to *why* and *how* an archangel could possibly lose his wings.

He knew Aurora conformed to no such unspoken etiquette. But gods, he didn't want to shatter this strange sense of peace by once again deflecting her curiosity.

She slid her fingers into his hair, caressed the nape of his neck. A gentle, soothing gesture, but instead of enhancing the abnormal warmth curling around the left side of his chest a dark, alien sensation twisted deep in his gut.

Muscles tightened and he lifted his head enough so he could see her face. Her eyes were half closed, her cheeks flushed and a small smile tilted her lips. She looked satisfied and happy and why that combination heightened his unease he had no idea. But it did.

Wouldn't it be better for her to fall for him, considering she had no option but to stay with him for the rest of her life? That had to be better than having a woman who hated the sight of him and threw verbal abuse his way every time they crossed paths.

But that tiny coil of panic continued to twist deep inside. He didn't want her to fall. Didn't want to witness her inevitable slide into bitterness and recrimination when she finally realized that he'd never return her feelings. Because unlike other lovers who'd made that fatal mistake, this time he couldn't just walk away. He was stuck with Aurora for as long as she lived.

The panic—an outrageous emotion for an archangel to experience—spiked deeper. But he might as well confront the issue now. If she made unreasonable demands on his time when he no longer desired her, his only alternative was exile from his own island.

Slowly she opened her eyes and looked up at him. The devastating terror that had consumed her in the seconds as he'd brought her back had vanished. No matter how unorthodox his methods at least they'd worked. She'd been so distracted by his seduction her sanity had failed to tip into the abyss.

Equally, there was no awe of his status in her sultry gaze. She looked at him as if they were equal. As if this crazy interlude meant something more than primal sex.

What was he waiting for? Any other time, with any other woman, he'd already be telling her how things were. But somehow he couldn't shatter this moment with the truth.

"Gabe." Her voice was as seductive as her eyes. He heaved himself up onto his hands, willing her to remain silent. With another mortal he'd not even hesitate to enter her mind and manipulate her into compliance. But this was Aurora. And he couldn't bend her to his will in such a way. A shudder inched along his spine as he realized he didn't even want to.

"Not now." With more reluctance than he cared to admit he withdrew from her enticing body and rolled onto his back beside her. "Go to sleep."

She wriggled onto her side, flattened her hand over his chest and pushed herself up. He closed his eyes so he didn't have to see her. So she'd realize this conversation was over before it could even begin.

"Gabe," she said again, completely ignoring his attempts at saving the fragile construct of her heart. "There's something we have to discuss."

"There isn't." To underline his point he flung his arm across his eyes and hoped she now took the hint. He didn't feel like having an argument. If he was honest he wanted to have her again, but to hell with that. He wasn't a slave to the lust Aurora aroused in him.

"It's important." She leaned against him and her breath drifted across his jaw, as if she was gazing down at his face. "At least it is to *me*."

This strategy wasn't working. He rolled on top of her once again, pinning her to the bed. He'd managed to save her sanity already this night. It would be no problem seducing her once again so she forgot about her declarations of love and devotion.

"Be quiet." His mouth grazed hers and his cock hardened in anticipation. Maybe this was the answer. Fucking her into compliance until she was too damn exhausted to think never mind speak.

"We might have got away with it twice," she said with an edge of panic. "But it's really pushing our luck three times."

Irritated that she'd managed to snare his interest with her bizarre comment he raised his head and frowned down at her.

"What are you talking about?" It didn't sound like a confession of love to him. And he'd been on the receiving end of some pretty strange ones over the centuries. "Got away with what?"

Her breath shuddered out between her teeth and she broke eye contact to focus on his nose. "We didn't use any protection."

For a second he thought he had misheard. But the fact Aurora refused to look at him, combined with the way the words were still ringing in his ears, confirmed the astounding truth.

She was concerned that he might have passed something on to her.

"Let me assure you . . ." He was doubly annoyed that her insult had done nothing to diminish the extent of his erection. "I don't carry diseases. It's impossible for me to have"—he resisted the urge to grind his teeth—"infected you."

Her eyes widened in apparent horror. "Infected me?" She sounded as shocked as she looked. What was she playing at?

"Yes." Now would be a good time to leave her. Except it felt too damn good wedged between her thighs. "But if that wasn't your problem then it applies equally the other way. You can't infect me, either."

From the late morning sunlight that spilled into his bedroom he saw her cheeks flame with mortification. Obviously that hadn't been her inference either. Not that he'd for one second thought it was. But the way she was now looking up at him unaccountably rubbed his phantom feathers the wrong way.

"I wasn't—" She bit off her words and avoided his gaze. He narrowed his eyes, waiting. He wasn't the one who'd started this. If anyone should be offended here it was him. Yet her clear distress at his accusation ate into him like acid.

By rights he should kick her from his bed. But still he remained where he was, as if he craved this excruciating torture.

"That didn't occur to me." She sounded hurt. "I was thinking more of . . . me getting pregnant."

A dull pain spiked through his heart and for a moment he embraced it, allowing the ancient agony to wash through him in a self-indulgent wave.

Helena. The child of his heart. The child of his love. His miracle.

"No." His voice was devoid of emotion while regret wrenched through his chest. "You won't get pregnant."

"But I might. I'm not on the Pill or anything. I mean, it's possible, isn't it?" Again he heard the thread of panic in her tone as if the possibility of conceiving the offspring of an archangel truly horrified her.

And she was right to be horrified. Except Aurora would—*could*—never conceive his child.

He closed his eyes and once again rolled onto his back. No other woman had ever thought or dared to raise this with him. It was no issue with those who possessed immortal blood, and as for the others they either knew the chances of conception were zero or else they harbored a secret desire to bear his child against all the odds.

"Archangels don't procreate." They hadn't done so for millennia. "Trust me. You don't have to worry about that."

She stirred and he knew she was once again looking down at him. He kept his eyes shut. Tried not to see Helena's sweet smile, the unruly curls that framed her face or hear her enchanting laughter echo through his brain.

"Why don't I? You've got all the right equipment. And you can't tell me angels don't procreate, because I know they do."

He looked up at her, but couldn't summon the energy to glare. Because she was right. But she had no *right* to throw that in his face. No right to question his word.

Had he really thought she would accept his denial without contradiction?

Resignation at the knowledge that Aurora would never simply accept his word without discussion weaved through his mind as he weighed up what to tell her. But then her eyes widened in apparent alarm and she brushed the tips of her fingers over his shoulder. Oddly, the gesture seemed conciliatory, but that made no sense.

"I'm sorry, I mean, well, if the myths of angels are true I'm just guessing so are the stories of the"—she hesitated for a second, clearly searching for the right word—"Nephilim?"

Fuck, would she not just shut up? This conversation was killing him from the inside out. And Aurora didn't have a clue.

"Yes." His voice was harsh and he sat up, dislodging Aurora's soothing caress. "But like everything from antiquity humankind has corrupted the truth." He knew the stories that polluted the histories of Earth when it came to the beloved Nephilim. It was one of the reasons why he had little time for those born on this planet. "Despite the fact that we have all the right *equipment* archangels were never intended to procreate. And yet some did. But only with what you might quaintly refer to as their soul mate."

Soul mate. The words tasted sour on his tongue but the appalled look on Aurora's face told him she had instantly understood all the implications associated with that hated term.

"I'm sorry." Her whisper brushed against his shoulder and something in her tone pierced through the memories that threatened to overtake him.

"It's all right." It wasn't all right. It would never be all right. But Aurora sounded so genuinely distressed, and looked so convincingly contrite, that he couldn't help but try to reassure her.

Didn't make sense. Neither her reaction to his admission or his instinctive need to convince her there was nothing for her to apologize for. He dragged his fingers through his hair and craved alcohol to deaden the ache in his brain.

"I didn't mean to pry." Her voice was soft, as if she confessed to a great sin. He sighed heavily. She had not the first conception of how mightily *he* had sinned. Or how horrific a price his loved ones had paid.

She never would.

"Go to sleep, Aurora." He looked at her then, as she sat facing him on his bed. She was only a mortal, a human from Earth, and yet in the last few moments he had shared more with her than he had with anyone in millennia.

The knowledge caused his gut to tighten and again that inexplicable rope of panic coiled like a poisonous serpent. Before he could be tempted to pull her into his arms and lose himself once again in the welcoming heat of her flesh he turned, picked up the dagger and left the bed.

She didn't say anything. Didn't try to stop him. At the door he battled against the urge to turn once more and look at her. To see if she was watching him.

But he didn't. Instead he went into his office, his haven, and pulled open the top drawer in his desk.

Helena laughed up at him from the one and only picture that remained of her. His gaze slid to her mother and even now, even after all these endless centuries, the familiar pain of futile fury and hopeless devotion ripped through his heart. He had been unable to save either of them. They were gone. And they could never return.

Eleni. His first love. His only love.

Eleni had driven him insane with her smart mouth and inability to acknowledge his archangelic superiority. But then, Eleni hadn't been a mere human. She'd had the right to question him and insult him. She possessed noble blood and status of her own. Her pride in her Nephilim heritage shone through everything she said, everything she did. She bowed to no man and no immortal, and despite fighting her charms for more than three years, his surrender was inevitable.

He'd irrevocably fallen the moment he looked into her fearless dark eyes. Had fallen more surely every time they spoke, every time she refused his advances, and every time she laughed at his attempts to dominate.

Because she'd known. Right from the start she'd known they belonged together and theirs was a partnership of equals.

Forty years. That's all they'd had together. And the miracle of creating Helena.

He shoved the memories back into the dark corners of his consciousness and opened his laptop. Eblis, who had no compunction listening into the thoughts and telepathic communication of those who frequented his den, recalled a group of pirates had been discussing the home solar system of the missing child, Evalyne. Gabe logged on and accessed all the information he could find on the small galaxy of Fornax, where Eblis said the pirates had originated from.

It wasn't much to go on, but at least it was a start.

Chapter Twenty

AURORA stretched and a muffled groan escaped. Her entire body ached, inside and out, and as she gingerly curled back into a ball a flicker of heat warmed her heart.

That was the price demanded after hours of raw, uninhibited sex.

It took a few seconds for her brain to realize that she was smiling like an idiot instead of . . . Well, how was a girl supposed to feel after spending the night with an archangel? *Absolutely knackered* seemed to sum it up perfectly.

Finally she forced open one eye. She was still lying at the wrong end of the bed, and she was alone. Hadn't Gabe returned at all after he'd left her this morning?

She chewed her lip and rolled onto her back, wincing at her protesting muscles. At some point she must've pulled a cover over herself, and she wrapped it around her breasts as she sat up, pushing her hair off her face.

Sunlight streamed in through the wide glass doors that led to the balcony, and for a moment she gazed at the distant rainforest. A tiny corner of her mind wondered at the sheer impossibility of everything that had happened over the last couple of days. But it was faint, insubstantial, as if that section of her consciousness did not quite belong to her. Because what did it matter how impossible everything was?

The only thing that did matter was it *had* happened and it *was* possible. She needed to focus on that. After all, she was living proof that one person's fantasy was another person's reality. How many people did she know who would have believed her if she'd told them of her mother's true heritage?

The ruined fishnet stockings were still tied around her wrists, and as she tugged at the knots she wondered where Gabe was. Had he gone out? What exactly did an archangel do all day? Finally giving up on the knots, she slid out of bed and picked up Gabe's discarded shirt. It smelled darkly erotic and seductively dangerous and she smothered a sigh as she pulled it over her head.

He fascinated her and aroused her like no other man she had ever met before in her life. Sure, he had the added advantage of immortality but it wasn't that. It was the flashes of the *man* she saw beneath the archangel that really intrigued her.

But even then, there was more. He'd not only rescued her from the Guardians but had then openly given her his protection. She knew Mephisto had been goading Gabe. Knew the winged bastard was only out to cause trouble. But Gabe, despite his foul mood, hadn't deserted her. And while it might gall that she'd been at his mercy there was no point wasting energy on useless anger. She was a mortal in a world of angels and demons.

On Eta Hyperium, when she'd thought herself safe from the Guardians, she'd been so desperate to escape that she'd decided to put her theory of traveling without breaching dimensions to the test. She'd focused her psychic energy on her home in Ireland, but that was as far as she'd got before Gabe had pulled her back. Had saved her *ass* yet again. He could be impossibly arrogant at times, but until she could work out a way of returning home without alerting the Guardians she'd make allowances for Gabe's occasional egotistical outbursts.

As she slowly made her way toward the bedroom door, pain enveloped her breast. How could she not make allowances after his heartbreaking confession during the night? She had almost admitted to having gone through his personal treasures. Resentment had bubbled at his barefaced lie that angels didn't procreate. Then her wounded pride crumbled as the depth of agony that underpinned his every word finally hit her.

It didn't matter how long ago his woman and child had died. He still loved them. Would always love them. And he loved them so fiercely that he still couldn't speak about them.

The door to his office was open. Gabe was asleep, arms folded on his desk, head cradled on his arms. She sagged against the doorframe, unable to tear her gaze from him.

He didn't look like an archangel. He looked like a man exhausted by grief and ancient heartache.

No. She wouldn't fall for him. She wanted him, yes. She could accept that. He fascinated her and despite his lord-and-master routine she kind of . . . liked him, too.

If all they shared was smoking sex and a casual friendship then there was nothing to stop her from walking away when the time came. *And that time would come.* She knew it wouldn't be easy. Gabe wasn't the type a girl could walk away from without regrets but at least she would be able to.

But if she fell in love with him? How could she walk away then and expect to get her life back on track?

She wrapped her arms around her waist and still couldn't drag her eyes away from him. Panic knotted deep in her gut and her chest tightened as the alternative hammered through her mind.

He expected her to remain here for the rest of her life. *She would never see her family again.* As her mother had never seen *her* family again. And while her mother loved her father and was happy to stay with him, eventually her mind had closed down under the strain.

Her mother clung to the edges of sanity by insisting there was only one world. *This* world. But by denying her heritage she scrubbed her mind of all telepathic links, the precious link Aurora had shared with her since birth. But even that hadn't been enough to halt the fog that clouded her mind.

Fear wound through the panic, tightening the noose. She might not have traveled to another dimension like her mother had, but if she stayed here—secluded and isolated from the rest of the world— she might just as well have. Would she wake up one day and believe this was *all there was?* That her life up until meeting Gabe had been nothing but a strange, barely recalled dream?

Gabe expelled a heavy sigh, frowned and rolled his shoulders in a slow, languorous movement. She watched, fascinated by the poetic play of his muscles as he passed from slumber into consciousness.

It would be way too easy to fall for him. Way too easy to agree with his plans without pushing forward her own ideas and suggestions. But while her dad loved her mum with all his heart and soul and would do anything for her, all Gabe felt for *her* was lust and a sense of responsibility.

If she allowed herself to feel anything more than desire for him, eventually her heart would wither. She didn't want to think what might become of her after that. Because it wasn't going to happen. She wasn't going to *let* it happen.

And then she realized Gabe was looking at her.

Stay calm. Stay in control. *Control* was of paramount importance. She would not allow her emotions to rule.

"Hi." She hoped she sounded casual and not as if her brain was about to explode.

He didn't answer but he did give her a long, assessing once-over. The expression on his face suggested he didn't much care for the fact she was once again wearing one of his shirts.

She shifted self-consciously, and through force of habit her fingers went to curl around her necklace. Except her necklace was no longer around her throat. She smothered the sense of loss that stabbed through her at the realization that Mephisto had likely destroyed it and forced herself to remain still. Just because Gabe was perfectly comfortable wandering around his home completely naked didn't mean she intended to do the same.

Finally he grunted by way of greeting, swiveled the chair so he was facing her, and it was blatantly obvious he was more than ready for a repeat of that morning.

With more willpower than she knew she possessed, Aurora kept her gaze fixed on his face. It didn't stop her from noticing the size of his erection though, or prevent the sharp tug of desire low in her womb.

"I've been thinking." Her treacherous gaze flicked to his groin and she all but forgot about the half-formed plans that had drifted through her mind as she'd woken. *Concentrate.* She gave herself a sharp mental slap, jerked her head up and caught the half-smile on his lips, the smolder in his eyes. It was obvious what *he* was thinking.

"Come here." His voice was smoky, seductive, and she'd taken a step into his office before she even realized.

"Gabe." It was hard to speak. He always did that to her. Would she always find him this irresistible if, by some incredible chance, they stayed together for any length of time? "Do you have the Internet?"

His lazy smile faltered. "The *what?*" He sounded incredulous. As if it was inconceivable she could think of anything but him when in his naked presence.

Well, he wasn't exactly wrong. She struggled to remember her point.

"The Internet. Well, an email connection really." Her phone was still dead and she had a feeling it had nothing to do with the battery needing a charge. "So I can let my parents know I'm still alive." Then she could at least stop worrying about them thinking the worst and concentrate on formulating her plans.

He was silent for a moment as though it had never occurred to him that she'd want to do such a thing.

"I can hook up a connection for you. But you can't tell them what's happened."

"I know that." She wanted to reassure them, not frightened them half to death. "I'll just say I had to leave unexpectedly but I'll be in touch soon."

"Aurora." For a second she thought she saw regret in his eyes. "Don't go making plans to meet up with them. I can't guarantee your safety outside my island."

"I wasn't going to." And the reason she hadn't planned on doing any such thing was because her plans were aimed in another direction entirely. "So, about this Internet. Is it some kind of cosmic web?" She forced a smile and hoped it didn't feel as fake as it felt. "I don't think I'm going to find many answers on the regular net, do you?"

He was silent for a few seconds as if digesting her comments and finding them unpalatable. "What kind of answers?"

"I thought I'd research the Guardians. See if I could find a loophole in their logic or something."

"There is no loophole." Irritation filled the air. "Do you think I haven't thought of that?"

She glanced at his desk. It was as clear as it had been yesterday.

"You mean you—is that what you were doing this morning? Researching for a loophole?"

"Of course I wasn't." He sounded seriously rattled now. "I know a great deal more about the Guardians than you do."

Of course he did. He was an immortal and she was only a human. He'd had eternity to discover everything about the Guardians. But that didn't necessarily mean he had.

She took another few steps until she was standing by the side of his desk. Until she could, if she wanted, reach out and spear her fingers through his gloriously tangled hair.

Hair that she had tangled earlier that day.

"I'm not disputing that." She resisted the urge to press her thighs together in a futile attempt to dampen down the lust. She couldn't let sex dictate *every* single move between them, no matter how enticing the notion. "But I know next to nothing about them and I'd like to learn."

The silence vibrated between them as Gabe glowered at her as if she had asked for something outrageous. She stared back, refusing to break eye contact or utter another word. She'd told him what she wanted. It was up to him to respond.

Finally he muttered something under his breath. *What was that language?* She dearly wanted to know but now wasn't the time to distract him with a tangent.

"Fine." He sounded like he didn't care one way or the other. "But you're wasting your time. Their clauses are ironclad."

Despite his negative attitude, anticipation sizzled through her blood. No matter how pessimistic Gabe was of discovering something she could use to her advantage, she just knew she would. She had to.

AURORA HAD JUST finished a late lunch of exotic fruits as Gabe strolled into the kitchen. He'd showered, his hair still damp, and he looked completely edible.

Without meaning to she licked her lips and tried not to drool.

The legends might have got a lot wrong when it came to the angels but they'd certainly been right about the heavenly beauty. Only when he deposited a slender, faintly glimmering laptop on the table in front of her did she even realize he'd been holding something.

"I've reconfigured the language options. You need to imprint your DNA so it recognizes your commands."

Her DNA? Why would a laptop need that kind of information? "How does it work?" There was no keyboard so far as she could see. "Does it connect directly to my brain or something?" She was joking, but Gabe shot her an assessing glance.

"The DNA imprint is a security feature." He turned back to the laptop, and the screen suddenly blazed into rainbow-bright life. "I can access it psychically but I doubt you'll be able to, despite your"—he paused, as if weighing up his words—"probable telepathic abilities."

For a second she wondered why he assumed she was telepathic, and then remembered how he'd probed her mind when they'd first met. How staggered he'd been by the mental barrier she hadn't even known she possessed. The protective barrier that, she guessed, was a natural part of her mother's heritage to repel unwanted telepathic intrusion.

"Yes, I am telepathic. So's my mother." She hesitated for a moment then decided to share a little more. "All of my mother's people are telepathic." When Aurora had been growing up, her mother had loved telling her stories about her home. How people communicated telepathically as easily as they spoke aloud and how strange her mum found it that on Earth nobody did. Aurora and her mother had shared a telepathic link but Aurora had never discovered anyone else whose mind she could reach. Not that she'd exactly gone around trying. "But it's not something I, you know, tell everyone about." But she had the strongest urge to tell Gabe. To explain so he would understand why she had so desperately wanted to breach dimensions. "You see, the thing is—"

"You descended from witches. That's okay, I won't burn you at the stake." He flashed her a sardonic smile as if he actually meant it. She was so distracted by both his smile and the fact he appeared to find nothing odd in his remark that she forgot to correct him. "Place your thumbprint here." He indicated an indentation in the bottom right-hand corner of the screen. "You can gain access to the *cosmic web*"—his lips twitched with amusement—"with this." He placed a small crystal globe in front of her. "This is our version of the mouse." Finally he touched the bottom of the frame and a wafer-thin keyboard slid out.

"This is amazing." She ran her finger over the crystalline keyboard. "How's it all powered? Do you have your own generator?" He had lights, air-conditioning, hot running water. Where did he get his power source?

"Solar, hydro and wind."

Of course. She should have guessed.

"Environmentalists would love to get their hands on your technology." Because Gabe's version of harnessing the elements was light-years in advance of anything she'd come across before.

He stood back, folded his arms and frowned down at her, as if she'd just struck a nerve. "It's not my technology. It was ancient knowledge here before I ever discovered Earth. And it's a damn sight better than the so-called discoveries and advances made in your Age."

Ancient knowledge? *Before he had discovered Earth?* She stared up at him, a dozen questions ricocheting through her mind.

He was referring to lost civilizations. Great, unknowable cultures that had existed *before his time.*

"How—"

"I'm not discussing it."

She snapped her jaw shut. She wouldn't get mad at his high-handed manner because he'd already given her the means to discover anything she wanted. It was also likely the dark-haired woman and their child had lived during that ancient time. Did she really want to remind Gabe of that—of them?

Unsure of how she *did* feel about that, she pushed the thought aside and stood up.

"Okay." She could tell by the swift narrowing of his eyes that he'd expected more argument from her. For some reason that cheered her up and she managed a breezy smile. "Mind if I use your shower?"

"Go ahead." As she moved past him and tried not to breathe in his seductive scent, he reached out and tugged gently on her hair. "You don't have to ask, Aurora." His tone was odd, as though her question had somehow bothered him. "This is your home, now."

A strange pain lanced through her heart at his words. This would never be her home and they both knew it. And yet Gabe, in his own way, was trying to make her feel less alienated.

"Right." She couldn't look at him. Couldn't trust herself to look at him, in case he saw . . . something he shouldn't in her eyes. She focused on the door. He would see nothing in her eyes because there was nothing to see. "Thanks."

With that, she made her escape.

Chapter Twenty-one

FOR a moment Gabe remained rooted to the spot, staring at the door that Aurora had disappeared through. Had he just told her this was her home? His sanctuary?

Sure, he had faced the inevitable fact she would remain here for the rest of her life but that still didn't make this her *home*.

"Shit." He glared around the kitchen before focusing on the laptop. It hadn't occurred to him what Aurora might actually do with her time, but if she wanted to investigate the Guardians then at least that would keep her occupied.

Unsure why he felt so damned put out by what had just happened, he turned and followed her upstairs. She'd just reached the second-floor landing and he caught a seductive glimpse of shapely thigh and enticing pussy.

She needed clothes. He'd have a permanent hard-on if all she wore was a succession of his shirts. And since when had his shirts been so damn sexy on a woman in any case?

Since no other woman had ever worn his shirts since Eleni, he ignored the question and stamped up the stairs. Aurora had already vanished into the bathroom and he stared at the blue shirt she had worn yesterday, now crumpled on the floor next to the bed.

With a muttered curse he grabbed at it and saw a delicate golden chain tangled in the material. He tossed it onto the bed and his shirt down the laundry chute.

He was supposed to be hunting down abductors, but Aurora couldn't continue using his shirts. Gods, the simple necessity of clothing her hadn't even crossed his mind. He didn't have time right now to seek out enchanting outfits or enticing lingerie, no matter how much the image appealed.

There was only one thing he could do. He'd have to teleport to her house and bring back her personal belongings.

DESPITE HIS GLAMOUR that rendered him invisible to human eyes, the dogs sensed him the second he arrived in Aurora's kitchen. He ruffled their fur and telepathically commanded them to ignore him. From the sound of things he wasn't alone in the house, and the last thing he needed was inquisitive mortals investigating the dogs' mournful whines.

The silver-framed picture Aurora appeared so attached to was where he'd left it on the workbench. He picked it up, gave the ethereal flower another dubious glance before sliding it into the black rucksack he occasionally used on missions. As he turned to leave the kitchen a man entered, his blue eyes instantly reminding Gabe of Aurora. But they were shadowed with fatigue and he slumped down onto one of the kitchen chairs, propped his elbows on the table and cradled his head in his hands, as if his brain hurt.

He was obviously Aurora's father, and just as obviously sick with worry as to what had happened to her. A laptop was on the table and Gabe sent a subliminal message to the man. *Log on to your email account.*

Gabe left the kitchen without a backward glance and strode toward the stairs.

When Aurora sent her message, her father could stop worrying. She was safe, and Gabe intended to ensure she remained that way.

Upstairs he glanced at the first room, instantly dismissing it as not the one he sought. A woman lay on the double bed, her hand across her eyes, and as he turned to try the next room she gave a muffled sob.

She'd have a lot more to cry over if her daughter had been taken by the Guardians. He pushed open the second door. This was more like it. Within seconds he'd filled the rucksack with the contents of the chest of drawers by the wall, plus all the feminine bits and pieces that were strewn across various surfaces. He had no idea where Aurora was going to keep all this stuff. He'd probably have to commission another piece of furniture for her.

He pulled open the closet door and piled her clothes, including the hangers, over his arm. Mission accomplished. He backed up, turned around and saw the woman standing in the doorway, staring directly at him.

For a split second his heart jolted. He could see where Aurora got her hair and freckles. It was like he'd been given a glimpse of her thirty years into the future. Instead of teleporting right away he shifted his focus to examine her aura. If Aurora was descended from an immortal—which seemed a possible answer after her remark that all her mother's people possessed her telepathic abilities—there should be a residual element in her mother's aura.

A shiver inched along his spine. This woman's aura glowed, but it was shredded as though giant claws had ripped through the ethereal fabric of her existence. But despite its ruined state it was glaringly obvious she didn't possess even a trickle of immortal blood.

And then he realized she was still staring at him. Not through him; *at* him.

Not possible. Humans, even those who possessed a modicum of psychic ability, couldn't see through an immortal's glamour. But he'd known Aurora's abilities weren't usual. Obviously neither were her mother's. He should have gone for a level-two glamour just to be on the safe side.

"What are you?" Her voice was hushed, and he realized she didn't possess the soft Irish brogue Aurora did.

Reason dictated he teleport immediately. He owed this woman nothing. Yet the strange glitter in her dark eyes unnerved him and the question reverberated in his own brain. What are *you*?

Where have you taken my child?

Her voice, strong and sure, split through his skull and his muscles tensed in shocked disbelief. Even the foremost telepathic races in the universe wouldn't dare to take such a liberty without invitation. Only other immortals of similar status had that right.

She's safe. He used the channel she had opened up, and although he was tempted to scan the outer edges of her mind he knew what he would find.

The same barriers, but likely far more powerful than those that shielded Aurora. At least he now knew who had taught her to protect her mind.

Bring her back. It was an imperious command but panic threaded through every word. And a fleeting flicker of remorse stabbed through his chest.

He would never bring her back. He couldn't risk her safety.

"No." He spoke aloud with finality. And returned to his island.

HE'D DUMPED EVERYTHING on his bed when Aurora emerged from the bathroom. Dressed in his black shirt, she had damp hair, her face was freshly scrubbed and she'd finally got rid of the remnants of those fishnet stockings. There was no reason on earth why he should find her irresistible. And yet he did.

Despite how much her presence was encroaching into his personal life.

Her eyes widened when she caught sight of her belongings. He folded his arms, not at all sure whether she'd be grateful or furious. It was disorientating, not knowing which way she'd fall. But on the other hand it was addictively intriguing.

"They're my"—she hesitated, and stepped closer to the bed—"my *things*." She sounded incredulous. "You went back and collected my things?"

"Don't thank me. It was nothing." He heard the sarcasm in his words but couldn't help himself. He was an archangel, and here he was acting like a damn courier. What he couldn't understand was why he didn't feel more genuinely irked about it all.

He watched the blush heat her cheeks. It was clear she hadn't expected him to bother trying to make her feel more comfortable in her new life and equally clear she had no idea how she felt about it.

"Thanks." As gratitude went it was hardly mind-blowing, but since she appeared to be having trouble speaking he supposed it would have to suffice.

"You can hang your clothes in my closet. There's plenty of room." There wasn't, but he was sure Aurora would find a way to squeeze her things inside. "It's just temporary." Until he sorted out the furniture issue.

"Yes." The word rushed from her, as if she'd been holding her breath. "It's only temporary."

Satisfied, he relaxed and leaned back against the carved bedpost as Aurora gingerly peered inside his rucksack. The look of astonished disbelief on her face was priceless as she began to pull out all her personal bits and pieces.

He really didn't have time to stay and chat with her—not that he wanted Aurora to *chat with him* in any case—but his curiosity demanded satisfaction.

"Your mother is one of the most powerful mortal telepaths I've ever encountered."

The bottle of perfume she'd been holding slid through her fingers and she looked at him as if he'd just sprouted horns.

"You met my mother?" She sounded as if she couldn't imagine anything worse. Given the circumstances he supposed he couldn't blame her.

"Briefly. She not only saw through my glamour but she then telepathically demanded your return." It hadn't occurred to him before, but since Aurora also possessed that ability there should be nothing stopping Gabe and her from using a telepathic connection either.

Before he could put that theory into practice he realized she was staring at him as though he'd lost his mind. He should have kept his mouth shut. Why had he told her about her mother? Now Aurora would probably pounce on the comment and start another argument about how she had to find a way to return.

"She spoke to you *telepathically?*"

There she went again, veering off on strange tangents with her questions. Why was she so astonished that her mother had used telepathy? It had nothing to do with the etiquette of the situation since Aurora knew nothing of immortal etiquette. And even if she did he had the strongest suspicion it wouldn't make that much difference to her.

"You sound surprised." Shocked was closer to the truth. "You were the one who told me your mother's family possessed that psychic trait."

"Yes, but she's not used it for years." Aurora gripped the rucksack as she would a life-support system. "Are you sure she did, Gabe? You didn't sort of probe her mind and read her thoughts by accident?"

"No, I didn't." Irritated by her accusation, especially since he had contemplated scanning the outer reaches of her mother's mind, he shot her a scathing glare. "I don't probe minds without a damn good reason and that goes for reading thoughts too." She might descend from a long line of telepaths but it was obvious she hadn't the first clue about how her power worked.

If he probed a mind it was never by accident and the thoughts he harvested during such a probe were read by design. While her abilities paled by comparison to his, the principles remained the same throughout every telepathic race.

Then again, Aurora didn't come from a primarily telepathic race.

"I can't believe she did." Aurora's face flushed. Was she actually saying she thought he was lying? "She stopped speaking to me that way ten years ago."

And then he heard the underlying anguish in her voice. The sense of loss she had experienced over the last decade.

"Why?" He'd sensed no weakness in her mother's link. If he didn't know differently he'd be convinced she came from a species of pure telepaths. But on Earth humans had failed to explore that evolutionary option millennia ago.

He watched Aurora forcibly release her death grip on the rucksack. She put it back on the bed, folded her arms as if she was going into battle and finally looked up at him. Wariness clouded her beautiful blue eyes.

"You asked me, back in that demon's den, what I'd been doing before you suddenly arrived on my land. You asked if I'd been trying to breach dimensions."

He'd accused her. And she'd admitted her guilt. He didn't want to go over it all again and couldn't understand why she'd brought it up now. It no longer mattered. He was resigned to having her here. It wouldn't be that bad.

"What about it?" Gods, he couldn't understand why he was having this conversation now, when he needed to hunt down miscreants in the Fornax Galaxy. But he couldn't leave while she looked so tragic.

"The thing is . . ." She sounded nervous, although he couldn't think why. He already knew about her greatest crime. "My mother's slowly been losing her grip on reality. When I was a child she used to tell me stories about her family and home all the time. But then ten years ago she cut off our link—the link we'd shared all my life. It was like she'd cut off, I don't know, half my brain and one of my limbs. Suddenly she just wasn't *there* anymore."

He understood that. He and Eleni had been linked telepathically. But he still didn't get Aurora's point. What did any of this have to do with her breaching dimensions?

"You've no idea what it was like, Gabe. It was as if she needed to forget about her true heritage just to survive. But by doing that she was shutting everybody out." Her shoulders slumped as if in defeat. "I wanted something solid to show her that her past really existed. Theoretically I should have entered at the exact same location where the flowers grew. So all I intended to do was take some and bring them back as proof."

He could feel the glower on his face, could hear his heart pounding in his chest. And Aurora's words became a rising echo that hammered through his brain.

Where the flowers grew. So she could bring some back.

The flowers.

The silver frame with its strange, ethereal bloom, and the eerie certainty he'd experienced of something being not quite *right* with it, slashed through his mind. *No.* It was impossible. He couldn't fathom what she was trying to tell him, but it certainly wasn't that her mother came from *another dimension.*

He shoved himself from the support of the bedpost, snatched up the rucksack and pulled out the frame. Again the eerie sense of wrongness shuddered through him and he looked into Aurora's now bemused face.

"What are you talking about?" His voice was uncannily calm, considering the erratic state of his thoughts.

"My mother." Her voice was barely above a whisper. "I was trying to find her home, Gabe. To prove to her it really does exist. To try and bring her back to us again."

He jabbed the frame at her, denial stabbing through him. What Aurora was saying was impossible. And yet he knew she believed every single word.

"Are you trying to tell me . . ." The words lodged in his throat. "What are you trying to tell me?"

The tip of her tongue flicked over her lips and for a second he had the strongest suspicion she wasn't going to say another word. Then she stiffened her spine and he saw the apprehension in her eyes.

"My parents are from different dimensions." The words rushed from her as if she had never spoken them before. *Of course she had never spoken them before. Who would she say such a thing to?* "My dad's from Earth—this Earth—but my mum's . . . *not*. They met each other in their dreams while they were still children. They grew up together—but only in their dreams. And then they fell in love."

He let out a measured breath. *Theoretically* it was very possible to dream of those who existed in another dimension. The astral planes weren't confined to one dimension or another. They were potentially accessible to all sentient beings.

Except for the Guardians.

But Aurora wasn't talking about theories. She was telling him her parents had somehow, against everything he had believed possible, succeeded in a trans-dimensional physical union.

And then the truth slammed through him. *Aurora was the result of a trans-dimensional union.*

Something akin to awe shivered through his soul. It had been so long since something had so fundamentally shaken the core of his existence that he didn't know how to react. Didn't know what to say.

He could only stare at her as if he had never truly seen her before.

But still there was nothing that marked her as such an extraordinary being. Her damp hair curled around her face, the freckles that dusted her nose and cheeks were still ridiculously appealing, and her eyes were the prettiest shade of blue he had ever encountered.

"What happened?" His voice was hushed but he couldn't help it. Because despite knowing she told the truth he still couldn't fathom how it had come to pass.

"We don't know." An oddly guarded note entered her voice, as if his reaction wasn't quite what she'd expected. "One day my mother simply walked through from her world into this one—straight into my dad's arms. At the exact same place where you found me the other day."

"Just like that?" There had to be more. Maybe her mother's people had been experimenting with the dynamics of interdimensional travel.

"Gabe, she didn't do anything weird. She wouldn't have had the first clue how to deliberately breach dimensions. They were just doing what they'd done countless times before—communicating with their thoughts. My dad isn't at all psychic. That telepathic link with her is the sum total of his psychic ability. He couldn't even link telepathically with me."

"Your parents communicated outside of the astral planes? When they weren't dreaming?" Another eerie shiver inched over his flesh.

"When they became teenagers they developed the ability to communicate while they were still awake." Aurora gave him another odd look, as if his reaction still bothered her. "I mean, they could carry on a conversation with each other without having to be asleep or going into trance to enter the astral planes."

"What about the Guardians? How did she avoid them?" At least now he knew the reason for Aurora's extraordinary mental barriers. She had inherited them from a species of human he had never before encountered.

"They never mentioned anything about the Guardians. No violet lightning, nothing. She walked into this world and whatever gateway had opened for her closed straightaway. Permanently."

No Alpha Immortal, so far as Gabe was aware, had given the Guardians the right to patrol dimensional boundaries. They had done so for millennia. The Dark Matter of the universe, where the Guardians existed in ethnocentric isolation, was rumored to hold ancient secrets. Immortals surmised that, when dimensions were breached, it triggered a celestial alarm for the Guardians.

But the Guardians were of this dimension. Aurora's mother came from another. Was that how she had avoided detection?

Aurora took a step toward him. "I honestly had no idea I'd be breaking some kind of cosmic law, Gabe. I just wanted to find a way to prove to her that her world did exist. That she wasn't losing her mind. She just needed to *encompass* it all."

He understood what had driven her. Could even empathize. But he still couldn't fathom how she had actually intended to put her theories into practice.

"I'd already decided to study genetics at university, but then I decided I'd also research every aspect of astral projection I could. I mean, I'd always been able to project ever since I was a child but I'd never actually studied the phenomenon. Because it wasn't a phenomenon to me, you see? It was normal."

Aurora had entered the astral planes in the bathroom back on Eta Hyperium. She'd been trying to escape, even though escape was impossible. Yet her belief in her abilities had been absolute.

"Go on." He hoped she couldn't hear the awe in his voice. It wasn't dignified that a mere mortal could so unbalance an archangel.

"Eight years." There was a dreamlike quality to her voice. "It was my covert mission. Finally I decided there was no point wasting any more time in partial experiments and endless theorizing. I had to put it to the test."

Even after she had confessed to him on Eta Hyperium, he'd believed that she'd breached dimensions by some freaky accident. That she'd been dabbling in things she knew next to nothing about. But he couldn't have been more wrong.

Just as Mephisto had asserted, Aurora had known what she was doing. She had prepared for that moment for eight years. And now he knew why, could he blame her?

"Because of my unique DNA, I was sure I could gain access to my mother's dimension. And I was right." She hesitated for a second, obviously recalling that fateful moment when she had breached dimensions and caught the Guardians' wrathful attention. "Assuming I was successful, not only would the breach open in the spiritual realm but also simultaneously in the physical. So all I had to do was maintain that contact on the spiritual plane while I returned to my body and walked through the breach into the other dimension."

Chapter Twenty-two

EVEN theoretically he would never have believed it possible. But it had worked. And it had to be down to the combination of her unique psychic abilities and the fact she didn't belong solely to this dimension.

Yet something had interrupted her because when he'd arrived she was most certainly not strolling into another dimension.

Which brought him back to the burning question: *How the fuck had he arrived in Ireland?*

"You had it all worked out."

"I thought so." She offered him a small smile that, bizarrely, pierced his chest. "But I hadn't planned on being knocked off my feet by an avenging archangel."

He had no intention of admitting he still didn't have the first clue how that had happened.

"Just as well you were, considering the fallout." But there was no condemnation in his words. Because there was no longer any doubt in his mind that he'd done the right thing by disregarding ancient protocols and rescuing Aurora. The Guardians had taken it upon themselves countless millennia ago to ensure dimensions remained intact. Gabe was damn sure they had no provision for extenuating circumstances. If they had captured Aurora she wouldn't have been given the opportunity to defend her actions, and with a stab of guilt he remembered his caustic response when she'd asked about a fair trial or court of appeal.

There's nothing fair about it. He'd thrown the words at her, not really considering them, but they haunted him now. Because they were true.

"Gabe." The smile slid from her lips and there was no mistaking the thread of unease in her voice. "You must have come across this before. I mean, I can't be the only one whose parents are from different dimensions."

The odd compunction possessed him to reassure her that of course she wasn't the only trans-dimensional being he'd encountered. To somehow soothe her fear of being . . . The words hovered in his brain, loathed yet so apt.

The fear of being an anomaly of nature.

Yet he couldn't lie to her because it wouldn't change the truth. And as he stared into her eyes an outrageous notion rocked his mind.

Just because he had never known this to happen before, did not mean it had not.

Something of that magnitude should be common knowledge among the elite immortals. And like it or not, he was numbered among the elite.

But no one had known of Aurora.

"You . . ." He discovered he was at a loss for words and brutally pulled his reeling senses back into line. "You're the first I've encountered." *Admit it.* Strangely, it wasn't as hard as it should have been. "But that doesn't necessarily mean you're the only one, Aurora."

She flinched, as if she'd known what his answer would be and yet had desperately hoped otherwise.

"Thanks for being honest." She offered him a wan smile. "Nothing like having it confirmed that you're a complete freak of creation, is there?"

"You're in excellent company. I've been called worse."

As he'd intended, she stared at him in open astonishment, her own unique status temporarily forgotten. He even grinned back at her, and considering the subject matter that was a first. He didn't usually find anything amusing when he recalled the origins of his creation and the bitter fallout that followed.

"I find that very hard to believe."

He tugged gently on her damp hair and then, because it felt right, wound the chestnut strands around his finger. The overpowering urge to stay with her thundered through his mind. To take her in his arms and ensure that she really was . . . all right.

But no panicked waves of terror emanated from her. The truth was he didn't want to leave her. He wanted to stay for himself, not simply because Aurora might need his presence.

Unnerved by that flash of insight, he hastily untangled his finger from her hair. Aurora was here so the Guardians couldn't get their claws in her. It suited him because he wanted her sexually, but that was all. He'd be damned if he started putting that base need before everything else.

"Hard to believe but true." He handed her the silver frame and she hugged it to her breasts in a gesture that spoke volumes. He ignored the flicker of sympathy that attempted to ignite. Gods, he hadn't brought her here for nefarious purposes. If he could ensure her safety outside this island he'd be the first to allow her to go.

When he'd tired of her.

He ignored that thought, too.

"I'll be back later." It occurred to him that they could eat together. "I'll bring food."

"Where are you going?" She sounded surprised, as if she'd expected him to stay with her.

"Out." He wasn't in the habit of telling anyone of his movements, and in any case he doubted she'd even heard of the Fornax Galaxy.

"Out? Doing what?"

From the corner of his eye he caught a flash of distant wings approaching his villa from the forest. He took a couple of steps toward the balcony doors to get a better look at his unexpected visitor.

"Stuff." The figure looked like Azrael.

"Oh." There was a tight note in Aurora's voice. "Well, fine. You go and do your *stuff* and I'll see you later then."

He stifled the urge to kiss her goodbye, since that evoked an uneasy level of intimacy that caused his ancient scars to burn. And so he jerked his head at her in a gesture of farewell and teleported onto the front terrace.

AZRAEL'S IRIDESCENT FEATHERS shimmered in the sunlight as he landed next to Gabe. Folding his wings, he rolled his shoulders and squinted up at the villa as if he could sense something was not quite normal.

Either that or he'd spoken to Mephisto and had come to have a look at the mortal for himself. Gabe folded his arms. Aurora was not an exotic exhibit.

"Something," Azrael said, "is screwing with the astral planes."

Whatever he'd expected Azrael to say, it hadn't been that.

"What?" Unlike most of the archangels who had given up visiting the astral planes at the same time as they'd annihilated the celestial city of their creation, Azrael had become obsessed with that realm and with maintaining its harmonious balance.

Discounting the time Gabe had followed Aurora yesterday, he had only been in there once since. And even then it hadn't been willingly.

Azrael glanced up at the balcony and frowned before looking back at him. "I've never come across anything like it. Chaos is the only way to describe it."

Gabe recalled the sense of disharmony as he'd entered the astral planes. He knew who'd caused that echo of chaos. It was Aurora, when she had opened the breach between dimensions.

"The levels were collapsing," Azrael said, as if he found nothing strange in Gabe's continued silence. "If you can imagine a physical entity smashing its way through, you have a good idea of the mess that's left behind."

"Except you can't physically enter that realm." Aurora was more powerful than he'd imagined. But how could he know of her limitations when she was the child of two dimensions? Unlike anyone else who might've tried tampering with the laws of creation, Aurora possessed a unique weapon. Who could say what devastation she might have caused on the astral planes, when two parallel worlds claimed her DNA?

The astral planes, the ultimate haven of healing and renewal, would recover. But if Az or any immortal guessed Aurora was the one behind the chaos she would be held accountable.

He'd never let them take her to trial.

"But guess who was there, attempting a cover up?" Clearly Azrael considered Gabe's last comment too banal to even bother answering. "Mephisto."

What the hell was Mephisto doing there? "It could be a natural phenomenon. Mephisto's probably just poking around trying to find out what happened." Except Mephisto already knew who was responsible. So why hadn't he exposed Aurora already? What was he still playing at?

Azrael grunted and his fingers curled around the hilt of his katana. "If that was a natural phenomenon then the universe is fucked. It was an outside force and Mephisto knows more than he's telling me." Again Azrael shot him an odd glance. "So you don't know anything about it?"

Alarm stabbed through Gabe's chest. "Why would I know anything about it?" Had Mephisto said something to Az? Had Az discovered Aurora's interference on the astral planes and somehow traced her back to Gabe?

"A couple of hours ago I detected a lingering echo of your presence." Azrael sounded reluctant to admit it, as if he was as good as accusing Gabe of being the perpetrator of the disruption. "But it was distorted almost beyond recognition."

Gabe expelled a silent breath of relief. "I entered the astral planes briefly yesterday." There was no need to go into detail. "Doubt I'll be making a return trip any time soon."

Azrael didn't answer right away. Gabe had the uneasy feeling that the other archangel had read far more into Gabe's answer than he'd intended. "Are the rumors true? Did you really save a human from the Guardians' clutches?"

He should have guessed what had happened in Eblis's club was now common knowledge. Anyone who'd been there could have cobbled a juicy story together and managed to get at least some details right.

That didn't mean he had to tell Azrael what had really transpired, even if he was relieved by the change of subject. "I wanted her so I took her." It was the truth. In a way.

"Is she the reason you entered the astral planes?"

Fuck, so much for changing the subject. "Why would she be?" It took more effort than he wanted to admit to keep his voice nonchalant.

"No chance of meeting this irresistible female, then?" Azrael sounded keener to meet Aurora than he had any right to.

"I'm on my way out." And even if he wasn't, there was no way he'd let Azrael, with his insubstantial suspicions, near Aurora.

Azrael gave him a probing look that Gabe didn't like in the least. "Let me know when you're ready to share your little human. She must really be something for you to put yourself out so much." And with that he teleported.

Scowling, Gabe contacted Mephisto.

What did you discover in the astral planes? Mephisto would know exactly what he meant.

There was a significant pause, as if the other archangel was deliberating as to whether or not he would deign to respond.

Quit panicking. The insulting command only failed to rouse Gabe's ire because of the odd underlying sense of . . . unease. *I've cleaned up your crap. There's nothing to trace back to you.*

With that enigmatic statement Mephisto cut their line of communication. Gabe glanced up at his balcony, frowning. He knew Mephisto liked talking in riddles and he was more than willing to shoulder the blame if it saved Aurora's head. But why, when they both obviously knew the truth, had Mephisto made it sound as if the collapse on the astral planes was due to *him*—and not Aurora?

Chapter Twenty-three

ALTHOUGH Aurora knew she was being unreasonable she couldn't help feeling aggravated that Gabe had left without even the courtesy of telling her where he was going. She embraced the irritation, replayed every derogatory comment and look he'd shot her way since the moment they'd met, but her strategy just wasn't working.

How could she stay mad with him when he'd gone to the effort of bringing all her clothes and personal things for her? It was the last thing she'd expected and she was still having trouble processing what it meant.

As she pulled on a pair of shorts and a sleeveless top, she acknowledged it probably meant nothing. She was reading too much into it, even though she didn't want to. Because once a girl started dreaming that a hot guy was being considerate and caring because he felt something for her, she was in deep trouble.

Especially when the hot guy in question was an ageless archangel.

With a groan that sounded suspiciously like defeat she hauled her clothes into his dressing room. The exquisitely crafted timber wardrobe set into the wall was massive, but it was also pretty much full. She squeezed her things inside regardless. It was only a temporary arrangement, after all.

She held on to that thought with grim determination as she unpacked the rucksack and piled everything on the floor of his bedroom. And only then did she notice her necklace lying on the bed.

Relief streaked through her. Mephisto hadn't destroyed it after all. She picked it up by the delicate gold chain and went to the balcony doors. Sunlight streamed in, causing the tiny rainbows and flecks of gold to shimmer and glitter like a minuscule fantasy world. After emailing her parents, her first priority was to discover all she could about the Guardians. But it wouldn't hurt if she performed a quick search of angelic artifacts, would it?

NOTHING. SHE COULDN'T believe it. She'd been hunting the cosmic Internet for what seemed like hours and although there was plenty of stuff about angels, a great deal of it sounded the universal equivalent of an unverified Wikipedia. And that was after she'd taken account of the sometimes bizarre translations.

It was all generalized and frequently contradictory. As if everything relied on gossip and speculation according to whichever civilization happened to be the author of that particular entry.

If any information was out there, the ancient truth of the angels had been long buried in the cloudy stream of time. And when, feeling horribly guilty, she'd tried digging into the mystery of the Archangel Gabriel, she'd plowed through a dozen sites before finally accepting the frustrating truth.

It all appeared based on myth and speculation. None of it came close to the complex man—*archangel*—she knew.

She propped her elbows on the kitchen table and cradled her head. This was hopeless. Nothing had so far even come close to showing her a replica of her necklace, and she had the feeling nothing ever would. Because no one, apart from the angels themselves, knew anything about those precious artifacts.

Well, that was an odd thought. She sat back and curled her fingers around the butterfly wings but still the certainty persisted. And then another unassailable conviction gripped her.

The angels crafted the necklace as a token of their devotion for their beloved. And the tradition had evolved, and perished, in antiquity.

A shiver scuttled over her arms. *Where were those thoughts coming from? And why was she so certain that they were true?* It was kind of creepy and she hit the delete key, wiping the screen.

Discovering hidden secrets of the angels wasn't going to set her free. She needed to unearth something solid and usable about the Guardians.

EBLIS HADN'T KNOWN which pirate tribe had been discussing the Medana solar system in his den, so Gabe had visited the most disreputable. They were known for trading minors from the more primitive planets in the Fornax Galaxy, which was one thing, but taking them from another Galaxy altogether wasn't something that could be allowed to go unpunished, even if he hadn't been investigating Evalyne's disappearance.

He'd not got much from the first two he interrogated, whose minds were putrid and disintegrated like overripe fruit as he ripped them to shreds in search of information. The third pirate, desperate to save his skin and mind intact, spewed names and dates and garbled confessions of underground cults, none of which made any sense because who the hell could be after angel blood? The only piece of information that appeared likely to warrant further investigation was the brief mention of the largest planet in the seventh system of Fornax.

But he filed all the information away just in case. And then he severed the pirate's spinal column.

GABE TOOK A shower as soon as he returned to scrub the stench of the pirates from his body. It was good to be home where Aurora waited for him. She was clean, pure and would doubtless regale him with the myriad conflicting data she'd unearthed on the Guardians.

And then his mind stumbled and the half-smile on his lips froze. *Home?* When was the last time that word had so easily slipped into his consciousness?

He knew when. He refused to remember. Because the last time he'd had a home Eleni lived there.

AURORA KNEW THE exact moment Gabe returned, even though he didn't walk in through the front door. In fact, he didn't make any sound at all but that was irrelevant. His presence brushed through her, almost tangible, and she glanced over her shoulder, expecting to see him.

The kitchen was still empty. The villa was still silent. But even so, Gabe was home.

She stood up, stretching her cramped muscles, and realized how hungry she was. It had been hours since she'd eaten the fruit. It was getting dark already.

What had he been doing? She climbed the stairs, entered his bedroom and heard the shower through the open bathroom door.

What did she think he'd been doing? It wasn't as if he had a regular nine-to-five job, was it? And where had he gone the last time he'd left her?

A sex club.

She folded her arms and tried not to acknowledge the searing hurt in her chest. Honestly, she was pathetic to care that he'd most probably been out screwing other girls. It wasn't as if they had any kind of relationship here, was it?

He was an archangel. His sex drive was phenomenal, going by how quickly he'd recovered this morning, and he'd probably be amazed if he guessed how deeply his betrayal wounded her.

Except it wasn't betrayal. God, she had to get a grip on reality. He'd rescued her, taken her back to his villa and she, like an idiot, had tumbled into his bed with hardly a squeak of protest.

She had nobody but herself to blame for the way she was feeling.

The shower stopped. She straightened her spine and forcibly relaxed her tense muscles. She couldn't let him see how easily he could hurt her. This was, in fact, a great wake-up call because despite all her protests she knew damn well she was in serious danger of falling for him.

He strolled into the bedroom, a damp, gorgeous god of creation, and the smile he bestowed her way had her stomach tightening and skin tingling.

Just with a smile. Then again, his smile was a thing of heavenly magnificence.

"You're back." As inane remarks went, that had to take the cherry on the proverbial cake. She refused to break eye contact, even though she longed to feast her gaze on his semi-aroused cock. Which she knew, in spite of her best intentions of not looking, was thickening by the second.

Was that all he *ever* did? Indulge in sex all day and all night? She gritted her teeth into an approximation of a smile and ignored the treacherous tug low in her womb. She wouldn't fall into his arms the moment he returned. That would just make her look sex-deprived and desperate for his attention.

"And I'm starving." His eyes darkened, and it was obvious he wasn't talking about food. She curled her nails into the palms of her hands to stop herself from wrapping herself around him. She had *some* pride left.

"Good." Unfortunately her voice was husky and far from showing him that she, at least, didn't require endless sex in order to function. She dug her nails in harder to focus her ravenous libido. "So am I. What did you bring back?"

He blinked, glorious long eyelashes that he had no right possessing and certainly had no right flaunting in her direction. But still she stared, mesmerized, only vaguely acknowledging the bemused frown that now creased his forehead.

"Ah." He sounded uncharacteristically off-balance. "Food. I forgot."

Because he was too busy shagging every woman who crossed his path.

She kept on smiling even though every muscle in her face ached like an infected abscess.

"I suppose you ate while you were out." With difficulty she relaxed her fingers before her nails tore holes through her hands. "Well, don't worry. I'm sure I'll find something in your kitchen."

He came closer. She wondered how long she could hold her breath before passing out. Why did he have to smell so delicious? Like an exotic rainforest. Dangerous and forbidden.

"I haven't eaten all day." He curled one hand around the bedpost, an action she was positive he did deliberately in order to show off his perfectly proportioned biceps. She tore her fascinated gaze from his bronzed muscles and tried not to glare into his face. He appeared supremely oblivious to the fact she was seething with . . . *resentment.*

"Oh." It was getting harder to speak. She'd have to retreat because once he touched her she had the feeling she'd forget all the reasons why she had to make a stand with him.

"I'll go get something." His smoldering gaze drifted over her, from head to toe and back again, scorching her skin like a lick of flame. "Later."

Her nipples hardened and molten tremors attacked low in her belly. He could seduce her with barely a glance, make her come with scarcely a touch. She forced her feet to move. Away from him.

"Well, okay." She injected a breezy note in her voice but it sounded more like a breathless whimper. "I can tell you what I found out first if you like. I thought we could talk while we eat but I'm easy." *He already knew that.* It wasn't a happy thought.

For a moment he continued staring at her, as if he wasn't sure whether she was pulling his leg or was genuinely ignorant of his true intentions. Then he relinquished his grip on the bedpost and strolled toward his dressing room.

Her mouth dried. He had a seriously sexy rear. Her fingers itched to stroke his tight butt, to feel his warm flesh beneath hers. A tiny moan escaped and she hastily turned it into a cough. Gabe, thank god, didn't appear to notice.

"Discovered a loophole?" Gabe tossed a glance over his shoulder as he pulled on a pair of black jeans. She stared, and the only coherent thought she had was *he's going commando.*

When he turned around and slowly tugged the material over his far from disinterested erection, she let out a faint wheeze and struggled to regain eye contact.

He had a mocking grin on his face as if he knew full well the effect he had on her. Since that fact had already been well and truly established she didn't see why he had to act so smug about it.

"Not yet." Her voice was husky. She tried clearing her throat. "Does anyone actually police your net to make sure the information is accurate? Because for every so-called fact I discovered I then found another that said the exact opposite."

And she wasn't just referring to the Guardians. But he didn't have to know that.

Gabe shrugged and pulled out a black shirt. She'd never before considered watching a man get dressed could be an erotic experience but every casual move he made was tying her up into knots of sensual frustration.

"It works on a similar principle to the Internet here on Earth. You can't believe everything you read online." He appeared to find that amusing, as if she was incredibly naïve to have imagined otherwise. "It's a resource but it's not infallible. Occasionally it's just plain entertaining."

"Luckily I managed to work that out." She offered him a tight smile, irritated he hadn't thought to tell her that before he'd left the villa. It would certainly have lowered her expectations of tapping into a fantastical repository of mind-blowing revelations. "But one thing did keep cropping up. The Guardians apparently hate immortals even more than they do humans." She folded her arms. "Except they aren't allowed to abduct immortals. Isn't that convenient?"

"It is for us."

"So is it true their species was around for thousands of years before any of the gods or goddesses came into being?" That was another thing she'd found incredibly frustrating. She could follow a fascinating lead only for it to taper off into an insubstantial mist. So while several sources had categorically stated the Guardians' loathing of the Immortals, exactly *who* or *what* or *where* they might be was annoyingly unspecified.

"Yes. They've been a malignant curse of Creation for seeming eternity." Gabe no longer sounded amused, he sounded disgusted. "They should have died out long before the Alphas evolved."

Aurora forgot about being annoyed with Gabe's attitude. "The Alphas?" She took an unintentional step toward him. He'd mentioned them before but she still didn't know for sure what he meant. "What are they?"

He shoved his bare feet into black sneakers. "Megalomaniac pains in the ass. Grab some plates and glasses. Won't be long." And with that he tossed her a smile of pure evil, and vanished.

Chapter Twenty-four

BACK in the kitchen Aurora struggled against the surreal sensation of normalcy. Gabe had popped out for a takeaway and she was placing the finest porcelain and crystalware on the table. Anyone would think they were just a regular couple intending to enjoy a quiet night in together.

Except Gabe's version of *popping out* was anything but conventional, and only a seriously deluded woman would think there was anything in the least bit regular about her current situation.

She knew all that. But it made no difference. Because a tiny, obstinate core of her insisted that this was perfectly . . . normal.

Even when he reappeared without warning she didn't drop the heavy silver cutlery. She was getting used to his extraordinary method of transportation, as though she'd been aware of such things all her life.

If that wasn't a warning about how easy it was to lose her grip on reality she didn't know what was.

"Wild salmon with asparagus and tournedos of beef," he said. "I didn't know what you'd like so I bought the lot."

"American Express?" She was joking but only partially. *Did* Gabe pay for stuff? Why on earth would an archangel need to pay for things in any case? And, although she supposed it didn't really matter, did this food even originate on planet Earth?

"MasterCard," he said deadpan. "For the air miles."

She pulled off a lid and the breathtaking sight of a crown pavlova, topped with strawberries and blueberries, made her stomach growl.

"Yeah, I can see you need them." She flashed him a grin because it was so hard to remain mad with him. Especially when she knew that he didn't deserve it.

Charm radiated from him like a lethal pheromone. It probably wasn't even intentional. She could either spend the next who knew how long fighting the attraction between them or taking it all at face value and nothing else.

Like a holiday romance. No commitment. No strings. And she wouldn't let her imagination go wild every time he left the villa.

Great intentions. She doubted she'd live up to them.

"But seriously. Do you really have credit cards? *Money?*"

"Sure." He strolled to a door that earlier that day she discovered led to a cellar. She hadn't investigated further. She'd watched too many slasher movies as a teen to fall for that one. "My investments have the potential to topple governments both here and on a couple of other worlds. It's not that hard to amass a fortune when you're considered immortal." He disappeared through the door. "You could call it a hobby of mine."

"That and sex," she muttered as she sat at the table. Hardly aware of her actions, she pulled her chain from beneath her top and curled her fingers around the familiar pendant.

"I heard that." His voice echoed from the depths of the cellar, and she felt her face heat. He also, apparently, had supersonic hearing. "Are you offering hors d'oeuvres?" He stepped back into the kitchen, holding a couple of dust-covered bottles of wine and wearing a lascivious grin. "Because we can always reheat the food later."

Insatiable. Forlorn acceptance whispered through her mind, along with the resignation that she, a mere mortal, would never be able to satisfy his carnal cravings. So much for not letting her wild imagination run away with her. He didn't even have to leave the villa for her to agonize about his infidelity.

"Tempting, but no." Surreptitiously she crossed her ankles and pressed her legs together. Not that it helped alleviate the sensual throb radiating from between her thighs.

He pulled the cork from one of the bottles and then, with another smile forged from pure sin, wrapped his arm around the back of her chair and leaned over her shoulder to pour the wine into her glass.

"Try this. Tell me what you think."

She hoped he couldn't hear her uneven breath. Or rapid heartbeat. But since the vintage bottle of wine froze in place as if he had paused to savor her reaction, she had to assume he knew only too well. And that he was probably smirking with masculine self-satisfaction.

She kept her eyes fixed on her glass and tried not to hyperventilate as he slowly leaned into her neck. His warm breath sent erotic tremors across her flesh and she struggled against the overpowering urge to squirm.

But despite her best intentions, her eyes closed and she very slightly leaned toward him. To hell with her pride. She'd take what she could get and face any regret later.

There was a dull thud and she cracked open one eye to see the bottle on the table. Gabe scooped her pendant into his hand and the chain bit into her neck as he yanked it up to take a closer look.

"Careful." She looked up at him, but he was frowning at her necklace as if it personally offended him. "What are you doing?"

"Where did you get this?" He sounded as angry as he had soon after she'd first met him. Did he think she'd stolen it from him? Did that mean he still had his daughter's necklace somewhere in his villa?

"I had it specially commissioned for my twenty-first birthday." She tried to make her voice reassuring without giving away the fact she'd guessed what he was covertly accusing her of. "I was wearing it back in Ireland, remember?"

He looked at her then as if she had just uttered something incomprehensible.

"Yes, of course I remember you wearing a chain. But I didn't know . . ." His words died and for an eternal moment she saw raw, bleak longing in his eyes and could feel the cold abyss of loss drag icy fingers across her soul.

And a chilling certainty illuminated a dark corner of her mind.

They were not butterfly wings. How could she have ever mistaken them as such? They were angel wings. The gift from an angel to his beloved.

Deep in her heart a small chasm cracked open.

Slowly he let the chain slide through his fingers. "You had this specially commissioned?" He sounded as if her answer didn't matter one way or the other. She clenched her fists on her lap, tensed her muscles against her overpowering instinct to wrap her arms around him. To try and offer whatever comfort she could.

Because he wouldn't welcome it. Wouldn't understand why she even felt the need to offer him comfort. Because as far as he was aware she was ignorant of his loss.

"Yes."

"Why?" The hint of accusation in his tone caused another shaft of pain deep in her heart. How many centuries had he mourned the loss of his loved ones? How would it feel, to be loved so absolutely by an archangel?

By Gabe?

She recoiled from the thought, terror stabbing through her chest. She didn't want to know. Didn't want to imagine. Because it forced her to face the obvious counterpoint. *How would it feel to love Gabe?*

"I . . ." Her voice cracked and she cleared her throat, no longer able to look into those mesmeric eyes. Because now she'd glimpsed the suffering behind the beauty, and it ripped her apart. "Ever since I can remember I used to dream of rainbows and gold dust and"— *don't say angel*—"wings. I don't know why. The weird thing is once I started wearing this necklace the dreams stopped."

"You dreamed of this?" His voice was oddly harsh as if he disbelieved her, but when she glanced up at him she caught the anguish in his eyes. "How could you dream of *this*, Aurora? This exact design?"

"I don't know." Was there a connection between her dreams and the necklace she'd seen in Gabe's picture? It was an outrageous thought but everything that had happened over the last couple of days had been outrageous. "Why? What does it mean to you?"

She didn't think he was going to answer her. She braced herself for him to dismiss her question. Told herself she wouldn't be hurt. But she knew she lied, because she wanted him to confide in her. Wasn't that what lovers did?

She knew, in that second, that she was losing her struggle. *She was falling.*

"It's based on an ancient archangelic design." He sounded as if the words were being torn from him against his will. But at least he was answering her and she acknowledged just how great a concession he was granting her. Two days ago he would, she knew, have brushed her question aside as of no consequence. "We'd harness fragments of the rainbows that glinted over our city. Trap particles of the gold that glittered in the air. And bind them into our angel wings for all eternity."

It sounded beautiful. She had the absurd desire to weep.

"City?" Her voice was hushed. "You had a city, Gabe?"

He closed his eyes, his gorgeous long lashes hiding his expression. When he once again looked at her all trace of ancient pain had been concealed.

"We did." He picked up the bottle of wine. "It was the place of our creation, the hell of our incarceration. It no longer exists."

He poured her wine and she knew the moment for confidences had passed. She accepted her glass and returned his smile but still one thought hammered in the back of her mind.

For more than twenty years she had dreamed of magical rainbows, glittering gold dust and angel wings crafted into an ancient angelic design.

But the question was *why*?

Chapter Twenty-five

THE child's laughter was pure and carefree, and Aurora smiled, vaguely bemused although she wasn't quite sure why. *Who was this child?* She seemed oddly familiar with her curly blonde hair and kaleidoscopic eyes. An insubstantial thought drifted through her mind. *Was this a dream?*

"Finished." The little girl held up a seashell-encrusted picture frame. "Can we give it to him now?"

I can't understand what you're saying. Yet, bizarrely, the strange language made perfect sense.

"As soon as he gets home." She was thinking in English. And yet the words were exotic, foreign.

She glanced around the stone and timber kitchen. Unease trickled over her flesh. Had she been here before?

A shadow blocked out the sun and then *he* was there. Tall, golden-haired, and the world was filled with light and love as he pulled her and the child into his arms.

Silken feathers teased and caressed, belying their inherent

strength and she gasped, disoriented, as his wings embraced and claimed.

His wings.

"Aurora." The way he breathed her name, so husky and seductive, sent tremors of an entirely different nature dancing over her skin. She wound her arms around his neck, felt him tug his fingers through her hair, and the sun dimmed into a pre-dawn glow.

The dream fluttered through her mind, fading into mist-shrouded corners, and the elusive distinction between dream and memory merged, became one, as Gabe's mouth claimed hers.

SITTING IN THE shade on Gabe's terrace, elusive tendrils of Aurora's early-morning dream haunted the edges of her consciousness. Although a strange feeling of contentment cocooned her, the harder she tried to recall the details the fainter they became. It was frustrating because for some obscure reason she had the strongest certainty that the details were of the utmost importance.

But it was no good. All that remained was the intangible sense of joy, and with a sigh she forced her wandering attention back to Gabe's laptop.

But she couldn't concentrate, and she leaned back in the chair Gabe had hauled out from the kitchen, along with the table and a mobile air-conditioning unit, before he'd left.

She stared at the distant forest and tried not to imagine what he was doing. She hadn't asked where he was going and he hadn't volunteered the information. But despite all her good intentions she couldn't prevent the knot of resentment deep in her gut from tightening.

Even after having sex *three times* last night——not counting the quickie this morning when she'd been only half-conscious——he still went out for more. Was it for the variety? Or was it her lack of stamina? Because there was no denying the fact she could hardly keep her eyes open this morning.

Not that she was complaining. Exactly. But it was a thought, wasn't it? Gabe clearly had an insatiable libido and saw no reason to curb it just because she was staying with him.

She refocused on the laptop. She was an idiot to get so worked up over it. *It* was only sex. And that was all it ever would be. It wasn't as if she'd done something stupid like let her heart become involved. She might be falling, but she hadn't fallen irrevocably. There was still time to pull back.

Wasn't there?

AURORA CHECKED HER email account, expecting to see a reply from her dad. What she hadn't expected was to see one from her mum as well.

With a trickle of unease, she opened it. It must have been at least four years since her mother had felt up to emailing. Aurora was sure it was no coincidence this miracle occurred the day after her mother and Gabe had a telepathic exchange.

And what had they spoken about anyway? She'd been so staggered by his careless revelation that she'd forgotten to ask.

As she read the message she could feel her face heating. It was as if she'd slipped back fifteen years, and was listening to her mother chastising her for some childish misdemeanor.

Don't try telling me you've gone off to do RESEARCH with some guy you met at a psychic fayre.

Well, she'd had to tell them something, seeing as Gabe had communicated with her mother, but she'd never expected her mum to get so irate about it. In fact, she hadn't expected her mum to make much response at all. Wild hope flared. Could this be the cataclysm that brought her mother back from the shadows?

What have you done, Aurora? What sort of people just vanish into thin air?

What? Gabe had teleported in front of her mother? Was he *mad*? What was the point of her trying to tell her parents everything was fine and not to worry, when he'd gone and done *that* in front of them?

With a feeling of dread she opened her dad's reply. He was sure to be furious that she'd so upset her mum. Except he sounded perfectly fine and was relieved that she was okay.

Her mother hadn't confided in her dad. Was that because the events had faded into the far recesses of her mind as soon as she'd sent her email?

Or was it because with that thread of lucidity, her mother hadn't wanted to unnecessarily distress her father?

AFTER REPLYING TO her parents by saying a lot but telling them nothing, she decided to approach things from a different angle today. She focused on Guardian abductions and tumbled into a vortex of increasingly paranoid conspiracy theories. It was kind of shocking to discover that trait wasn't confined to humans of Earth. It appeared to be a universal obsession.

Speculation as to the Guardians' origin ranged across the spectrum of the imagination, as did the reasons why they abducted in the first place. None of the suggestions were palatable, but the one that really sickened her was the theory they did it to feed their insatiable drug habit. *Feeding on the terror of mortals.*

As with the so-called alien abductions on Earth, abductees generally—although not always—turned up again sooner or later. Their memories were hazy, their sanity compromised, and evidence of torture apparent but at least they were still alive.

And then she stumbled across the anomalies.

Hidden in obscure archives were scanty reports of those who

hadn't returned alive. Those whose throats had been slit and their bodies drained of all fluid. She dug deeper, her stomach churning with revulsion at the images scrolling across the screen.

And almost missed it.

Heart pounding, she scrolled back, zoomed in closer on the last unfocused image. She hadn't imagined it. Around the woman's neck was a chain. And although it was hard to see she was certain the pendant was in the shape of wings.

Involuntarily, she curled her fingers around her necklace. Coincidence. But she didn't believe it. Not for a second. There was a connection. *Had* to be. God, where was Gabe when she needed to talk to him?

From the corner of her eye she saw him materialize. Talk about perfect timing.

"Gabe, come here. You'll never—" Her words lodged in her throat as Mephisto, arms folded, regarded her through narrowed eyes.

"Aurora." Just that one word, but the menace in his voice caused a shudder along her spine. He made no move toward her, and yet his presence dominated the entire terrace, looming over her, suffocating.

She refused to squirm under his unblinking gaze. "Gabe's not here."

"It's not Gabe I want to speak with."

Nerves stabbed through her gut. Mephisto appeared far more intimidating when he wasn't flashing his evil smile around. She flattened her hands on her thighs to stop them from shaking. No way did she want this arrogant bastard to guess how much he unnerved her.

"What about?"

His mouth thinned as if her tone offended him. She forced a panicked breath into her lungs and reminded herself she was under

Gabe's protection. On his island. *So much for being a strong, independent woman of the twenty-first century.*

She hadn't been this terrified of Mephisto when he'd turned up before. But before he hadn't exuded this icy, deadly intent.

Intent for what?

Whatever it was, Aurora knew it wasn't good news for her.

"Tell me exactly what you did on the astral planes."

"You know what I was doing." He'd been at the club. Who else but Mephisto could have told Gabe she had been attempting to breach dimensions? And although she didn't have a clue how Mephisto knew she had no inclination to ask. "And so does Gabe."

Mephisto unfolded his arms and rippled his wings. An immortal predator stalking his prey.

"Tell Gabe whatever fucking fairy story you like. But don't try it on with me. I'll ask you one more time. What did you do on the astral planes?"

She could tell him the whole truth. Explain about her mother. But the thought of sharing such intimate details with Mephisto was abhorrent. He wouldn't give a damn about her reasons unlike Gabe, who'd been amazingly understanding about it all, now that she thought about it.

Before she could think better of it she pushed herself to her feet. Her knees shook and she gripped the top edge of the laptop screen for added stability. No point ruining her façade of courage by collapsing.

"I made a mistake." It hurt, having to confess that to Mephisto. "And I'm paying for it."

He moved so fast she hardly had time to blink before he was standing right in front of her. Before his arm shot out and knocked the laptop across the table, smashing onto the terrace.

"Paying for it?" His voice was still deadly low but his eyes burned scarlet. "I don't see you paying for anything. It's the Archangel Gabriel who's paying your debt and I want to know what the *fuck* you did to him on the astral planes."

Fear stabbed through her, but it wasn't fear of Mephisto for herself. What did he mean that Gabe was paying her debt? Immortals were beyond the grasp of the Guardians. She'd discovered that and Gabe had confirmed it.

But suppose they were both wrong?

"What do you mean? Is Gabe in danger? I thought he was safe from the Guardians?"

Mephisto stared at her as if he didn't have the faintest idea what she was talking about. As if her words were incomprehensible. Bizarrely, relief surged through her. If Mephisto considered her questions irrelevant then surely that meant Gabe wasn't in danger of abduction?

"*You're* his debt." Mephisto looked at her as though he'd like to incinerate her on the spot. "Manipulating your puny existence into his life."

Manipulating? "I'm not—"

"Last chance." He bared his teeth in a mirthless grin. "Tell me how you dragged Gabe through the astral planes without his knowledge. If I'd known that was your ultimate goal I would've fried your brain two years ago in London."

Mephisto thought *she* was responsible for Gabe's arrival on her land? Through the astral planes?

London? What did London have to do with any of this?

"I didn't. I don't have any idea how he—"

"Don't think I won't rip open your mind to find the truth if I have to, human."

She believed him. And he would leave nothing of her mind behind afterward.

"I am telling you the truth."

A phantom, psychic hand grasped her fingers and she staggered at the brutal grip. Mephisto's fiery glare scorched her flesh, and it took every particle of willpower she possessed to remain standing upright.

"*What are you?*" He ground the words between his teeth, as if they were forced against his will. As if something about her mystified him in a fundamental way.

He tightened his psychic grip on her fingers. Pain raced up her arm, speared through her chest, arrowing toward her heart.

Her vision was blurring. She refused to break eye contact. "Forget about me." She hitched in a crippled breath. "Why are you so concerned about Gabe?" Mephisto didn't strike her as the caring type. "What do you care about *anything?*"

"Who the hell are *you* to question *me?*"

He was going to kill her. At the moment he was playing, like a cat with a mouse, but within seconds he would tire of his game. He would rip through her mind, clawing for answers. And find nothing.

How easy it would be to fall to her knees. To grovel at his feet and beg for mercy. *He'd spare her then.*

The thought was absolute, as if it was ancient knowledge. And with it came a cold, white fury that ignited her paralyzed brain and pumped blood through her deadened fingers. She straightened her spine, pushed back *with her mind* and psychically felt Mephisto recoil in hideous, incomprehensible denial.

"Who the hell are *you* to intimidate *me?*" Her words, imbued with contempt, echoed in her ears. But where had they come from? It felt like she was continuing a conversation long since discarded.

Mephisto's eyes widened in disbelief. But it was more than that; it was something inexplicable. Because he looked, for one fleeting second, as if he'd been shaken to the core of his existence.

A dull thud echoed behind her and then Gabe was there, gripping Mephisto's biceps, and the unsettling connection severed.

"Back off." His voice was low. A deadly warning.

Mephisto wrenched himself free, his glare never leaving Aurora. "What the fuck"—Mephisto's voice was low, oddly hushed—"have you *done?*"

Shivers skated over Aurora's arms. Was he talking to her? What did he mean? That there were further repercussions of breaching dimensions that she had yet to learn?

Gabe appeared oblivious to Mephisto's strange behavior. "Don't come near Aurora again."

Finally Mephisto tore his gaze from Aurora. "She's just a human." Was it her imagination or did he sound as if he was trying to convince himself as much as Gabe? Then he stepped back, unfurled his wings and clenched his fists. "Think about it, Gabe. Is it really worth it?"

"Get out of here." Gabe sounded feral.

Mephisto gave her one last condemning glance. And then he teleported.

Chapter Twenty-six

GABE battened down the rabid desire to follow Mephisto's trail and hammer the crap out of him. *How dare he manhandle Aurora?* Even the thought was enough to twist his guts and cause his blood to steam with impotent rage.

But even as he took her hand and saw the way she gritted her teeth against the pain, he knew it was more than rage. More than fury that another archangel had dared to disregard the ancient bonds of ownership and touch a mortal under his protection.

He tried to ignore it. Rage he could deal with. But not fear. Not the fear that he might have arrived too late to save her. That Mephisto might, despite everything, have pillaged Aurora's mind and left a vacant, broken creature in her place.

"This might hurt." He enveloped her injured hand between his. Mephisto, the sadistic bastard, had partially torn fragile tendons and muscle. Nothing he couldn't fix but that wasn't the fucking point. "You'd better sit down."

"I'm all right." She glanced at his hands before looking back up at him. "You can heal." It wasn't a question. Then she sucked in a sharp breath and his frown deepened. He was trying to go slow, trying to be gentle, but until he'd finished her brain would register acute pain. "Can you bring back the dead as well?"

"No." For a second he broke his concentration to look at her. Her teeth were clenched and her face was drained of color but she met his gaze and even offered him a grimace that she clearly believed resembled a reassuring smile. For some reason it caused an odd stabbing sensation through his chest. "Bringing back the dead doesn't tend to go too well. Healing others is just a side benefit of our innate ability to rejuvenate."

She let out a huff of laughter. "Good job Meph didn't go straight for the mind-suck then."

Meph? Had she just called Mephisto *Meph*? No one called the other archangel that, apart from Zad. Gabe wasn't even convinced Mephisto liked Zad abbreviating his name but he'd definitely not heard anyone else use the term.

Except for Eleni. And the only reason she had used the name was because she knew how much it rankled.

"He won't come near you again." Again the rage surged, but it was more than rage. *Less* than rage. Because the fear fed on the rage and diminished it until only the fear remained. *Shit.* He focused on her healing injuries, slowly released his psychic grip. "He had no right coming here frightening you."

"Good job the cavalry arrived in time, huh?" She flexed her fingers and he saw the awe on her face. "Wow. You're good."

The color was returning to her cheeks, her eyes were no longer shadowed with pain, and she wasn't shivering in terror that the most powerful archangel in existence had almost destroyed her.

Probably because she had no idea how close she'd come. Just as well. He didn't want her worrying about Mephisto as well as the Guardians.

"Should be as good as new. Let me know if you get any twinges."

She curled her healed hand against her breasts and flattened her other hand against his heart. Such a light touch yet he felt the imprint of her palm and fingers scorch his flesh through his shirt.

Gods, he wanted her. Wanted to hold her and touch her and know that she really was all right. Wanted to lose himself inside her again, to reach that elusive pinnacle where, for a few blissful moments, his guilt receded and peace bathed his soul.

"Thanks, Gabe." Her voice was soft and her blue eyes hypnotized him. "I might have held him off for a few seconds but I know how close he was to pulverizing my brain."

For a second he was tempted to tell her that of course Mephisto had no intention of truly pulverizing her brain. It was odd, this compunction he had to protect Aurora from the harsh truths. And it didn't even make any sense. Because she already knew the truth.

"He won't make that mistake twice." He and Mephisto would most likely never cross paths again until Aurora—

The thought seared his brain. *Until Aurora was dead.* And a human lived only a few score years at most. No time at all when compared to the lifespan of an archangel. He would have his island back and Mephisto would put this day into the archives and resume their previous relationship as if nothing had come between them.

A few score years. A fleeting lifespan. *An eternity alone.*

"I'm sorry about your laptop." Aurora's hands were now on his shoulders, her warm body all but touching him. *Alive.* She was alive now and now was all they had. But instead of scooping her into his arms and taking her inside and fucking her until this unnatural knot of panic subsided, he sat on her chair and cradled her with his thighs.

"It's fixable." And even if it wasn't, so what? It was only a piece of technology, manufactured by one of the most advanced civilizations in the Andromeda Galaxies. An irreparably damaged laptop could be replaced. But if Aurora had died—

There was only one Aurora.

He molded the seductive curve of her hips and cradled her waist. She was human, a mortal. So fragile that if he held his breath he could hear the beat of her heart, the rush of her blood in her veins. By rights he should have tired of her already and yet he couldn't get enough. Even this morning he hadn't wanted to leave the bed. Had wanted to remain, basking in the afterglow. Had wanted to take her again.

Only her clear exhaustion and inability to keep her eyes open for longer than a few sleepy seconds had prevented him from following through with his insatiable lust. A lust he hadn't experienced for millennia. When was the last time a single female had so ensnared his libido?

But she *was* only human. And he couldn't expect her to match his desire. Not unless he wanted her permanently semi-conscious with fatigue.

Once, that was exactly all he wanted from her.

"Gabe." There was an unmistakable note of concern in her voice and his fingers tightened involuntarily around her waist. He didn't want her permanently worrying, either. "Is the fact you saved me from the Guardians causing you problems with—well, anyone?"

She was worrying about *him*? "Wouldn't matter to me even if you were." He tugged her closer, breathed in deep, relishing her purity. It had been forever since someone had showed such simple concern for him. "The only ones who might have complained gave up all pretense at responsibility millennia ago."

Aurora framed his face with her hands, stroking her thumbs over his cheekbones. His overnight shadow grazed her skin, erotic and evocative. It had never occurred to her before that archangels might shave.

But it was hard to remember he was an immortal when he held her like this. When, every time she looked at him, she didn't see the archangel but the man.

Despite his fantastical eyes. And despite the scene that had so recently taken place when he had resembled anything but a normal, mortal male.

"You mean the Alphas?" He'd mentioned them twice in passing, but she'd not come across any references to them while researching. She still didn't know exactly how they fitted into Gabe's personal world except for the fact that compared to them he didn't consider himself immortal.

"You don't need to worry about them. They never come anywhere near this side of the universe anymore. Too primitive for them."

She hadn't been worrying about them for herself but it appeared she didn't need to worry on Gabe's behalf, either. Maybe all Mephisto had meant was he considered she, personally, was a burden to Gabe.

Weird. Almost as if Mephisto actually cared about someone other than himself.

"But what—who—are they? Kind of like your ancestors?"

He sighed heavily as if he didn't want to talk about it but was prepared to humor her. A strange little pain weaved through her heart at the knowledge he was slowly opening up to her. Maybe without him even realizing it.

"The Alpha Immortals are ancient. The forebears of all immortals alive today."

A tiny warning in the back of her mind urged her to show some level of restraint. But she wanted to touch him. Wanted to feel his hands on her, holding her as if she belonged to him. And on this island they did belong to each other. No matter what her head kept telling her, she couldn't help the overwhelming sensation that Gabe felt more than base lust.

It had been in his voice as he'd healed her hand. In the furtive glances he shot her every time she'd winced. It wasn't love and it couldn't lead anywhere permanent. But for now, it was enough.

Because now was all they would ever have.

He rolled his shoulders, as if his muscles ached, and then looked directly at her. His gaze was intense, focused entirely on her, and she knew that *now* would never be enough.

"Are there many of them? The Alphas?" She loved his eyes. She could drown in their mystical depths and die in ecstasy.

"Countless." There was a husky note in his voice. But he didn't slip his hands beneath her T-shirt or tug her closer. "They're all wasting away on the far side of the universe." His eyes darkened and again she waited for him to pull impatiently at her clothes. Except he didn't.

"So who's in charge?" She forked her fingers through his hair, tugging his head back. The heat from his hands enveloped her waist and desire kicked in hard and brutal low in her womb. No matter that they had spent most of the night having sex, or that he'd possibly just returned from another woman's bed.

She still wanted him again.

He gave her a mocking grin as if her question was amusing. But still he didn't make any attempt to take up her unspoken offer. It was almost as if he was deliberately holding back. Except why would he do such a thing? He never had before.

And it wasn't because he'd lost interest. Arousal thudded in the air between them, thick and sensuous, and if *she* could feel it then she was damn sure he could.

"Who's in charge? What of, the universe?" He was laughing at her, but she didn't mind because the way his eyes crinkled and lips curved entranced her. "No one. Everyone. You know how it is."

She had no idea how it was, and yet in a way she knew exactly what he meant.

"Fate and destiny?" She'd never really believed in either, despite the extraordinary way her parents had met and come together. But now she was willing to seriously consider almost anything.

"Why not." It wasn't a question and his hold on her relaxed as he shifted restlessly on the chair as if her touch disturbed him. He glanced at the shattered laptop. "I'll order a new laptop. Shouldn't take long to arrive. I have contacts." He offered her a mocking grin.

He was putting her off. But he wanted her. It was obvious by the tension in his muscles and the erratic rise and fall of his chest. Intrigued, she trapped his jaw between her palms and forced him to look at her. His eyes were dark, his teeth clenched. And as she leaned in closer the tantalizing scent of hot, aroused male flooded her senses.

There was no hint of feminine perfume, tang of sex or residual damp from a recent, hasty shower. No evidence at all that he'd spent the time away from this island today in the arms of another woman.

Slowly she speared her fingers into his hair, cradling his temples with her palms. He looked up at her, his expression indefinable, but awareness sizzled in the air, electrifying the light touch of his fingers at her waist.

"Your contacts"—her voice was low, breathless and appeared to hypnotize Gabe—"can wait."

"Are you giving me another order?" As he spoke he finally slid his fingers beneath her top and tremors of pure sensation raced over her skin. The muscles of his already rock-hard thighs tightened, enslaving her. "You do know who I am, don't you?"

She leaned in closer, their breath mingling, and raked her fingers through his silken hair before grasping handfuls and jerking his head back.

"Yes." He was the Archangel Gabriel. But he was so much more than that. "You're the man I want. You got a problem with that?"

He laughed and wound his arms around her waist as if he imagined she might try and escape.

An insubstantial thought flickered through the back of her mind. She did need to escape this island. *But she never wanted to escape Gabe's arms.*

"Do I look like I have a problem with it?"

He looked utterly irresistible when he laughed with her, when it was a struggle to recall he wasn't just an ordinary guy but an immortal. Looking at him now, as he grinned up at her as if he hadn't a care in the world—the universe—how easy it would be to think he had no concept of suffering or loss.

But she'd seen beneath his arrogant façade to the mortal beneath. His loss, no matter how long ago it had occurred, was still raw.

Was this moment of carefree laughter another façade?

Pain, as deep and desolate as any pain she had experienced while watching her mother's mind slowly fade, squeezed her heart. She wanted to believe that, when he was with her, Gabe could forget his past.

The irony seared her soul, but it was true. She wanted her mother to remember and for Gabe to forget. And the chances of her achieving either were remote.

All she had was now. All she might ever have was now. She wouldn't waste it with regrets of what could never be.

"I'm not sure." She smiled back, hoped he couldn't see how much of an effort it took for her to match his flippant mood. "I think further investigation might be called for."

He laughed again, this time without the underlying impression that it had escaped without him quite expecting it. This time his laugh sounded as if he was genuinely enjoying their exchange.

"I can spare you an hour or so." He began to get up, clearly intending to take matters into his own hands. She untangled her fingers from his hair and shoved roughly at his shoulders.

"Sit still."

His eyes widened. But he didn't attempt to ignore her. Instead, after his initial flash of surprise, his lips quirked in clear amusement.

"Another order? Not even demi-gods are that brave around me."

"Good job I'm not a demi-god then, isn't it?"

He snorted and began to pull off her shirt. She slapped his hand, gripped his wrists and pinned him to the arms of the chair.

"Don't touch. Or do I have to hurt you?"

Gabe choked on another laugh. "I'd like to see you try."

She trailed her hands up his arms. He didn't move a muscle. Or break eye contact.

"Be careful." Her voice didn't sound like her own. It sounded scandalously sexy, sultry even. "What you wish for." Heart pounding, making it hard to draw breath, she concentrated on unbuttoning his shirt. "Because you never know your luck. You might just get it."

Chapter Twenty-seven

GABE stifled the primal urge to rip off their clothes, drag Aurora into his arms and slake the molten lust that surged through his blood. He was as desperate for her body as if he'd been celibate for years. As if this was their first time. As if he hadn't already sampled what she had to offer; hadn't already taken her more frequently than any other woman in centuries.

Sex was an entertaining way to pass the time. Enjoyable, satisfying. And ultimately forgettable.

He remembered every frenzied moment of every single time he'd been with Aurora. It seemed that far from diminishing his need, every time he had her only left him more ravenous for more.

Instead of obeying his natural instincts to assert control, to take what she offered on his terms, he gripped the arms of the chair, his biceps straining with the effort.

"What do you have in mind?" He watched the way she slid each button free with maddening deliberation, an enchanting frown of concentration etched on her brow. He wasn't sure whether she was doing it deliberately or not, but either way it was stoking his lust like nothing he could recall.

"Wait and see." She glanced up at him then and the blush on her cheeks, giving her an intriguing aura of innocent seductress, stretched his frayed self-control to its limits. "Not used to the woman taking over, are you?"

He heard the hint of triumph in her voice and it was obvious that thought gave her a great deal of satisfaction. That she wanted to be the first who had ever had him pliant beneath her searching fingers.

A feral grin split his lips and she smirked, clearly pleased by his reaction. Even if it wasn't the truth. Even if he'd lost count millennia ago of how many women had stripped him and worshipped him, while he lay there basking in their adoration.

Because with every other woman, except Eleni, who had taken the initiative, he'd been content to let them feed their curiosity. He'd not had to rein in his desire as he was doing for Aurora. Hadn't needed to remain agonizingly still while she grappled with a simple thing like removing his shirt.

And unlike any of them, Aurora was far from incoherent with awe or speechless with the honor of being in his company. She was with him because . . .

Despite himself a pained grunt escaped as she tugged his shirt from his pants. But still his thought hovered.

Aurora was with him because he was the *man she wanted*.

Not an immortal. Not an archangel. Not because of his reputation as a ruthless mercenary. But just because of *him*.

She grasped the ends of his shirt in her fists and looked as if she wasn't too sure what she was supposed to do next. Gods, he hoped she opened his pants. His cock was fucking killing him.

"Take off your shirt." Her voice was uneven and she still clung onto the edges of his shirt as if it was her lifeline.

It would be so much easier to rip off his shirt, open his pants and pull her onto him. The image scalded his vision, blurred reality. He wanted her now. But she needed this more.

"No." He barely recognized his voice. He sounded like a desperate addict craving his next fix.

Aurora.

He grimaced, pushed through the fog enslaving his sanity and searched for the words she needed. "You want me naked, you strip me."

Her pupils, already huge, expanded further and her blatant arousal fueled his own. She dropped the ends of his shirt and slid her hands up his abdomen, her touch light but sure. He instantly regretted his benevolence.

"Is your body naturally perfect or do you work out?" The tip of her tongue slid across the seam of her lips and he stared, mesmerized. Had she just done that on purpose?

"Both." If he gripped the damn chair any harder it was going to splinter. He tried, without much success, to relax his rigid muscles. "How about you?"

Her fingers halted a whisper from his nipples. "Me?" She sounded as though she thought he might be mocking her. "My body's hardly perfect, even if I do go to the gym."

He released a pained breath. Why had he thought it a good idea to let Aurora take over? She was talking way too much. She always talked way too much.

Despite her poor timing he realized he'd have her no other way.

"It's perfect"—he ground the words between his teeth in an attempt to keep focused—"to me."

For a moment she stared at him as if he was her entire world and something deep inside twisted, the pain corkscrewing through his chest. He'd sworn she would look at him with adoration, but he'd never envisaged a look like this. He couldn't even place it, only knew it had nothing to do with mindless worship of an immortal being.

And then she let out a breathless laugh and stroked her thumbs over his nipples. He damn near came in his pants. How much more of this could he take?

"I bet you say that to all the girls."

What? That he was seconds from a major embarrassment?

"Yeah." The word was feral. "Right."

She flattened her hands over his chest, over his erect nipples, molding his body in her palms. Her warm breath feathered his mouth, her breasts rose and fell with tantalizing promise but still she remained fully clothed when he wanted her naked and screaming his name while he—

"I'd like to watch you work out." She slid her hands over his shoulders, beneath the fabric of his shirt, and despite his good intentions a groan of pure frustration razed his throat. She appeared to enjoy his discomfort if her evil smile was anything to go by. "I can just see you pumping iron."

He could see him pumping something else. And damn soon, too.

She eased his shirt off his shoulders, then concentrated on attempting to tug it from his body.

"Need some help?" Gods, it hurt to think, never mind speak. When was the last time he'd been so insanely aroused?

"Yes." He heard the thread of frustration in her voice. Clearly she'd wanted to strip him without any assistance. "Just come forward a bit so I can—that's it."

He closed his eyes and drew in a deep breath, his face cushioned in the gentle swell of her breasts. He could hear the frantic rush of her blood, feel the erratic hammer of her pulses, but still she insisted on focusing her attention on his damn shirt.

Or not. As she pulled the material down his back her hands spent more time clinging to his flesh and digging into his muscles than was strictly necessary. Erotic torture. He turned his head and flicked his tongue over the peak of her breast, and a seductive quiver rippled through her body.

"Told you not to touch." She plunged her fingers into his hair but didn't attempt to drag his head back. If anything, she pressed him closer. "Not good at taking orders, are you?"

"No." He fastened his teeth around her nipple. Even through her top and bra he could feel the tantalizing nub harden under his tongue.

"Stop." It was a choked gasp and he was tempted to ignore it. Especially when her fingers dug into his scalp as if the last thing she wanted was for him to *stop*.

Air hissed between his teeth as he drew back from her luscious breasts. Her nails gouged his head in response, as though she hadn't believed he would do as she asked.

She dragged her fingers through his hair and he stifled another groan. Every fucking thing she did aroused him, and if she did much more he'd damn well combust.

"Lift your arm." Her order was hardly coherent and he smiled grimly. At least her performance was causing her a degree of the discomfort he was experiencing. He unhooked his fingers from the chair and suffered in acute silence as Aurora then slid both hands over his taut biceps. Except she did it again, as if the texture of his flesh fascinated her. And then again, sculpting his musculature with the tips of her fingers.

"What," he ground out, "are you doing?" Not that he wasn't enjoying it in a vaguely masochistic way. But he'd enjoy it a whole lot more if she would release his agonizingly trapped cock from his pants.

"Exploring your body." The words were husky, provocative and speared straight through his shaft. "If it wasn't too close to the truth I'd say you were built like a god."

He laughed. Didn't mean to but couldn't help himself. "Don't insult me at a time like this, sweetheart. I'm built like an archangel, not a god."

This time she was the one who laughed, a sexy, sultry laugh that sank into his blood and filled his mind. With an endearingly inelegant tug she finally managed to pull off his shirt and dropped it onto the terrace with a sigh of clear relief.

He sat back and once again gripped the arms of the chair. It was either that or grab Aurora, but despite his need he wanted to know what else she had in mind. It was odd. All she had done was removed his shirt and yet he couldn't remember when anything, no matter how sexually breathtaking, had so ensnared his libido.

She stood before him, still entrapped by his thighs, and her reverential gaze enchanted him. Women without number had looked this way at him and yet, conversely, not one of them had.

Because not one of them had ever affected him the way Aurora was affecting him now. He waited until she finally lifted her gaze to his, and offered her his most decadent smile.

"Do you think . . ." She trailed off, and he wanted to tell her the time for thinking was past. That he didn't care what she intended, that she should just *do* it. "Do you think you'll have any more unexpected visitors? Should we go inside?"

He heard an unmistakable crack as he finally splintered one of the timber arms.

"No. To both." He sounded rabid. If anyone did turn up he'd fucking slaughter them. "Are you done now?"

Instead of quaking at his tone, as any other mortal with a shred of sense would have, she just smirked, like he'd said something that greatly amused her. Then she began to inch her T-shirt up from her waist, daring him to break eye contact.

He didn't.

"Do I look as if I'm done?" The hint of mockery, that she was virtually throwing his own words back in his face from their first sexual encounter, was electrifying. His thumbs were hooked into the top of her shorts and tugging them down her thighs before he even realized he'd moved. Her arousal scented the air, her damp pussy the most enticing sight he'd glimpsed in millennia.

"Gabe." Her breathless whisper dragged his mesmerized gaze from between her legs. Her lips were parted, her eyes glazed, and her T-shirt was bunched over her breasts, hiding her cleavage but showing the sexy lace of her bra and dark hint of erect nipples. "Sit back."

He couldn't sit back. He was in agony. Every move a fiery torture. And every breath was saturated with her evocative, sultry scent.

Slowly he unhooked his fingers from her shorts. "Satisfied?" The word rasped into the heated air. Maybe Aurora had discovered a way to kill an archangel after all.

"Not yet." Her voice was uneven. "Patience isn't one of your virtues, is it?"

"Never said it was." Riveted, he watched her pull her T-shirt over her head, her breasts lifting provocatively in the lacy cups that cradled them. She dropped it on top of his shirt and then slid her hands over her breasts, across her belly to the apex of her thighs.

"Wasn't going to strip right off yet." Her hands slid lower, pushing her shorts down her legs. "Was going to make you wait for it."

She bent from her waist, slowly sliding her shorts from her body, giving him an unobstructed view of her tempting breasts and captivating cleavage.

And for once, words failed him.

She kicked off her shorts, then slid her hands over his rigid thighs, a slow, torturous caress, and his chest constricted as if that might ease the excruciating throb devouring his entire groin.

No chance. Not when Aurora's fingers drifted over his erection as if she was measuring his length.

Another frustrated groan escaped. "You are making me wait for it. Since when have you been a sadist?"

Her gaze was fixed on the bulge in his pants. "Since I met you." Finally she tugged at his belt and he hitched in a painful breath in an attempt to give her some leverage. "Lift up." Her voice was an intoxicating blend of command and awe and he obeyed without a second thought.

Bracing his weight on his hands, he watched Aurora go to work on releasing him from his current state of purgatory. Through the lust thundering inside his brain a thread of amusement ignited. Her brow was creased in concentration as if she was engaged in a task of monumental complexity.

He couldn't remember the last time he'd been *amused* during such an encounter. Then she let out a frustrated hiss and yanked.

"Fuck!" Still clutching the chair he reared up, almost knocking Aurora onto her ass. "You damn near castrated me."

She slapped her hand across her mouth and her eyes widened. His vision was blurred but he could have sworn she was on the verge of giggling.

"Sorry." The word was muffled. She slid her hand from her mouth and cradled his jaw. "I've never manhandled such an impressive weapon before."

Gods, damn, she *was* laughing. He was so staggered even the volcanic throb of his abused cock faded. It had been forever since a simple fuck had become so mystifyingly complex.

The thought drifted through his mind, instantly dismissed. There was nothing complex about it. *Nothing.*

"My impressive weapon." Hell, it was hard to keep a straight face. Then he wondered why he was even trying. "Despite being immortal is also made of flesh and blood. And it damn well hurts." Fuck, had he said that aloud? Admitted a weakness?

"I'm really sorry." This time she sounded genuinely contrite. "I didn't mean to hurt you. I didn't *really* hurt you that badly, did I?"

In the great scheme of things he wasn't hurt at all. But in all of his long existence no woman had ever managed to pinch the sensitive skin of his cock *in a zipper*.

A snort of laughter erupted at the sheer incongruity of the situation. He unhooked his fingers from the chair and it dropped to the ground.

"You did," he told her as he finished her botched attempt and finally freed himself. Relief punched through his groin and he shoved his pants down his legs before she had the chance to protest. "The question is: What are you going to do about it?"

Chapter Twenty-eight

SHE didn't answer right away. He wrapped his hand around his engorged cock, a brutal grip, but it did nothing to ease the need thundering in his veins. She watched him, mesmerized, as if she had never witnessed such a thing before, and air hissed between his teeth.

He reached out with his free hand but before he could wind his fingers in her hair and drag her toward him, she gripped his wrist.

"Stop that." Her gaze was still transfixed between his thighs, and he squeezed his sensitive glans, enjoying not only the physical sensation but Aurora's reaction.

"Why? You got a better offer for me?"

She slid her fingers from his wrist to his elbow. Rivers of fire ignited beneath his skin, burning through his blood, and a fractured thought occurred to him. *Since when had his forearm been such an uninhibited erogenous zone?*

"If you don't stop"—she finally looked up at him, her eyes dark with passion, her cheeks flushed with arousal and never had he seen such a bewitching sight—"you'll never know."

His grip tightened around his shaft and shallow breaths seared his lungs. He was torn between the need to pull her into his arms and thrust his cock deep inside and the rapidly diminishing *want* to know what she had in mind for him.

"Tell me."

One hand gripped his biceps and her other flattened against his chest. He collapsed back onto the chair, his gaze never leaving hers.

"I thought I'd start off here." She feathered a kiss across his lips, her breath warm and enticing. Without conscious thought he wound his arm around her, trailed his fingers across the smooth skin of her back, the curve of her waist, and cradled her delectable ass. Her eyes widened but she didn't protest.

Instead her hands curled over his shoulders to brace her weight. She nibbled kisses along his jaw, the tip of her tongue flicking his flesh between every teasing kiss. He molded the rounded curve of her ass and she answered his unspoken demand by sinking against him as her mouth fastened on his throat.

Her teeth claimed his flesh and erotic darts of pleasure thundered through his blood. Even through her bra—*why the hell was she still wearing her bra*—her erect nipples grazed his chest. He pumped his cock, pressing her closer, wanting to feel her skin against his.

"No." Her jagged whisper inflamed him further. So did the touch of her hand as she slid between their bodies and covered his. "I want to make you come, Gabe. By myself."

He nearly came right then. It took monumental effort to loosen his grip and let her thread her fingers through his and drag his hand to her waist. How easy it would be to push her to her knees. But it wouldn't be the same as her doing it in her own sweet time.

If that was even what she had in mind.

Her fingernails scraped over his chest, raked across his nipples, scored threads of fire over his abdomen. Finally she sank onto her knees between his thighs. His heart thudded in erratic arousal against his ribs, as if this was the first time a woman had ever been on her knees before him instead of times without number.

But it was the first time with Aurora.

She looked up at him through her eyelashes, an intoxicating combination of innocence and wanton seductress. Her rich chestnut hair tumbled around her shoulders, and he fought the desperate urge to plunge his fingers through those silken curls, to hold her close, to force her to his will.

He gripped the chair arms once again. An unlikely implement of torture.

"Where did I hurt you?" Her breathless words fanned his erection as she took him in her hand as if afraid he might break. He gritted his teeth against the order burning his tongue for her to *grip*. If she wanted to touch him as if he was made of spun glass, then he would suffer it. "Was it here?" The fingers of her free hand dusted his length and an agonized growl rumbled through his chest.

"Yes." Not that he could recall now. His entire body throbbed with ecstatic anticipation, which was a sensation he'd not experienced in . . . eternity.

He watched, mesmerized, as she bent over him, her hair caressing the insides of his thighs. Her wet mouth brushed against his rigid length, her lips fastening, her tongue teasing. She sucked and kissed and licked and his hands were in her hair, cradling her head. *Wanting more.*

She pulled back, panting, and despite his inclinations he relaxed his hard grip on her. She looked up at him, her head resting on his thigh, her lips parted in blatant invitation, his cock in her hand. And he damn near forgot how to breathe.

"I thought"—each word was an erratic gasp—"I might use my mouth on you. Do you like oral sex, Gabe?"

Was she serious? And did she seriously expect him to *answer* her?

He managed a primitive grunt. His cock jerked within her light grasp.

"Except," she added, and he glared at her, unable to believe she was still talking at a moment like this. "I'm not sure my mouth is *big* enough."

"Your mouth is plenty big enough."

"A girl could take that the wrong way." Then she slowly, deliberately, licked the tip of her tongue across his gleaming slit.

"Aurora." It was a warning. But it was also an entreaty. He, who never asked for anything much less begged. "For gods' sakes, let me in."

Her hand tightened around him, exquisite agony, and her other hand cradled his aching balls. She shuffled unsteadily between his thighs as if she was in discomfort, and he faintly recalled she was kneeling on hard, unforgiving stone. And then he forgot about everything as her mouth enslaved him.

Silken heat enveloped the head of his cock and he reared upward, instinctively, the need to penetrate pounding through his senses. She sucked hard, her teeth grazing his flesh, and he plunged both hands through her hair, twisting her curls around his fingers, forcing her along his rigid length.

Gods, it was exquisite. Her head nestled between his thighs, her hot breath erratic against his shaft. The erotic feel of her mouth surrounding him, her tongue cushioning him, her teeth claiming him. *Her nails digging into the hard muscles of his thigh.*

A strangled groan scraped his throat and he eased his grip on her head. Instantly she slid up a couple of inches, the friction a new kind of sensual torture. And then she gripped him, her fingers tightening around his cock, and it took all his willpower not to shove himself down her tempting throat and empty into her.

Panting with restrained exertion, he wound her hair around his fists. He watched, transfixed, as she worked the head of his cock with her mouth and tongue. Sucking him so hard his vision blurred and senses shattered. And still she tortured him with her fingers, as she trailed over his rock-hard balls, cradled them in the palm of her hand and then, shockingly, squeezed.

Fuck. It was too much. He couldn't hold back any longer. And while the image of her on her knees worshipping his cock was blowing his sanity, he wanted to feel her come around him as he pumped into her tight sheath.

Aurora could barely breathe, barely think as Gabe filled her mouth and filled her hands. He tasted of sex, of sin, of primal desire and forbidden delights. Already her jaw ached, yet she'd only taken the tip of him into her. Tremors flooded her womb as she recalled how he had thrust deep, choking her, and yet a secret part of her hadn't wanted him to pull back.

He gripped her jaw. Her hair was tangled around his hands and she tried to relax, waiting for the thrust. *Wanting* it. But instead of holding her head still for his further invasion he withdrew.

His cock, wet from her mouth, mesmerized her, and raw, jagged desire speared through her sensitized sheath. But he didn't give her the chance to admire any longer as he gripped her forearms and hauled her to her feet.

"Finished?" The word was breathless, incoherent. Her jaw didn't feel as if it quite belonged to her and a decadent smile curved her lips at the thought.

"No." There was a savage glow in his eyes as if he was on the outer edges of control, and her pulses hammered.

God, he was beautiful. Unblemished bronze flesh molded his strong, perfectly defined musculature and his golden hair brushed his shoulders. He lifted her roughly in his arms and for one surreal moment she imagined him unfurling his glorious wings, enveloping her in the magical cocoon of softness and strength, the scent of arousal and devotion intoxicating her senses.

It was just a fantasy. But it felt so real. As if she was remembering another time . . .

Mephisto. Disappointment cascaded, even as Gabe hoisted her onto the table. She was only recalling the feel of Mephisto's wings and superimposing the sensation with Gabe.

Except it wasn't that at all. And it had nothing to do with Mephisto. It was fading like a distant dream but the fleeting sensation had been so visceral, as if . . .

It was a memory.

Gabe palmed her bottom and balanced her on the edge of the table. His gaze scorched her, his touch inflamed, yet goose bumps prickled her skin.

"You can't," he panted, "be cold."

She clamped her legs around his waist. She was so desperate to feel his wings her mind was conjuring tricks. But it didn't matter. She didn't need his wings because right now she had *him.* And he was all that mattered.

"I'm burning." She wound her arms over his shoulders and buried her fingers in his glorious hair. "For my archangel."

For a second he became absolutely still, and the look on his face was impossible to define. As if her words had been not only unexpected but had touched him in a way he hadn't imagined.

Or maybe it was just her own imagination, looking for something that simply wasn't there.

"Then you'd better hold on." His words were raw with warning or promise; she couldn't tell and didn't care. His cock nudged her swollen pussy, a teasing, tantalizing kiss. Anticipation sizzled through every cell but still he kept her waiting.

"Gabe." She was begging. *She didn't care.* "For god's sake, I need you inside me."

His grin was pure evil, forged in heaven and honed in hell. Incoherent moans spilled from her lips but she didn't even care about that, either. Because Gabe was torturing her in a way she had never believed possible. Slowly, inch by magnificent inch, he eased into her when she desperately craved a brutal possession.

"Now," he said, a thread of triumph licking his voice, "who's the impatient one?"

She gripped his waist in a vise, dug her heels into his taut butt and lifted herself from the edge of the table. The sensation of shoving herself along his erection, of feeling her body stretch to accommodate his size, sent ripples of pure lust from her clit to her womb.

"Me." Her voice was hoarse, her heart stampeding. He filled her so completely and it felt so utterly right. "And I'm about to make you come."

So fast she barely had time to comprehend, he pinned her to the table. Her fingers were still tangled in his hair; his hands were now imprisoning her hips. And with a thrill of dark delight she saw raw savagery gleam in his eyes.

"But I," he growled, sounding wild and inhuman, "intend to make *you* come first."

A couple of well-aimed thrusts was all it would take. She squirmed helplessly beneath him, but his hold was absolute.

Did it matter? She raked her fingernails over his head and felt his big body shudder. Oh, he was close. As close as she. The knowledge inflamed and she slid her legs higher, clamping around his back, jerking him closer. Her internal muscles tightened around his invading length, a mind-blowing caress of silk and flame and spirals of fire licked low and deep.

Mindlessly, she dragged her hand from his hair, scored the skin of his waist and hip with her fingernails. Feverishly, she reached for him, grasped his taut balls, and his primal groan echoed through her blood. Reality blurred as he rammed into her, brutal and savage.

He came, hard and fast, the pleasure so fierce it bordered on agony. She gripped him tight, forgot how to breathe, to think. She could only feel him inside her and see him above her. Sensation consumed, enslaved, and finally only one coherent thought filled her world.

Gabe.

EYES CLOSED, GABE fought for breath. His forehead rested against Aurora's and her orgasmic scream still echoed in his mind.

His name. She had screamed his name in the exquisite moment that she had come.

Her erratic breath panted against his mouth, her heart hammered against his chest. She was soft and warm and her legs still entrapped him in a silken embrace. Slowly he raised his head and looked at her. Her eyes were closed, her lips parted and she looked utterly enchanting.

A faint flicker of unease drifted through his mind. How many times had he taken her? Why did he still find her so irresistible? Even now, seconds after climax?

He should be craving distance. Feel suffocated by her intimate touch. But even as he probed the thoughts, attempted to ignite them, they slid away, insubstantial and unimportant.

What did it matter how he should be feeling? The truth was plain. He didn't just want Aurora for the sex. He enjoyed her touch even when they weren't fucking. Revelation trickled along his spine. Because it was even more than that.

He liked her company. In the short time they'd been together he'd got used to having her here, in his own private sanctuary. It was crazy, but he even liked the way she'd turned his life upside down with her innocence of his world and her incessant desire to assert her own authority.

Gods, she could have no idea just how radically she'd messed with his existence. He never lost control during sex, yet so far he had every time with Aurora.

He'd never brought a mortal to this island. Yet here he was stark naked on the terrace outside his villa, still impaled within her tempting heat.

Her eyelashes flickered. Her blue eyes were glazed. She looked sated and exhausted and guilt stabbed through him. He'd taken her again. After he'd vowed not to. But damn, all she had to do was look at him and he wanted her.

No excuse. He could have resisted. *Except their time together was so inevitably brief.*

"Nice." She sounded half asleep. Her leg muscles flexed. "Want another go?" And then she winced and rolled her shoulders, as if she was uncomfortable.

He wrapped his arms around her and lifted her from the table. There was no earthly need, yet he kept her secured onto his cock.

"Later. You need to rest first." He stepped over the large timber chest he'd dropped after seeing Mephisto looming over Aurora and took her into the villa. Every move he made caused her slick sheath to rub with agonizing temptation along his burgeoning erection. It was with a sense of relief he finally laid her on the bed.

She groaned. "I can't believe I'm having an afternoon nap." She opened one eye and peered up at him. She looked positively edible. "You having one too?"

"Sure." He lay beside her, on top of the covers, and propped his head in his hand. With any other woman he would have given her a helping nudge into slumber. But Aurora wasn't any other woman. And if she was, he wouldn't be in this unbelievable position in the first place.

Silence settled, and with it an odd kind of comfort. He watched her sink into oblivion and only then did he realize their fingers were entwined. With a heavy sigh he began to free himself. Before he started work on the contents of the chest he would sort out acquiring another laptop. He couldn't be without one in his line of work and besides Aurora needed one too. As his fingers slipped from hers she stirred, frowned, and momentarily tightened her grip on him.

"My beloved archangel."

The words were soft but completely coherent. A shudder clawed along his spine but still her whispered endearment branded his brain and pierced his hardened heart.

My beloved archangel. Only Eleni had ever called him that. Only Eleni had ever dared.

Only Eleni had ever possessed the right.

With a tangled sense of fascination and dread-filled hope Gabe stared at Aurora's sleeping face. It wasn't possible. He knew that. Eleni was dead, and dead forever. Aurora's words meant nothing.

Meant everything.

He raked his hand through his hair, mind reeling. He couldn't shift the feeling that somehow there was a connection between Eleni and Aurora, no matter how crazy the idea was.

There was only one other he could talk to about it. Only one other who could understand.

Zad.

Chapter Twenty-nine

AFTER contacting Zad it didn't take long to track him down. He was knee deep in the latest devastating earthquake that had recently hit the Pacific.

Gabe stood on a bank of steaming rubble and watched the other archangel, second only to Mephisto in age, leave the medical team he'd been organizing and make his way across the broken buildings and shredded vegetation toward him.

Gabe could see through the glamour that rendered Zad's wings invisible to mortal eyes, but nothing could disguise the aura of quiet authority Zad exuded without even trying. No wonder he was always roped into positions of leadership despite his reluctance.

"Is it worth it?" Gabe narrowed his eyes against the gritty atmosphere and stared across the ruined city. Zad haunted natural disasters on Earth as if they were a drug.

"Got to be worth a try."

They'd had this conversation a million times in the past. Gabe had never been able to get over his natural inclination to let humans just get the hell on with it. Somehow or another their species always survived, no matter what the Earth or cosmos threw at them.

They survived, whether they deserved to or not.

Strange. He and Zad had both lost those who meant everything to them. Yet while Gabe had turned his back on humanity for their ignorant involvement Zad had embraced them.

Gabe would never again open his arms to the human race.

Aurora.

Her face filled his vision, obliterating the ravaged landscape. She was a human and he'd done more than open his arms to her. He'd broken ancient covenants for her.

But then, she wasn't strictly indigenous to Earth. She was a unique, incredible hybrid who possessed the genetic material from two dimensions. He'd never lay the blame of the past on her shoulders.

Yet he'd saved her, offered her sanctuary, before he'd known her true heritage.

Her true heritage. Again the futile hope that she was so much more than she could ever be echoed through his heart. It would answer his insatiable desire and would be the reason why he hadn't minded her irreverence. It would also explain the unacknowledged fear that he could easily have arrived too late today to save her from Mephisto's rage.

"Gabe," Zad said. "Is this still about the woman you rescued from the Guardians?"

There was no point denying it. Aurora was the only reason he'd sought out Zad. "Yes."

Zad cast him a speculative look. "You aren't pissed off by the inconvenience anymore." It wasn't a question. "The sex must be spectacular."

"It's not the—" He clamped his jaw shut. He wasn't about to discuss his sex life with Zad, of all people. "She has a necklace, Zad. Obviously its quality is inferior but apart from that it's an exact replica of the ones we gave our beloveds. And do you know why she has it? Because she used to dream of angel wings and rainbows as a child. She had it specially commissioned to her specific design."

Zad squinted into the distance and shoved his hands in the pockets of his dusty jeans. For long moments Gabe thought he wasn't going to acknowledge his words. But finally the other archangel turned to him, his face an inscrutable mask.

"It doesn't mean anything, Gabe. Children throughout the ages, throughout the universe, dream of rainbows and angels for no other reason than both are"—he shrugged and a mirthless smile tugged the corners of his mouth—"fantastical."

Gabe forcibly relaxed his clenched fists. Buried in the back of his mind an insistent voice of logic urged him to shut up, to leave, to forget about this insanity.

Except he couldn't let it go. Not yet.

"That's not all. When she was asleep she said—" The words lodged in his throat. How could he repeat them, after so long? To anyone, but most of all to Zad, who had also loved Eleni?

Zad's mahogany wings rippled in the breeze, and Gabe saw his muscles tense as if he struggled against the instinct to soar to the heavens.

"It doesn't matter what she said." His voice was still even but a harsh note of finality underlined every word. "She's not Eleni, Gabe. Neither first-generation Nephilim nor their descendants have souls to return to us. We've always known that."

He knew it. Had always known it. The offspring of an archangel and a human and all their descendants was eternally damned. But still the irrational hope had flared that somehow, against every possibility and despite her Nephilim heritage, his Eleni had been reborn.

It was a fool's dream, and while he was many things, he was no longer a fool. The similarity between the necklaces was a coincidence. There was no universal convergence, no karmic confluence. Aurora was not Eleni. He would never be given the chance to love her again, hold her again. Would never have the chance to save her life the way he'd been unable to save her life so many years ago.

Aurora had never said she dreamed of *angels'* wings, after all.

He glanced at Zad. "How long must we serve penance?"

"Gabe." Zad didn't look at him. "Forget about the vow we made in our rash youth. It's not a sin to love again. You're not betraying Eleni's memory."

Gabe gave a harsh laugh that did nothing to ease the fathomless despair consuming his chest. Archangels rarely fell in love and when they did it was forever. "You know we can have only one beloved. Like you said"—he flung Zad a bitter glance, the words already eating into his battered heart like foul acid—"it's only spectacular sex."

"With the right one." Zad finally turned to look at him, and Gabe gritted his teeth against the fleeting desolation he glimpsed in the depths of Zad's dark eyes. "Sex heals the soul."

AURORA STRETCHED, FROWNED and opened her eyes. Unbelievable. She'd fallen asleep in the middle of the afternoon. As reality came back into focus, so did a sense of unease. There was something she needed to tell Gabe. Something important. Already knowing she was alone in the bed, she still turned to see if he was beside her. But of course he wasn't.

She sat up, propped her elbows on her knees and speared her fingers through her tangled hair. What had possessed her to seduce him? Apart from the obvious. Which was she couldn't keep her hands to herself whenever he was near her.

A defeated groan escaped. Her number one priority was discovering a way she could return home. But, as she had feared, being with Gabe was eroding her sense of urgency.

He only had to look at her for her to forget how impossible this situation between them was. And when he looked at her with concern, when he touched her with tenderness, the thought of leaving, of never seeing him again, twisted her heart.

It was more than sex. More than lust. But she'd known that, almost from the start. And now she had to deal with the consequences of being stupid enough to fall for an archangel.

It would be so easy to simply accept her situation. She was a mortal. How could she hope to stand up to an alien species that was older than anything she could imagine?

Gabe no longer appeared to resent her presence. He had changed, too, over the last couple of days. Although she wasn't going to delude herself that he was falling for her. But at least she could imagine, or fool herself into imagining, that a future with him wouldn't be intolerable. She could stay on his island and be safe.

Isolated from everyone and everything she had ever loved or known. Becoming crippled with guilt over abandoning her parents. Growing old and decrepit while Gabe stayed forever in his gorgeous, irresistible prime. *And she would never have the chance of a family of her own.*

It was a future, but not a future she could willingly embrace. Not when she knew how fragile a person's sanity was; when she knew that even an overwhelming love like that of her parents for each other sometimes just wasn't enough.

She would focus on her self-imposed mission. It was all she could do. Find a loophole in the ancient laws governing the Guardians' rights and discover a chink in their armored protocols. Just because no one else ever had didn't mean it was impossible. Maybe no one had ever tried before. As she pushed back the covers a half-forgotten idea glimmered in the back of her mind and she froze.

The mysterious force field—or whatever it was—that surrounded Gabe's island repelled the Guardians. When she had sneaked into his office she'd wondered if it could be adapted to protect individuals.

Unsurprisingly, after discovering his true identity, the possibility had fled her mind.

But now it glowed with renewed hope, and threaded through the vision of freedom another hope blazed.

If she was protected and free to choose her own path outside of Gabe's jurisdiction, *would he still want to be with her?*

BY THE TIME she'd had a quick shower and was back in the kitchen she'd managed to convince herself it was completely possible to modify the force field to her own specifications. The only thing she couldn't work out was why Gabe hadn't thought of it right away.

And where had he gone *again*? She glanced outside and caught sight of a large timber chest. Frowning, she went onto the terrace and crouched beside it. It hadn't been there earlier. Dimly she recalled a thud, just before Gabe had launched himself at Mephisto. This must have been what he'd dropped.

Well, it was none of her business. But still she remained where she was, as if the chest contained answers to unasked questions. She trailed her fingers along the top and they slid into a concealed groove. Before she quite realized what was happening the entire top folded up on itself and disappeared down the back of the box.

Great. If Gabe came back now he'd think she was prying into his personal stuff. But much as she really *didn't* want to go through his things behind his back she held her breath and peered inside.

An eerie shiver chased over her arms, as if she had intruded into his most private of places, a sacred relic of his previous life. Whatever she'd expected to see it hadn't been a chest filled with a child's beloved toys and books and items of clothing.

She sat back on her heels and closed her eyes. She felt like the worse kind of voyeur. As if she'd wrenched open Gabe's heart and was rifling through his pain, probing into his long-buried wounds.

With a sigh she propped her elbow on the edge of the chest and looked inside again. She couldn't help herself. It didn't matter how much it hurt to know how deeply Gabe still missed his child. She needed to dig further, to discover all she could about his past. It might, in some strange way, help her understand the man—*the archangel*—he was today.

And then he materialized in the kitchen, just feet from her. Heat swamped her and she jerked back, as if that might fool him into believing he hadn't caught her rifling through his personal possessions.

His daughter's personal possessions.

He strode toward her, unsmiling and grim, and for the life of her she couldn't think of an adequate excuse to justify her behavior. He stepped over the opened chest and placed something on the table, and then sat on the chair and faced her.

Obviously he was waiting for her to say something. Her mind was scarily blank. How pathetic would it sound to tell him she'd opened the chest without meaning to?

"I pulled some strings," he said bizarrely. He continued to look at her as if he wasn't even aware of the chest between them. "And we have a new laptop."

A new laptop? She glanced at the slender package on the table, then back at him. Was he messing with her?

"Uh . . . good?" Her voice was unnaturally high and she tried clearing her throat but her heart was pounding so frantically she could hardly breathe, never mind anything else.

A frown of apparent bafflement flicked over his gorgeous features. "Yes. The last one shattered, remember?"

Aurora risked shooting the chest a doubtful glance. Gabe was acting as if it was invisible. But all *she* could see was an enormous great elephant.

"Yes." It was no good. Even if Gabe was willing to overlook the situation she didn't want him thinking the worst of her. "Look, I'm really sorry, Gabe. I didn't mean to pry. I mean, I haven't pried. I haven't looked at anything at all." She sounded guilty, defensive and completely pathetic. She knew a good half of her guilt was because of the time she really had gone through his things. And found the picture of his family.

Thank god he didn't know about that.

He shrugged as if it didn't bother him one way or the other what she'd done. "So long as you haven't lost anything I don't see why you're getting so wound up over it."

She spread her fingers across her thighs and attempted to make sense of that last odd sentence. He made it seem that the chest held no personal significance to him at all.

"Of course I haven't lost anything." Had she jumped to the wrong conclusion about the contents of the chest? Now that she thought about it, the stuff didn't even look very old. "What is it?"

"Just work related."

He said it so casually that for a moment she wondered if she had misheard him. *Work* related? He *worked*? What in the name of god would an archangel do for *work*?

"There's no need to look so staggered." Gabe sounded as if he couldn't decide whether he was offended or amused by her disbelief. "What did you think I did with my time? Endless clubbing across the universe?"

Since that was horribly close to what she had imagined, she didn't answer. But she had the feeling her red face spelled it out all too clearly.

"Thanks." His sarcasm was palpable. "Good to know your high opinion of me."

"Well, you can hardly blame me. And it's not as if you've ever told me what you do when you leave the island, is it?"

He didn't answer right away, and she got the distinct impression that just days ago he would have given her one of his arrogant glares for daring to question him. But the expression on his face wasn't haughty or dismissive. Had it really never occurred to him that she might be interested in where he went or what he did?

"It's been a while since I've told anyone my reasons for coming and going." A frown creased his brow, and she had the absurd desire to curl up on his lap and give him whatever comfort she could. Would he never be able to talk to her without seeing or thinking of the dark-haired woman he had loved so long ago?

She forced the image to the back of her mind. Why was she torturing herself with something that could never be?

"So what is it you do, exactly?" She glanced into the chest, so Gabe wouldn't see the hopeless wish in her eyes.

"I track the missing."

Whatever she'd expected him to say it hadn't been that. Even her pathetic self-pity receded and she looked up at him, entranced. The old myths hadn't got everything wrong. He really was the Angel of Mercy.

"You mean you're like a private investigator?"

The look on his face suggested he didn't think much of her comparison. At all.

"Do I look like a PI?" The disgust in his voice confirmed her suspicion. "Trust you to pick the least glamorous term."

"It doesn't matter what you call yourself. What's important is what you *do*."

He scowled as though her admiration for his occupation rubbed him the wrong way. "I don't do it out of the goodness of my heart. My fees are astronomical."

He charged? For some reason that hadn't occurred to her. Then again, she supposed he had to live, and considering he'd already told her he amassed fortunes as a hobby it shouldn't come as that much of a surprise.

"Well, I suppose that's only fair. You need to cover expenses."

God, what was she saying? He was an archangel. What sort of expenses would he incur? It wasn't as if he needed a travel allowance.

"I don't charge to cover expenses. I charge so potential clients are fully aware of the magnitude of their request."

Gabe resisted the undignified urge to shift on the chair. *He never squirmed.* But the look of unadulterated reverence on Aurora's face, far from casting a satisfied glow across his ego, irritated him.

And to make it worse he wasn't irritated at *her*.

"Oh." She sounded completely baffled. "Okay."

The fact she wasn't even questioning him further only deepened his black mood. He wanted her to question him. To push his patience to its limits. Wanted her to annoy him, to give him the excuse he needed to put her in her place. To turn his back on her.

To continue as he had done so for countless centuries.

And since when did he need a fucking *excuse* to put a mortal in their place?

"Guess," he said, torn between wanting to pull her into his arms, to hold her and forget his past, his present and eternal future, and wanting to wipe that enchanting expression from her face for good. "Give it your best shot. What do you think I demand as payment, Aurora?"

Chapter Thirty

FOR a long moment she continued to gaze at him. It was clear she didn't have a clue what he charged and thought he was crazy to expect she might. And then a shocked comprehension clouded her eyes and her lips parted as if she was having trouble processing those thoughts.

"You don't." She sounded torn between awe and horror. "Tell me you don't demand a person's soul."

"Fine." He had no idea why her disgust bothered him. Wasn't this what he'd wanted? "I don't demand a person's soul."

"But you're an *archangel*." She made him sound like some kind of benevolent god. An oxymoron if ever he'd come across one. "Only the devil demands the soul in payment."

"Define your definition of *devil*." He'd been called that and worse in his time. It was all a matter of perspective.

A frown flashed across her face as if she didn't think much of his flippancy. He resisted the urge to tell her that he was deadly serious. What did it matter what she thought?

It mattered.

He throttled the knowledge before it could fully form. But the echo remained; a haunting reminder that no matter how he denied it to Zad, his attachment to Aurora was a lot more than *spectacular sex.*

"So let me get this straight." She pushed herself from the floor and perched on the edge of the chest. "There really are souls and that's your price?" She sounded disbelieving, although he couldn't tell whether that was because she didn't believe in souls or she didn't believe he deprived people of them. *"Why?"*

Now she was asking the right questions. Now she was pushing the boundaries and by rights he should remind her of the reason she was with him. And it wasn't because they were equals.

It wasn't her place to question his judgment. Wasn't her place to make him doubt his own integrity. He owed her no explanation for his actions. So why did he have this gnawing urge to wipe the condemnation from her eyes?

"Proof." She was only a mortal and it *didn't matter* what she thought of him. "If a potential client is willing to sacrifice the possibility of ever being reborn, just to save the one they love in this life, then maybe—just maybe—the missing one is worth searching for."

"Reborn?" It was obvious she'd never seriously considered that possibility before. "Are you telling me people really do *reincarnate?*"

"Only if they possess a soul." He heard the thread of bitterness in his voice and didn't even try to disguise it. "Otherwise once you die, that's it. You're gone forever. No second chances."

She was silent for a moment, an enchanting frown creasing her brow. He rapped his fingers on the table, waiting for her further condemnation. And had no idea why he didn't just get up and get out of there.

"So you return the one they love." Aurora sounded doubtful but he was sure she understood perfectly. "And then take away the chance they may have of getting together in a future life?"

That was exactly the conclusion he wanted her to draw. She would retreat, and this strange sense of connection he was beginning to feel with her would shatter. Their relationship would be based entirely and exclusively on sex. Just as it should be.

Except the suicidal desire to leap to his feet, to drag her into his arms and tell her the truth hammered through his brain. Did she really think so little of him that she could believe he'd do that?

Despite the price his clients believed they paid, all he did in reality was wipe their minds. They retained no memory of ever having approached him, let alone what he'd done for them. But despite the rumors that he demanded not only his client's soul but also their life as payment, still the desperate sought him out.

He battened down his illogical urge. Let her believe the worst of him.

"That's right." To his disgust he sounded belligerent. As if he, an archangel, was on the defensive.

"But that's awful." Finally she sounded shocked. It was what he wanted but he derived no depraved pleasure from her reaction. "I mean, after what you've just told me about reincarnation that sounds even worse than if you just killed them outright."

"Like I said"—he offered her a feral smile but, typical Aurora, she didn't flinch—"it's the ultimate proof."

"That's ridiculous." If any other mortal—or even another immortal if it came to that—had taken that tone with him, they'd feel the full force of his ire. But instead he remained mute, and took a morbid satisfaction from her obvious distaste. "There's got to be other ways someone could prove their love was genuine. I can't believe you'd do anything so"—she hesitated, clearly struggling for the right word to describe her utter revulsion—"*extreme.*"

He'd expected a far more vitriolic adjective from her, but for some reason the way she said *extreme* stung. "What criteria would you use?" The demand issued before he could prevent it. Gods help him, did he really seek justification? "How would you prioritize which case to take and which to leave?"

The silence stretched between them, into infinity, shattering forever the fragile threads that had inexplicably woven them together. A flimsy bond he had no use for, no need of and no desire to see flourish.

With the right one, sex can heal the soul. But Aurora was not the right one. And his soul was beyond salvation.

Finally she broke eye contact and looked into the chest. She trailed her fingers over the contents as if she was clairsentient and could discover secrets from touch alone. He braced himself for her complete condemnation. Even though her condemnation meant . . . nothing.

"You would need harsh criteria." To his disbelief, he detected a thread of reluctant acceptance in her voice. Or was he simply irreparably delusional? "Otherwise I imagine you'd be swamped with requests."

He forcibly unclenched his fist. A fist he couldn't recall making. Aurora wasn't leveling accusations his way. She wasn't looking at him as if he was something unspeakable. She wasn't behaving at all the way he had envisaged.

He'd been prepared for her disgust. Had anticipated it. *Welcomed* it. But as always Aurora had caught him off guard and, gods help him, *he was relieved.*

"That's why I've never suppressed the rumors." The words were out before he could stop himself. Except the truth was—he didn't want to stop himself. Didn't want Aurora thinking the worst of him, despite the way he'd attempted to delude himself. He wanted her to know the truth because she hadn't condemned him. "What the hell would I do with a million souls, Aurora?"

When she looked up at him she had the same look on her face as when he'd first told her he tracked the missing. And this time it wasn't irritation that clawed through his chest. It was an odd sensation of . . . peace.

"You're looking for a child, aren't you?" She didn't wait for him to answer. There was no need when the contents of the chest told its own tale. "How old is she?"

"Four years old."

"Do you"—she hesitated, as if unsure how he might react to her question—"want me to help, Gabe? I'd like to. If you didn't mind."

He stared at her as a surreal sense of disbelief enveloped him. She wanted to *help* him?

No matter her good intentions her request was impossible. For a start she couldn't understand the Medan language. What possible use could she be to him?

Apart from the obvious obstacles that she had no idea what to look for, he didn't need her help. But despite that logic he acknowledged, with a sense of fatality, that he wanted her help.

Even if all her help amounted to was simply keeping him company while he sifted through endless potential evidence.

CURLED UP ON the sofa, Aurora stifled a yawn. She had no idea what the time was but it had been dark for what seemed hours. The remains of another mouth-watering meal Gabe had brought back a while ago was strewn across the floor, and he was at the other end of the sofa, focused on his laptop.

For a few moments she indulged her obsession and merely gazed at him, soaking in the glow of his hair, the sculpted perfection of his face, his total concentration on the task he'd set himself. She'd been touched that he'd accepted her offer, even if it was apparent that he didn't think she would be of any help to him at all.

But he hadn't thrown her shortcomings in her face. Instead he'd delegated the task of scrutinizing hundreds of pictorial evidence. At least for that she didn't need to be able to decipher a strange, alien language.

Except no one in the pictures looked like an alien. The small child Evalyne, whose existence was catalogued in loving detail from the moment of her birth, looked like any adorable little girl from Earth.

With a sinking sense of failure, Aurora faced the truth. She wasn't helping Gabe at all. How were they supposed to discover anything from looking at all these images? It was a total waste of time.

She picked up the next sheaf, since there was hardly anything else she could do, and gave the top picture a tired glance.

And froze.

Shivers raced across her arms and the nape of her neck. She clutched the picture, peered closer, and her heart hammered high in her breast, restricting her breathing.

"Oh my god." The words tumbled into the silence and Gabe glanced up, a frown of concentration still etched across his brow. "I've found something." She crawled along the sofa, uncaring of the pictures that fluttered to the floor. "Look. Look at what she's *wearing*."

Gabe looked, and didn't comment. She edged closer until she was practically plastered across his chest, and jabbed her finger at the relevant spot. "Her necklace, Gabe. Can't you see it? It's the *image* of mine."

"Yes." His voice was emotionless, as if her discovery meant nothing. She glanced up at him, then looked back at the picture. There, around the little girl's neck, was a replica of Aurora's own necklace. It was opened and the vibrant shimmer of rainbows and gold dust was clearly visible. How could Gabe just sit there as if her discovery meant nothing?

"Well, but don't you find that really amazing? I mean, it has to mean something, doesn't it?"

He shifted under her weight and slid one arm around her.

"Children always dream of angels and rainbows." He sounded as if he was reciting ancient knowledge. "It's of no significance."

No significance? She twisted in his arm and flattened her free hand against his chest. Against his heart.

"Of course it's of significance. My one might be a fake but what are the chances this one is, too?" Her hand cradled his jaw and she forced him to look at her once again. "Don't you see?" Why couldn't he see? "It means Evalyne is descended from an *angel*."

She felt him go rigid beneath her, coiled tension and granite-hard muscles clearly denying her words.

"That's impossible." His tone was final. "It's a coincidence. Nothing else."

Coincidence? In the space of three days she'd come across *three* necklaces identical to her own. God, she still needed to tell Gabe about that other one she'd discovered just before Mephisto had turned up.

No way was this simply a coincidence.

"Okay, I'm not saying this was made for Evalyne's mother or grandmother or whatever. Obviously we're talking generations ago here." Her fingertips trailed over the rough stubble grazing his jaw. "But the original beloved would have passed it down to her daughter, who would have passed it down in her turn, a continuing chain of endless devotion."

His hand tightened at her waist and the look on his face caused the words to dry in her throat.

"What?" His voice was oddly hushed, at odds with the savage glare on his face. "How do you know about that?"

Unease trickled along her spine.

"You told me." Just the other night, when he had first looked at her necklace. And yet for an unfathomable reason it seemed she had known that fact for so much longer.

"No, I didn't." The words were uncompromising and she stared at him, baffled. Of course he had. Otherwise how would she have known? And there was no doubt in her mind. She was right about this. "I told you your necklace was based on an ancient archangelic design but I didn't say who we gave them to or the tradition of passing from mother to daughter."

"Well, so it was a good guess." Except she couldn't shake the feeling it was so much more than a mere guess on her part. "I mean, it's pretty obvious that's what would happen, isn't it? And I'm just saying I'm positive that's what happened in Evalyne's case. She has angel blood, Gabe. I know it."

"No." There was a dread finality in his tone, but his gaze was riveted on the picture of the child. "There are no Nephilim left, Aurora."

She didn't want to disagree with him, not when it was agonizingly obvious that when he looked at the picture of Evalyne he was thinking of his own long-dead daughter. But she couldn't let it go. He had to look at this objectively.

"How can you be so sure?" Her voice was soft and once again she pressed her free hand against his chest, against his wounded heart. "You can't know for certain."

Finally he looked at her, and the sorrow of ages glowed in his eyes.

"I'm certain." There was no doubt in his voice, only ancient resignation. "Gods and mortals had children together ever since the Alphas discovered they were sexually compatible. At our most basic level all of us—gods, archangels, mortals—are made of the same stardust."

"Yes." She wasn't sure what he was getting at, but the important thing was he was talking to her about his past. Would he tell her about his own daughter? She hoped he would. Desperately. Because it would mean Gabe thought her important enough to entrust with his most precious memories.

"Our goddess, for reasons known only to herself, wasn't inter-ested in procreating with her fellow Alphas. She wanted more than that. She wanted to create her own unique species."

"The angels," she whispered, awed, despite knowing how deeply Gabe disliked his goddess. "She made you in her image." Was that how the myths went? Although admittedly, the myths had got a lot wrong.

"No," Gabe said. "Surprisingly, considering the size of her ego. She stole DNA from all the Alphas for her baseline, found this planet and experimented for millennia until she was satisfied with the outcome."

From *all* the Alphas? Without their consent? She imagined the other mighty gods and goddesses would have been furious.

"And created the angels?" Her voice was still hushed, still awed.

This time Gabe offered her a crooked smile, and it pierced right through her heart.

"Again, no. She created, for want of a better word, our cousins. You met one. Eblis."

"Oh." She could feel her eyes widening in shock but couldn't seem to help herself. "I thought he was a demon, not an angel." That would teach her to jump to conclusions.

"He is." Gabe didn't appear to notice her confusion. "There was just one problem with the demons that became apparent some time after they hit maturity. They bred like rabbits with the humans of Earth."

Chapter Thirty-one

I SUPPOSE that would be a problem," Aurora said, but her mind was reeling. Was half the Earth swarming with the descendants of demons? On second thoughts, that would explain a *lot*.

Gabe grunted, whether in agreement or not she couldn't tell.

"The problem, so far as our goddess was concerned, was her demons were spending far too much time indulging in earthly pleasures and not nearly enough in worshipping at her feet. And she loathed their offspring with a passion."

"Well, it always makes sense to blame the innocent."

His fingers caressed her waist, seemingly unaware of his action, and he shot a sardonic smile her way. "Demon spawn are many things, sweetheart, but they're never innocent." Then he gave a heavy sigh. "She banished her demons and as many of their children as she could find. Turned them loose in the universe and began Version II." His eyes narrowed. "The archangels. And this time she ensured there would be no messy distractions in the form of . . . offspring."

Chills inched along her skin at his words and at the shocking implication behind them. "She created you sterile?" But it didn't make sense. He had already admitted some archangels had children. *He* had a child.

"She thought she did." He leaned his head against the back of the sofa and gazed at the ceiling. "As we matured we, too, indulged in earthly pleasures. There was a magnificent civilization back then, Aurora. A thriving culture based on science and mathematics that had evolved over ten thousand years or more. We were the immortal ones and yet we learned so much from them."

"And this"—Aurora hesitated, not wanting to interrupt his reminiscences but unsure if she had missed something vital—"was on *Earth*?"

"In time," Gabe said, as if he had not heard her question, "it became apparent that, with the one who claimed our heart, we could have children. But despite the joy they brought us we were always consumed with guilt."

"Because you were going against the word of your goddess?"

He looked at her, frowning.

"No." His expression suggested that was the last reason he would feel guilt and couldn't imagine why she thought he should. "It was because our beloved Nephilim possessed no souls. Unlike the offspring of gods and mortals who suffered from no such curse, our children—children we loved with all our hearts—could never be reborn. We were condemned to know that because of us, our precious children were destined for one life. And one life only."

His daughter.

A hard knot of anguish filled the center of her chest. She couldn't even begin to imagine the depth of Gabe's despair. And he had existed for who knew how long, consumed with misplaced guilt.

"I'm so sorry." The words were barely audible and hardly adequate. But she meant them. With everything she was.

"It happened long ago." He drew in a deep breath, his magnificent chest expanding beneath her. "But that's the reason why Evalyne can't be descended from an archangel. We only ever procreated on Earth, and that was millennia ago. When we finally left the place of our creation and ventured into the rest of the universe we all made a vow. We would never fall again."

His words stabbed through her, but she refused to allow the devastation a foothold. She knew he didn't love her. Knew now why he could never love her. Except . . .

Something was missing. Something he still wasn't telling her, apart from the fact he had once had a daughter. A piece of his history between the time archangels had children and when they had made the decision to never love again.

But she could hardly question him on it. Not when he'd shared so much of his past with her. Not when she didn't even know why she was so convinced he'd withheld something of vital significance.

Slowly she sat up so she could face him properly. She knew he considered the matter of Evalyne's heritage closed and maybe it was. Or maybe he was just blinded by his preconceived notions.

"Gabe." She kept her voice soft, despite the overwhelming certainty that she was right and needed to make him see that. "I understand what you're telling me. But"—she hesitated, took a deep breath and plunged ahead—"there's something I want to show you. I found it earlier today, just before Mephisto turned up." *Had that really been earlier today?* It seemed like a lifetime ago. She smothered her impatience as Gabe reconfigured the laptop to accept her DNA, and she trawled through her mind, trying to recall the specific pathways she'd followed.

Gabe didn't question her, but neither did he seem especially interested in what she was searching for. Minutes crawled by as she scrolled through endless obscure snippets of information. Finally, just as panic began to nibble around the edges of her mind, she hit gold.

"There." She turned to Gabe, who still appeared lost in another world. "Look. She was abducted by the Guardians but murdered before they returned her. And she's wearing a necklace identical to Evalyne's."

He glanced at the screen, as if he imagined she was hallucinating. Within a second his focus sharpened and he took the laptop from her as he scrutinized the image with a fierce intensity.

"Shit." The word hissed between his gritted teeth, but still his gaze remained transfixed on the image before him. *"Angel blood."* He said the words as if disjointed pieces of the puzzle had suddenly fallen into place. "It can't be."

"What can't be?" She gripped his biceps, willed him to look at her. "What is it, Gabe?"

He dragged his gaze from the laptop, a wild look in his eyes. "Something one of the pirates said when I interrogated him." He sounded distracted, his attention only partially on her. "I discounted it. *Shit.*"

Nausea churned in the pit of her stomach. She'd been so focused on connecting the necklace with an angelic heritage that she'd missed a huge, obvious link.

"You don't think Evalyne's been taken by the Guardians, do you?" But even as she asked the question a dreadful certainty gripped her heart. "It doesn't mean they'll kill her though, does it? They don't usually drain their victims. . . ." The words dried in her throat as the full impact punched through her heart. "They only take the blood of the descendants of *angels.*"

Gabe jerked his head as if in denial. "There has to be another explanation. Another connection." He shoved the laptop at her and stood up. "I'm going to question Jaylar about his immortal heritage."

She pushed the laptop onto the sofa and followed him. "Let me come, Gabe."

"No. It's too dangerous."

"What are the odds the Guardians'll know where I am? We won't be that long, will we?"

"You're not coming with me."

She gripped his hand. Now was hardly the right time to broach her suggestion but she had a feeling there never would be a right time. And she needed to know, one way or the other.

"Isn't there some way you can adapt the force field that protects your island so it can protect me? Like a mobile unit or something?"

"What?" He sounded as if she had just said something completely incomprehensible.

"The force field repels the Guardians. Surely it must be possible to rig something I can use so I can be protected outside your island?"

"No."

Was that it? No discussion? "But—"

"Aurora." It was obvious he was battling the instinct to simply ignore her questions and continue his mission without her. "It's not something I can manipulate to my will. It exists, but I didn't consciously create it. I could no sooner remove its presence as I could re-create its power."

He hadn't *consciously* created it? "Then how—"

"I don't have time now." Impatience threaded his voice. "I'll be back as soon as I can."

No. He had to see that she wasn't a liability and she didn't deserve to be pushed aside. "I might be able to help."

For a moment she saw another denial glowing in his eyes. But the truth hovered between them. Against all the odds, against both of their expectations she had already helped him. How could he deny the possibility, no matter how slender, that she could help again?

Air hissed between his gritted teeth, as if she drove him to the edge of endurance.

"Stay close." Then he wound his arms around her and teleported.

·

———————

MEPHISTO FOUND ZAD at a primitive Taoist retreat hidden deep in the sacred mountains of China. He leaned against a timber support of the hut Zad had acquired and scowled at the mountainous panorama before him.

It had been millennia since he'd been so genuinely shaken. And it had taken a *mortal* to bring him to such an undignified pass.

Not just any mortal. But then, Eleni had never been *just a mortal*.

No wonder he'd been intrigued by Aurora when he'd found her in London. Somehow, something in him had recognized her true character. It explained the odd glow in her aura after Gabe had given her his protection at Eblis's club. Because her aura hadn't shown the usual glow of a mortal claimed by an archangel. Mephisto hadn't recognized the signature at all, but then again he hadn't been looking for a sign of unbreakable archangelic devotion.

But when she had stood up to him earlier, when she'd had the audacity to thrust into his mind, the image of Eleni had burst through his brain. It was so visceral that for one terrifying second he had feared for his sanity.

It wasn't possible. He'd battled with that absolute for hours. But it didn't change the fact.

Eleni had been reborn.

Zad emerged from the hut and propped himself against the other timber support. He was covered in dust and stank of whatever disaster he'd recently returned from. The silence stretched between them, as silences had often stretched between them. But this time he found no solace, no comfort, as this silence hung like a thick blanket of fog, suffocating his thought processes.

Finally he could stand it no longer.

"Demon spawn are soulless. That was ancient knowledge when we discovered Earth, right?"

Still glaring at the imposing mountain ranges, from the corner of his eye he saw Zad's profile tense.

"Right." The word was guarded. It was like Zad knew what Mephisto was about to say. Except that wasn't possible. Even Gabe, the poor bastard, hadn't guessed the truth.

"By default so were the Nephilim."

This time Zad didn't answer. Just folded his arms and unfurled his wings by the smallest degree.

"Nephilim," Mephisto said, turning to the other archangel whose expression might have been carved from marble, "could never be reborn. That's a fundamental, irrefutable fact."

"What's with the potted history?" There was an edge to Zad's voice. "Think I need a refresher?"

Molten rage pumped through Mephisto's veins. Rage and frustration that something he had believed in, had failed to question, had taken as absolute truth—*was a lie.*

"Eleni"—the name he had once been so familiar with tangled on his tongue—"is *back*, Zad."

Zad shot him a smoldering glare. "Told Gabe that, did you?" For once his voice wasn't even. It pulsed with a bitter fury.

"Gabe doesn't have a fucking clue." *And neither, apparently, did Eleni.* Mephisto clenched his fist and pounded the timber support. It splintered, and the hut sagged like a drunken goblin. "If he's lucky, he never will." He glared at Zad. "Her death almost destroyed Gabe once. He can't find out who she really is, Zad. I don't think we could bring him back from the abyss a second time."

Chapter Thirty-two

AURORA pried open her eyes and relaxed her death grip on Gabe. Teleportation might be a great way to travel but her stomach didn't appear to agree. She took a deep breath and stepped back, only to have Gabe slide his fingers through hers and jerk her swiftly back to his side.

They were in an elegantly appointed room reminiscent, more than anything, of a drawing room of an eighteenth-century French château. Except interspersed with the luxurious furnishing was evidence of super-sophisticated technology.

A tall man, who looked completely human, stood in front of them. He gave a half-bow, his gaze fixed on Gabe, and uttered foreign words. All she recognized was *Gabriel.*

Her heart sank further when Gabe replied in the strange language. It hadn't occurred to her she wouldn't understand anything that was being said.

"What are you saying?" she whispered urgently. Was it too much to hope he had the equivalent of a Babel Fish handy?

Gabe glanced down at Aurora. How had he forgotten she couldn't understand the Medan language? He knew the demons had developed technology to address this problem for their high-ranking half-bloods; those who, unlike archangels and demons, hadn't inherited the ability to process a multitude of complex languages from their Alpha forebears. If they had a telepathic connection he could instantaneously translate the conversation to her. *And there was no reason why they couldn't establish a telepathic connection.*

He pulled himself back to the present. Now wasn't the time to initiate such a connection, not when he had to negotiate around Aurora's unique brain structure.

"I'll translate." He turned back to Jaylar. "Where did your daughter get her angel wings necklace?"

"My Lord?" Jaylar glanced at Aurora as if she might hold the answer then back at him. "Her what?"

Before he could translate, Aurora pulled her necklace from beneath her top. Jaylar's focus riveted on her outstretched palm.

"Angel wings?" He sounded confused. "We've never called it such. My mother gave Evalyne a necklace much like this one on her fourth birthday. Just days before she disappeared."

"Where did your mother get the necklace?"

"My Lord, I fail to see how the origin of a necklace can have any bearing on—"

"Answer the question."

"Gabe." Aurora flattened her free hand against his chest. "Ask him if his ancestors came from Earth."

Irritation flared that she dared to interrupt him, dared to question his methods. And instantly died. Because she was right.

He relayed the question.

"No." There was a thread of defiance in Jaylar's tone, as though he expected Gabe to take issue with his denial. Then he shot Aurora another glance and appeared to reconsider his answer. "But our fam-

ily history has always hinted that our esteemed demi-goddess ancestor spent time on that far-flung planet before she settled on Medana.
The necklace originates from her. We've always believed it was
forged by the gods themselves."

Gabe translated for Aurora as he trawled through ancient memories. In those enlightened days demi-gods and goddesses had been
plentiful on Earth and many had taken archangels as their lovers.
But it still didn't answer the vital question: How had Jaylar's ancestor
been in possession of such a precious artifact?

"He's almost right," Aurora said, making no sense at all. He
stared at her and she raised her eyebrows, apparently surprised he
couldn't follow her obscure train of thought. "About the necklace.
Except it wasn't forged by gods, but by archangels."

Since he was the one who had told her that, Gabe couldn't work
out why Aurora thought she might have unearthed a great revelation.
"And Jaylar's descended from the gods, not archangels." Theoretically, the fact that Evalyne had a drop of immortal blood in her
veins should have been protection enough against the Guardians
grasping claws. But, just as the ritual to effect an archangel's protection over a mortal required the spilling of blood, a similar ritual was
needed before descendants of immune immortals were also granted
the same invulnerability. Eleni had undergone the ritual at birth, and
she and Gabe had bestowed the protection onto Helena.

But he knew how easy it would be for that knowledge to be lost
through countless ages. The gods, like the demons, had never experienced any problems with procreating and only acknowledged their
offspring when it pleased them to do so. If Jaylar's demi-goddess
ancestor hadn't bestowed the protection on her own child, or told
anyone else on Medana of it, then the knowledge hadn't been lost. It
had never been shared in the first place.

He returned his attention to Aurora and the enigma of the necklace. "There's no reason why she should be in possession of the wings."

"Unless an archangel *gave* that demi-goddess the necklace while she was still on Earth."

"That," Gabe said with finality, "would never have happened."

"Well, unless you think it likely that she stole it, then as far as I can see the only answer is an archangel gave it to her because she was his beloved."

Had Aurora lost her mind? "That's impossible." No archangel would have fallen for a demi-goddess. That was as infeasible as an archangel falling for a *demon.*

"Why is it impossible?" Aurora frowned. "It seems perfectly possible to me. And what's more I bet she was pregnant with that archangel's child before she left Earth, as well."

Gabe had the insane urge to laugh out loud. "She couldn't have been." They would have known. *Surely they would have known.* "We only conceive with our beloveds."

"Yes." Aurora sounded as if they had already established that was what had happened. "It's all making sense now, isn't it?"

The denial choked in his throat. It wasn't making any kind of sense at all. The offspring of gods were—had always been—exciting and enjoyable as lovers. But never anything more. Because at their core they regarded archangels as an anomaly of nature. A freak of creation. The physical manifestation of an Alpha goddess's insatiable ego. They were the ultimate unwanted, bastard children of the original immortal pantheon.

A fuck was one thing. Falling was something else entirely.

But Aurora knew nothing of their history. She had simply heard the facts and drawn an obvious conclusion. A conclusion that might have eluded him, purely because of his own ingrained prejudices.

Was it possible a Nephilim had been born in another galaxy, after the great destruction that had decimated Earth?

Could Evalyne—could Jaylar—be descendants of an archangel?

Aurora herself was proof that the impossible could happen. Who was he to say that bonds of eternal devotion had never existed be-tween an archangel and demi-goddess?

He looked back at Jaylar. Scanned his aura. It was clear he pos-sessed immortal heritage but after so long impossible to decipher. Gabe gripped Aurora's fingers, as if she was his anchor in a rapidly disintegrating reality.

"Do you have your daughter's necklace? I need it."

"No." Anguish seeped into Jaylar's voice. "She was wearing it when she disappeared."

So there was no way to prove whether it was genuine or simply another fake, like Aurora's. But what were the chances that, after millennia, he would come across two fakes within days?

There was nothing else he could learn here. He jerked his head at Jaylar, tightened his grip on Aurora and teleported.

Home.

AS DAWN SLID delicate ribbons of pink and peach into the bedroom, Aurora propped her head on her hand and gazed down at Gabe. He was sprawled on his front, the sheets tangled around his hips, and his back was clearly displayed.

The parallel scars that distorted his flesh, despite their obvious age, still looked as if they caused untold agony.

How had he lost his wings? Why hadn't he been able to repair whatever dreadful injuries he'd sustained? Or didn't archangels' powers of rejuvenation extend to their wings?

Slowly she trailed her fingertips along the length of his back, perilously close to the deep gash, yet not quite touching the mangled flesh. Was the accident or attack that had injured him linked with the death of his beloved?

Stupid question. Of course it was. It had to be.

A dull pain cradled her heart. It was crazy and useless to be jealous of a woman who had been dead for thousands of years, and yet here she was. Envious of a love that could never be hers.

She braced her weight on her hand and leaned over him. The juxtaposition of perfectly sculpted muscle and bronzed, unblemished skin contrasted with the brutal slashes that had once ripped open his body. Instead of detracting from his beauty the imperfection only enhanced it. And at the same time made him seem, somehow, more human and less . . . immortal.

Tenderly, she pressed her lips against the knotted seam of flesh where, unknown millennia ago, his wings had been ripped from him. Her eyes drifted shut and in her mind she saw once again their glorious majesty. Yet the flecks of gold, which had highlighted each individual cream feather, had been so pretty. Delicate, even. Not majestic at all.

She knew, in her head, she was recalling the image she'd found in his office. But in her heart it was so much more. It was as if she could remember his wings herself. Could recall the feel of him wrapped around her. The exhilaration of him holding her as they flew through the skies while such incredible power and deceptive softness imbued each individual feather.

Her head sank lower and she breathed in deep, savoring the scent of sexual satisfaction, of elusive rainforests and the tantalizing hint of ages old familiarity. Was this how it began? The gradual erosion of the memories of her previous existence, until all she recognized was life with Gabe?

She wound her arm across his back, pressed her cheek against his scar. She couldn't give up in her quest. She had to discover a way of safely returning to her life, for the sake of her parents.

But god. If not for them she would willingly take her chances in Gabe's world. Take however many years she had, before her memories faded. Because she would make those years count. And maybe, unlike her mum, this time love really would be enough.

Even if it was only one-sided.

Gabe stirred, and she shoved her foolish thoughts into a dark corner of her mind. This morning they were going to follow up on the information Gabe had extracted from the pirate he'd interrogated, but it wasn't quite morning. Not yet.

She molded her body to his as he rolled onto his back, her nipples grazing his chest as she stared down at him. His eyes were still closed, his breathing still even, and he looked like every fantasy lover she had ever dreamed of.

He was so achingly familiar. But she had known him for only four days. She had to remember that. She hadn't known him all her life, no matter how the certainty slid with insidious intent through her senses.

Still bracing her weight on one hand she trailed her fingers along his jaw, over his lips. His body was hard beneath hers and she felt his cock stir against her thigh.

Stealthily, just in case he really was still asleep and not faking, she slid over him and trapped his hips between her knees. Palms spread on his chest she sank onto him and delicately caressed the length of his rapidly thickening cock with her damp sex.

Her clit ached with the delicious friction and she pressed down harder, tremors of pure delight racing straight into her trembling womb. She wanted him inside her, filling her, possessing her, but she wanted to prolong this moment of anticipation. The heady sensation of having Gabe, her beloved archangel, powerless beneath her while she tormented him with sensual pleasures.

A fantasy, for sure. But her lack of finesse didn't seem to matter. Because already his heart thudded with a satisfyingly erratic rhythm and his breath was anything but even.

"You finished?" His voice was low, gravelly, insanely arousing.

"What makes you think that?" Thank god his eyes were still

shut. Because she had the tragic certainty that if he could see her now, he would see just how much he meant to her.

"You stopped." He finally cracked open one eye, long lashes concealing his expression from her. "I thought I should check. In case you needed some help."

Slowly she slid down his length once again, her nails digging into his rigid pecs. "Think I can manage."

His hands cradled her breasts, but his eyes meshed with hers. Slowly he slid his hands along her body, and everywhere he touched ribbons of flames ignited and smoldered beneath her sensitized skin.

"After last night I thought you'd sleep in." His voice was uneven and he palmed her bottom, his grip hard and sure. "I was counting on you sleeping in."

She bared her teeth, leaned into him and gently rubbed the tip of her nose over his. He had done that to her only once, and she never had to him. And yet the gesture seemed so intimately familiar.

"I know you were." After they'd finally got to bed—and she doubted it had been more than three or four hours ago—he'd ravished her. No other word for it. But the way she felt right now, anyone would think she'd been without sex for years. "But tough luck. I'm going to the Fornax Galaxy with you today whether you like it or not."

His fingers slid under her exposed bottom and trailed with tantalizing promise toward her aching clit. She panted into his face and raised her hips, and with a grin of triumph Gabe cupped her wet pussy.

"We'll see." He teased her swollen lips, dipped inside her slick sheath, and a moan of frustration rasped along her throat. They would see, but she had no intention of discussing it now.

She kissed him, open-mouthed, ravenous and demanding, and his grip on her butt tightened as his fingers penetrated deeper. *But not deep enough.* She wanted more, needed more, and only his magnificent cock would satisfy.

He massaged her tender flesh, probing deeper, angling his penetration and she squirmed, her teeth ripping his lower lip. He growled, a primal sound that vibrated in her mouth and through her veins, heightening the need and fueling the desire. The taste of his blood flayed her reason.

Her muscles contracted around him but still he probed, still he massaged with erotic intent. She hissed with rabid frustration against his bloodied lip and surged upward, shuddering with pleasure as his fingers dragged against her trembling channel.

"Are you sure," she gasped as she sank slowly onto his engorged cock, "that you're not some kind of sex god?"

His grin was feral. "I'll be your sex archangel if you want me to."

"I'm serious." With agonizing deliberation she lowered herself another inch onto his shaft. "I only have to look at you and I want to jump on you and screw you senseless."

He snorted with laughter and his cock shoved further inside her, a delicious sensation of penetration and possession. She tensed her muscles around him, squeezing him tight, and thrills pulsed through her at the way he gritted his teeth as if she pushed him to the very edge.

"I'm happy to say"—he sounded as if every word caused untold pain—"the feeling is mutual."

Palms spread on his chest she pushed herself up. Kneeling on the bed, imprisoning his hips, her calves cradled his thighs as she looked down at him.

Bronze flesh, taut muscle and a face that could make . . . gods weep. Slowly she raised her hips, felt him slide from her embrace. And then she sank back down again, quivering at the sensation of how completely he filled her. As if they were two parts of the whole. As if they belonged together.

The thoughts fluttered through her mind, silly and romantic, yet utterly compelling.

He bucked beneath her, spurring her onward. The breath rushed from her lungs as his size expanded her tender flesh, as he filled her body and heart and soul. Intermingled, they became one, and she couldn't feel where she ended and he began because there was no divide.

There had never been any divide.

As she convulsed around him, as he came with brutal ferocity within her, his arms encircled her waist and he ground out words in his strange language. Words she couldn't understand but that captured her heart, regardless.

For eternity.

Chapter Thirty-three

SPRAWLED on Gabe's chest, Aurora listened to the comforting thud of his heart as it gradually slowed its erratic thunder. He held her close, one arm around her waist, his other hand curled around her shoulder. Did he fear she might try to escape?

She pressed her lips against his damp skin, closed her eyes. She had to stop imagining his every gesture meant so much more than it did. She was the one who feared he might escape. And her heart would never recover.

Dawn had broken and the sun had risen. Any moment Gabe would shatter this tranquil interlude and there would be no time for her questions. She snuggled more securely against him, smiled when he merely tightened his embrace. As if abandoning this cocoon of serenity was the last thing on his mind.

"Gabe." She traced her fingertips over his impressive biceps. "What's that language you sometimes speak?"

She felt his surprise vibrate through his body. It was obvious that was the last question he imagined she might ever ask.

"It's unknown on Earth nowadays." His fingers played with her hair, seemingly unaware of what he was doing. "It eventually evolved into what's now referred to as archaic Sumerian."

Eventually evolved? Archaic Sumerian was one of the oldest languages ever discovered. But Gabe was referring to a civilization that had existed further back in the past. A civilization she knew nothing about.

The civilization he had mentioned when he'd told her how Evalyne could not possibly be descended from an angel.

"What happened?" Her voice was scarcely above a whisper. "Why haven't we discovered any archaeological evidence?"

Still he didn't push her away. But instinctively she felt his mind recoil, and beneath her, his muscles tensed as if readying for battle. She squeezed her eyes shut, cursed her tongue. But still couldn't regret her questions. If he couldn't share his past with her, she could forget all of her half-formed dreams of some kind of future together.

"Traces did survive. But mankind chose to ignore their history. As far as humans are concerned, nothing of importance happened on their planet more than five thousand years ago."

She crossed her arms over his chest and gazed down at him.

"Are you saying we've missed something? That a great civilization flourished during that time?"

"No. Five thousand years ago humans were back to scrabbling in the dirt." He sounded grimly satisfied by that fact. "I'm talking about the end of the last so-called Ice Age, Aurora. That was when we discovered Earth. That was the true golden age of technological advance and enlightenment."

For a horrible moment she thought he was mocking her. But he looked deadly serious.

"But"—she cleared her throat, tried again—"people were hunter-gatherers then, Gabe."

His hand trailed from her shoulder and gently cupped her face.

As if she was something fragile. Precious. This time she didn't even bother smothering the thought. Because, no matter how improbable, deep in her heart she knew Gabe did think she was something precious.

If she was still nothing more than a toy to him he wouldn't be laying here, suffering her questions. He wouldn't be trying to explain an impossible past to her. He would have dismissed her, the way he'd dismissed her concerns and opinions on the day they'd first met.

"Yes, that's true. For the most part."

His agreement threw her, and she frowned, completely confused. "The most part?"

"Eleven thousand years ago," he said, "there was a vast continent where the culture was rich and diverse. That's where we made our playground. The scholars of that time were our teachers, our lovers. They taught us about the stars and the celestial cycle of the Earth."

Enthralled, Aurora stared into his mesmeric eyes. They were glazed, as he recalled living in that far-off time, in that fantastical land.

"Our goddess was fine with this. At least we weren't polluting the human gene pool with countless offspring." This time his smile was bitter. "She'd got some serious shit from the other Alphas over her *experiments*. They would have ripped her apart if they'd been able to. Not only were we created from them all, but she'd given us wings. The ultimate indulgence."

"They were *jealous*?" *Gods* had been jealous of *archangels*?

He shrugged, like it didn't matter and he no longer cared. "They rarely interacted with us. We were content to remain on Earth. And eventually some of us discovered love."

"And your goddess wasn't fine about *that*." It wasn't a question, and when he gave her a probing look she knew she was right.

"She didn't like it." He paused, frowned, and for a moment she had the certainty that he wasn't going to tell her anything more. She brushed her lips across his, a butterfly kiss, and hoped with all her heart he wouldn't stop now. "But she tolerated it."

"Because as far as she was concerned," Aurora said, the words spilling from her before she could stop herself, "the love of an archangel for their beloved was nothing compared to the eternal love you bore for her."

The look of shock on Gabe's face mirrored the shock ricocheting through her chest. *Where had that come from?* Why was she so sure that she was right?

"Something like that." His voice was guarded, and it was obvious he was having trouble processing her last comment. That made two of them. "We never chose to enlighten her."

A chill inched along Aurora's arms, not at what Gabe had just said. But at what he had left unsaid.

"But souls are reborn." Her voice was hushed as the implication thundered through her mind, illuminating dark fragments of long forgotten dreams . . . *memories?* "She thought the love died when your beloved died. She didn't know you waited for them to come back to you."

His hand tightened around her waist and his intense gaze roved over her face, searching for something. Something elusive; something unimaginable. Her breath stalled in her throat as his eyes darkened and then he slowly blinked, and the moment shattered.

"It never occurred to her we were capable of undying devotion for a mere human. Never crossed her mind that despite her best manipulations and sacred edict, a few precious Nephilim had been born."

Dread scraped a skeletal claw along her spine. She had wanted to know what had happened that had made archangels decide to never love again. But now that it seemed Gabe was willing to tell her she realized she didn't want to know.

Was afraid to know.

But Gabe was looking at her, waiting for her to ask the question. He wanted her to ask . . . so that he could continue.

Did he believe that by sharing the past with her, the magnitude of his misplaced guilt might diminish?

She had no choice. She was being ridiculous and melodramatic because no matter how awful whatever had happened was, why would knowing it make her afraid?

"What did she do?"

He didn't answer. Just continued to look at her, as if he had no idea who she was or why she was in his bed. But he didn't release his possessive hold on her, either.

"Why am I telling you all this?" He speared his fingers through her hair, held the back of her head. "I've never told anyone of my past. Why you? Why now?"

"I don't know." She mirrored his actions, spearing her fingers through his hair and cradling his temple. "Why not?"

For long moments he didn't reply. She could feel the internal battle that raged in his mind—the desire to confide and the millennia-old conditioning that demanded eternal silence. But he hadn't entered her mind. They weren't sharing thoughts. And for once there was no fear hovering on the edges of her consciousness that an insidious insanity lurked.

She just knew.

Finally he released a heavy sigh, and she knew he'd come to a decision. One that might damn him forever.

"She walked the Earth. To see for herself why we were so enamored. She found those willing to betray our secrets. They told her of the Nephilim, told her how those archangels who fell waited, life after mortal life, until their beloved was reborn."

A terrible certainty gripped her. If so many myths and legends had basis in truth, then so too did the stories of the great flood that had all but wiped out humankind.

And the heavens opened and the seas rose and escape was denied to all those with tainted blood.

It was more than a thought. It felt like ancient knowledge that she had always known but never before been able to access. Images of tsunamis, of erupting volcanoes, of devastating earthquakes saturated her mind in terrifying detail. She clutched Gabe's hair, anchored herself in this moment. She was not recalling those events. She was only imagining how it must have been.

"So she"—her mouth was dry, her tongue felt like it didn't belong to her—"sent the flood to wipe out everything?"

His hard grip on her head eased and he let out a long breath. It sounded almost like regret.

"It's ironic how the flood lives on in the collective consciousness." His hand curled around the back of her neck, a potentially threatening gesture, which conversely brought her odd comfort. "Yet the reasons behind it have been lost to antiquity. No, she didn't send the flood. No single deity sent the flood, Aurora. The geophysical upheavals of that time were simply a part of the natural cycle of the Earth's clock."

She relaxed her panicked grip on his hair. That made a lot more sense to her than the vindictive actions of a spurned goddess. Or god, if it came to that.

But Gabe loathed his goddess. And the only reason she could imagine for such hatred was because that Alpha Immortal was, in some way, responsible for the death of his beloved and daughter.

"What did she do, Gabe?"

"There was originally another planet in this solar system," he said, seemingly oblivious to her question. "The ancients called it Nibiru. But it was more than a planet. It was the City of Angels where we'd been created, where our goddess occasionally resided. More important, it was immune to the natural forces that govern any normal planet."

They would be safe on Nibiru. Although many would perish on Earth, with the exodus enough would survive to start again, to re-create their society, to pass on their knowledge to future generations . . .

The thought wasn't hers. Couldn't be hers. Yet it was so powerful, so absolute. *What was happening to her?* Or was this how it had started with her mother? Not the gradual fading of her old life but the certainty that she had lived *another life* altogether?

"You wanted to save the people. By taking them to your city."

"We couldn't have saved them all." It was obvious that memory razed his soul. "You have to understand something. Their civilization was ancient long before we discovered their continent. They had studied the heavens for millennia, passing on their knowledge from one generation to the next. They'd unearthed the past and with mathematical precision gained foreknowledge of the future. The apocalypse would come."

He said it with such finality. As if it was a foregone conclusion and nothing could prevent it.

"But they tried to find ways to stop it?" Any advanced civilization would try to prevent the destruction of their way of life if they possibly could.

"No. That was never their design. It was carved into their consciousness that they wouldn't all survive. It had been an accepted facet of their future for countless generations." He dragged in a heavy breath. "I'm not saying they were happy about it. But they channeled their energy into preserving what they could. What could be passed down through the ages to descendants far in the future."

But nothing had survived. No one had ever heard of this great, doomed civilization. A strange sorrow pierced her at that forlorn knowledge.

"What happened?" she said softly, although a part of her didn't want to know. And again the fear gripped her. A fear she didn't quite understand but still couldn't ignore.

"We offered the chance of escape." A trace of bitterness edged his voice. "For a select few thousand. But the plan leaked and it was like a dam exploded. While the people had accepted their predestined fate and the odds of perishing, they absolutely weren't ready to accept the kind of intervention we offered. Not when we couldn't offer it to everyone."

"They turned against the Nephilim," she whispered, unsure why she was so certain of that, only knowing she was right. And that vilification of the archangels' beloved children had survived countless ages, twisting something that was pure and beautiful into a monstrous travesty of the truth.

"And sold us out to our goddess." His voice was eerily calm. "We didn't discover this until afterward. If we'd known we would never have answered her call. Never have returned to Nibiru. Never given her the chance to neutralize us while on Earth the continental plates shifted and magnetic poles reversed. While life as we had known it was all but annihilated."

Chapter Thirty-four

SILENCE vibrated in the air, but frantic fragments of disjointed thoughts—*memories?*—tumbled through her mind.

She had always known he had not forsaken them . . . He had not willingly severed their telepathic link . . . One day she would return to him . . .

They were crazy thoughts. A sign of desperation. Was she trying to fool herself that she, Aurora Robinson, had in a previous life been Gabe's *beloved?*

It was dreadfully seductive. How easily she could let herself believe it. But it was a fantasy. Not real. *She would not allow her reality to blur.*

Tenderly, she cradled his face between her palms, their bodies meshed as if they were one. He had promised to save the ones he loved, and been unable to keep his word. This was the crux of Gabe's guilt, and he had never been to blame. How could he have known the extent of his goddess's wrath?

No wonder he loathed her.

"And when it was over"—she hesitated, wondering if she should continue to probe—"she released you?"

"No." His voice was devoid of emotion. "We rose up against her. Destroyed our City, annihilated the whole damn planet in our battle for freedom. But we were too late. Earth had reset her clock. And the human gene pool had been . . . cleansed."

"I'm so sorry." They were trite words but not meaningless. What else could she say?

He rolled onto his side, still holding her, so they faced each other.

"It was my fault. We'd long ago decided to save our own—our beloveds, the Nephilim and current lovers. But I suggested we try and preserve the nucleus of the civilization as well. If I hadn't done that then there wouldn't have been the uprising. Our goddess wouldn't have discovered our plan until we'd executed it." A trace of bitterness seeped into his voice. "Until it was too fucking late for her to do anything about it."

The Archangel Gabriel. The Angel of Mercy. The stories had been right, after all.

"It wasn't your fault." If only there was some way she could make him believe that. But after so many centuries what hope did *she* have of changing his conviction?

"I've never forgiven humans for how they betrayed us to our goddess. For how, as the Earth shifted around them, they turned their wrath on our Nephilim and murdered them." He offered her a mirthless smile that ate into her heart. "After the destruction of Nibiru we avoided Earth. Utilized our Alpha powers and explored the universe, which was something we'd never been inclined to do before then."

"But you live on Earth." The words slipped out before she could stop them and she bit her lip. "I mean, you came back to Earth . . ." Her voice trailed into silence. Not because she didn't know what to say, but because she was unable to say it.

"It's our curse." He sounded resigned. "No matter where we travel or make our so-called permanent base, the Earth calls to some primitive core deep inside us. Whether we live here or not, few of us can stay away for more than a few decades or so. Ironic, isn't it?"

It wasn't ironic. She knew why he couldn't stay away. Mentally she steeled her nerve. "It's because you all know, even if it's only subconsciously, that one day your beloveds will be reborn."

This time the silence was so profound she thought she'd pushed him beyond his limits. She threaded her fingers through his, willed him not to turn from her or tell her it was none of her business. It didn't matter how every word pierced her heart. All that mattered was Gabe speak of his past in the futile hope that, somehow, it would help heal his wounded soul.

"The knowledge isn't subconscious." He raised their joined hands and focused on their entwined fingers. "We knew it would take millennia for the human race to recover from the brink of extinction. Knew that, eventually, the odds would once again be in our favor." Finally he looked back up at her and the raw despair in his eyes caused her heart to compress in hopeless empathy. "But the odds have never been in our favor, Aurora, because we were never meant to exist. Humans were never supposed to fall in love with us. We watched our beloved Nephilim die, knowing our blood in their veins damned them for eternity. How could we put the ones we loved through that, life after life? How could *we* keep going through that, again and again?"

Her throat ached with unshed tears for all that he'd told her. And all that he had not. And again the seductive, insidious feeling of having known Gabe in another time haunted her. She tried to suppress the thought because it wasn't just crazy it was insensitive, but she couldn't help it.

He'd just told her that, in time, their loved ones would be reborn. Aside from encroaching madness how else could she explain the flashes of knowledge she'd experienced? The eerie certainty that she had once understood the language of the ancients; that she had once known the beauty and splendor of Gabe's incomparable wings as he wrapped them around her?

Was it possible she was the one Gabe had loved so fiercely, so long ago? He had irrevocably lost his daughter, but wouldn't he embrace the chance of loving his child's mother once more?

"But what about you?" She pressed his knuckles against her breast. Against her heart. "Have you never searched for your beloved?"

"No." There was a chilling finality in his tone and shivers scuttled over her exposed flesh, as if the temperature had just dropped several degrees. Why had she asked him that question? Because a terrible certainty clutched her. *She didn't want to know the answer.* "Eleni— my beloved—wasn't a full-blood human like most of the beloveds. She was part Nephilim—descended from an archangel. Our beloveds were our soul mates but because of her heritage Eleni didn't possess a soul. If she had I would have searched for her until the end of time."

Pain enveloped her heart, the sensation so heavy and all-encompassing it compressed her lungs, crushed her chest. Fragile hopes and elusive dreams crumbled into dust, as if they had never existed.

Because they never had existed outside of her frighteningly vulnerable mind.

She had never loved Gabe in a previous life, because his beloved had been part angel. And although he couldn't search for Eleni, he would never stop loving her until the end of time.

"I know what you're thinking." He stirred restlessly, and panic clawed through her, magnifying her pain. He couldn't know what she'd been thinking. *Please let him not have guessed the stupid hopes she'd harbored.* "Eleni wasn't immortal. She would have died eventually and there would have been no hope of us ever being together again. I know that. Always knew it. But she was taken before her time." His fingers tightened around hers, willing her to understand. But she did understand. He didn't have to try and justify his love to her.

She envied that love. And knowing how deeply he adored Eleni only made her, masochistically, love him all the more.

"Nephilim, even when their blood is diluted by generations as Eleni's was, still lived longer than pureblood humans. We could have had a thousand years or more together. Not long, not for me, but longer than we had."

She closed her eyes against the bleak expression that clouded his eyes, against the hollow knowledge that this was all he could ever give her, and kissed his knuckles. It wasn't enough, but maybe it was enough to know that once he had been capable of a love she had only dreamed could exist. And maybe it was enough to know that she, too, was capable of such love.

For her beloved, damaged Archangel of Mercy.

Chapter Thirty-five

DRESSED in long black pants, leather boots and black top, Aurora figured she looked the part for a trip into a pirate's lair. Not that Gabe was any more willing about taking her to the Fornax system as he had been last night but at least he'd stopped arguing. They were sitting in the kitchen, facing each other, and now he was painstakingly initiating telepathic contact with her.

Unlike the day they'd met, when his intrusion had been the equivalent of a casual glance, this time he was penetrating inside her mind. It was electrifying and utterly erotic, although by the tortured frown of concentration on Gabe's face he was totally missing the sexual connection.

She clamped her lips together before she said anything that might incriminate her. For sure, she knew the brain was the most erogenous zone of the body but for god's sake, it was almost impossible to sit still when every nerve ending trembled on the precipice of orgasm.

"Am I hurting you?" He ground the words between his teeth. He gave the impression he was in physical pain. "I'm going as slow as I can. Your brain is beautiful."

For a second she gaped and then an incredulous laugh escaped. "Okay, and now I've heard everything." She trailed a finger along his jaw. "No one has *ever* told me that before." What's more, Gabe meant it literally. For some reason that was even more of a turn-on.

His frown intensified, as if he didn't appreciate her levity. "I don't want to inadvertently damage you. I have no idea how deep inside your brain your protective network penetrates."

And until she'd met Gabe she had no idea she'd possessed such a thing. Did her mother even know about it? Or was it such a part of her people's biology that it was hardly worth commenting on?

Gabe bit out a curse in his ancient language and reared back. Alarm streaked through her and she grabbed his hands and pulled him back toward her. "What's wrong?" Had he discovered something terrible lurking inside her brain? "What happened?"

He let out a frustrated grunt and jerked his head in denial. "Nothing. Just had a message from Zad—another archangel. He's at the beach and on his way here." Gabe sounded disgusted. "Talk about crap timing."

Had Zad turned up to continue what Mephisto had started? She never had told Gabe everything the other archangel had said to her. Mainly because she had no idea what he'd been going on about. But clearly, he had meant *something*. And hadn't, as far as she could make out, told Gabe.

From the corner of her eye she saw a figure emerge from the edge of the forest, and she followed Gabe onto the terrace. He threaded his fingers through hers and pulled her to his side, a blatantly possessive gesture. It was as though he was expecting a less than benevolent exchange with the approaching archangel and didn't want there to be any misunderstanding as to her status.

Although what, exactly, that status might be she wasn't sure.

Trepidation fluttered in her chest as Zad drew nearer. She didn't know why she was so nervous. Zad was hardly likely to try and fry her mind when Gabe was right by her side, was he?

"Zad." Gabe didn't sound overly friendly. "Caught me at a bad time. I'm running late."

Mesmerized, Aurora stared at Zad as he came to a halt by the edge of the terrace. His mahogany wings were coated in fine dust and were ragged around the edges as if he'd just escaped from a falling building. He was dressed casually enough in black jeans and shirt but understated power radiated from him, as tangible as a living entity.

Oddly, she found that thought comforting.

"I was passing," Zad said, his voice deep and melodic, and Aurora still couldn't tear her gaze from his dark eyes. "Thought I'd stop by."

She felt tension spike from Gabe. He clearly took exception to the way Zad hadn't yet taken his intense stare from her. But unlike the way Mephisto had looked at her, there was nothing predatory in Zad's gaze. He looked at her as if he was *seeing her.*

What a crazy thought. She blinked a couple of times to shatter the moment, and thankfully Zad finally transferred his attention to Gabe.

"Like I said." Gabe sounded a little defensive, although Aurora couldn't think why. "I have a date with Kala. You know how she is if kept waiting."

Was Kala the pirate they were scheduled to meet? She'd better be.

"Not personally." Zad shot Aurora another glance before returning his attention to Gabe. "Don't let me keep you. I'll stay here and entertain your guest."

In the same second that Gabe shoved her away from Zad, Aurora realized there was no sexual undertow in the other archangel's words. He meant, literally, he would entertain her while Gabe was gone. And the weird thing was she was almost tempted.

"No need." There was a definite edge in Gabe's voice. "Aurora's coming with me."

"You're taking a human to the Fornax Galaxy?" Zad's voice remained even but Aurora could feel the fury vibrating beneath each word. Fascinated, she glanced between Zad and Gabe. What was going on? Why did Zad give the impression he was concerned about her welfare when he'd never even met her before? And equally, why wasn't she irritated by his interference?

"She's under my protection." Gabe was obviously irritated enough for the both of them, if the glare he was directing at Zad was any indication. "*No one* touches her."

Neanderthal or not, there was no denying the jolt of pleasure that seared her chest at his blatant declaration of possession. Although why he felt the need to stake his claim to Zad she couldn't imagine. If *she* knew Zad had no interest in her sexually then why on earth didn't Gabe?

Zad turned to her and held out his right hand, palm up. His gaze meshed with hers and his challenge was blatant.

"Zadkiel," he said.

Gabe's grip on her right hand became painful. His message was obvious.

But he didn't own her. And while she had no idea what Zad was up to, she was absolutely clear on one thing. Gabe was completely wrong if he thought Zad wanted to seduce her.

She placed her left hand on top of Zad's. "Aurora Robinson."

Briefly, he squeezed her hand before he stepped back and turned to Gabe. Who looked murderous.

"Occasionally," Zad said, "I have been known to be wrong. But whatever the truth is, any mortal woman who defies you has my blessing."

Gabe growled. Zad unfurled his wings and took another step back.

"Let her in, Gabe." Was that a command or a plea? And what the hell did he *mean*?

She watched, awestruck, as Zad soared into the sky and disappeared. And then she turned to Gabe, who was glowering at the distant forest as if he'd like to incinerate it.

"Who *is* he? What did he mean?"

"You know who he is." Gabe sounded pissed. "The Archangel Zadkiel."

"No." She frowned at his obtuse attitude. He knew she was asking for more than Zad's name. "I mean, who *is* he?"

He transferred his glare to her and she was certain he wasn't going to answer her. She folded her arms and glared back. After a moment his expression transmuted from frustrated anger into something that looked like disbelief.

"Why do you defy me at every turn?" It wasn't a threat. He sounded as if it was a revelation that not only she dared to defy him, but he'd not struck her down long ago for doing so.

"I don't know." She decided she might as well be honest, since the look of bemusement on his face had dissolved her flare of irritation at his attitude. "It just comes naturally."

For a second she thought he was going to take issue with that comment. And when she thought about it, it *was* hard to believe that she treated Gabe like a regular human man. She doubted she'd forget his immortal status if he still possessed his wings. Yet would it really make that much difference? No matter how she should behave in the presence of an archangel, he'd still be the same to her however he looked.

Finally he let out a measured breath, clearly deciding to let the matter go. Probably because he couldn't figure out the answer any better than she could.

"Zad was the first archangel to fall. Centuries before any other of us did. Zad and his beloved"—Gabe hesitated for a second, and a ghostly finger of presentiment trickled along her spine—"were Eleni's distant ancestors. Eleni was almost the last of Zad's direct bloodline. He adored Eleni."

GABE WOUND HIS arm around Aurora and teleported to the largest planet in the seventh system of Fornax, directly into the outer sanctum of Kala's personal penthouse suite. It wasn't strictly protocol, but it effectively bypassed the numerous security measures set up to block a multitude of lesser beings from entering the building. The female guard who gave him a piercing once-over was a high-grade half-blood demon and didn't appear impressed with his arrival.

"The Primus is expecting me." He tightened his grip on Aurora's hand and hoped that, for once, she'd do as he'd asked and keep her mouth shut while they were here.

"Wait here." The guard flicked a disinterested glance at Aurora and her lip curled in clear affront that he'd dared to bring a mere human, uninvited.

He still couldn't believe it himself. He'd fully intended to leave her behind but Zad, damn him, had forced his hand. As soon as the door swished shut behind the guard Aurora let out a ragged breath.

"This isn't quite what I was expecting." Her voice was scarcely above a whisper. "I was imagining the pirates would live in a dodgy dive somewhere."

He completed his third scan of the room since arriving before looking at her.

"Don't, under any circumstances, refer to Kala as a pirate." Gods, when had he ever given Aurora the impression Kala was a pirate? "She's third-generation pureblood demon and doesn't let anyone forget it."

"Oh." For one misguided second he thought she was going to leave it at that. "So, I don't really understand. What's the connection between the demons and the pirates?"

He swallowed a groan of frustration. Aurora really picked her moments.

"When the demons were banished from Earth, a lot of them ended up in the Fornax Galaxy. So too did a lot of their half-blood descendants—those who survived the initial banishment, that is." He attempted to psychically penetrate the inner sanctum, to discover what Kala was playing at by keeping him waiting. His mental probe bounced off the wall and exploded in his mind, like deadly shrapnel. He gritted his teeth and struggled to remember what he'd been saying. "But over millennia the chasm between the demons and those they considered unworthy of acknowledging as their descendants widened. Remember I told you they breed indiscriminately? They only claim parentage if the offspring is exceptional. Most of the time demon spawn is left to its own devices." If demons, like archangels, were able to procreate only with the one they loved would they also cherish every child? "The crème of the hierarchy spread throughout this Galaxy, conquering worlds populated by primitive mortals. Their abandoned descendants, for the most part, merged into the mortal population. But a segment carved out lucrative careers in piracy."

Her eyes widened in comprehension and her lips parted as another inevitable question formed in that irresistible brain of hers. But the door to Kala's inner sanctum swished open, and the guard beckoned with one autocratic jerk of her head.

Twilight slanted through the faceted glass wall that gave panoramic views over the impressive sky city, bathing the luxuriously appointed room in a surreal glow. Kala, tall, sleek and demonically beautiful, stood in front of her desk, arms folded, pale gold wings partially extended. She always confronted him that way. Flaunting their haunting beauty, the cream highlights threading through the gold in a perfect inverse of his own long lost wings.

For the first time the sight didn't make him want to demolish something.

"Primus Kala." He inclined his head in a gesture of greeting, acknowledging her rank.

"Archangel Gabriel." She flicked Aurora a glance. "I see the rumors are true. You are ensnared by a human female." Chilly amusement tinged her words. "How quaint that you felt the need to bring it with you."

Gabe refused to rise to the bait despite the fact Kala had deliberately used the one language in the universe that Aurora could understand. He wanted answers from Kala and he'd get nothing if he pissed her off.

"I've heard there's a pirate tribe based in the Seventh System who trade in minors from the Andromeda Galaxies. Heard any of *those* rumors?"

Kala didn't rise to his bait, either.

"Those that specialize in minors have no need to raid the Andromedas. We have plenty of our own ripe for harvesting in the lesser Sectors."

Aurora made a choking sound and her nails dug into his hand. He tightened his grip, a silent warning to bite her tongue. She was under his protection but they were in Kala's jurisdiction, and if Aurora annoyed the demon it was doubtful Kala would give a shit about ancient protocols.

He hadn't been giving a shit about them just lately either.

"My intel was clear." At least, Eblis had been clear that pirates from Fornax had been discussing a solar system located in Andromeda. His informant who'd named *this* planet had been virtually incoherent with terror and hadn't categorically stated anything much that made sense. But fortunately Kala was unable to penetrate his mind, just as he was unable to penetrate hers.

"Your intel," Kala said, "is faulty."

"If the Higher Councils in the Andromeda Galaxies discover the trade they'll turn Fornax inside out."

"There is no trade, Gabriel." Kala rolled her shoulders and her wings expanded a fraction more. "The dickless wonders who rule the Andromedas would stand no chance against Fornax. And they know it."

"But this isn't any ordinary child, is it?" Aurora said. Damn, she just couldn't help herself, could she? Fortunately Kala completely ignored the interruption, acting like Aurora's outburst was as meaningful as a pet cat stretching.

"If you have solid evidence, by all means do share. Otherwise you know what you can do with your *intel*."

He wouldn't give her Eblis's name, but he could project an image of the pirates he'd eliminated. It was a long shot that Kala would know of them personally but her connections in this Galaxy were legion.

If there was a tribe specializing in such abductions, Kala was his best shot in hunting them down. No matter how much she despised the people of the Andromeda Galaxies, she wouldn't be inclined to go to war over something she had no personal involvement or investment in.

Unless the order had come from her direct. He wouldn't put it past her but his gut feeling was she was as completely in the dark as he was. And beneath that icy exterior she was steaming mad that something of this magnitude might be happening in the Seventh System without her spies having discovered it.

"This child," Aurora said, her voice higher than usual, disregarding the glare he shot her way, "was taken because she has angelic blood."

Great. She'd now blown to hell any hope of Kala's cooperation. No matter what tenuous connection Aurora might believe existed between an ancient necklace and recent abductions—or the insidious knot of doubt in his own heart—it had been millennia since any mortal possessed a trace of angelic blood. Kala would conclude he was pissing her about.

Kala turned to Aurora and looked her up and down as if she was a disgusting cockroach that had just landed at her feet. If he didn't appease the demon right now she was likely to liquefy Aurora's brain.

"Kala." He'd play on her disdain for humans. And deal with Aurora's inevitable fury later.

He never got the chance. Kala raised one hand in an imperial gesture, her gaze now fixed on Aurora's face. "The Andromeda minor has *angelic blood*?"

Fuck. She wasn't going to make this easy. "It's one theory we're considering."

"Yes." Aurora's voice was breathless but her conviction rang through. "She does."

"The Nephilim were annihilated in the Great Cleansing." Kala looked back at him, an unmistakable gleam of malice in her eyes. He tensed, knowing the majority of demons considered the genocide of archangelic offspring was something to be celebrated. "They haven't existed for millennia before my time." She paused, and her wings undulated in a sensual play of power. *"Officially."*

Chapter Thirty-six

OFFICIALLY? Shock stabbed through his chest at her blatant implication.

"What do you know?"

"Never been proved." Kala shrugged one shoulder. "But there's an underground cult. It goes back generations and we've never given them much credence. They're obsessed by the notion that Nephilim still survive. Fuck knows why. But if your minor really does have angelic blood, and they found out"—she paused and exchanged a significant glance with the guard who'd accompanied them—"then it's likely they risked abducting her. And if they have I'll personally hang them with their own entrails. No filthy pirate tribe goes behind *my* back."

"Not before I've interrogated them. We need the girl back."

After Kala gave orders for the cult leaders to be rounded up, Aurora stood beside Gabe as a deadly silence descended. It didn't appear to affect either Gabe or Kala but it screeched along her nerve endings like fingernails scratching across a chalkboard.

Finally, after what seemed like eternity, the guard reentered the room.

"Primus. The accused have been located." Oddly, she spoke in English just as Kala had. It appeared the demon wanted Aurora to understand exactly what was going on.

"Bring them in." Kala jerked her head at Gabe. "My jurisdiction, Gabriel. Don't interfere."

The guard, after another significant glance at Kala, handed Gabe what looked like a glittering earpiece.

"For your pet," the guard said.

Gabe's jaw tightened in obvious distaste at her being referred to as his pet, before he handed the earpiece to her.

"It's a translator." His tone implied that was a bad thing. Slightly awed, Aurora picked it up between finger and thumb. *Was this her Babel Fish?*

Ten warriors, male and female, marched in, herding a motley group of six, and arranged themselves between the prisoners and the doors.

Kala strolled toward the one who appeared to be the leader. He sank to his knees and the others followed. Kala kicked the leader in the face, and blood spurted from his shattered nose.

"Found any Nephilim lately?" She tapped her bloodied boot on the floor. Taken aback, Aurora glanced at Gabe to see how he was reacting to the interrogation but he looked as if everything was just fine.

She had to remember where she was. Kala was a demon. Obviously this was the Fornax idea of justice.

The man babbled in an unintelligible language and Aurora tapped her earpiece. Wasn't it working properly? Kala kicked him again, and Aurora heard the sickening crunch as his cheekbone splintered.

"Don't address me in your barbaric lexicon."

The man spat blood onto the floor and Aurora glanced away. She couldn't work out how she felt about this treatment. If he'd really kidnapped a small child then he deserved everything Kala dished out. But she just didn't want to witness it.

Kala appeared to be enjoying herself. Did that make the demon worse than her? Or did it just make *her* a hypocrite—wanting justice but not wanting to get her hands dirty?

"Nuh-nuh Nephilim," the man spluttered between broken teeth and bone. "Leh . . . Legend." The words were muffled but perfectly understandable even though Aurora knew, logically, he wasn't speaking a language she had ever heard before.

Kala strolled to the next quivering pirate and gripped the female's hair, jerking her almost off her knees in the process.

"We can do this the easy way," she said, sounding deceptively pleasant. "Or I can hand you over to the archangel. If he gets inside your mind there won't be anything left to salvage afterward."

All the prisoners turned toward Gabe and their eyes showed their terror. God, what kind of reputation did an archangel have to cause such a reaction? Or was it because of the Nephilim connection?

Both?

"My Lady Primus," gasped the captured female. "It's our life's work to seek out those descended from the cursed Usurpers of our forebears. To ensure justice for the wrongs against our ancestors. To stand up for—"

"If I wanted your manifesto I'd read your fucking literature." Kala pulled a glinting stiletto from her ankle boot and casually sliced the tip across the prisoner's exposed throat. A line of crimson appeared.

Involuntarily, Aurora gripped Gabe's hand and he squeezed her fingers, probably to reassure her she was safe no matter what happened. But really, was this torture necessary? Why couldn't Gabe just slide into their minds and extract the information they wanted?

Because this happened to be Kala's jurisdiction?

The prisoner slapped her hand across her throat, eyes bulging with fear, and blood seeped between her fingers. Kala wiped her blade on the woman's worn leather tunic.

"Where's the Andromeda minor?" She released the woman's hair and examined the tip of her stiletto as if searching for microscopic droplets of blood.

"We don't have her, Lady Primus." A third pirate shuffled forward on his knees and held on to the bleeding female. "For seven generations our lineages have searched for a Nephilim descendant. But it was never our intention to keep the creature. We searched by order of another."

"Another?" Kala directed her blade within an inch of the male's left eye. "Explain."

He shuddered, but didn't back off. "The Guardians."

Gabe, still gripping her hand, was by Kala's side before the male finished speaking. "You gave a child of archangelic descent to the Guardians?" His voice vibrated with incandescent fury. "You fucking piece of shit. You—"

Kala held up her hand. Incredibly, Gabe shut up. Aurora unclenched her free hand and tried to stop hyperventilating but her lungs wouldn't cooperate. She'd been right about the connection. But now, as it was confirmed, she wished desperately that there had been another reason, another answer.

"Let me get this straight." Kala sounded perfectly calm but her eyes glowed scarlet. "For seven generations your cult has been spewing the word of retribution for our demonic Fall from Grace. Right?" She didn't wait for an answer. "But all the time it was a cover while you searched on behalf of the Guardians?"

"No. We've always believed in our Word. But the blood search, yes, Lady Primus. That was for the Guardians."

Kala turned to Gabe. Her eyes were still red, her pupils slits of pure gold.

"They're yours," she said. "Destroy them now or take them back to the Andromedas. I'll issue a hunt. Not one of their followers will remain alive in any of my Sectors. You have my word. Ensure it's conveyed to the Andromedas."

Gabe released her hand. He didn't say a word, but the male who had just spoken suddenly collapsed onto his back, writhing in agony and clutching his head, foam bubbling from between his clenched teeth, blood trickling from eyes and ears.

She backed off, wrapped her arms around her stomach. The other prisoners appeared frozen, the warriors watched with avid interest and Kala appeared utterly unmoved by proceedings.

And she'd thought Gabe's method of extracting information would be less brutal than Kala's? More civilized?

He wasn't human. He had his own moral code and it wasn't hers, would never be hers. He was an archangel, and he was seeking vengeance for the abduction of one of his own.

She couldn't watch. She turned away, disgust and sorrow and a bleak despair churning through her blood at this irrefutable knowledge of how fundamentally different she and Gabe were. But did it change the way she felt about him? Could anything ever change the way she felt about him?

Didn't these pirates deserve all this and more for taking a small, frightened child and handing her over to those monsters?

From the corner of her eye a flash of violet split the room in half. She whirled around, watched in paralyzed disbelief as the jagged scar wrenched open and a familiar silvery arm slid through, enlarging the gap.

She opened her mouth, tried to call Gabe but her lungs weren't working, her throat closed up and nothing emerged but a strangled gasp.

Its body appeared. Its arm extended. And then it froze, and its silver-gray body began to dissolve as if it was some kind glamour, and for one eternal, terrifying second she saw the creature beneath. Flicking in and out of her conscious vision, as if it was in two places at once, in front of the shadow of its solid image and behind, super-imposed on her retinas and yet impossible to get a concrete grip on in reality.

But it was there, behind its mask. And waves of unadulterated loathing smashed into her, causing her to stagger, and then unbeliev-ably the creature began to retreat.

For a second she couldn't comprehend and then, without even thinking about what she was doing, she darted forward.

There was no mistake. The creature recoiled, spitting mental venom, a horrific screech across her psyche.

Adrenaline pumped through her, banishing the last straggling remnants of terror. Something had happened, something had changed. *The Guardians could no longer touch her.*

"*No.*" Gabe's roar of denial vibrated around the room, and he gripped her arm, jerked her back. She knew she had less than a sec-ond before he teleported her to safety and she pulled herself free, panting as if she'd just run the four-minute mile in full combat gear.

"They backed off." She chanced a glance over her shoulder and the rift had vanished. "They could have got me, Gabe, but it was like they changed their minds at the last moment."

"The Guardians"—Kala was clearly holding on to her temper by the flimsiest of threads—"are prohibited from my domain. That wasn't a random probe. They're searching for your pet, Gabriel."

"What do you mean, they backed off?" Gabe glowered at her as if he didn't believe her or the evidence of his own eyes. "They never back off."

"Yet they did." Kala's wings shimmered in outrage. "The question is why?"

Chapter Thirty-seven

I DON'T know." Aurora's glance snagged on the prisoners sprawled on the floor and her heart jackknifed. Had Gabe killed them *all?* She dragged her focus from the broken bodies and looked back at the archangel in front of her. And despite the evidence to the contrary that littered the floor, she saw only the man.

She would only ever see the man.

"I'm taking you home." The look on Gabe's face told her that once he had her there, nothing would induce him to let her leave the island again.

She backed up another step.

"No. Wait. Don't you see what this means? Your protection *is* working." He'd told her she had negated his protection by breaching dimensions. But clearly that wasn't the case, despite the way it hadn't held back the Guardians on Eta Hyperium. She had no idea why the dynamics had shifted but, incredibly, it appeared Gabe didn't either. "It means I can come with you into their—wherever it is they live— to rescue Evalyne."

"Is this really a *human*?" Kala sounded torn between disbelief and fascination. "It behaves like a fucking goddess. I've seen the aura of archangels' pets before but they've never looked like *this* one."

"You're going nowhere near the Guardians' Voids," Gabe said, ignoring Kala's remarks. There was a savage gleam in his eyes and a chill snaked along her spine. *What had he discovered from the pirates?* "It's too late for Evalyne. Too fucking late."

No. She wrapped her hand around his biceps, whether to give or seek comfort she wasn't sure. "They killed her before handing her over?"

"No." The word sounded like he'd wrenched it from the pit of his being. "I saw everything when I invaded that pirate's mind. They handed her over three months ago."

It was horrible and she didn't even want to imagine what terrors that poor child had been through, but why was he so sure they were too late to rescue her? "But you can't know for sure she's dead."

"A *human*," Kala said, "is questioning the word of the Archangel Gabriel and is still in possession of all its faculties? What's going on?"

Gabe bared his teeth but didn't respond to Kala's demand. He kept his focus on Aurora.

"The Voids are devastating to archangels. We can't enter and survive. If Evalyne truly possesses our blood then she died weeks ago."

"What?" Had she misunderstood? "You mean you'd *die* if you tried to rescue Evalyne? How is that possible?"

He gripped her arms, pulled her close. "Through an agonizing process of disintegration until there's nothing left." He turned to Kala. "Let me know when you've exterminated the cell responsible." And with that he teleported them back to his island.

GABE HELD ON to Aurora after they arrived home, as if by releasing her she might somehow vanish. She didn't try and escape, didn't question why his grip was so hard she'd likely have bruises later. She simply kept her arms around him, her head against his shoulder, her body warm against his.

He closed his eyes and her scent sank into his senses, a soothing balm for his outrage against the pirates. But nothing could soothe the frantic thunder in his mind or the ugly fear that gripped his heart.

The Guardians had come for her again. And he, intent on exacting justice from the guilty, hadn't been aware.

Ice shivered through his veins and he slid his arms around her, holding her so tight against his body that he could feel her heart as though it was his own. One frenzied thought pounded through his brain. *He could have lost her.* And would have lost her, if the Guardians hadn't backed off.

In that second when he'd turned, when he'd seen the violet fracture, terror had exploded through his heart. He'd put Aurora in danger by taking her with him. He wouldn't—couldn't—lose her in such a way. And bound inextricably with the terror was a soul-destroying truth.

If he lost her to the Guardians, if she died because of his negligence, the fabric of his existence would unravel.

But it was more. He knew it even as he fought to deny it. Because it wouldn't only be guilt at having failed to protect her that corroded his existence. It was the horrifying prospect of simply *losing her* that clawed through his heart and ate into his reason.

He didn't need to question why the Guardians had retreated. He didn't need to shift perspective and examine her aura in order to see what Kala had seen. He knew why the Guardians could no longer touch Aurora. He knew Kala had seen the glowing halo of love and devotion in her aura; something the demon would never have come across before. Archangels took mortals as lovers and gave them their protection, but not for millennia before Kala's birth had an archangel . . .

Fallen.

The only way Aurora could be safe from the Guardians' clutches outside his island was if she was an Immortal's beloved.

Eleni was his beloved.

There was no ancient decree written in blood, but he'd always believed archangels could have only one beloved. Wasn't that the way it should be? Archangels didn't fall lightly. Surely such a love could be given just once in their long existence?

But it didn't matter what he had once believed. Because against all the odds he had fallen again. For Aurora. And by so doing had given her the ultimate protection.

His love.

Guilt scored through him despite Zad's assurance, that by loving Aurora he did not betray Eleni. Yet at the same time a deadly resignation unfurled. Buried deep in the black abyss of his heart, he had known of this outcome from the moment Aurora had tried to save him back in Ireland.

Why else would he have put up with her endless questions and refusal to accept his authority? Why else had he told her things that he had never told another living being? It was because, at primal level, he'd recognized she was his equal.

But he couldn't tell her. Not yet. Not until he'd had time to come to terms with it himself. Telling her would force home the knowledge that she was mortal and he an archangel, and unlike his Eleni Aurora didn't even have the advantage of archangel blood to extend her fleeting, fragile existence.

Vertigo stabbed through him, vicious and raw. This was why he'd denied it. Why he hadn't wanted to acknowledge it.

Because Aurora would die, and he would once again have to endure.

Except she possessed a soul. That fact punched through him, a faint pinprick of light in a dank tunnel of eternity. *She could be reborn.* And he would search for her, life after life, eternal.

But he still didn't want her to die.

Aurora stirred and with deep reluctance he loosened his grip on her. She eased back just far enough so she could look at him and her eyes enslaved, just as they had enslaved him the first moment he'd seen her.

"How do you know about the Voids, Gabe?" Her voice was soft as if, somehow, she knew the answer to her question.

He had told her so much of his life. As his beloved, she had the right to know everything.

Even if she didn't know what she was to him. And whether she knew or not how long could he delude himself that she was anything less than the reason for his existence?

He didn't want to talk about it. But knew he must. "After Eleni and . . ." *Helena.* He should tell her about Helena but he couldn't. Because he still couldn't come to terms with her death. "After she and the others perished, I lost my mind. Rampaged through the universe. Finally ended up on an obscure planet in the Fornax Galaxy just so I could plague the hell out of an obnoxious demon called Eblis."

Her eyes widened. "Eblis?"

"I won't bore you with the details of our decades-long feud. But during this time he was involved with a mortal who had a small daughter. Eblis was besotted with the kid. Anyone would think she was his own—except demons aren't renowned for their great parenting skills."

"What happened?" Trepidation filled her eyes and he knew that she had partially guessed.

"The Guardians abducted her. It was random. They had no idea a first-generation demon watched over her and even if they did it would have made no difference. She didn't possess demon blood, Eblis hadn't given her his formal protection, so in their eyes she was fair game."

"So the ancient protocols apply to both archangel *and* demon?" The look on her face suggested that hadn't occurred to her before.

"Yes. The big difference between us was every Nephilim birth was a rare and precious gift. Whereas demons rarely fell in love and the males more often than not had no idea how many offspring they'd spawned."

"Did Eblis try and get her back?"

"He wasn't there. But I was. Stoned out of my skull as usual. This little kid—she was cute for a mortal. Seeing her dragged into their teleportation device—the violet lightning—turned my guts. I could barely see straight but I plunged after her with only one thought in my mangled head."

"To save her," Aurora whispered.

He slid his hands along her arms and threaded his fingers through hers. So much of what had happened during those early centuries after he'd failed Eleni and Helena was a drug- and alcohol-induced blur. But he remembered leaping into the Voids. He'd never forget the time he'd spent in that hell.

"I fought the Guardians for her. Not something I'd recommend. But they finally relinquished their grip and I tossed her through the rapidly shrinking fracture. Right into Eblis's arms. Then the fracture closed up and I was catapulted into the center of their cursed Voids."

"Christ, Gabe." Aurora sounded horrified. "You were trapped in there with them? What did they *do* to you?"

He knew what she was thinking. She was wrong. "Nothing. They can't touch us, remember? Old protocols. They wanted me out. I was polluting their domain but here's the thing. I refused to leave."

"But what—I thought—"

"Within seconds of entering the Voids my skin started smoldering. But that's nothing to what that place did to my wings. It was like acid seeping into the root of each feather, corroding it from the inside. Agony like nothing I'd ever imagined. And I embraced it."

Her fingers tightened around his, trying to give comfort. Did she know that just being here, listening to him, was giving him more comfort than he'd known in millennia?

"With Eblis's help, Zad, Mephisto and another archangel, Az, finally managed to track me down. It's not easy breaking into the Guardians' realm. By the time they found me I was half mad with the pain but still refused to leave. But they've always been stubborn bastards."

"But you recovered." He heard the anguish in her voice. He pressed her hands against his heart and offered her a tired smile.

"I was a mess. Not just physically. I'd gone beyond anything our archangelic powers of rejuvenation could handle. In the end they took me into the astral planes. The ultimate realm of healing and renewal."

"The astral planes healed you." Awe threaded her voice.

"It was a long shot but nothing else had worked. It took years. My soul in the astral planes, my physical body here, on this island, absorbing the healing vibes through the spiritual connection. Eventually I healed enough to return to my body but there'd been an unexpected side effect."

Chapter Thirty-eight

FOR a moment she looked confused, and then awed comprehension illuminated her beautiful blue eyes.

"This island's protective shield."

"I was like a nuclear reactor in meltdown. We didn't know it until later, but when I returned to my body the essence of the astral planes couldn't be contained in a physical entity. It flooded into the atmosphere, encasing this island. The Guardians can't ascend into the astral planes, and that's why they can't gain access to this island. But equally, it acts as an effective barrier against anyone wanting to ascend into that realm from the island." He sighed heavily. "Like I told you before. I'm responsible for the protective force field but I can't manipulate it. It just is."

She slid her fingers from his and tenderly cradled his jaw. Such a light touch, yet he could feel it deep in the heart of his being.

"But your wings . . . were beyond repair?"

His wings. Ancient sorrow surfaced but it was no longer all-consuming.

"They were gone long before I was dragged from the Void. There was nothing left to salvage. When I finally regained my senses I was bitterly glad they'd gone. They were the one thing our goddess loved above all else about us. Our glorious wings. Her own unique creation." He rolled his shoulders, felt the phantom tug of long-destroyed muscle and feathers. Yet still the dull ache did not consume. "That's how we discovered the Voids weren't archangel friendly."

Her thumb caressed the corner of his mouth. He resisted the urge to suck her inside, to finish this discussion, to try and scrub his soul of the knowledge that he had failed to save a child who was, perhaps, the last but one Nephilim in the universe. Evalyne was so small, so fragile, how could she possibly have survived more than a few days in the Voids?

"You didn't know before?" Aurora's whisper curled through his jagged thoughts, dragging him back to reality.

"Why would we? We never traveled beyond Earth. We knew of the Guardians but not through personal experience. And of course we were protected as the Alphas were protected, not because we were beloved but because our DNA was pure first-generation Immortal."

"But Evalyne's bloodline is diluted," Aurora said, and he instantly understood her meaning. Evalyne's mortal heritage might be the one thing that had kept her alive in the Voids. The knowledge crucified him. To know she might still be suffering and yet he had no way of finding her. "And now I'm protected through you."

He stared at her as disbelief thundered through his brain. Did she seriously still think they stood a chance of saving Evalyne?

"No, Aurora." His voice was harsh. He had to make her understand the impossibility of her conviction. "Dark Matter doesn't behave in the same way as the rest of the universe. It's not easy entering those vast sectors of space, and even if I did manage it, I'd still have to break into the Guardians' Voids. The chances of finding Evalyne in that endless abyss are virtually nonexistent. The only way Zad and the others found me was because the Guardians were so desperate to get rid of me they laid an energy trail. Even then it took a couple of years. Evalyne, if she's still alive, doesn't have that kind of time on her side."

"But if there was some way of pinpointing her location, couldn't you just teleport in quickly and grab her?"

Hadn't she been listening to anything he'd said?

"There's no way of discovering where she is." Frustration hammered through every word. "And even if by some miracle we could, teleportation doesn't work in the Voids. Their physics are completely alien to ours."

She pulled back, gripped his hands and there was a strangely wild look in her eyes.

"I have an idea." Her voice was breathless and he could hear the elevated beat of her heart. He stiffened, not sure what was on her mind but certain he wasn't going to like it. Why did she have to be so stubborn? Why could she never accept his word? And knew, if she did, she would not have captured what remained of his heart. "Hear me out, Gabe. When I tried reaching my mother's dimension I was in the exact place where she'd entered our world. I had the flower she'd worn on that day and I was focusing on that flower *and* the meadow of flowers she used to talk about. Do you see what I mean? I was attempting to psychically connect this world with hers."

He did see what she meant. Could it be possible to locate Evalyne in a similar way? But even as hope flared, reality crashed down.

"But that's different. Your DNA is of two dimensions. You're talking about trying to create a connection between two points in *this* universe."

"I know there's no guarantee of success. But I think there's a good chance of finding her this way."

She sounded so hopeful. But there were so many drawbacks to her plan he hardly knew where to start. "Just because you could connect with your mother's world doesn't mean you could even penetrate the Dark Matter, never mind locate Evalyne in the Voids. We know the Guardians can't enter the astral planes. It might be impossible for a connection to exist between that realm and the Dark Matter."

"It's got to be worth a try, hasn't it?"

Frustration coiled deep in his gut. "For any hope of success we'd need some kind of gateway to exist in the physical world."

"But we would have." She sounded surprised, as if she'd thought he already knew that. "The breach is simultaneous in both the astral planes and here in the physical world." Of course. Now he remembered she'd told him that before. "There's no reason why I couldn't have breached dimensions without entering the astral planes at all."

"Then why bother with the astral planes?"

Her eyes widened. Had that thought never crossed her mind before? "Well, I don't know. The idea to find my mum's dimension came to me when I was there and it just seemed the right place to attempt such a journey. I find it easy to concentrate there. Besides, I *like* the astral planes. They're . . . beautiful."

It didn't matter where Aurora made the connection. So long as she could. *Was he seriously contemplating such a crazy idea?* "Do you really think you can do this?"

"Yes. But." She hesitated for a second, and looked unsure as to whether she should continue. "It would help if I had something to focus on, something unique and precious, something to connect with Evalyne."

"There's sure to be something we can use in the chest of belongings her father gave me." What kind of thing did Aurora need? "If we're going to do this we can't waste any more time. Every second in that place could be her last."

"Yes." For some reason he couldn't fathom, Aurora sounded nervous. "The thing is I don't think there's anything in that chest that has the kind of connection I need."

He frowned, his mind clawing through the possessions Jaylar had sent. "What do you need? Whatever it is we can get it."

"That's not what I mean." She cleared her throat and he stared at her. What was she finding so hard to say? "Honestly, please believe me. I'd use mine if I thought it'd work but we both know it's only a cheap fake of the real deal."

For a second he continued staring at her and then icy suspicion inched through his veins. No. She couldn't mean that. She didn't even know about that. *What was she talking about?*

Except he knew what she was talking about. Guilt seeped from her every pore, from her every breath. But still he couldn't find the words to articulate his tangled thoughts.

"I'm sorry." Her whisper drifted through his mind, strangely disconnected. "I discovered the picture of you with your family the day I arrived. I saw your daughter wearing her necklace."

Aurora held her breath as Gabe's eyes slowly refocused on her. Her timing sucked. She'd never intended letting him know that she'd poked through his most private things. Would never in a million years have brought up the fact that she knew he'd once had a daughter.

But, although she couldn't explain it, she knew if they had any chance of rescuing Evalyne they needed that precious archangelic artifact. It was a link across time and the cosmos between two beloved Nephilim.

"She was four years old." The words were bleak and pain stabbed through her heart. *She had been little more than a baby.* "We never expected we'd have a child. Nephilim could conceive with mortals but not easily. What were our chances, when we were both cursed by the same vindictive goddess? But finally—*finally*, we held our baby in our arms. *And I couldn't save her.*"

"Because your goddess betrayed you. It's never been your fault, Gabe."

"I was sworn to protect them." Had he even heard her? Would he ever hear her, when it came to trying to assuage the guilt that corroded him? "Would've torn the universe apart to snatch them from danger. They were my beloveds. I'd have laid down my immortality for them but instead"—he gritted his teeth and his eyes glittered like raindrops bathing a fractured rainbow—"they died and I survived."

A tiny piece of her heart withered. He would never forgive himself. No matter what she said. The necklace was too precious to him. He'd never allow her to use it for something that she couldn't even prove would make a difference.

"Evalyne is only four years old." He sounded as if he was speaking to himself.

"Yes." She'd find something else to use. There had to be something in that chest. Something that called to her. Something she could get a psychic grip on.

He brushed his lips across her clenched knuckles. "I'll get the necklace."

THEY TELEPORTED TO Kala's planet, to the underground headquarters of the pirate cell that had abducted Evalyne. According to the information Gabe had extracted, this was the exact place where the Guardians had come to collect the child.

The place was wrecked, and Kala's warriors looked pissed at having to cut short their plans at total demolition. But finally she and Gabe were alone and with infinite tenderness he removed her necklace and placed his treasured one around her neck.

With a sense of awe she curled her fingers around the ancient pendant. Its shape was familiar but an ethereal vibration seemed to emanate, as if it possessed a fragile heartbeat of its own. Her breath caught in her throat and instinctively her fingers tightened as a surreal glow of tranquility washed through her.

After years of nurturing a poor substitute, she felt she had finally discovered a long lost piece of her soul.

"Do you want me to come with you into the astral planes?" Gabe's husky whisper against her ear dragged her back to the present. He stood behind her, his arms wrapped around her, and she leaned her head against his shoulder.

"No, it's okay." If Gabe was right and a connection was impossible to forge between the astral planes and Dark Matter, she'd try again on the physical realm. But one way or another she was determined to succeed. And when she located Evalyne, Gabe would reach through the gateway she created and rescue the child.

THE ECHOES OF chaos that had disturbed the astral planes the last time she'd been there had vanished. She concentrated on the precious angel wing necklace Gabe had entrusted to her, the token of devotion from an immortal to his beloved. And simultaneously focused on the image of Evalyne in her mind, anchoring her with an identical angel wing necklace.

This time no raindrop-encrusted spiderweb materialized. Instead energy, raw and primal, throbbed and instinctively she knew it originated from Gabe's necklace that she cradled in the palm of her hand. A blazing trail of starlight shot from the necklace and collided with an identical glowing trail that emanated from a place beyond her comprehension—from Evalyne's archangelic artifact.

She was aware that Gabe loosened his hold on her and moved toward the shimmering darkness that had materialized on the physical plane. Waiting for the moment Aurora's psychic energies connected with Evalyne.

Distortion took on form and the terrifying sensation of nothingness receded. And there, in a stark tomb-like chamber, was the child restrained by her wrists, hanging from a wall.

Chapter Thirty-nine

Gabe plunged into the Void and Aurora gripped the psychic connection with such fierce concentration her mind trembled. She watched him stagger toward the child and was horrified when his skin began to smolder.

He'd assured her he would be fine for the few moments it would take to rescue Evalyne. But he was wrong. He wasn't fine. *He wasn't going to make it.*

For a few agonizing seconds she continued to watch as Gabe ripped the restraints from the wall and pulled Evalyne into his arms. He turned and stumbled back toward the fracture, then fell to his knees. She heard his agonized groan, saw him lift the child and catapult her through the rift before he fell onto his hands.

God, no. Without conscious thought she tumbled back into her body. Disoriented, she lurched toward the rapidly shrinking rift and fell into the deadly Void.

Panting, she gripped Gabe's biceps. "Move!" she screamed, but she didn't know if she screamed only in her mind. The oppressive atmosphere tightened her throat and seared her lungs but still she tugged uselessly at Gabe.

"Get out of here," his voice rasped as if his vocal cords had been burned through.

"Not without you." Her palms scorched with the contact but she refused to let go.

Looming, shadowy creatures from primeval nightmares swarmed in her peripheral vision, their hideous psychic hisses shredding her brain. *She was still wearing the demonic earpiece, and she could understand them.* And their hate-filled vitriol wasn't directed at her. It was directed at Gabe.

He bared his teeth, gripped her wrist and shoved her forward, and together they fell through the narrow fracture. The jagged edges slashed through her flesh and blood trickled down her arms but they were out. From the corner of her eye she saw the violet fracture seal shut. Obviously the Guardians couldn't wait to be rid of them.

"What the hell do you think you were doing?" Gabe panted, propping himself up on one hand as he gently brushed Evalyne's tangled hair from her face. "You were supposed to stay out of the Voids. Can't you ever do as you're told?"

She peered at Evalyne's face and saw the child's eyes flicker. Relief spun through her. The little girl was going to be all right.

"You fell down," Aurora whispered, turning to look at him. Her heart squeezed at his scorched flesh, but at least he didn't seem about to collapse. "I thought you needed some help."

He pushed himself back onto his knees and gripped her shoulders. "You were helping. Until you jumped through and scared the shit out of me."

She huffed out a shaky laugh. "I'm sorry. I was just afraid of losing you. I didn't want you to be trapped in there again, that's all."

For a moment she thought he was going to retort that they were *both* almost trapped inside the Voids because she'd abandoned her post. And now she thought about it she couldn't believe she'd done something so incredibly stupid. Not only had she put both Gabe and herself in danger but what would have happened to Evalyne?

"Gods, Aurora." He dragged her into his arms and buried his face in her hair. "Just promise me you'll never do anything like that again. Don't ever put yourself in danger for my sake. Do you hear me? I'm a fuc—I'm an archangel, remember. I can take care of myself."

She sniffed into his neck. She was not going to cry. She would wait until Evalyne was safely reunited with her parents before she indulged and slid into relief-induced shock.

He exhaled, as if it hurt, and then lifted Evalyne in his arms. "Hold on," he said, looking at Aurora. And then he teleported.

"MY LORD GABRIEL." Jaylar sank to his knees in the luxurious room where they'd met before, and kissed Gabe's feet. It was an ancient custom of homage. One he'd never thought twice of before. But now, with Jaylar, it felt wrong.

His gaze slid to Evalyne, who was wrapped in her mother's arms. The last shred of doubt as to the child's heritage had vanished in the Voids, when the Guardians hadn't tried to reclaim her. Gods and goddesses might not acknowledge their descendants or care what happened to them. But no archangel would turn their back on a Nephilim, no matter how diluted the heritage—and now the Guardians knew that, too.

"Thank you." Jaylar looked up. Tears glittered in his eyes. "My soul is yours, my Lord." And again he bowed his head. Waiting to pay the price.

Jaylar had no idea he was descended from an archangel. Had no idea he didn't possess a soul.

Gabe wouldn't have taken his soul in any case. But what right did he have to wipe the minds of this small family? He had no rights over Jaylar. Except to love and protect him and his daughter as Nephilim.

Who was their archangelic ancestor?

He drew back, dragging Aurora with him.

"Stand up." His voice was hoarse. From the corner of his eye he saw Evalyne's mother flinch as if she expected dire retribution now the mission was completed.

Jaylar stood and looked him fearlessly in the eye. He would give whatever Gabe demanded because he would do anything to save his daughter.

"She was taken by the Guardians." He waited a moment to allow Jaylar to comprehend. "They wanted her for her diluted archangel blood." He recalled the other victim Aurora had discovered. The one who'd been wearing an angel wing necklace. He didn't want to make the connection but how could he not? Had she been another Nephilim? *How many others were scattered throughout the universe?* While archangels had blindly believed all their beloved children had perished in the Great Cleansing, the Guardians had discovered differently.

But why did they hunt such an elusive prey? Guardians abducted mortals so they could feed on their terror. Did an archangelic heritage give an added edge? Or was there another reason?

Jaylar gripped Gabe's arm, as an equal might. *They were equals.* "They'll return for her, is that what you're saying? How can we protect her, my Lord? What must we do?"

"They won't be back for her." But in the distant future they might well return for one of Evalyne's descendants, unless the ancient protocols were once again resurrected. "We'll let you know what you have to do to ensure continued immunity."

"Angel blood?" Evalyne's mother said, looking at Jaylar. "You're descended from the *angels*?"

Mephisto needed to be informed and the archangel responsible for Jaylar and Evalyne's protection found. But right now he needed to heal Aurora's injuries.

"My payment"—instantly their attention returned to him—"is this. Keep your child safe." With that he teleported home.

BACK IN HIS kitchen as Gabe healed the bloodied gashes on her arms, Aurora silently marveled at how quickly the burns on his skin were fading. Was it from his powers of rejuvenation? Or did the healing aspects that enveloped this island have something to do with it?

"How's that feel?" He looked up at her.

"Good." Her skin was as smooth as it had been this time yesterday. She entwined her fingers through his and for several moments they sat in contemplative silence. Then she remembered something and pulled out the earpiece. "Impressive," she said as she placed it on the table.

He grunted but didn't seem inclined to elaborate further. This time the silence wasn't nearly so comfortable.

She was no longer confined to this island for her safety. Would Gabe bring it up or was he waiting for her to? Did he want her to stay with him, or could he not wait until his island was his own once again?

Was she deluding herself by thinking he cared about her?

She cleared her throat and wasn't encouraged by the dark frown he shot her way.

"Have you always lived here on this island? Since, uh, discovering Earth, I mean?" *Did you used to live here with Eleni and your daughter?* That's what she really wanted to know. Not that it made any difference whether he had or not. She just wanted to *know*.

"This island didn't even exist back then." He looked vaguely bemused by her questions. "I found it a couple of decades before I became the uninvited guest of the Guardians. That's why the others brought me here afterward."

It was stupid, but relief sank through her at the knowledge Eleni had never lived here. How selfish could she get? But it was a small pettiness, when Eleni still held the one thing Aurora craved.

Gabe's love.

"I thought maybe you'd always lived here. The villa . . ." Her voice trailed off and she averted her gaze. It was bad enough he knew she'd rifled through his personal possessions without reminding him yet again.

"In the picture," he said. He didn't sound mad. "That was where I lived with Eleni and Helena. I rebuilt a replica here after I recovered from the Voids. I told you once I never brought women here. It was the truth. You're the first."

Warmth encased her heart. That was something to hold on to. And his daughter's name was Helena. What a pretty name. She'd always liked it.

"Don't you like the villa?" His voice was gruff and she frowned up at him. What made him ask that? She'd never given that impression, had she? "I can shift things around. Just let me know."

He was willing to *shift things around*? For her?

Was she jumping to conclusions here or did it sound as if he wanted her to stay with him?

"No, I'm—everything's fine." Well, the upstairs balcony was a bit dodgy without a barrier but she didn't quite feel up to mentioning that at the moment. *He wanted her to stay.* It hammered through her mind, a crazy refrain, and she bit the inside of her lip so she wouldn't grin like a deranged clown.

"Let me know. If you change your mind."

"I will." *He wanted her to stay.* That meant he wanted her in his life. And while she couldn't stay permanently on his island that didn't really matter. What *mattered* was Gabe didn't appear to want to lose her. "Now the Guardians are no longer after me, can you drop me back at my parents? I want to make sure my mum's all right." Would her mother remember the email Aurora had sent? More important, would she remember her *response*?

Gabe didn't answer right away. He just continued to look at her, and although he didn't move a muscle she had the strangest sensation that he was retreating. She tightened her fingers around his, but he didn't reciprocate.

"Is that okay?" Did he think she wanted to leave for good? If so, he certainly wasn't pleased about it. Would she make a complete dick of herself if she told him how she felt? Did it even matter? She loved him. She wanted him to know she had every intention of trying to make this improbable relationship work. Somehow.

"Sure." His voice was flat and he untangled his fingers. "You collect your things. When you're ready I'll take you back."

She frowned. His attitude was all wrong. And what was all that about collecting her things? Didn't he want her coming back here after all?

"No, look, Gabe. I didn't mean that." He'd obviously got the wrong end of the stick. "It's not that I want to leave your island, but—"

He stood up and tossed her a disinterested glance. "It's okay, Aurora. You don't have to explain. There's no reason for you to be imprisoned on my island any longer. You're free. Isn't that what you've always wanted?"

"Well, yes." Of course she wanted her freedom. She could hardly make a choice about her future if she wasn't free to do so. Gabe would forever wonder whether she was with him only because she had to. "But—"

"Fine." He jerked his head. "I'm going to have a shower. Will you be ready to leave when I'm done?"

For a second she stared at him in mute disbelief. Not only did he want her off his island, he couldn't *wait* until she was off his island.

Except she didn't believe it. Wouldn't believe it. She took a deep breath and as he turned and strode from the kitchen she pushed herself to her feet.

"I don't think you understand." She knew he didn't understand. "I mean, obviously I can't live here permanently because—"

"Obviously." Derision dripped from every syllable. "It's no big deal. You have a life to get back to." And with that he disappeared.

Chapter Forty

PALMS flattened against the stone-tiled wall of the shower, Gabe glared at the floor as the water jets pummeled his back and shoulders. He'd been so sure Aurora would chose to stay with him. But the moment she knew she was free she'd wanted to go.

He could keep her here. She could never leave without his help. But what fucking good was that? For the past week she'd been imprisoned because freedom equaled capture by the Guardians. But the Guardians would not dare touch her now.

Do I have to hurt you? Aurora's teasing words floated in his mind.

I'd like to see you try. He'd been so sure she never could.

Be careful what you wish for.

The steam rose, obscuring his vision, and he blinked rapidly, the moisture stinging his eyes. He'd feared the time when Aurora would grow old and die and he would be left behind. But he didn't even have those few blissful years ahead. Because she wanted out, right now.

He knew she wanted him. Knew she still desired him. But it wasn't enough.

He wanted it all.

She was his beloved. He would give her anything that was within his power to make her happy. But the one thing she wanted was the one thing that would destroy the fragile vision he'd harbored of them forging a future together.

WHEN HE ENTERED the bedroom she'd already packed and was standing awkwardly by his bed. Something cracked deep in his chest. His heart, maybe. He'd always thought he no longer possessed a heart but Aurora had proved him wrong.

She'd proved him wrong about so many things. Gods, how could he let her go? How could he not?

How the hell was he going to survive?

"I've left your necklace on the bed." She avoided eye contact and made a vague gesture with her hand. "Sorry, I just need to use the bathroom." She sidled past him like they were strangers. She had no idea every word she uttered tore into his heart and lodged with agonizing intent.

He pulled her necklace from the pocket of his shirt and then picked up the one he had created for Eleni, so many centuries ago. He loved Eleni. Would always love Eleni. But now he also loved Aurora. And his love for Aurora did not diminish his devotion for Eleni. In a strange way he couldn't explain the one love enhanced the other, as if they were entwined.

Tenderly he kissed the ancient angel wings before sliding it into Aurora's purse. Maybe when she discovered what he had given her she'd understand how he felt. Understand why he'd let her go.

She came into the bedroom and he dropped her necklace back into his pocket. Against his heart.

It was a poor substitute for her love, but the only piece of her he could keep with him for all time.

———————

HE TELEPORTED DIRECTLY to her bedroom and it was hell letting Aurora go. She didn't help by keeping her arms around him for a few seconds longer, as if she never wanted them to part.

"Are you going to come downstairs and meet my parents?" She looked up at him, her blue eyes as enchanting as the first time he'd seen her.

"Better not." He dumped her clothes on her bed and tried not to imagine Aurora under the rainbow-patterned duvet. But he knew the vision would plague him for all eternity.

"Am I going to see you again?" She sounded defensive, and he briefly closed his eyes before turning to face her.

"Friends with benefits you mean?" He saw her stiffen, and he forced a dismal smile. Where was his archangelic radiance when he needed it? "Wouldn't work, would it?"

"No." She folded her arms and lowered her lashes so he could no longer drown in the haunting innocence of her eyes. "So this is it, is it? Just like a holiday romance after all."

His jaw tensed. A holiday romance. "Something like that." The words just about choked him. Why was she making this so hard? He'd given her what she wanted. Didn't she know it would destroy him if they continued to see each other on a purely casual basis? If he knew she was seeing—*screwing*—other men? Didn't she know how easily he'd hunt them down and pulverize their brains for daring to touch the woman he loved?

"Aurora." A man's voice, uncertain and questioning, called from downstairs. "Is that you?"

"My dad." Aurora offered him a smile that didn't reach her eyes. If that wasn't a cue for him to go he didn't know what was. But he couldn't leave without touching her one more time. Without kissing her one more time. And so he took her clenched fist, uncurled her fingers and kissed the palm of her hand before he teleported back to his island.

"WHAT IS THIS?" Eblis sounded disgusted. "A fucking archangel retreat?"

Gabe glowered at Zad and Azrael as they strode into the dimly lit alcove. That had to be a first. He couldn't remember either of them setting foot on Eta Hyperium before.

"You need to upgrade your security," he said to Eblis. "It can't tell the difference between archangel and demon DNA."

"What the hell are you doing here?" Zad, who rarely raised his voice or emerged from his façade of tranquil acceptance of the randomness of the universe glared at him. He looked ready to leap across the table and throttle Gabe.

"Getting pissed." Gabe downed the remainder of his tankard and it still didn't lessen the hard knot of desolation buried in the pit of his gut. It had been two days since he'd taken Aurora back to Ireland. Two days of constant drinking with Eblis. And still the alcohol hadn't numbed any part of his anatomy.

"Got a problem with that?" Eblis sounded like he hoped Zad did have a problem with it. One that involved fighting.

"You look like shit, Gabe," Azrael said. "Tell me it's got nothing to do with that interfering human you picked up."

"You abandoned her." Zad glared at Gabe as if he had committed an unforgivable sin. Gabe gritted his teeth. Zad was one of the few archangels he'd never physically fought. Partly because of his connection with Eleni but mainly because Zad just never got that riled.

But one more fucking word—

"Tossed her out of your life as soon as you could. Left her to fend for herself—"

"Shut the fuck up." Gabe shoved the table out of the alcove with his booted foot. "What's it to you anyway?"

"Looks like he's attached to this female himself," Eblis said. "That right, archangel?"

Disgust and fury and raw, primitive possessiveness slammed through Gabe's chest. He'd suspected Zad wanted Aurora from the moment he'd met her the other day. And now he knew.

"You touch her . . ." For a moment words failed him. To know that some day Aurora would take another man, might fall in love with another man—*bear his children*—corroded his soul. But the thought of another archangel having her was beyond intolerable. "I'll fucking neutralize you."

Instead of going for his throat, Zad looked bizarrely self-satisfied. Azrael, on the other hand, had a look of horrified disbelief on his face.

"Gabe." Azrael's tone was urgent. "She's just a human. Nothing special. Right?"

Nothing special? She was his everything. And he'd let her go without telling her.

"You left her because that's what she wanted," Zad said as if that was a revelation and not a particularly welcome one. "You didn't try and change her mind."

"Change her mind?" Azrael slung Zad a look of outrage. "Why the hell would Gabe want to change a human's mind if she's ignorant enough to turn him down?" He flung himself back against the sofa, his wings partially extending. A frown creased his forehead. "Since when have *mortals* ever turned down an archangel?"

She hadn't turned him down. Because he hadn't asked her to stay. All she'd wanted was to check on her parents. And he'd taken that as irrefutable evidence that she wanted her life back, without any restrictions.

"Is this what you want?" Zad's attitude was back to normal.

Calm, almost indifferent. Except for the inexplicable glitter of intensity in his eyes. "The knowledge that for the next three score years or more she's alive and you're not with her?"

No. It twisted his reason that he wasn't with her. He wanted nothing more than to ignore her protests and take her once again to his island.

His prisoner.

How long would it be before her *want* and *desire* turned not to endless love but to resentment and loathing?

"Zad, what the fuck are you on?" Azrael glowered at the other archangel. "Gabe can find another human easily enough if that's what he wants. One that doesn't have an unhealthy obsession in meddling with the astral planes."

So Azrael had figured out Aurora's connection with the disruption in that realm. Not that it mattered. Gabe staggered to his feet. Shit, all that alcohol had affected him after all.

"I don't want another human." He looked at Zad. "Aurora is the only woman I want."

Azrael leaped up, infuriated incomprehension flickering in his eyes as he grabbed Gabe's shoulders.

"You *love* her?" He made it sound something obscene. "How could you do that again, Gabe? It all but destroyed you after Eleni. Don't you understand? She's mortal. She's destined to die. No matter how many times you find her in the future she'll always fucking *die*. And each time your heart will die as well."

Did Azrael think he didn't know that? It was the reason he'd fought his love for Aurora. But it made no difference if he acknowledged it or not. He loved her, even if she didn't love him back. And he was a deluded fool if he thought he could've stayed away from her for the rest of her life. What price was his pride? What use was his ego? If he told her how he felt, told her what he wanted, she might refuse.

But if he gave her the choice . . . she might just accept.

"It's a small price to pay, Az." Yes, it would destroy a piece of him every time she died. But the love would survive.

"How can a few fleeting years possibly compensate for that kind of heartache?"

"Shut your mouth, archangel." Eblis stood, unfurled his wings. "Before any more shit comes out of it."

"What the hell do you know?" Azrael said. "You're a fucking demon."

"And you," Eblis said, contempt dripping from every word, "have never fallen."

Chapter Forty-one

IT had been two days since Gabe had dumped her. Aurora sat on the edge of her bed and stared sightlessly at the half-packed case at her feet.

This afternoon she was returning to London. To her post-graduate studies and the house she shared with three others. She'd stayed on in Ireland an extra day in the pathetic hope that Gabe might change his mind and come back for her. Or at least visit her.

But there had been nothing. The previous week might just as well have been a fantastical dream. The only proof she had that it had been real was the constant ache in her chest, reminding her that despite her good intentions she'd given Gabe her heart. And allowed him to trample all over it.

Her dad had wanted to know all about the psychic fayre she had supposedly gone to, and because she felt so awful about lying she'd been deliberately vague. But for some reason her dad had honed in on her *single* mention of Gabe and now appeared to think she was in the middle of some great love affair. *If only.*

She heard her mother at her bedroom door and futile guilt washed through her. Far from remembering their email exchange her mother didn't appear to realize Aurora had gone missing at all. It was as if the last few days had been gently airbrushed from her consciousness.

And that was that. She'd failed in her dearly cherished hope of helping her mum regain her memories. And after everything she'd learned during the last week there was no way she'd risk trying to cross dimensions again.

Her mother leaned against the dressing table that had been passed down through countless generations and idly fingered Aurora's bag.

"It's been nice having you home," she said.

"Mm." Aurora pushed herself to her feet. Her packing wouldn't do itself. From the corner of her eye she saw her mum begin to poke through the contents of her bag and she sighed. She'd long ago stopped keeping anything too personal in her bag when she came to visit. Her mum didn't seem to comprehend that what she was doing was an invasion of privacy.

"Well, that's strange." Her mum sounded surprised. "Why aren't you wearing your necklace? You always wear it."

Instinctively her fingers went to her bare throat. She hadn't put her necklace back on after returning to her parents. The urgency to have it next to her skin had died. Somehow, after touching the real archangelic token of devotion, she couldn't bear the thought of an inferior, human-crafted imitation.

On her knees she glanced over at her mother as she pulled the glittering chain from her bag. Her mum frowned and peered at the pendant cradled in the palm of her hand as if she had never seen it before. Oh, god. Was her mother's condition worsening further?

"What is this?" There was an odd note in her voice and Aurora dug her nails into the palms of her hands. There was no point getting upset. There was nothing she could do about it.

"You know what it is." She forced herself up and went over to her mum, who was now looking at the necklace like it was a rattlesnake readying to attack. "Here, do you want to put it on me?"

"No, I don't know what this is." Her mother's voice was firm. She sounded as lucid as she had in that recent email. "I know what it *looks* like, but that's neither here nor there."

Aurora pulled her mum's hand down so she could see. And her heart jackknifed.

She didn't need to touch it to feel the ethereal pulse. Didn't need to open the wings to see the magical rainbows or gold dust from a long-destroyed City of Angels.

Gabe had given her his beloved's necklace. And kept hers for himself.

She clutched her mother's arm before she collapsed onto the floor. There was no way in hell this was a mistake. Gabe had deliberately given her his treasured necklace.

Why would he do that?

"Give it to me." Her voice sounded reedy, as if it didn't belong to her. Her mother ignored her and opened the pendant, and Aurora's breath escaped in a silent sigh.

There was only one reason why Gabe would have given her something so precious. But why hadn't he said anything? Stupid, stubborn man. *Archangel.* How was she supposed to contact him? How was she supposed to tell him how much she loved him and wanted them to spend whatever time they had together?

Why hadn't she told him back in his kitchen, when she'd wanted to?

"This isn't yours."

Aurora unhooked her nails from her mum's arm. "No, it—it belongs to a friend of mine."

"A friend?" Her mother looked up at her and silence spun between them. "You mean that man who came here and collected all your clothes?"

"What?" Her mother remembered? "Uh, yes. That's the one." Did her mum remember that Gabe had teleported in front of her? She hoped not.

"He vanished right in front of my eyes." Her mum sounded accusing. "I don't mean he jumped out of the window. I mean he vanished. People don't vanish like that in this world, Aurora."

In this world?

"No," Aurora said, her voice so faint she wondered if her mum would hear it. "He—he isn't from these parts." That was putting it mildly.

Her mum tilted her hand so that the rainbows and gold dust glittered, as if they were illuminated by their own tiny sun.

"I spoke to him." There was a faraway quality in her mother's voice. *"Why did I forget I could do that, Aurora? I've missed you so much."*

Aurora's heart twisted. Her mum was sliding away from her again.

"But I'm right here," she said. "And I'll—" Belated comprehension slammed into her and she stared, slack jawed, at her mother. *"Mum?"* Tentatively she asked the question in her mind. *"Can you hear me?"*

Her mother's eyes were glazed. But not as if she was slipping back into her own safe world. She looked as if she was trying to remember . . .

"This is what I was afraid of." Her voice was barely above a whisper. "That you'd find someone the same way I found someone. That one day you'd leave this world the way I left mine. I couldn't face that, Aurora. *I tried to forget, so none of it was real."*

"Why didn't you tell me?" It had never occurred to her that her dad's greatest fear was also her mother's. By trying to help her mum regain her memories, she had attempted to do the one thing her mother had feared above all else.

"You were too young. And then . . . it was too late." Her mother's fingers closed over the angel wings. "You're going to leave with him, aren't you." It wasn't a question. "You're going back to his dimension."

"Listen to me." Aurora held her mother's hands. "He's from this dimension, mum. Just not from this world. I won't ever leave you, but I need to be with him. If I can find him again."

Her mum pulled free and once again gazed at the necklace. Then she straightened her spine, seeming to come to a decision.

"You'll need this." She fastened the clasp around Aurora's neck and then cradled her face between her palms. "You know where to find him, Aurora. The same way you did before." And then she whispered, mind to mind. *"He's in your heart."*

AURORA RETURNED TO the same place Gabe had made his unorthodox entry into her life. *Seventeen steps east of the ancient oak, three steps north.* Logic told her it made no difference where she was. Gabe would either hear her or not. But her heart knew differently.

This was how she would reach him.

She sank to the ground, heart thudding against her ribs. She wasn't going into trance. She wasn't going to enter the astral planes. She was going to try and connect her mind to Gabe's.

"What the fuck do you think you're doing now?" Mephisto's infuriated voice suddenly sliced through her concentration and she glared up at him. He towered over her, his midnight wings fully extended like an avenging angel of death. "Haven't you caused enough trouble?"

She pushed herself up. Mephisto still loomed over her but at least she didn't feel quite as vulnerable as she had while sitting at his feet.

"I wasn't trying to cross dimensions." She hated the defensive note in her voice. "I was just trying to contact Gabe."

Mephisto took one step toward her. Oddly, she didn't find it threatening despite the wild gleam in his eyes.

"If you love him, E," he said, "set him free. Don't let him find out who you really are."

E?

"He knows who I am." A trans-dimensional child. An anomaly of nature. "And he doesn't care about that. If he loves me what's it got to do with you?"

For a moment the archangel stared at her as though she'd just said something unbelievably stupid. And then a strange expression crossed his face. A combination of disbelief and incredulity. As if her words had suddenly taken on another meaning.

"You really don't know, do you?" He folded his wings and raked a condemning glance over her. "You're as in the dark as Gabe."

An eerie shiver trickled along her spine and she curled her fingers around the necklace, drawing comfort from the ethereal sensation of life that pulsed within. And for the second time she had the strangest sensation that she and Mephisto had confronted each other numerous times in the past.

Had her fragile hope been true? Mephisto had called her E. Did that stand for *Eleni?*

The earth rumbled and as she staggered a violet streak of lightning appeared and a dozen foul Guardians emerged.

Mephisto gripped her arm and slung her behind him. She gasped and terror snaked through her. What were the Guardians doing here?

"Explain." Mephisto's voice was low. Deadly. He did not speak in English. He spoke the language of the ancients.

And she could understand him.

A horrific screeching hiss scraped through her nerves but deep in her brain she could *feel* dormant synapses reconnecting, primal pathways reactivating. And then the hisses and shrieks formed substance and cohesion and ancient words clawed through her mind.

It belongs to us—

Anomaly of nature—

Outside your jurisdiction—

"No matter what the parentage," Mephisto said. "You touch the beloved of an archangel and you risk war against all Immortals."

Shock slammed through her. It was one thing to guess Gabe had fallen in love with her. It was something else to learn that he had elevated her to the status of a beloved. *That* was why the Guardians had backed away in Kala's suite.

That was why he had given her his precious archangelic necklace.

Section 188, Sub-Section 52, paragraph nine point three hundred of the—

"Don't quote the protocols at me."

We have the right to take all anomalies in order to maintain the integrity of the universe—

Such abominations cannot be allowed to survive—

The anomaly must be given to us for neutralization—

Slowly he turned and looked at her, his wings outstretched, as if protecting her from the Guardians' sight.

"I don't believe it. Nothing's straightforward with you, is it? Not only did you come back but you had to be the one thing outside of an Immortal's protection."

Fear stabbed through her. "What do you mean?" And instantly she remembered how she'd torn her arms, left traces of her blood in the Voids when they'd rescued Evalyne. Was that how the Guardians had discovered her dual heritage? "Because of my *parentage?*"

Mephisto's eyes turned scarlet with rage. But for once the rage was not directed at her.

"Isn't it fucking always?"

AS GABE PULLED on a fresh shirt in his dressing room a sudden, disconnected image of Aurora flashed through his brain. He froze. That image didn't come from him. Had Aurora created a telepathic link with him? But even as the thought formed he discarded it. No matter how strong her telepathic ability, no one could forge such a link with an archangel. The link always had to be initiated from their end.

And then he remembered her mother and his conviction crumbled.

He picked up her necklace and slipped it into his shirt pocket and vertigo slammed through him. So sudden, so violent, he staggered against the wall and doubled over, panting as if he had just had the oxygen vacuumed from his lungs.

Primal terror struck him, twisting his gut and squeezing his heart. He tried to analyze the terror but it was formless. For a split second he saw the repellent shadows of the Guardians in his mind's eye. It didn't make sense, because *his love protected her*, yet a certainty ground through him that it wasn't over and it would never be over. Aurora, his beloved, was in deadly danger.

Chapter Forty-two

ARE you telling me there's nothing you can do?" Aurora took an involuntary step closer to Mephisto as the Guardians began to fan out around him. "You're the top archangel and you're *powerless* against them?" She didn't question how she knew Mephisto's rank. It didn't matter. All that mattered was that he somehow get her out of this mess.

"If you were Nephilim, but you're not."

If she was Nephilim. An ancient certainty unfurled in her mind. Mephisto would find a way if she was Eleni because all Nephilim were loved and protected, no matter what the personal feelings might be between individuals.

If she was Eleni. Gabe was convinced that Nephilim didn't possess souls. That it was impossible for them to be reborn. But Mephisto had just as good as told her that, in a previous life, she had been Eleni. She gripped his arm, ignored the glare he arrowed her way, and recalled everything Gabe had told her about the Nephilim. She didn't know for sure she had once been Eleni. But if that was the only way Mephisto might be persuaded to save her skin in this life, she'd do everything she could to touch his conscience.

"Gabe and I were always soul mates. How can you say I'm not Nephilim, if my soul is Eleni's? What *is* Nephilim, Mephisto? Flesh and blood only? Or is it something more, something that you've never before encountered?"

He glowered at her. But he didn't pull away. Didn't tell her she had no idea what she was talking about. Because her words had touched a nerve, and Mephisto never liked not being in full control of any situation.

"It might work." He ground the words between his teeth, as if it went against everything he was to agree with something she had said. "If I twist enough of the sub-sections, dig deep enough into the ancient protocols. But there's no guarantee. And if it's a case of you or the universe, do yourself a favor and slit your own throat."

He swung around, wings fully extended, to face the enemy. Aurora hitched in a relieved breath and then, from the corner of her eye, saw a lone Guardian beyond Mephisto's peripheral vision. And it was pointing a lethal-looking weapon directly at her.

GABE TELEPORTED TO the exact place where he'd first met Aurora. In the fleeting second it took for his molecules to reconnect he saw the Guardians surrounding her, saw Mephisto turn his back on her . . . and the weapon aimed at her.

He didn't think. Just reacted. He teleported in front of her to deflect the beam, There was no longer any option. He had to take her back to his island.

As their gazes collided he saw fear, denial and endless love reflected in her eyes. Then, so swiftly he didn't even feel it coming, she shoved at him with her mind. A psychic punch, trying to push him out of the path of danger, just as she'd physically tried to protect him from the Guardians on the day they'd met.

Time balanced on the precipice; suspended; forgotten. With her barriers gone, their minds linked together, connecting in a way he had never imagined. Vivid images smashed through his mind, memories saturated with Eleni, her eyes, her laughter, her fragrance. Vibrant visions of their life together. Flashes of memory that were familiar, but they weren't his.

They were Eleni's.

And instantaneously the memories he'd lost came flooding back. Last week at the club the psychic core that forever bound him to his beloved had reignited because Eleni was in danger—*and this time he could save her.*

Heedless of logic or reason, instinct had taken over, following the primal connection. He'd honed in on the pure essence of Eleni—*of Aurora*—on the astral planes. And against all laws of physics he'd crashed through them, with only one thought thundering through his being.

To protect her from certain death.

And, consistent with the fucked-up humor of the universe, the second he'd arrived in Ireland he'd suffered instant amnesia.

The knowledge shattered through him in less than a second, and as he wrapped his arms around her a cosmic blast smashed into his back and arrowed through his chest. Uncomprehending, he glanced down, saw Aurora's necklace glow from inside his shirt pocket. And as blackness descended the glow expanded, connecting to an identical white-blue beacon of light that radiated from the angel wings around Aurora's throat.

Chapter Forty-three

A RED-HOT psychic flame seared through Gabe's brain and he shot upward, heart pounding, mouth dry, every bone in his body aching. Two things pierced his blurred vision. One, he was attached to a drip. And two, Mephisto, whose primitive psychic prod had slammed through his brain, was glaring down at him as if he'd like to rip his head from his shoulders.

A drip? He curled uncoordinated fingers around the needle and pulled. It hurt like shit and he collapsed back onto the bed with a muffled curse. But then he realized he was in his own bedroom and Aurora was by his side. She was also hooked up not only to a drip but to various human medical monitors.

He shoved himself up once again and leaned over her, fear spiking through his chest. Why was she unconscious? Had the blast from the Guardians gone right through him and injured her?

"Don't pull out her needles." Mephisto sounded rabid. "I need to talk to you."

"Fuck that." Gabe began to ease the needle from her arm, only to have Zad appear from nowhere and grip his wrist. The fear punched deeper. "What's the matter with her? Why couldn't you heal her?"

"She's no longer injured," Zad said. "We were just keeping her unconscious. Same as you."

"Me?" He pulled his wrist free. *Damn, that hurt.* Felt like Zad had cracked a bone. Disjointed fragments of memory surfaced. *Aurora was Eleni.* But somehow that wasn't important right now. The only thing that mattered was that Aurora wasn't critically injured. "She's safe here from the Guardians, right?" There was only one reason why they'd come back for her and that was if they'd discovered her unique heritage. It wasn't what he wanted for Aurora, but if the only way to keep her alive was to keep her on his island then that's the way it would have to be.

Mephisto unfurled his wings and clenched his fists.

"Forget about E for just two seconds, will you?" He loomed over Gabe, and his eyes flickered scarlet. "The Guardians fired on an archangel. According to the ancient protocols, that gives us the right to decimate their ranks. But since they claim this fucking archangel appeared from nowhere after the beam was fired, the case is not clear-cut."

"Aurora is not being sacrificed to the Guardians." Gabe glared at Mephisto and ignored the worrying fatigue that snaked through his body. "If Armageddon is what they want, then Armageddon is what they'll get."

"Like I said." Mephisto offered him a feral grin. "Not that clear-cut. I've spent the last six weeks negotiating with those bastards. Six weeks while you lay here, oblivious. And I finally managed to broker a deal."

Gabe reared off the bed and grabbed hold of Mephisto's shirt. "Six weeks?" It was the only thing his bruised mind could latch onto. Because what the hell did Mephisto mean by saying he'd *negotiated* with the Guardians? "Cut the crap. What's going on?"

"The blast from the Guardians went straight through you and hit Aurora," Zad said. "You were knocked out cold and she almost died. She *would* have died—there was nothing we could have done to save her, Gabe. Except—we're not sure how—your souls entwined. You kept her alive. Gave her time to heal."

A shudder inched along his spine. Souls didn't entwine. It wasn't possible.

He released Mephisto, who oddly hadn't retaliated, and looked down at Aurora. She looked as if she was just asleep. Since the moment he'd met her so many long-held convictions had crumbled. Just because he'd never before come across the phenomenon of entwined souls didn't mean it was impossible.

Just as it wasn't impossible for Nephilim to be reborn.

"He kept her alive"—fury sizzled in every word Mephisto uttered—"but at what cost? *His fucking immortality.*"

Gabe staggered back and sat heavily on the bed as Mephisto's words pounded through his brain. They made no sense. His immortality? He'd given up his immortality so Aurora could live?

"We don't know how it happened." Zad gripped his shoulder. "We tried to separate you but it wasn't simply a case of you keeping Aurora alive. The connection went both ways. Your life forces were as one."

He was mortal. He couldn't comprehend the magnitude. But if he was mortal, he wouldn't have to exist for countless centuries after Aurora died. If his and Aurora's souls were entwined, neither could live without the other.

Wild hope flared deep inside, heating his blood, illuminating the dark abyss of his no-longer endless future. Aurora would be reborn, and so would he. And they would find each other, *life after life, for eternity.*

"In exchange for holding off your Armageddon—and let's face

it, you'd be fucking useless in that battle as a mortal—the Guardians have agreed to relinquish all rights over Aurora and her direct bloodline." Mephisto folded his wings and slung Aurora a black glare. "I also told them I made you a mortal as a consequence of your actions. And the fucking idiots believed me."

"It doesn't matter what they believe, Meph. All that matters is they'll never dare touch Aurora or her descendants." Zad finally tore his gaze from Aurora and glanced at Gabe. "Her parents are safe, too. Meph constructed a magnificent defense. He argued that they were immune from the Guardians' jurisdiction because it was love alone that had allowed her mother to breach dimensions. And since the Guardians have no concept of love, they had no rebuttal."

"Shut the fuck up, Zad." Mephisto sounded livid. Obviously he hadn't wanted Gabe to know of his involvement in protecting Aurora's parents. "Everything I did was for the sake of a fellow archangel and reincarnated Nephilim. On the other hand you watching over a couple of oblivious humans for six weeks, just to ensure they don't fall apart over their missing daughter, smacks of inanity to me."

Gabe gave a hoarse laugh. "The universe is a screwed-up bitch." He'd wanted a second chance to save his beloved. He'd wanted to be with Aurora. He'd never imagined his wish would be granted so completely.

So perfectly. For once the universe had got things right.

AURORA STRETCHED LANGUOROUSLY, her muscles feeling oddly disconnected as if she hadn't used them in a while. Arms held her securely around her waist, strong, comforting. Familiar. With a half-smile she opened one eye.

She was lying on top of Gabe. She raised her head and saw they were in the exact same place where Gabe had first entered her life. A week ago? She frowned, trying to remember. The last thing she could recall was being here with Mephisto, and then Gabe suddenly appearing in front of her. So what had happened? Where were the Guardians?

"Hey." Gabe tightened his hold on her. "Are you feeling okay?"

She felt fine. Just a bit . . . disoriented.

"Where did Mephisto go?" She levered herself up so she could look at Gabe properly. "It's the strangest thing, but I have this weird feeling of Zad—oh my *god*." She gripped his shoulders and stared at him, shock thudding through her senses. "Your eyes, Gabe. What's happened to your *eyes*?"

"Huh?" His grin faded. "What's wrong with them?"

"They're *blue*." A beautiful blue to be sure. But where was the swirling kaleidoscope of greens and silvers?

He grunted. "That's not the only thing that's changed. Do you remember—in the second the Guardians fired on us—our minds connected?"

Memories flooded through her mind, like a dam had burst deep in the mysterious, unexplored sectors of her brain. Memories of another life, another time. Memories of Gabe, of Helena, of Zad.

Eleni's memories.

Her memories.

"I came back." Her voice was awed. And then she tried linking to him telepathically. *"And you found me."*

"If I'd known"—his voice in her mind was tortured—*"I would have searched for you, Aurora. I would have found you years ago. You would never have put yourself in danger with the Guardians if only I'd found you sooner."*

"Stop it." She speared her fingers through his glorious hair. "You know what this means. You're stuck with me forevermore. Since I obviously possess a soul you can bet your life I'll be back on a regular basis."

"Aurora—"

"Gabe." She cradled his temples, gazed deep into his eyes. It didn't matter what color they were. Because they were his. "Don't you see what this *really* means? It means everything we believed—everything we were told—about Nephilim and their descendants not having a soul isn't true. I don't know if it's got anything to do with my trans-dimensional heritage. Maybe it takes an extraordinary pairing of DNA or something. But the point is—we *can* be reborn. Helena—our baby—she could come back, too. It's possible. You know it is."

She saw the hope, the longing, glitter in his eyes. Felt his struggle as he attempted to overcome millennia of ingrained inevitability. Finally he rolled her onto the ground so they faced each other.

"Yes." So much heartache echoed in that one simple word. "It's possible. Anything's possible." He heaved a sigh. "I'm no longer an immortal."

"What?" How could that be? She pressed her hand against his heart and something grazed her palm through the material of his shirt. "But you're an archangel. How can you not be immortal?"

Gabe was no closer to understanding how that had happened than he had been an hour ago when Mephisto had told him. "I don't know. All that matters is I'm here. We're together." With the fortune he'd accumulated over countless years they could enjoy a luxurious, decadent lifestyle anywhere Aurora wanted.

And then he remembered his limitations. *So long as it was on Earth.*

Somehow he knew that no matter how wealthy they were, she'd be happiest here in Ireland—or maybe London. Somewhere she could continue with her research, even if physically breaching dimensions was off limits.

"You're right. That is all that matters." As she spoke she slid her fingers into his shirt pocket and pulled out a delicate chain.

"Shit." He focused on the blackened pendant that dangled from the chain. It had once been her substitute angel wings. Now it resembled a shard of fossilized charcoal.

Aurora curled her fingers around the necklace at her throat. No ethereal pulse warmed her flesh. "Gabe?" She didn't know what she was afraid of, but she was afraid anyway. "What's happened?"

Frowning, he unclasped the pendant and opened the wings. She peered down and saw the scorched rainbows, the black specks. There was nothing magical or beautiful about it anymore. It looked as if all the life within had been extinguished by fire.

"Oh." The word choked her throat. "I'm so sorry, Gabe. You kept this safe for so long and now—now I've ruined it—"

"Gods." He sounded awed, shaken. "It was the angel wings. That was the conduit between us. Somehow, in the moment the Guardians fired, your necklace and this one fused our life forces together." He gave a disbelieving laugh. "The spark of eternity within the rainbows and gold dust reversed. It sucked out my immortality in order to save you." He looked up at her, as if she was his everything, and her heart ached. "My beloved."

"I love you." She whispered the words that filled her soul. "I'll always love you."

He tangled his fingers in her hair. "I fell in love with you, Aurora, before I ever knew you were Eleni. It was *you* I wanted to save from the Guardians. Do you believe me?"

"Yes." Of course she believed him. He had fallen for her, believing he betrayed Eleni. And now, finally, he could begin to let go of the past, unburden the guilt that was never his to carry.

"And you love me, do you?" He brushed the tip of his nose across hers, and deep in her ancient memories she remembered all the other times they had touched like this. "Even though I'm no longer an archangel? Even though I'm just a normal, regular man?"

She shook her head and sighed. "I don't know, Gabe. I don't

think you could ever be *normal* or *regular* no matter how hard you tried." And then she wrapped her arms around his neck in a fierce, protective hug. "You'll forever be the Archangel Gabriel. But I fell in love with the man. Haven't you always known that? It's always been the *man* I've loved."

About the Author

Christina Ashcroft is an ex-pat Brit who now lives in Western Australia with her high school sweetheart, their three children, an eccentric Maltese-cross and three regal cats. She can't remember a time when she didn't write, and always managed to include an element of fantasy or the paranormal in her English essay homework. Luckily her English teachers didn't mind, despite the fact that these stories generally finished with the hero or heroine (or both) coming to a dire end. Thankfully, by the time she hit fourteen she discovered romance novels and the wonder of a Happily Ever After. She now writes about hot archangels and the women who capture their hearts for Penguin/Berkley Heat, and her books always have a happily ever after. Visit her online at www.christinaashcroft.com.